ALIENS:
RECENT ENCOUNTERS

OTHER WORKS BY ALEX DALLY MacFARLANE

The Mammoth Book of SF Stories by Women

ALIENS:
RECENT ENCOUNTERS

ALEX DALLY MacFARLANE

PRIME BOOKS

ALIENS: RECENT ENCOUNTERS

Prime Books
www.prime-books.com

For more information, contact Prime Books:
prime@prime-books.com

ISBN: 978-1-60701-391-4

CONTENTS

INTRODUCTION

ALEX DALLY MacFARLANE

—◆—

Whether extremophile bacteria under the ice plumes of Enceladus or sentient life on worlds orbiting distant stars, aliens could take many forms. Research throughout our solar system has not yet found life beyond Earth, though it has raised fascinating possibilities. What will we encounter? Will we be able to encounter it at all?

Writers have been exploring those questions for over a hundred years. This anthology takes a modern approach: collecting the best recent answers, from authors who engage with the present day and futures that encompass the breadth of global human experience.

One of the greatest strengths of stories about aliens is their ability to create life and worlds as we have never imagined them. Consider the hollow, four-legged parts of the alien planet Golubash used to age wine in Catherynne M. Valente's "Golubash, or Wine-Blood-War-Elegy," or the copper, hourglass-shaped Quatzoli of Ken Liu's "The Bookmaking Habits of Select Species," or the tetrahedron that arrives in New Delhi in Vandana Singh's "The Tetrahedron," unfathomable to almost everyone.

Other stories consider the limitations on our ever having meaningful encounters with aliens. The star-faring humans of Nancy Kress' "My Mother, Dancing" live by the wisdom of Fermi, whose famous paradox (If it is so statistically likely that sentient life exists on other worlds, why haven't we heard from them by now?) suggests the non-existence or scarcity of life beyond Earth. Elizabeth Bear's "The Death of Terrestrial Radio" dwells on the difficulties of distance between the planets in our galaxy.

It is no surprise that several stories are about the consequences of aliens successfully reaching us. The possibility has excited and frightened countless people, providing the subject matter of numerous movies from the global invasion of *Independence Day* (1996) to the South London troubles of the recent *Attack the Block* (2011). An Owomoyela's "Frozen Voice" is also about a catastrophic invasion—by aliens with unfamiliar concerns—while Sofia Samatar's "Honey Bear" shows a slower, more unsettling take-over. Not all alien arrivals are violent, however: some are the small, personal encounters of Nisi Shawl's "Honorary Earthling" and Molly Gloss' "Lambing Season." Other aliens have come to our aid, as in Karin Tidbeck's "Jagannath" and Paul McAuley's "The Man." The Styonkars of Pervin Saket's "Test of Fire" are simply unimpressed with what they find on Earth.

When we are the ones arriving on inhabited worlds, the outcomes are rarely straightforward. Often, they are informed by the violent legacy of colonialism on our world and a tendency among science fiction writers to use aliens as a stand-in for Othered peoples. Greg van Eekhout's "Native Aliens" makes the metaphor explicit, as the descendants of Brevans and humans face difficulties caused by the humans' colonial legacy. Children fighting for their right to remain on an alien world are forced to deal with uncomfortable truths in Karin Lowachee's "The Forgotten Ones." Zen Cho's "The Four Generations of Chang E" looks at a different aspect of life affected by uneven international relations in our world: immigration, though the Chang E of her story moves not to another country but to the moon.

Not all alien stories need to centre humans. The Ansarac of Ursula K. Le Guin's "Seasons of the Ansarac," who have cut themselves off from human visitors, continue to lead their lives according to seasonal patterns. The Goxhat of Eleanor Arnason's "Knapsack Poems" never meets a human, instead composing poetry and dealing with the vagaries of life as a person of many bodies. While Jeremiah Tolbert's "The Godfall's Chemsong" begins with the arrival of a human, the nutrition supplied by that man—impacting on the relationships between individual members of the planet's sentient aquatic species—is the extent of his importance.

Some stories take entirely individual approaches: the varied forms of space travel in Yoon Ha Lee's "A Vector Alphabet of Interstellar Travel," the dogs of Brooke Bolander's "Sun Dogs," the fraught, hopeful message of Alastair Reynolds' "For the Ages," and more.

This anthology, then, presents stories that span our fictional theorising about alien life. There are many people—alien and human—to be met here, the relationships between them complex and unexpected: fitting predictions of any real encounters in our future.

FROZEN VOICE

AN OWOMOYELA

They've made us speak Hlerig.

They've made us wrestle sounds slippery as fish or burly as bears through our throats. They've made us stumble through conversations, even human-to-human, that we can hardly say. We can't pronounce our names. They named me *Ulrhegmk*, which in Hlerig means *little mountain thing*.

My mother named me Rhianna.

The things that brought us Hlerig are called *mklimme*. Us humans, they call *hummke*, and all our languages share the descriptor *rhlk*, a term which means *soft* or *runny*. I use *rhlk* terms to describe Hlerig: *Viscous* in rhlk English, *lipkiy* in rhlk Russian, *klebrig* in rhlk German. They mean that Hlerig sticks like glue in your mouth.

We have a term for mklimme, too: *daddy longlegs*.

A longlegs came walking through my part of the city on a muggy night while my mother was gone later than usual. Thirty, forty feet above us, its eyes flashed like cats' eyes and its spindly legs crossed blocks in three, four steps. One of its feet put down right across the street, big around as a trashcan and still delicate because it was so tall, and the other two feet stood in front of the low dome of the granary and at the common park at the end of the path. Three feet, two hands. One head which descended through the air and twitched from window to window, its faceted eyes angling back and forth until it came to ours. It put its hands, wide as splayed-open dictionaries, on the sill, and looked at us and the rest of the room.

Who is watching you children? it said, in a language my mother called "whalesong." Hlerig isn't their only language, and they prefer the whalesong speech humans can't hope to pronounce. I answered in Hlerig, pushing my brother out of the way.

"My mother watches us, but she's with friends."

She shouldn't be away, the longlegs said, and its head went up and back away from our window toward the sky. *We'll find her.*

Longlegs all think they're so helpful.

I watched it walk away, and grabbed my brother. My mother had told us where she was going; after making sure we had food in the cooler, just before she walked us to class in the park two days before, she'd told me exactly where she'd be. When the longlegs went looking they wouldn't find her with friends, and then they'd look elsewhere.

I pulled my brother up to the second floor of the house, where the walls had been ripped away and rebuilt like a paper wasp nest. "We're going to find her," I said.

My brother clapped to get my attention, and then made a clumsy sign with his hands. The longlegs tried to teach him to sign like they did, with their seven digits and two opposable thumbs, but his hands were no more made for their sign language as my mouth was made for their words. I had to squint in the darkness to understand him.

"We'll tell her they're out looking and bring her into the city a back way," I told him. "We just have to make sure she's not coming over the plains."

I was young, then, and I thought that would be easy.

My brother nodded and began to prepare, picking up what he thought we'd need—scarves and a flashlight and a compass with no letters on it, only tick marks around the circumference. The needle wobbled from North to Northeast whenever we used it, but it was the only one we had.

When we were sure the longlegs wouldn't see us, we went downstairs and pushed open the door. I grabbed my brother's hand, and we ran for the edge of the city.

The mountain by our city is called *Etrhe,* and the rocky hills and destroyed roads leading up into them are called *ulrhe*—not foothills, not exactly, but little mountains. In the ulrhe are ruins. And the cairn.

Our mother went to the cairn whenever she could sneak out at night—whenever the mklimme in our city were few enough in number, or when the skies rumbled with thunder and crackled with lightning. Storms confound the longlegs. They can't see or hear.

She came back from the cairn with books: old books, lost books, books we hid the instant we had them.

I'd never been out to the cairn. I didn't know my way out of the city like my mother did. She knew how to evade the longlegs and their sympathizers. (*Sympathizers* have little to do with *sympathy*, and we could never tell them anything.) I just ran with my brother, past houses, past the longlegs' paper-wasp structures, doing our best to look like we were on an errand whenever a longlegs turned its body and brought its all-seeing head our way.

Soon we were in the outskirts of the city, where old houses that hadn't been repopulated stood. And all the ruins began to look the same: wrecked walls, decaying doors and wooden floors, swept eerily clean of furniture and furnishings and all the detritus of domestic life. Humans had gone through, under the longlegs' watchful eyes, long ago. They'd brought everything to the cairn.

The night deepened and we were picking our way around the buildings, backtracking when roads were blocked, trying to find our way past buildings that had crumbled over their yards. Now and then shadows would move through the rubble, or seem to move, or a sound would be caught by the skeletal landscape and come twisting out at us so warped and strange that my brother had to clap a hand over my mouth to keep me from screaming. It was no wonder we got lost, and with that sense of being lost came fear. Then exhaustion.

We went into an old building. I didn't want to—the war left a lot of buildings crumbling, and every few months you'd hear about someone who got caught in one, broke a leg or their skull or their spine trying to scavenge some piece of a pre-war life. Almost without exception, those pieces were taken to the cairn anyway.

But it was cold, and we couldn't risk the mklimme finding us out there, so I smoothed the broken glass away from a windowsill and climbed inside. I told myself that when the sun rose, I'd go up to the roof and plot a course to the edge of the city. But for that night, we went up a set of groaning wooden stairs and found a bathroom—no windows—to hide in.

We didn't sleep. We huddled there for hours, my brother pressed against my side, and just as I thought he might drift off, the Hum began. The longlegs have a language for calling from city to city. Humans can't hear it but we can feel it in our bones, and certain houses amplify it. It felt like the tile floor was trying to skitter under us, trapped in the instant before the skitter, and I felt sick to the bottom of my gut.

My father used to tell us, before he was taken, that the longlegs don't sleep. They go about their business at night, walking through the cities or from city to city, with their long legs and their earth-skittering Hum. The ones inside the cities would peek in windows, make sure their humans were sleeping. And if there weren't humans sleeping there, they'd check back the next day, then look until they found them.

I couldn't understand the Hum, but I felt down to my bones that the mklimme were discussing my mother, my brother, and me.

I turned to hug my brother. His eyes were closed, his mouth pressed into a thin line that made him look much older than he was. "Don't worry," I said in pidgin rhlk. "Pretend we're playing hide-and-seek. Remember when we hid in the fireplace? Before mom brought home those encyclopedias and we had nowhere else to put them?" I brushed my hands against his hair. He has dark hair, almost black. It's a hobby in my family to name each other, because names are forbidden. Human names, at least.

When I was born, our longlegs looked from us to the mountain bordering our city and then bent down to say the words in Hlerig. *Your name is Ulrhegmk. Little mountain thing.* When I talked to other longlegs, they made noises and said my name was beautiful.

I used to stand over my brother's bed and say *Your name is Dougal. It means "dark stranger."* I'd say *Your name is Wyatt. It means "hardy" and "brave."* Or I'd say *Your name is Avalon. It's a name from a far-away place. I'll teach you to read about it one day.*

"Remember when we hid in the fireplace all day?"

The far wall of our living room was false. My mother and my father covered up the shelves along the mantlepiece. The false wall wasn't hard to get into: it was held on with construction gum, and if you knew where to look, you could slide your hand into a handhold and pull it out. Even my brother could, if he planted both feet and tugged; my mother wanted us to have access.

I hugged my brother against me. "We'll just be quiet. They can't see in."

Our fireplace had never been used for fire. No one in the city cleaned chimneys and we didn't want to ask the longlegs, so my parents called it a fire hazard and left it alone. If you were very careful, after the false wall went up, you could climb into the fireplace and ease the wall into place behind you. Sitting in the fireplace wasn't comfortable, but it was the safest place to read. You had to position yourself into a corner with your legs tucked to one side, then you could put a candle in the corner left over, and you could read.

"We'll be very quiet," I told my brother, who was always quiet. "In the morning we'll find mom, and then we'll go home."

Our longlegs, the one who caretakes our neighborhood, has a name we can't pronounce. The name it gives us in Hlerig is *Gnheg*, but in secret we call it *Eroica* because the unpronounceable name reminded my father of part of a song by that name. Eroica saw our living room before the false wall was put in, but my father wasn't worried. He and my mother painted a fireplace on the false wall when they put it up, and Eroica never noticed the difference. It was depth perception, my father explained to me; all the longlegs had problems with depth.

But their vision was fine.

They saw him running home with a book one day. A bound book, bound for the hidden fireplace, my father bounding over all the things in his path. It's funny how some things come together.

They caught him.

He must have thought he could hide the book, explain his running away, but they broke a window after he closed the door. My brother screamed, like he'd never scream again, and I held him back on the stairs. From the stairs I saw Eroica's hands (wide-open dictionaries) groping after my father (and I *hate* that word, grope, *oshchupyvat'*; it's as gummy in any language as its Hlerig word *botb*, as stupid and unfeeling) until they found him, standing not quite six feet from the tip of his head to his feet on the ground, and when one of those hands wrapped around him and the other touched the book, I heard Eroica scream too.

Zenig-hrie. Frozen voices. That's the Hlerig word for books; nothing frightens them more. When they came, mother said, they stomped over our armies and our nuclear waste sites and even natural terrifying things like volcanoes and steep cliffs and the tornado alley, but on pulling a roof from a library they would scream, like Eroica screamed, and they would run away on their long long legs until certain ones, special ones, came and took the books away. Brave people, then, like fighter pilots, followed them and saw them doing strange things to the books, and later on they saw them doing the same strange things to their own dead.

You hear stories about people who tied books to tanks and cars and their own bodies so that the longlegs couldn't touch them. At first it was the big religious books, the ones that are easy to find even now because so many people hid them: the Bible, the Qur'an. Then it was anything. Then the longlegs came back with fire, and the books burned, and the people burned, and in the end (my mother used to tell me stories ending with *The End*, but this one wasn't like those; she explained to me the difference between *The End* and *in the end*) even the books didn't save them. The world lay down and we lost our voices, the frozen ones and our *rhlk*, our beautiful liquid tongues.

I was born later. And my brother, who snuggled into my arms in that muggy, Humming night, had been born even later than that.

I searched around in my mind until I found Aesop's fables. They're easy to remember, because as long as you know the moral at the end you can say anything that comes to mind to get you there. I told him, as I held him, about the tortoise and the hare. I told him about the ant and the grasshopper. I told him about the boy who cried wolf, and somehow, he found sleep.

Somehow I slept for a little too, and my dreams were full of words: dancing words, warning words, words as slick as the melting wax from our candles and as dark as the fireplace in the home we'd left behind us.

Longlegs congregated away from the city. They liked the wide-open spaces where they could stretch their legs without worrying about where to put their feet down in the tangle of broken-down fixed-up houses.

The wide-open space east of our city in the foothills used to be part of our city, too. They tore it up. The cairn in the middle *was* the city around it: chunks of asphalt and brick wall and siding and telephone wires and telephone poles and light poles sticking out of the mess like toothpicks, a mountain among the ulrhe. Underneath that pile is where all of our books went, along with dead longlegs and the dead soldiers the longlegs took away. My mother said there were ways to get under it, using the old sewer systems, but they were dangerous and grim—you never knew when you'd find a skeleton instead of a book, and the sewers hadn't been maintained in so long that parts of them were always collapsing.

The cairn was still where they took the books and dead longlegs, but they only seemed to put them on top and pile more things on top of them. No one could tell if that's where they took the human dead; they mostly left us alone, digging graves in our usual cemeteries, unless they found corpses with no one to claim them. That didn't happen often. No one was homeless after the longlegs took over; everyone was fed, everyone had shelter. There were even some people who loved them for that.

My mother said it was easy to feed everyone after you'd killed most of them anyway.

The good thing about the cairn was that the longlegs never went there. The bad thing was that there weren't even old buildings left; it was all torn-up ground and wild weeds, broken streets rambling through the grass. Longlegs could see you, the same way you'd see a mouse running across your floor. And sometimes you'd see movement in the grass and remember stories about wild dogs.

When we found our way out of our city in daylight, everything, even the sunlight, frightened us. Whenever we saw longlegs we hunkered down into the long grass and watched until we were sure they were moving away. Then we'd run for the cairn again, swelling larger and larger against the horizon as we neared, like a bruise rising out of the ground to overshadow us.

The sun rose too. I started calling out. My brother put his hand to my mouth but I pulled it away; even my voice sounded small in the empty hills, and the far-off longlegs didn't turn our way. Even if they'd heard me, I wonder how I would have sounded to them—maybe my plaintive rhlk cries would be no stranger than the calling of birds, out here.

We ran to the edge of the cairn, then up, into and over it, around disturbed piles of rocks, past pieces of pre-war things I could only identify because I'd read about them. After a while I got to thinking that we *were* like the birds around the mountain, and our voices were part of the world out here, speaking forbidden words in this world the longlegs built but didn't control.

Then I heard my mother's cry.

I froze. I grabbed my brother's hand, because the sound I'd heard was not language, not any language she'd taught me. My brother pulled his hand away and ran. I ran after him, tumbling rocks, scrambling over debris.

She was lying on her back. Our mother. Her head was tilted up toward the sky, and she tried to move it to look at us when we came near. When I knelt down next to her I could see a white crust at the corners of her eyes. I took her hand, and felt cold all over.

She had ink on her fingertips. Her knapsack had burst and books were scattered across the cairn with their pages flapping in the breeze. And the side of her shirt was dark with blood. I kept looking at the books, the knapsack, because I was afraid to look at the blood.

"Where are you?" she whispered, in English. It was her first language, and ours, Hlerig be damned. Then she whispered, *"Non, non,"* and her fingers curled around mine.

My brother put his hand on her shoulder, and she took one long, shuddering breath.

"The longlegs are looking for you," I said. It seemed like such a stupid thing to say, but I had to say something. No other words came.

She took another breath. "I fell," she said, answering what I hadn't been strong enough to ask. Her head moved, and she looked up at a part of the cairn tan with sandstone. "It was dark, and . . . "

She swallowed. It sounded like it hurt her to swallow.

"Darling, darling," she said, "they won't find me here. You have to go home."

It was in her voice, not her words, that I heard she wasn't coming with us.

I gripped her hand. "You have to show us the way back in," I said. "How to get through the old city. We'll go through the ulrhe so they don't see us on the plains."

She was quiet for a while, frowning, her eyes closed. She looked a little like my brother had the previous night; she knew, and I knew, and I think even he knew, that I was lying to myself, thinking she would come back with us.

Carefully, painfully, she raised her other hand to touch my cheek. I remember how cold her palm was. "Go back," she said. "The mklimme will take care of you."

Sometimes I wondered why my mother called them *mklimme*—that ugly, hard Hlerig word to say. She said they had the right to name themselves. Just as we wanted.

My brother was picking up the books from her knapsack, turning over the covers to see them in the full sunlight, and stacking them from biggest to smallest on the ground next to us. He was doing that not to look at her, I think.

She rolled her head to the side to watch him. Then she reached out for one of the books, and he handed it over. Her lips pressed together, and a pained noise escaped them.

"Don't bring them home," she whispered. "Let the mklimme find you."

"I want to take them," I told her. I meant, *I don't want to leave you here.*

"I want you safe," she said.

I held mother's hands on top of the book. Her skin was as cold as the cover, or the cover was as warm as her skin. I remembered when she brought my first book home, a thin volume with large illustrated pages and breaths of text on each page. It was so lively, so easy to read, that I forgot why they called it a *frozen voice*. I'd closed my eyes, and believed I could feel it breathing.

I closed my eyes, and felt my mother's hands rise and fall unsteadily with her breath.

The Hlerig word *zenig* can mean *frozen* or *dead*. "I wonder," my mother told me once, when I'd wondered why books frightened the longlegs so much, "if they don't think we've done something horrible to produce them. If when they saw us wearing books like armor, they didn't react the way we would if we saw people walking around wearing human bones and skin."

I wondered if there was a way to show them that every time the covers opened the voices lived again. Show them how to hear them, whispering stories inside you.

My mother squeezed my hand. "They think they're doing the best for us."

In Hlerig there's a word for everything, but the words don't fit us well. I can't wrestle my mouth around *chlkrig* and still think *love*, and my brilliant, warm mother, whose hand I held tight, was nothing like egg-laying *yntig*. But there are moments of synchronicity. The Hlerig word *kpap*, which means *enduring* or *venerable*, sounds a little like *kitap* in rhlk Arabic—the word for "book." And the derivation *chldn* from *chlkrig* sounds almost like *children* does. In Hlerig it means "loved."

"There will be more books, I promise you," she said.

They have made us speak Hlerig. But I wouldn't use the Hlerig words. I wouldn't speak them then.

To my mother I said, *Spasibo, xie xie, thank you, děkuju*. And I held my brother's hand as he mouthed, *Au revoir, annyeonghi-geseyo, má`a al-salaama, goodbye*.

THE BOOKMAKING HABITS
OF SELECT SPECIES

KEN LIU

—◆—

There is no definitive census of all the intelligent species in the universe. Not only are there perennial arguments about what qualifies as intelligence, but each moment and everywhere, civilizations rise and fall, much as the stars are born and die.

Time devours all.

Yet every species has its unique way of passing on its wisdom through the ages, its way of making thoughts visible, tangible, frozen for a moment like a bulwark against the irresistible tide of time.

Everyone makes books.

The Allatians

It is said by some that writing is just visible speech. But we know such views are parochial.

A musical people, the Allatians write by scratching their thin, hard proboscis across an impressionable surface, such as a metal tablet covered by a thin layer of wax or hardened clay. (Wealthy Allatians sometimes wear a nib made of precious metals on the tip of the nose.) The writer speaks his thoughts as he writes, causing the proboscis to vibrate up and down as it etches a groove in the surface.

To read a book inscribed this way, an Allatian places his nose into the groove and drags it through. The delicate proboscis vibrates in sympathy with the waveform of the groove, and a hollow chamber in the Allatian skull magnifies the sound. In this manner, the voice of the writer is re-created.

The Allatians believe that they have a writing system superior to all others. Unlike books written in alphabets, syllabaries, or logograms, an Allatian book captures not only words, but also the writer's tone, voice, inflection, emphasis, intonation, rhythm. It is simultaneously a score and a recording. A speech sounds like a speech, a lament a lament, and a story re-creates perfectly the teller's breathless excitement. For the Allatians, reading is literally hearing the voice of the past.

But there is a cost to the beauty of the Allatian book. Because the act of reading requires physical contact with the soft, malleable surface, each time a text is read, it is also damaged and some aspects of the original irretrievably lost. Copies made of more durable materials inevitably fail to capture all the subtleties of the writer's voice, and are thus shunned.

In order to preserve their literary heritage, the Allatians have to lock away their most precious manuscripts in forbidding libraries where few are granted access. Ironically, the most important and beautiful works of Allatian writers are rarely read, but are known only through interpretations made by scribes who attempt to reconstruct the original in new books after hearing the source read at special ceremonies.

For the most influential works, hundreds, thousands of interpretations exist in circulation, and they, in turn, are interpreted and proliferate through new copies. The Allatian scholars spend much of their time debating the relative authority of competing versions, and inferring, based on the multiplicity of imperfect copies, the imagined voice of their antecedent, an ideal book uncorrupted by readers.

The Quatzoli

The Quatzoli do not believe that thinking and writing are different things at all.

They are a race of mechanical beings. It is not known if they began as mechanical creations of another (older) species, if they are shells hosting the souls of a once-organic race, or if they evolved on their own from inert matter.

A Quatzoli's body is made out of copper and shaped like an hourglass. Their planet, tracing out a complicated orbit between three stars, is subjected to immense tidal forces that churn and melt its metal core, radiating heat to the surface in the form of steamy geysers and lakes of lava. A Quatzoli ingests water into its bottom chamber a few times a day, where it slowly boils and turns into steam as the Quatzoli periodically dips itself into the bubbling lava lakes. The steam passes through a regulating valve—the narrow part of the hourglass—into the upper chamber, where it powers the various gears and levers that animate the mechanical creature.

At the end of the work cycle, the steam cools and condenses against the inner surface of the upper chamber. The droplets of water flow along grooves etched into the copper until they are collected into a steady stream, and this stream then passes through a porous stone rich in carbonate minerals before being disposed of outside the body.

This stone is the seat of the Quatzoli mind. The stone organ is filled with thousands, millions of intricate channels, forming a maze that divides the water into countless tiny, parallel flows that drip, trickle, wind around each other to represent simple values which, together, coalesce into streams of consciousness and emerge as currents of thought.

Over time, the pattern of water flowing through the stone changes. Older channels are worn down and disappear or become blocked and closed off—and so some memories are forgotten. New channels are created, connecting previously separated flows—an epiphany—and the departing water deposits new mineral growths at the far, youngest end of the stone, where the tentative, fragile miniature stalactites are the newest, freshest thoughts.

When a Quatzoli parent creates a child in the forge, its final act is to gift the child with a sliver of its own stone mind, a package of received wisdom and ready thoughts that allow the child to begin its life. As the child accumulates experiences, its stone brain grows around that core, becoming ever more intricate and elaborate, until it can, in turn, divide its mind for the use of its children.

And so the Quatzoli *are themselves* books. Each carries within its stone brain a written record of the accumulated wisdom of all its ancestors: the most durable thoughts that have survived millions of years of erosion. Each mind grows from a seed inherited through the millennia, and every thought leaves a mark that can be read and seen.

Some of the more violent races of the universe, such as the Hesperoe, once delighted in extracting and collecting the stone brains of the Quatzoli. Still displayed in their museums and libraries, the stones—often labeled simply "ancient books"—no longer mean much to most visitors.

Because they could separate thought from writing, the conquering races were able to leave a record that is free of blemishes and thoughts that would have made their descendants shudder.

But the stone brains remain in their glass cases, waiting for water to flow through the dry channels so that once again they can be read and live.

The Hesperoe

The Hesperoe once wrote with strings of symbols that represented sounds in their speech, but now no longer write at all.

They have always had a complicated relationship with writing, the Hesperoe. Their great philosophers distrusted writing. A book, they thought, was not a living mind yet pretended to be one. It gave sententious pronouncements, made moral judgments, described purported historical facts, or told exciting stories . . . yet it could not be interrogated like a real person, could not answer its critics or justify its accounts.

The Hesperoe wrote down their thoughts reluctantly, only when they could not trust the vagaries of memory. They far preferred to live with the transience of speech, oratory, debate.

At one time, the Hesperoe were a fierce and cruel people. As much as they delighted in debates, they loved even more the glories of war. Their philosophers justified their conquests and slaughter in the name of forward motion: War was the only way to animate the ideals embedded in the static text passed down through the ages, to ensure that they remained true, and to refine them for the future. An idea was worth keeping only if it led to victory.

When they finally discovered the secret of mind storage and mapping, the Hesperoe stopped writing altogether.

In the moments before the deaths of great kings, generals, philosophers, their minds are harvested from the failing bodies. The paths of every charged ion, every fleeting electron, every strange and charming quark, are captured and cast in crystalline matrices. These minds are frozen forever in that moment of separation from their owners.

At this point, the process of mapping begins. Carefully, meticulously, a team of master cartographers, assisted by numerous apprentices, trace out each of the countless minuscule tributaries, impressions, and hunches that commingle into the flow and ebb of thought, until they gather into the tidal forces, the ideas that made their originators so great.

Once the mapping is done, they begin the calculations to project the continuing trajectories of the traced out paths so as to simulate the next thought. The charting of the courses taken by the great, frozen minds into the vast, dark terra incognita of the future consumes the efforts of the most brilliant scholars of the Hesperoe. They devote the best years of their lives to it, and when they die, their minds, in turn, are charted indefinitely into the future as well.

In this way, the great minds of the Hesperoe do not die. To converse with them, the Hesperoe only have to find the answers on the mind maps. They thus no longer have a need for books as they used to make them—which were merely dead symbols—for the wisdom of the past is always with them, still thinking, still guiding, still exploring.

And as more and more of their time and resources are devoted to the simulation of ancient minds, the Hesperoe have also grown less warlike, much to the relief of their neighbors. Perhaps it is true that some books do have a civilizing influence.

The Tull-Toks

The Tull-Toks read books they did not write.

They are creatures of energy. Ethereal, flickering patterns of shifting field potentials, the Tull-Toks are strung out among the stars like ghostly ribbons. When the starships of the other species pass through, the ships barely feel a gentle tug.

The Tull-Toks claim that everything in the universe can be read. Each star is a living text, where the massive convection currents of superheated gas tell an epic drama, with the starspots serving as punctuation, the coronal loops extended figures of speech, and the flares emphatic passages that ring true in the deep silence of cold space. Each planet contains a poem, written out in the bleak, jagged, staccato rhythm of bare rocky cores or the lyrical, lingering, rich rhymes—both masculine and feminine—of swirling gas giants. And then there are the planets with life, constructed like intricate jeweled clockwork, containing a multitude of self-referential literary devices that echo and re-echo without end.

But it is the event horizon around a black hole where the Tull-Toks claim the greatest books are to be found. When a Tull-Tok is tired of browsing through the endless universal library, she drifts toward a black hole. As she accelerates toward the point of no return, the streaming gamma rays and x-rays unveil more and more of the ultimate mystery for which all the other books are but glosses. The book reveals itself to be ever more complex, more nuanced, and just as she is about to be overwhelmed by the immensity of the book she is reading, she realizes with a start that time has slowed down to standstill, and she will have eternity to read it as she falls forever towards a center that she will never reach.

Finally, a book has triumphed over time.

Of course, no Tull-Tok has ever returned from such a journey, and many dismiss their discussion of reading black holes as pure myth. Indeed, many consider the Tull-Toks to be nothing more than illiterate frauds who rely on mysticism to disguise their ignorance.

Still, some continue to seek out the Tull-Toks as interpreters of the books of nature they claim to see all around us. The interpretations thus produced are numerous and conflicting, and lead to endless debates over the books' content and—especially—authorship.

The Caru'ee

In contrast to the Tull-Toks, who read books at the grandest scale, the Caru'ee are readers and writers of the minuscule.

Small in stature, the Caru'ee each measure no larger than the period at the end of this sentence. In their travels, they seek from others only to acquire books that have lost all meaning and could no longer be read by the descendants of the authors.

Due to their unimpressive size, few races perceive the Caru'ee as threats, and they are able to obtain what they want with little trouble. For instance, at the Caru'ee's request, the people of Earth gave them tablets and vases incised with Linear A, bundles of knotted strings called *quipus*, as well as an assortment of ancient magnetic discs and cubes that they no longer knew how to decipher. The Hesperoe, after they had ceased their wars of conquest, gave the Caru'ee some ancient stones that they believed to be books looted from the Quatzoli. And even the reclusive Untou, who write with fragrances and flavors, allowed them to have some old bland books whose scents were too faint to be read.

The Caru'ee make no effort at deciphering their acquisitions. They seek only to use the old books, now devoid of meaning, as a blank space upon which to construct their sophisticated, baroque cities.

The incised lines on the vases and tablets were turned into thorough-fares whose walls were packed with honeycombed rooms that elaborate on the pre-existing outlines with fractal beauty. The fibers in the knotted ropes were teased apart, re-woven and re-tied at the microscopic level, until each original knot had been turned into a Byzantine complex of thousands of smaller knots, each a kiosk suitable for a Caru'ee merchant just starting out or a warren of rooms for a young Care'ee family. The magnetic discs, on the other hand, were used as arenas of entertainment, where the young and adventurous careened across their surface during the day, delighting in the shifting push and pull of local magnetic potential. At night, the place was lit up by tiny lights that followed the flow of magnetic forces, and long-dead data illuminated the dance of thousands of young people searching for love, seeking to connect.

Yet it is not accurate to say that the Caru'ee do no interpretation at all. When members of the species that had given these artifacts to the Caru'ee come to visit, inevitably they feel a sense of familiarity with the Caru'ee's new construction.

For example, when representatives from Earth were given a tour of the Great Market built in a *quipu*, they observed—via the use of a microscope—bustling activity, thriving trade, and an incessant murmur of numbers, accounts, values, currency. One of the Earth representatives, a descendant of the people who had once knotted the string books, was astounded. Though he could not read them, he knew that the *quipus* had been made to keep track of accounts and numbers, to tally up taxes and ledgers.

Or take the example of the Quatzoli, who found the Caru'ee repurposing one of the lost Quatzoli stone brains as a research complex. The tiny chambers and channels, where ancient, watery thoughts once flowed were now laboratories, libraries, teaching rooms, and lecture halls echoing with new ideas. The Quatzoli delegation had come to recover the mind of their ancestor, but left convinced that all was as it should be.

It is as if the Caru'ee were able to perceive an echo of the past, and unconsciously, as they built upon a palimpsest of books written long ago and long forgotten, chanced to stumble upon an essence of meaning that could not be lost, no matter how much time had passed.

They read without knowing they are reading.

Pockets of sentience glow in the cold, deep void of the universe like bubbles in a vast, dark sea. Tumbling, shifting, joining and breaking, they leave behind spiraling phosphorescent trails, each as unique as a signature, as they push and rise towards an unseen surface.

Everyone makes books.

GOLUBASH, OR WINE-BLOOD-WAR-ELEGY

CATHERYNNE M. VALENTE

The difficulties of transporting wine over interstellar distances are manifold. Wine is, after all, like a child. It can *bruise*. It can suffer trauma—sometimes the poor creature can recover; sometimes it must be locked up in a cellar until it learns to behave itself. Sometimes it is irredeemable. I ask that you greet the seven glasses before you tonight not as simple fermented grapes, but as the living creatures they are, well-brought up, indulged but not coddled, punished when necessary, shyly seeking your approval with clasped hands and slicked hair. After all, they have come so very far for the chance to be loved.

Welcome to the first public tasting of Domaine Zhaba. My name is Phylloxera Nanut, and it is the fruit of my family's vines that sits before you. Please forgive our humble venue—surely we could have wished for something grander than a scorched pre-war orbital platform, but circumstances, and the constant surveillance of Château Marubouzu-Débrouillard and their soldiers have driven us to extremity. Mind the loose electrical panels and pull up a reactor husk—they are inert, I assure you. Spit onto the floor—a few new stains will never be noticed. As every drop about to pass your lips is wholly, thoroughly, enthusiastically illegal, we shall not stand on ceremony. Shall we begin?

2583 Sud-Côtê-du-Golubash (New Danube)

The colonial ship *Quintessence of Dust* first blazed across the skies of Avalokitesvara two hundred years before I was born, under the red stare of Barnard's Star, our second solar benefactor. Her plasma sails streamed kilometers long, like sheltering wings. Simone Nanut was on that ship. She, alongside a thousand others, looked down on their new home from that great height, the single long, unfathomably wide river that circumscribed the globe, the golden mountains prickled with cobalt alders, the deserts streaked with pink salt.

How I remember the southern coast of Golubash; I played there, and dreamed there was a girl on the invisible opposite shore, and that her family, too, made wine and cowered like us in the shadow of the Asociación.

My friends, in your university days did you not study the manifests of the first colonials, did you not memorize their weight-limited cargo, verse after verse of spinning wheels, bamboo seeds, lathes, vials of tailored bacteria, as holy writ? Then perhaps you will recall Simone Nanut and her folly: she used her pitiful allotment of cargo to carry the clothes on her back and a tangle of ancient Maribor grapevine, its roots tenderly wrapped and watered. Mad Slovak witch they all thought her, patting those tortured, battered vines into the gritty yellow soil of the Golubash basin. Even the Hyphens were sure the poor things would fail.

There were only four of them on all of Avalokitesvara, immensely tall, their watery triune faces catching the old red light of Barnard's flares, their innumerable arms fanned out around their terribly thin torsos like peacocks' tails. Not for nothing was the planet named for a Hindu god with eleven faces and a thousand arms. The colonists called them Hyphens for their way of talking, and for the thinness of their bodies. They did not understand then what you must all know now, rolling your eyes behind your sleeves as your hostess relates ancient history, that each of the four Hyphens was a quarter of the world in a single body, that they were a mere outcropping of the vast intelligences which made up the ecology of Avalokitesvara, like one of our thumbs or a pair of lips.

Golubash, I knew. To know more than one Hyphen in a lifetime is rare. Officially, the great river is still called New Danube, but eventually my family came to understand, as all families did, that the river was the flesh and blood of Golubash, the fish his-her-its thoughts, the seaweed his-her-its nerves, the banks a kind of thoughtful skin.

Simone Nanut put vines down into the body of Golubash. He-She-It bent down very low over Nanut's hunched little form, arms akimbo, and said to her: "That will not work-take-thrive-bear fruit-last beyond your lifetime."

Yet work-take-thrive they did. Was it a gift to her? Did Golubash make room, between what passes for his-her-its pancreas and what might be called a liver, for foreign vines to catch and hold? Did he, perhaps, love my ancestor in whatever way a Hyphen can love? It is impossible to know, but no other Hyphen has ever allowed Earth-origin flora to flourish, not Heeminspr the high desert, not Julka the archipelago, not Niflamen, the soft-spoken polar waste. Not even the northern coast of the river proved gentle to grape. Golubash was generous only to Simone's farm, and only to the southern bank. The mad red flares of Barnard's Star flashed often and strange, and the grapes pulsed to its cycles. The rest of the colony contented themselves with the native root-vegetables, something like crystalline rutabagas filled with custard, and the teeming rock-geese whose hearts in those barnacled chests tasted of beef and sugar.

In your glass is an '83 vintage of that hybrid vine, a year which should be famous, would be, if not for rampant fear and avarice. Born on Earth, matured in Golubash. It is 98% Cabernet, allowing for mineral compounds generated in the digestive tract of the Golubash river. Note its rich, garnet-like color, the *gravitas* of its presence in the glass, the luscious, rolling flavors of blackberry, cherry, peppercorn, and chocolate, the subtle, airy notes of fresh straw and iron. At the back of your tongue, you will detect a last whisper of brine and clarygrass.

The will of Simone Nanut swirls in your glass, resolute-unbroken-unmoveable-stone.

2503 Abbaye de St. CIR, Tranquilité, Neuf-Abymes

Of course, the 2683 vintage, along with all others originating on Avalokitesvara, were immediately declared not only contraband but biohazard by the Asociación de la Pureza del Vino, whose chairman was and is a scion of the Marubouzu clan. The Asociación has never peeked out of the pockets of those fabled, hoary Hokkaido vineyards. When Château Débrouillard shocked the wine world, then relatively small, by allowing their ancient vines to be grafted with Japanese stock a few years before the first of Salvatore Yuuhi's gates went online, an entity was created whose tangled, ugly tendrils even a Hyphen would call gargantuan.

Nor were we alone in our ban. Even before the first colony on Avalokitesvara, the lunar city of St. Clair-in-Repose, a Catholic sanctuary, had been nourishing its own strange vines for a century. In great glass domes, in a mist of temperature and light control, a cloister of monks, led by Fratre Sebastién Perdue, reared priceless Pinot vines and heady Malbecs, their leaves unfurling green and glossy in the pale blue light of the planet that bore them. But monks are perverse, and none more so than Perdue. In his youth he was content with the classic vines, gloried in the precision of the wines he could coax from them. But in his middle age, he committed two sins. The first involved a young woman from Hipparchus, the second was to cut their orthodox grapes with Tsuki-Bellas, the odd, hard little berries that sprang up from the lunar dust wherever our leashed bacteria had been turned loose in order to make passable farmland as though they had been waiting, all that time, for a long drink of rhizomes. Their flavor is somewhere between a blueberry and a truffle, and since genetic sequencing proved it to be within the grape family, the monks of St. Clair deemed it a radical source of heretofore unknown wonders.

Hipparchus was a farming village where Tsuki-Bellas grew fierce and thick. It does not do to dwell on Brother Sebastién's motives.

What followed would be repeated in more varied and bloodier fashions two hundred years hence. Well do I know the song. For Château Marubouzu-Débrouillard and her pet Asociación had partnered with the Coquil-Grollë Corporation in order to transport their wines from Earth to orbiting cities and lunar clusters. Coquil-Grollë, now entirely swallowed by Château M-D, was at the time a soda company with vast holdings in other foodstuffs, but the tremendous weight restrictions involved in transporting unaltered liquid over interlunar space made strange bedfellows. The precious M-D wines could not be dehydrated and reconstituted—no child can withstand such sadism. Therefore, foul papers were signed with what was arguably the biggest business entity in existence, and though it must have bruised the rarified egos of the children of Hokkaido and Burgundy, they allowed their shy, fragile wines to be shipped alongside Super-Cola-nade! and Bloo Bomb. The extraordinary tariffs they paid allowed Coquil-Grollë to deliver their confections throughout the bustling submundal sphere.

The Asociación writ stated that adulterated wines could, at best, be categorized as fruit-wines, silly dessert concoctions that no vintner would take seriously, like apple-melon-kiwi wine from a foil-sac. Not only that, but no tariffs had been paid on this wine, and therefore Abbé St. Clair could not export it, even to other lunar cities. It was granted that perhaps, if taxes of a certain (wildly illegal) percentage were applied to the price of such wines, it might be possible to allow the monks to sell their vintages to those who came bodily to St. Clair, but transporting it to Earth was out of the question at any price, as foreign insects might be introduced into the delicate home *terroir*. No competition with the house of Débrouillard could be broached, on that world or any other.

Though in general, wine resides in that lofty category of goods which increase in demand as they increase in price, the lockdown of Abbé St. Clair effectively isolated the winery, and their products simply could not be had—whenever a bottle was purchased, a new Asociación tax would be introduced, and soon there was no possible path to profit for Perdue and his brothers. Past a certain point, economics became irrelevant—there was not enough money anywhere to buy such a bottle.

Have these taxes been lifted? You know they have not, sirs. But Domaine Zhaba seized the ruin of Abbé St. Clair in 2916, and their cellars, neglected, filthy, simultaneously worthless and beyond price, came into our tender possession.

What sparks red and black in the erratic light of the station status screens is the last vintage personally crafted by Fratre Sebastién Perdue. It is 70% Pinot Noir, 15% Malbec, and 15% forbidden, delicate Tsuki-Bella. To allow even a drop of this to pass your lips anywhere but under the Earthlit domes of St. Clair-in-Repose is a criminal act. I know you will keep this in mind as you savor the taste of corporate sin.

It is lighter on its feet than the Côté-du-Golubash, sapphire sparking in the depths of its dark color, a laughing, lascivious blend of raspberry, chestnut, tobacco, and clove. You can detect the criminal fruit—ah, there it is, madam, you have it!—in the mid-range, the tartness of blueberry and the ashen loam of mushroom. A clean, almost soapy waft of green coffee-bean blows throughout. I would not insult it by calling it delicious—it is profound, unforgiving, and ultimately, unforgiven.

2790 Domaine Zhaba, Clos du Saleeng-Carolz, Cuvée Cheval

You must forgive me, madam. My pour is not what it once was. If only it had been my other arm I left on the ochre fields of Centauri B! I have never quite adjusted to being suddenly and irrevocably left-handed. I was fond of that arm—I bit my nails to the quick; it had three moles and a little round birthmark, like a drop of spilled syrah. Shall we toast to old friends? In the war they used to say: *go, lose your arm. You can still pour. But if you let them take your tongue you might as well die here.*

• • •

By the time Simone Nanut and her brood, both human and grape, were flourishing, the Yuuhi gates were already bustling with activity. Though the space between gates was vast, it was not so vast as the spaces between stars. Everything depended on them, colonization, communication, and of course, shipping. Have any of you seen a Yuuhi gate? I imagine not, they are considered obsolete now, and we took out so many of them during the war. They still hang in space like industrial mandalas, titanium and bone—in those days an organic component was necessary, if unsavory, and we never knew whose marrow slowly yellowed to calcified husks in the vacuum. The pylons bristled with oblong steel cubes and arcs of golden filament shot across the tain like violin bows—all the gold of the world commandeered by Salvatore Yuuhi and his grand plan. How many wedding rings hurled us all into the stars? I suppose one or two of them might still be functional. I suppose one or two of them might still be used by poor souls forced underground, if they carried contraband, if they wished not to be seen.

The 2790 is a pre-war vintage, but only just. The Asociación de la Pureza del Vino, little more than a paper sack Château Marubouzu-Debrouillard pulled over its head, had stationed . . . well, they never called them soldiers, nor warships, but they were not there to sample the wine. Every wine producing region from Luna to the hydroponic orbital agri-communes, found itself graced with inspectors and customs officials who wore no uniform but the curling M-D seal on their breasts. Every Yuuhi gate was patrolled by armed ships bearing the APV crest.

It wasn't really necessary.

Virtually all shipping was conducted under the aegis of the Coquil-Grollë Corporation, so fat and clotted with tariffs and taxes that it alone could afford to carry whatever a heart might desire through empty space. There were outposts where chaplains used Super Cola-nade! in the Eucharist, so great was their influence. Governments rented space in their holds to deliver diplomatic envoys, corn, rice, even mail, when soy-paper letters sent via Yuuhi became terribly fashionable in the middle of the century. You simply could not get anything if C-G did not sell it to you, and the only wine they sold was Marubouzu-Débrouillard.

I am not a mean woman. I will grant that though they boasted an extraordinary monopoly, the Debrouillard wines were and are of exceptional quality. Their pedigrees will not allow them to be otherwise. But you must see it from where we stand. I was born on Avalokitesvara and never saw Earth till the war. They were forcing foreign, I daresay alien liquors onto us when all we wished to do was to drink from the land which bore us, from Golubash, who hovered over our houses like an old radio tower, fretting and wringing his-her-its hundred hands.

Saleeng-Carolz was a bunker. It looked like a pleasant cloister, with lovely vines draping the walls and a pretty crystal dome over quaint refectories and huts. It had to. The Asociación inspectors would never let us set up barracks right before their eyes. I say *us*, but truly I was not more than a child. I played with Golubash—with the quicksalmon and the riverweed that were no less him than the gargantuan thin man who watched Simone Nanut plant her vines three centuries past and helped my uncles pile up the bricks of Saleeng-Carolz. Hyphens do not die, any more than continents do.

We made weapons and stored wine in our bunker. Bayonets at first, and simple rifles, later compressed-plasma engines and rumblers. Every other barrel contained guns. We might have been caught so easily, but by then, everything on Avalokitesvara was problematic in the view of the Asociación. The grapes were tainted, not even entirely vegetable matter, grown in living Golubash. In some odd sense they were not even grown, but birthed, springing from his-her-its living flesh. The barrels, too, were suspect, and none more so than the barrels of Saleeng-Carolz.

Until the APV inspectors arrived, we hewed to tradition. Our barrels were solid cobalt alder, re-cedar, and oakberry. Strange to look at for an APV man, certainly, gleaming deep blue or striped red and black, or pure white. And of course they were not really wood at all, but the fibrous musculature of Golubash, ersatz, loving wombs. They howled biohazard, but we smacked our lips in the flare-light, savoring the cords of smoke and apple and blood the barrels pushed through our wine. But in Saleeng-Carolz, my uncle, Grel Nanut, tried something new.

What could be said to be Golubash's liver was a vast flock of shaggy horses—not truly horses, but something four-legged and hoofed and tailed that was reasonably like a horse—that ran and snorted on the open prairie beyond the town of Nanut. They were essentially hollow, no organs to speak of, constantly taking in grass and air and soil and fruit and fish and water and purifying it before passing it industriously back into the ecology of Golubash.

Uncle Grel was probably closer to Golubash than any of us. He spent days talking with the tall, three-faced creature the APV still thought of as independent from the river. He even began to hyphenate his sentences, a source of great amusement. We know now that he was learning. About horses, about spores and diffusion, about the life-cycle of a Hyphen, but then we just thought Grel was in love. Grel first thought of it, and secured permission from Golubash, who bent his ponderous head and gave his assent-blessing-encouragement-trepidation-confidence. He began to bring the horses within the walls of Saleeng-Carolz, and let them drink the wine deep, instructing them to hold it close for years on end.

In this way, the rest of the barrels were left free for weapons.

This is the first wine closed up inside the horses of Golubash: 60% Cabernet, 20% Syrah, 15% Tempranillo, 5% Petit Verdot. It is specifically banned by every planet under APV control, and possession is punishable by death. The excuse? Intolerable biological contamination.

This is a wine that swallows light. Its color is deep and opaque, mysterious, almost black, the shadows of closed space. Revel in the dance of plum, almond skin, currant, pomegranate. The musty spike of nutmeg, the rich, buttery brightness of equine blood and the warm, obscene swell of leather. The last of the pre-war wines—your execution in a glass.

2795 Domaine Zhaba, White Tara, Bas-Lequat

Our only white of the evening, the Bas-Lequat is an unusual blend, predominately Chardonnay with sprinklings of Tsuki-Bella and Riesling, pale as the moon where it ripened.

White Tara is the second moon of Avalokitesvara, fully within the orbit of enormous Green Tara. Marubouzu-Débrouillard chose it carefully for their first attack. My mother died there, defending the alder barrels. My sister lost her legs.

Domaine Zhaba had committed the cardinal sin of becoming popular, and that could not be allowed. We were not poor monks on an isolated moon, orbiting planet-bound plebeians. Avalokitesvara has four healthy moons and dwells comfortably in a system of three habitable planets, huge new worlds thirsty for rich things, and nowhere else could wine grapes grow. For a while Barnarders had been eager to have wine from home, but as generations passed and home became Barnard's System, the wines of Domaine Zhaba were in demand at every table, and we needed no glittering Yuuhi gates to supply them. The APV could and did tax exports, and so we skirted the law as best we could. For ten years before the war began, Domaine Zhaba wines were given out freely, as "personal" gifts, untaxable, untouchable. Then the inspectors descended, and stamped all products with their little *Prohibido* seal, and, well, one cannot give biohazards as birthday presents.

The whole thing is preposterous. If anything, Earth-origin foodstuffs are the hazards in Barnard's System. The Hyphens have always been hostile to them; offworld crops give them a kind of indigestion that manifests in earthquakes and thunderstorms. The Marubouzu corporals told us we could not eat or drink the things that grew on our own land, because of possible alien contagion! We could only order approved substances from the benevolent, carbonated bosom of Coquil-Grollë, which is Château Marubouzu-Débrouillard, which is the Asociación de la Pureza del Vino, and anything we liked would be delivered to us all the way from home, with a bow on it.

The lunar winery on White Tara exploded into the night sky at 3:17 A.M. on the first of Julka, 2795. My mother was testing the barrels—no wild ponies on White Tara. Her bones vaporized before she even understood the magnitude of what had happened. The aerial bombing, both lunar and terrestrial, continued past dawn. I huddled in the Bas-Lequat cellar, and even there I could hear the screaming of Golubash, and Julka, and Heeminspr, and poor, gentle Niflamen, as the APV incinerated our world.

Two weeks later, Uncle Grel's rumblers ignited our first Yuuhi gate.

The color is almost like water, isn't it? Like tears. A ripple of red pear and butterscotch slides over green herbs and honey-wax. In the low-range you can detect the delicate dust of blueberry pollen, and beneath that, the smallest suggestion of crisp lunar snow, sweet, cold, and vanished.

2807 Domaine Zhaba, Grelport, Hul-Nairob

Did you know, almost a thousand years ago, the wineries in Old France were nearly wiped out? A secret war of soil came close to annihilating the entire apparatus of wine-making in the grand, venerable valleys of the old world. But no blanketing fire was at fault, no shipping dispute. Only a tiny insect: *Daktulosphaira Vitifoliae Phylloxera*. My namesake. I was named to be the tiny thing that ate at the roots of the broken, ugly, ancient machinery of Marubouzu. I have done my best.

For a while, the French believed that burying a live toad beneath the vines would cure the blight. This was tragically silly, but hence Simone Nanut drew her title: *zhaba*, old Slovak for toad. We are the mites that brought down gods, and we are the cure, warty and bruised though we may be.

When my uncle Grel was a boy, he went fishing in Golubash. Like a child in a fairy tale, he caught a great green fish, with golden scales, and when he pulled it into his little boat, it spoke to him.

Well, nothing so unusual about that. Golubash can speak as easily from his fish-bodies as from his tall-body. The fish said: "I am lonely-worried-afraid-expectant-in-need-of-comfort-lost-searching-hungry. Help-hold-carry me."

After the Bas-Lequat attack, Golubash boiled, the vines burned, even Golubash's tall-body was scorched and blistered—but not broken, not wholly. Vineyards take lifetimes to replace, but Golubash is gentle, and they will return, slowly, surely. So Julka, so Heeminspr, so kind Niflamen. The burnt world will flare gold again. Grel knew this, and he sorrowed that he would never see it. My uncle took one of the great creature's many hands. He made a promise—we could not hear him then, but you must all now know what he did, the vengeance of Domaine Zhaba.

The Yuuhi gates went one after another. We became terribly inventive—I could still, with my one arm, assemble a rumbler from the junk of this very platform. We tried to avoid Barnard's Gate; we did not want to cut ourselves off in our need to defend those worlds against marauding vintners with soda-labels on their jump-suits. But in the end, that, too, went blazing into the sky, gold filaments sizzling. We were alone. We didn't win; we could never win. But we ended interstellar travel for fifty years, until the new ships with internal Yuuhi-drives circumvented the need for the lost gates. And much passes in fifty years, on a dozen worlds, when the mail can't be delivered. They are not defeated, but they are . . . humbled.

An M-D cruiser trailed me here. I lost her when I used the last gate-pair, but now my cousins will have to blow that gate, or else those soda-sipping bastards will know our methods. No matter. It was worth it, to bring our wines to you, in this place, in this time, finally, to open our stores as a real winery, free of them, free of all.

This is a port-wine, the last of our tastings tonight. The vineyards that bore the Syrah and Grenache in your cups are wonderful, long streaks of soil on the edges of a bridge that spans the Golubash, a thousand kilometers long. There is a city on that bridge, and below it, where a chain of linked docks cross the water. The maps call it Longbridge; we call it Grelport.

Uncle Grel will never come home. He went through Barnard's Gate just before we detonated—a puff of sparkling red and he was gone. Home, to Earth, to deliver-safeguard-disseminate-help-hold-carry his cargo. A little spore, not much more than a few cells scraped off a blade of clarygrass on Golubash's back. But it was enough.

Note the luscious ruby-caramel color, the nose of walnut and roasted peach. This is pure Avalokitesvara, unregulated, stored in Golubash's horses, grown in the ports floating on his-her-its spinal fluid, rich with the flavors of home. They used to say wine was a living thing—but it was only a figure of speech, a way of describing liquid with changeable qualities. This wine is truly alive, every drop, it has a name, a history, brothers and sisters, blood and lymph. Do not draw away—this should not repulse you. Life, after all, is sweet; lift your glasses, taste the roving currents of sunshine and custard, salt skin and pecan, truffle and caramelized onion. Imagine, with your fingers grazing these fragile stems, Simone Nanut, standing at the threshold of her colonial ship, the Finnish desert stretching out behind her, white and flat, strewn with debris. In her ample arms is that gnarled vine, its roots wrapped with such love. Imagine Sebastién Perdue, tasting a Tsuki-Bella for the first time, on the tongue of his Hipparchan lady. Imagine my Uncle Grel, speeding alone in the dark towards his ancestral home, with a few brief green cells in his hand. Wine is a story, every glass. A history, an elegy. To drink is to hear the story, to spit is to consider it, to hold the bottle close to your chest is to accept it, to let yourself become part of it. Thank you for becoming part of my family's story.

I will leave you now. My assistant will complete any transactions you wish to initiate. Even in these late days it is vital to stay ahead of them, despite all. They will always have more money, more ships, more bile. Perhaps a day will come when we can toast you in the light, in a grand palace, with the flares of Barnard's Star glittering in cut crystal goblets. For now, there is the light of the exit hatch, dusty glass tankards, and my wrinkled old hand to my heart.

A price list is posted in the med lab.

And should any of you turn Earthwards in your lovely new ships, take a bottle to the extremely tall young lady-chap-entity living-growing-invading-devouring-putting down roots in the Loire Valley. I think he-she-it would enjoy a family visit.

THE FOUR GENERATIONS OF CHANG E

ZEN CHO

—◆—

The First Generation

In the final days of Earth as we knew it, Chang E won the moon lottery.

For Earthlings who were neither rich nor well-connected, the lottery was the only way to get on the Lunar Habitation Programme. (This was the Earthlings' name for it. The moon people said: "those fucking immigrants.")

Chang E sold everything she had: the car, the family heirloom enamel hairpin collection, her external brain. Humans were so much less intelligent than Moonites anyway. The extra brain would have made little difference.

She was entitled to the hairpins. Her grandmother had pressed them into Chang E's hands herself, her soft old hands folding over Chang E's.

"In the future it will be dangerous to be a woman," her grandmother had said. "Maybe even more dangerous than when my grandmother was a girl. You look after yourself, OK?"

It was not as if anyone else would. There was a row over the hairpins. Her parents had been saving them to pay for Elder Brother's education.

Hah! Education! Who had time for education in days like these? In these times you mated young before you died young, you plucked your roses before you came down with some hideous mutation or discovered one in your child, or else you did something crazy—like go to the moon. Like survive.

Chang E could see the signs. Her parents' eyes had started following her around hungrily, for all the world as if they were Bugs Bunny and she was a giant carrot. One night Chang E would wake up to find herself trussed up on the altar they had erected to Elder Brother.

Since the change Elder Brother had spent most of his time in his room, slumbering Kraken-like in the gloomful depths of his bed. But by the pricking of their thumbs, by the lengthening of his teeth, Mother and Father trusted that he was their way out of the last war, their guard against assault and cannibalism.

Offerings of oranges, watermelons and pink steamed rice cakes piled up around his bed. One day Chang E would join them. Everyone knew the new gods liked best the taste of the flesh of women.

So Chang E sold her last keepsake of her grandmother and pulled on her moon boots without regret.

On the moon Chang E floated free, untrammelled by the Earth's ponderous gravity, untroubled by that sticky thing called family. In the curious glances of the moon people, in their condescension ("your Lunarish is very good!") she was reinvented.

Away from home, you could be anything. Nobody knew who you'd been. Nobody cared.

She lived in one of the human ghettos, learnt to walk without needing the boots to tether her to the ground, married a human who chopped wood unceasingly to displace his intolerable homesickness.

One night she woke up and saw the light lying at the foot of her bed like snow on the grass. Lifting her head, she saw the weeping blue eye of home. The thought, exultant, thrilled through her: *I'm free! I'm free!*

The Second Generation

Her mother had had a pet moon rabbit. This was before we found out they were sentient. She'd always treated it well, said Chang E. That was the irony: how well we had treated the rabbits! How little some of them deserved it!

Though if any rabbit had ever deserved good treatment, it was her mother's pet rabbit. When Chang E was little, it had made herbal tea for her when she was ill, and sung her nursery rhymes in its native moon rabbit tongue—little songs, simple and savage, but rather sweet. Of course Chang E wouldn't have been able to sing them to you now. She'd forgotten.

But she was grateful to that rabbit. It had been like a second mother to her, said Chang E.

What Chang E didn't like was the rabbits claiming to be intelligent. It's one thing to cradle babies to your breast and sing them songs, stroking your silken paw across their foreheads. It's another to want the vote, demand entrance to schools, move in to the best part of town and start building warrens.

When Chang E went to university there was a rabbit living in her student hall. Imagine that. A rabbit sharing their kitchen, using their plates, filling the pantry with its food.

Chang E kept her chopsticks and bowls in her bedroom, bringing them back from the kitchen every time she finished a meal. She was polite, in memory of her nanny, but it wasn't pleasant. The entire hall smelled of rabbit food. You worried other people would smell it on you.

Chang E was tired of smelling funny. She was tired of being ugly. She was tired of not fitting in. She'd learnt Lunarish from her immigrant mother, who'd made it sound like a song in a foreign language.

Her first day at school Chang E had sat on the floor, one of three humans among twenty children learning to add and subtract. When her teacher had asked what one and two made, her hand shot up.

"Tree!" she said.

Her teacher had smiled. She'd called up a tree on the holographic display.

"This is a tree." She called up the image of the number three. "Now, this is three."

She made the high-pitched clicking sound in the throat which is so difficult for humans to reproduce.

"Which is it, Changey?"

"Tree," Chang E had said stupidly. "Tree. Tree." Like a broken down robot.

In a month her Lunarish was perfect, accentless, and she rolled her eyes at her mother's singsong, "Chang E, you got listen or not?"

Chang E would have liked to be motherless, pastless, selfless. Why was her skin so yellow, her eyes so small, when she felt so green inside?

After she turned sixteen, Chang E begged the money off her dad, who was conveniently indulgent since the divorce, and went in secret for the surgery.

When she saw herself in the mirror for the first time after the operation she gasped.

Long ovoid eyes, the last word in Lunar beauty, all iris, no ugly inconvenient whites or dark browns to spoil that perfect reflective surface. The eyes took up half her face. They were like black eggs, like jewels.

Her mother screamed when she saw Chang E. Then she cried.

It was strange. Chang E had wanted this surgery with every fibre of her being—her nose hairs swooning with longing, her liver contracting with want.

Yet she would have cried too, seeing her mother so upset, if her new eyes had let her. But Moonite eyes didn't have tear ducts. No eyelids to cradle tears, no eyelashes to sweep them away. She stared unblinking and felt sorry for her mother, who was still alive, but locked in an inaccessible past.

The Third Generation

Chang E met H'yi in the lab, on her first day at work. He was the only rabbit there and he had the wary, closed-off look so many rabbits had.

At Chang E's school the rabbit students had kept themselves to themselves. They had their own associations—the Rabbit Moonball Club, the Lapin Lacemaking Society—and sat in quiet groups at their own tables in the cafeteria.

Chang E had sat with her Moonite friends.

"There's only so much you can do," they'd said. "If they're not making any effort to integrate . . . "

But Chang E had wondered secretly if the rabbits had the right idea. When she met other Earthlings, each one alone in a group of Moonites, they'd exchange brief embarrassed glances before subsiding back into invisibility. The basic wrongness of being an Earthling was intensified in the presence of other Earthlings. When you were with normal people you could almost forget.

Around humans Chang E could feel her face become used to smiling and frowning, every emotion transmitted to her face with that flexibility of expression that was so distasteful to Moonites. As a child this had pained her, and she'd avoided it as much as possible—better the smoothness of surface that came to her when she was hidden among Moonites.

At twenty-four, Chang E was coming to understand that this was no way to live. But it was a difficult business, this easing into being. She and H'yi did not speak to each other at first, though they were the only non-Moonites in the lab.

The first time she brought human food to work, filling the place with strange warm smells, she kept her head down over her lunch, shrinking from the Moonites' glances. H'yi looked over at her.

"Smells good," he said. "I love noodles."

"Have you had this before?" said Chang E. H'yi's ears twitched. His face didn't change, but somehow Chang E knew he was laughing.

"I haven't spent my *entire* life in a warren," he said. "We do get out once in a while."

The first time Chang E slept over at his, she felt like she was coming home. The close dark warren was just big enough for her. It smelt of moon dust.

In H'yi's arms, her face buried in his fur, she felt as if the planet itself had caught her up in its embrace. She felt the wall vibrate: next door H'yi's mother was humming to her new litter. It was the moon's own lullaby.

Chang E's mother stopped speaking to her when she got married. It was rebellion, Ma said, but did she have to take it so far?

"I should have known when you changed your name," Ma wept. "After all the effort I went to, giving you a Moonite name. Having the throat operation so I could pronounce it. Sending you to all the best schools and making sure we lived in the right neighbourhoods. When will you grow up?"

Growing up meant wanting to be Moonite. Ma had always been disappointed by how bad Chang E was at this.

They only reconciled after Chang E had the baby. Her mother came to visit, sitting stiffly on the sofa. H'yi made himself invisible in the kitchen.

The carpet on the floor between Chang E and her mother may as well have been a maria. But the baby stirred and yawned in Chang E's arms— and stolen glance by jealous, stolen glance, her mother fell in love.

One day Chang E came home from the lab and heard her mother singing to the baby. She stopped outside the nursery and listened, her heart still.

Her mother was singing a rabbit song.

Creaky and true, the voice of an old peasant rabbit unwound from her mouth. The accent was flawless. Her face was innocent, wiped clean of murky passions, as if she'd gone back in time to a self that had not yet discovered its capacity for cruelty.

The Fourth Generation

When Chang E was sixteen, her mother died. The next year Chang E left school and went to Earth, taking her mother's ashes with her in a brown ceramic urn.

The place her mother had chosen was on an island just above the

equator, where, Ma had said, their Earthling ancestors had been buried.
When Chang E came out of the environment-controlled port building, the
air wrapped around her, sticky and close. It was like stepping into a god's
mouth and being enclosed by his warm humid breath.

Even on Earth most people travelled by hovercraft, but on this remote
outpost wheeled vehicles were still in use. The journey was bumpy—the
wheels rendered them victim to every stray imperfection in the road.
Chang E hugged the urn to her and stared out the window, trying to
ignore her nausea.

It was strange to see so many humans around, and only humans. In the
capital city you'd see plenty of Moonites, expats and tourists, but not in a
small town like this.

Here, thought Chang E, was what her mother had dreamt of. Earthlings
would not be like moon humans, always looking anxiously over their
shoulder for the next way in which they would be found wanting.

And yet her mother had not chosen to come here in life. Only in death.
Where would Chang E find the answer to that riddle?

Not in the graveyard. This was on an orange hill, studded with white
and grey tombstones, the vermillion earth furred in places with scrubby
grass.

The sun bore close to the Earth here. The sunshine was almost a tangible
thing, the heat a repeated hammer's blow against the temple. The only
shade was from the trees, starred with yellow-hearted white flowers. They
smelled sweet when Chang E picked them up. She put one in her pocket.

The illness had been sudden, but they'd expected the death. Chang E's
mother had arranged everything in advance, so that once Chang E arrived
she did not have to do or understand anything. The nuns took over.

Following them, listening with only half her attention on their droning
chant in a language she did not know to a god she did not recognise, she
looked down on the town below. The air was thick with light over the
stubby low buildings, crowded close together the way human habitations
tended to be.

How godlike the Moonites must have felt when they entered these skies
and saw such towns from above. To love a new world, you had to get close
to the ground and listen.

You were not allowed to watch them lower the urn into the ground and
cover it with soil. Chang E looked up obediently.

In the blue sky there was a dragon.

She blinked. It was a flock of birds, forming a long line against the sky. A cluster of birds at one end made it look like the dragon had turned its head. The sunlight glinting off their white bodies made it seem that the dragon looked straight at her with luminous eyes.

She stood and watched the sky, her hand shading her eyes, long after the dragon had left, until the urn was buried and her mother was back in the Earth.

What was the point of this funeral so far from home, a sky's worth of stars lying between Chang E's mother and everyone she had ever known? Had her mother wanted Chang E to stay? Had she hoped Chang E would fall in love with the home of her ancestors, find a human to marry, and by so doing somehow return them all to a place where they were known?

Chang E put her hand in her pocket and found the flower. The petals were waxen, the texture oddly plastic between her fingertips. They had none of the fragility she'd been taught to associate with flowers.

Here is a secret Chang E knew, though her mother didn't.

Past a certain point, you stop being able to go home. At this point, when you have got this far from where you were from, the thread snaps. The narrative breaks. And you are forced, pastless, motherless, selfless, to invent yourself anew.

At a certain point, this stops being sad—but who knows if any human has ever reached that point?

Chang E wiped her eyes and her streaming forehead, followed the nuns back to the temple, and knelt to pray to her nameless forebears.

She was at the exit when remembered the flower. The Lunar Border Agency got funny if you tried to bring Earth vegetation in. She left the flower on the steps to the temple.

Then Chang E flew back to the Moon.

THE TETRAHEDON

VANDANA SINGH

⊰⊱

The story of the Tetrahedron—its mysterious appearance in the middle of a busy street in New Delhi, India—is known in the remotest corners of the globe. There are pictures of it everywhere, towering over the trees and buildings while an anonymous crowd stands outside the fenced area, staring up at it in awe. But few know the story of one of the witnesses of this extraordinary event—an apparently ordinary young woman by the name of Maya, who stood waiting at a bus-stop near the intersection known as Patel Chowk on the fateful morning when the Tetrahedron first appeared. To understand her story we must look upon her with the gaze of someone who cares, so she becomes more than a face in the crowd. The way her brother Manoj considers her, perhaps, when he imagines her standing at the bus-stop at the start of it all—the thin, heart-shaped face, the wistful curiosity in her brown eyes, like a child in a china shop that has been told not to touch things . . .

She was dressed in a somewhat gaudy red patchwork tunic over narrow black trousers; a cloth bag hung over her shoulder, declaring her unequivocally a student of Delhi University. She was late for Accounting class, had long since given up hope of arriving in time, and was therefore letting buses bound for the University pass her by. It was this philosophical resignation, and her preoccupation with her thoughts, centered at that moment on her fiancé, Mr. Perfect Kartik, that resulted in her witnessing the manifestation (for lack of a better word) of the Tetrahedron.

She stood a little apart from the crowds at the bus-stop: young, sleek-headed men with cell-phones, steely-eyed women in saris carrying brief-cases, students in a colorful knot discussing politics. It was a cool morning in February and the crows were hunched on the neem trees over her head, watching the peanut-seller with beady eyes. The air smelled of traffic fumes and roasting peanuts, and somebody's flowery perfume.

What she was thinking about at this moment was how Kartik was beginning to irritate her. Maya's engagement to Kartik represented her final surrender to the demands of respectability. Every foray she had made into the out-of-the-ordinary—playing cricket with the boys, climbing trees, buying an entire tray of bangles from a beggar girl in the market, making friends with the girl in the next apartment block who rode a motorbike and was reputed to be "wild"—had been met with parental consternation, lectures on family honour and marital prospects, and had left her with busloads of guilt. So she felt like a traitor even thinking about how Kartik was starting to annoy her . . .

Lately, whenever she met Kartik (under the watchful eyes of some elderly relative or other) he would lecture her on her failings. The halwa she had made for tea was a little too sweet, that sari was a little flashy— and by the way, could she bring him the newspaper? But the worst was the way her mother and father acted around Kartik, as though he were some minor deity that must be kept in a constant state of appeasement. If only her brother Manoj, two years her senior, had been there—he would understand, but he had escaped many years ago. He was in the Merchant Navy, stationed now in Vishakhapatnam. Her three elder married sisters were harried mothers and quite useless. As for her friends in college, Maya no longer found their obsession with the latest fashions, jewellery and eligible young men diverting. These days she had been feeling very much alone.

At precisely 10:23 A.M. IST, her musings were interrupted by the appearance of an enormous tetrahedron in the middle of the street before her. It came suddenly and incongruously into existence—a monstrous black thing, about two stories high, broad enough on its triangular base to span all four lanes of the road. There was a chorus of screeches as cars and scooters and motor-rickshaws braked in desperation, and then a series of prolonged metallic crashes as vehicles behind them made contact. A woman near Maya dropped her bag and began screaming.

Curses, exclamations, invocations to various gods, the sounds of running feet as a stampede began—then a fearful, wondering silence fell upon the crowds that remained on the sidewalk and the people emerging slowly from the vehicles. Even those who had started to run slowed down and turned back to stare. Faces peered out of windows in the building on both sides of the street. The crows themselves stood silent on the branches of the old trees.

Astonishingly, nothing had crashed into the tetrahedron itself, which stood quietly in the street. To Maya's amazement it seemed as though the two buses, the cars and bicycles that had been in the place now occupied by the tetrahedron had simply ceased to be.

Moments later Maya found herself walking towards the Tetrahedron with a straggle of other bold onlookers. They stood gazing at its opaque sleekness, its geometrical perfection, wondering, but too afraid to touch. Until a small street urchin held out a dirty hand and touched the thing; then everyone followed suit, patting and feeling the smooth, unyielding surface. Behind them the crowd grew as people emerged from cars and buses to gaze open-mouthed at this unexpected sight and proffer theories. Depending on which religion the theorist professed, it was a signal from the gods that the end of the era of kalyug was come, and destruction was imminent, or that the one true God was about to emerge and pass judgment on the sinners . . . It was a government ploy (from a disgruntled clerk who refused to speculate as to how or why). It was a bomb from a neighbouring country that would explode any minute now and why were they standing there anyway. It was a new secret weapon the government had developed. It was an invasion by Martians (from a boy in school uniform) or by Egyptians (from his friend, who was contradicted by another schoolboy: "it's a tetrahedron, not a pyramid, stupid!"). Arguments broke out regarding the possible validity of each theory. Some bemoaned the fate of the people who had been in the space occupied by the tetrahedron. They must lie crushed flat under this monstrous thing, they said, shaking their heads ghoulishly. Well, well, who knew where you'd end up when you left your doorstep of a morning?

Then the press came, eager-eyed TV cameramen, the All India Radio people, and, following at their heels, the police. The latter were rather at a loss—there was nothing in the Indian Penal Code about this. The police officer fell back on old ground and began waving his baton at the crowd, "Move on, you're obstructing traffic!" while some responded, "what about that thing, it's obstructing traffic, are you going to arrest it?" But finally, in the anarchistic, reluctant way of a large beast, the crowd was pushed back and railings set up around the tetrahedron. Sirens wailed discordantly while stalled traffic was diverted, and finally army trucks rolled in.

Soldiers leaped out and took their places with clockwork precision, rifles agleam, but the Tetrahedron answered no questions or challenges. On the sidewalks a large crowd still stood and stared, and pickpockets and vendors of spicy and sticky concoctions did a roaring trade. Maya was interviewed by a reporter from The Statesman ("Did you really touch it? What do you think it might be?").

When she went home (who could sit in a class after this?) her parents were watching the whole thing on TV. The TV was blaring because her mother had the sewing machine going, trying to finish an order from the tailoring shop where she worked. The youngest of her married older sisters, who was here for a visit, was cooking something in the tiny kitchen of the flat, while her firstborn, little Chanchal, babbled in her grandfather's lap. Maya's parents were horrified when she told them she had been there and had touched the thing, but when she mentioned that The Statesman had actually interviewed her, their horror knew no bounds. What would Kartik say?

Fortunately Kartik did not subscribe to The Statesman. When he came for tea on the following weekend, he talked at length about the Tetrahedron, unaware that Maya had actually been there when it appeared. Kartik's theory was that it was a Pakistani secret weapon. Gratified by the attention of his hosts (his future father-in-law had nodded several times) he grew expansive, dandled little Chanchal on his knee (ignoring her outraged cries) and gave Maya a significant look. Maya, lost in thoughts of her own, stared blankly back at him, although her sister gave her a dig in the ribs and blushed and simpered. Maya had cause to be distracted.

The day after the Appearance, she had gone back to the Tetrahedron as though pulled by an invisible string. There were officious looking policemen guarding it from the public and a small army contingent occupying an entire block. Within the cordon, a group of people had been busy with instruments, in the important, oblivious manner of scientists. Among them she recognised Samir, a Ph.D student of astrophysics, who sometimes used the same University bus as Maya. He had once been introduced to her by an acquaintance on the bus, and she remembered his intense, intelligent gaze sweeping over her then with no more than a polite interest.

She had gone over to the cordon and called impulsively out to him, to his considerable surprise—but he was just finished and it had been only natural to go to the university together and to talk about the whole thing at the tea-shack. Nursing her tea in the chipped glass, Maya had told Samir about her witnessing of the tetrahedron's arrival. "It didn't arrive," she'd said. "I didn't see it come down from the sky, or through the trees. One moment it wasn't there, and the next moment it was." Samir had listened with great interest.

Now, as she poured Kartik more tea (the best Darjeeling her parents could buy), she thought about the past two days of drinking strong, cheap masala chai with Samir on the old wooden benches in front of the tea shack. She imagined her parents' shock and horror. What would Kartik say to that?

Samir had told her that the night before the arrival of the tetrahedron there had been an unusual event—a series of radio pulses from the vicinity of an ordinary yellow star that was not known for such activity. He hypothesised that the tetrahedron was an alien device, travelling at near-light-speed through space via some unknown mechanism. He was disarmingly frank about his bias towards an astronomical origin for the tetrahedron—he was a student of astrophysics after all—but next to the Pakistani-American secret weapon-theory, the astronomical one was the most popular. The people whose relatives had been in the buses and cars that had disappeared were demanding a complete investigation of every possibility. Foreign scientists had flocked to Delhi in droves, as had New Age groupies, end-of-the-world cults, members of the international press and ordinary gawking tourists. The President of the United States had been restrained with difficulty from declaring war on India for possessing secret weapons of mass destruction, and had only been placated with promises of a substantial American presence among the investigators. Other suspicious governments from the West had also sent their representatives. Suddenly New Delhi had become one of the most popular travel destinations in the world. Maya and Samir had laughed over newspaper headlines—the government was building more hotels! The Western press was floundering, unused as they were to reporting anything but disasters and political unrest from the third world! A tabloid reported that India had been chosen for a special reason by a wise alien race, and would shortly receive a message of epic importance concerning the next elections!

But what Maya relived most often in her mind was the feeling when she had touched the tetrahedron—the feeling of how useless and insignificant her life was against the unending mystery of the universe. Now, with Samir talking eloquently about aliens traversing the distances between stars, she had felt it again, the pointlessness of a life lived small. In a few years she would be like her sisters, plump and resigned, children running at her feet while Kartik gazed benignly at her from the sofa over the evening paper. "Maya, you know that sari does not suit you . . . " Maya this and Maya that. Could she take a lifetime of it?

Of course, she had only herself to blame, choosing Kartik. Her parents had left the final choice up to her, from an army of eligible bachelors of the appropriate class and caste. Dressed in her best, serving tea to a succession of potential in-laws and their self-conscious offspring, she had been dazzled by Kartik's assurance. Her parents had approved whole-heartedly—Kartik had a good future in a small company that manufactured shoes, and his parents' flat was huge—large enough to accommodate a young, married couple. But now she was no longer sure of her feelings.

She stopped going to class. Every day she went dutifully to the university, where she hung around the tea shop, waiting for Samir, listening to old film songs that the proprietor, Ramu, insisted on playing loudly on the radio. They drank strong tea in ancient glasses that had seen better days, and speculated about the tetrahedron. The scientists had found nothing. The object was made out of an unbelievably hard substance that could not be chipped off for testing. X-rays bounced merrily off it. It was much too heavy to be moved (this to the disappointment of an American software billionaire who wanted to transport it to his mansion in the U.S.). Neither controlled explosives nor corrosive chemicals had the slightest effect on it. Digging under it for the remains of the unfortunate bus and car passengers, the authorities found nothing—no bodies, no crushed bones or flesh, no evidence of charred remains, just dirt and the impenetrable substance of the tetrahedron standing over it. It stood implacable, a question with no answer.

When she was not at the tea-shop, Maya began to spend her time gawking at the Tetrahedron with the large crowd that was always there. Like others in the crowd she felt as though she, too, was waiting for something. The road where the Tetrahedron stood was now blocked to traffic, of course, and its immediate vicinity was patrolled by a now international team of soldiers on permanent alert. Meanwhile a series of shops had sprung up as if overnight in the parking lot of an adjacent building. Soft drinks, tea, hot samosas, cameras, film, knick-knacks such as plastic replicas of the tetrahedron were being sold at exorbitant prices. Foreign languages from all over the world mingled with radio music from the shops and live commentary from TV station crewmen. Rich businessmen rubbed shoulders with hippies and street urchins; Americans and Middle-Easterners, Japanese, Koreans, Kenyans all stood gawking and chattering in little groups. People-watching became Maya's hobby. Her favourite pastime was to eavesdrop on the conversations that sprang up in her vicinity—fragments of arguments, discussions, both academic and untutored—it was a feast for the ears.

" . . . the heat, the dust . . . Why here?"

" . . . the weapons theory has been more or less defused by now, no pun intended . . . except for the politicians, paranoid as usual . . . "

"Beats me . . . Place wasn't even what I expected. No elephants, or dancing girls, or any of that shit . . . Got my camcorder along and for what . . . All that thing does is to sit there while we sweat our butts off."

"Reason . . . there's a reason it's special, if you read the paper by MacArthur . . . "

" . . . and they don't even eat monkey heads, man, so much for Indiana Jones . . . bunch of vegetarians . . . "

"Don't grumble, dear, it was your idea . . . "

" . . . what do you expect Hollywood to do, make documentaries . . . "

"Well, the Johnsons, they went all over this country . . . couldn't stand their boasting . . . "

" . . . the term synchronicity? Meaningful coincidence . . . "

" . . . got some shots of the cows on the roads, weird enough for me . . . "

" . . . yes, like when you're thinking of a song and the DJ starts playing it—what's that got to do with . . . "

" . . . even the fast food joints aren't the same . . . "

" . . . only in a place like this, look at the traffic. By Western standards, with conditions like this, most people ought to be dead or dying. What keeps them going, eh? How anything functions here is a small miracle. A modification of the Jungian concept of synchronicity . . . "

" . . . did you hear what happened to the Gustafsons? The hotel didn't have any record of their reservations, poor things. They ended up you'll never guess where . . . "

" . . . Never in Japan, no. Far more disciplined people. There's something in the air over here, as though the chaos is intrinsic to the place . . . "

" . . . in the home of the student they'd hosted ten years ago, back when they were in Tucson . . . "

" . . . dimensional anomalies . . . fellow called Bhaskar, native—I mean Indian mathematician, cosmologist . . . yes, in the Times . . . no, no, the London Times . . . theorises that dimensional anomalies must exist in this region, hence the Tetrahedron . . . "

" . . . intrinsic anarchy, I like that, no wonder we couldn't hold on to the Empire . . . "

Maya would listen, fascinated. Sometimes a tourist would come up to her and ask if she'd agree to be photographed in front of the Tetrahedron. She was always discomfited by these requests and would back away with a muttered "sorry." Mostly she kept a low profile, watching, listening, sipping a drink or two, letting her thoughts drift, wondering at the silence, the serenity of the Tetrahedron in the midst of all the noise and bustle.

At home, nobody guessed what was going on in Maya's head as she pounded spices in the little kitchen, or hung wet laundry on the nylon clothesline in the balcony. In the evenings the tiny flat was full of the sound of the sewing machine. Her mother's scissors went snip-snip as iridescent piles of cloth accumulated on the drawing room floor. She would put some of the bright cloth aside to make a dress for Chanchal or a patchwork salwaar kameez for Maya. Her customers never found out. "Your mother is a marvel," her father said one day, when the dress was ready. "She can add two and two and get five!" "Dimensional anomalies!" Maya said with a small smile, and went into the kitchen to wash dishes. She gazed moodily out of the window at a view of rooftops and TV antennas, crowded streets, music and conversations blaring from tiers of lit open windows—over all this, in a hazy, dark sky, glimmered a faint star or two. Maya wondered what she was going to do with her life.

Tea with Kartik. Endless teas and breakfasts and dinners with Kartik. When he came the next evening he looked tired and a little vulnerable, and she felt a small pang. But seeing her parents bustling about him, deferring to his every wish, she felt her old irritation arise again. To make matters worse Kartik started talking about the Tetrahedron. This time he was convinced China had something to do with it too. After all, why stop at Pakistan? Maya set the teapot on the table down so loudly that everyone stopped talking and stared at her in amazement.

"What do you know about it?" she snapped at Kartik. Her heart was hammering in her chest. She was conscious for a moment that she was opening a door she would not be able to shut again. But her anger and confusion, held back as long as it had been, surged over what was left of common sense.

"China! Pakistan! Has it occurred to you that nobody—not anybody— can understand what that thing is? None of the foreign scientists, none of ours. Can't you see anything outside your own damned backyard?"

She turned on her heel and went into the kitchen, shaking violently, leaving a dead silence behind her.

Then a clink as her mother set down her cup, and her apologetic voice saying desperately to Kartik,

"Please understand, she is just . . . you know, sometimes young women . . . that time of the month . . . she doesn't mean it . . . "

And her father now beside her, looking at her in shock and hurt, saying "What have you done, child?"

What had she done? Insulted the man who was going to be her husband, damaged the fragile alliance between Kartik's parents and her own, lowered the family honour by behaving like a squabbling fish-wife instead of a girl from a respectable family. She looked at her father's upset face, at his shoulders stooping from disappointment, and burst into tears. She went blindly into the room she shared with her visiting sister and the child. Her sister patted her head.

"Listen, you donkey, that is no way to behave before marriage. You can quarrel all you want afterwards; look at Ashish and me—I shout at him all the time . . . "

"I don't want to marry Kartik," she said between sobs. It was a relief to have said it at last. But she could hear her parents in the drawing room, anxiously trying to placate Kartik. She heard his chair scrape on the floor as he rose, heard him say,

"I hope I have not been mistaken in her. If she comes to her senses . . . "

Then the front door shut.

After that, for some days, she really tried. She hadn't understood before how vulnerable her parents were, how frightened at the thought that their youngest daughter might never get married. Three daughters had slowly depleted them of their meagre savings, and Kartik's family had not even asked for gifts (the euphemism for the illegal dowry). They'd never find anyone like him. So the very next day she went to the phone booth at the corner of her street, called Kartik and apologised rather stiffly. He did not say anything except to tell her that he was going out of town on business for two weeks, and he would think about this when he returned.

Three days of attending classes and bearing with the questions of her friends put her in such a black depression that she returned to Patel Chowk. One day when the square seemed particularly crowded she fought her way to the edge near the parking area, clutching her soft drink in her hand, to stand beneath the generous shade of an ancient tree. It was then that she noticed a white van marked with the words "Ravindra Refrigeration Systems" parked near her. It looked familiar—she must have seen it there before without really noticing it. The side door of the van was open and a motley group of people were gathered around it, talking.

They were all so different from each other that it took her a moment to realise they were a group—three elderly men, two young women who looked Japanese, a lean young man who could have been from the Middle-East, and most incongruous of them all, an old lady in a beige salwaar-kameez perched in the open doorway of the van, knitting away. There was something indefinably different about them compared to the rest of the crowd—they seemed relaxed, they hardly glanced at the tetrahedron, they spoke to each other in low, easy tones.

Maya wondered why she had never really noticed them before. But the tetrahedron attracted so many kinds of people that perhaps it was no wonder. Now someone with a loudspeaker was shouting; policemen were pushing the crowds aside with batons. Another politician? No, it was a movie star, said a plump woman in a purple sari excitedly to Maya. Look, Malini Mehra herself in a glittering pink sari with a daring backless blouse, at the souvenir booth, waving flirtatiously at the gawking, camera-clicking onlookers. Maya turned away in exasperation. There, behind the trees, was the tetrahedron, the cause of all the excitement. As she glanced at its pinnacle rising into the sky above the treetops, she thought she saw one of the ubiquitous crows flying directly towards it. What was the bird doing? She squinted up at it but the sun was in her eyes. She thought she saw the bird reach one edge of the tetrahedron; then it disappeared.

She rubbed her eyes and blinked. The plump woman was still beside her, chattering away about Malini Mehra. "Did you see that?" Maya said. "Of course," said the woman, "Malini Mehra likes reds, they suit her skin, don't you think?" Maya looked away again, but the tetrahedron was just as before. Turning back she met the eyes of the old woman knitting in the doorway of the white van. The old lady smiled at her. Maya wondered if the woman had seen the crow vanish into the tetrahedron . . .

Later she met Samir at the tea-shop. He did not ask her where she had been the past three days. It was a relief to sit with him and watch old Ramu boil the tea in a battered saucepan over a kerosene stove. He added a thick pinch of powdered tea and cardamom to the simmering mixture of water and milk. The aroma filled her nostrils. Ramu's radio, tuned to a station that played only classic Hindi film songs, sat perched on the stained wooden counter.

She told Samir about what she had seen.

"I know, I wasn't quite close enough to see clearly if the crow did disappear. But so many strange things have happened, no?"

Samir was looking at her thoughtfully. As he started to answer, a sleek grey car stopped in the road across from them. A bright, confident, charming face leaned out of the back window, radiating ethnic chic—from the casually scooped up hair to the embroidered collar of what was probably a very expensive designer salwaar-kameez.

"Bhaiya, don't forget to be on time tonight!"

Bhaiya—Elder brother. Samir waved and looked faintly embarrassed. "My sister," he said apologetically as the car drove off in a puff of dust. "It's her birthday today."

It occurred to Maya suddenly that Samir was from a quite different stratum of society than herself. She had known this all along—he lived in Greater Kailash, after all, probably in one of those obscenely big houses—but it had never mattered, never seemed important, until now. His English was polished, hers just fluent enough to get by. She remembered meeting a friend of Samir's on their way to the tea shack some days ago, and the way the friend had looked at her and then again at Samir with astonished surprise. Samir hadn't introduced her. The friend had smiled at Samir and dug him in the ribs and muttered something to him before sauntering off. Something about fraternising with the vulgar proles? Words she only half caught and did not understand. After that Samir had kept talking to her as though nothing had happened, but just for a fleeting moment he had looked discomfited . . . Abruptly Maya was aware of herself as hopelessly lower-middle-class, belonging to the petty-tradesmen-uncultured bhainji sub-culture with all its implications. She didn't know anything about Samir's life, nor he about hers—what was she doing here with him?

But he was talking on, oblivious.

" . . . and maybe it was nothing, but maybe, just maybe, you've hit on something here. There's been a lot of speculation about this. Look," he drew out his notebook and tore off two pages. He tore one into a rough disk and put it against the edge of the other sheet, at right angles.

"Suppose you were a two-dimensional creature living on the surface of this rectangular sheet of paper. Would you know that this disk existed? No, because it is in the third dimension, right, which is not accessible to you. You would only see the straight line that is the intersection between the disk and the sheet where you exist."

She concentrated, pushing back her other thoughts.

"Achha, so if I put the edge of my hand against my face," she said, doing so, "my face feels only the edge. It has no idea of the extent or shape of my hand."

"Yes, something like that. You see, it may be that the Tetrahedron is only a projection of a more complicated object in our three-dimensional world. This object extends in a dimension that is inaccessible to us—all we perceive is the Tetrahedron. To us it appears closed. But in another dimension, there may be doors . . . "

He stopped, lost in thought. Maya was fascinated.

"You mean that somehow the crow I saw got through into another dimension, got into the Tetrahedron? But . . . "

He took a sip of his tea and set the glass down on the edge of the bench.

"Do you know what topology is?"

She shook her head.

"Simply put, it's a branch of mathematics that concerns itself with very general, basic properties of objects or spaces. Topologists look at what happens if you continuously deform the space or the object without breaking or tearing it . . . Here, let me give you an example."

He held the page he had torn from his book in one hand, and the paper disk in the other.

"This rectangular page and this disk of paper are topologically identical, because you can shrink or stretch one to become the other. And your chai glass is identical to them both because I can theoretically deform the sides until it's flat. But—"

He tore a small hole in the middle of the page.

"Now this is no longer topologically equivalent to the disk, because by the rules of topology, however much you deform this page, you can't get rid of the hole. So the page without the hole is a simply connected two-dimensional surface, and the page with the hole is what we call multiply-connected . . . "

"Oh . . . Like a tea-cup . . . I mean one with a handle, not Ramu's chai glasses."

"Yes, yes," he smiled delightedly at her, immensely pleased. "Topologically you and I are identical to a teacup, or a vada, if you like South Indian food—the human alimentary canal is the analogue of the hole in the vada!"

She was staring at him, wide-eyed.

"Achha, but what has all this to do with—"

"The Tetrahedron? Plenty. Topology is relevant in two ways. One, if the topological structure of the Universe is non-trivial, multiply connected in several dimensions, then it might provide shortcuts for faster-than-light travel. Like the wormholes in space that the newspapers keep talking about. Two, the true shape or structure of the tetrahedron itself. If we could see it completely in all the dimensions that it inhabits, we might see something topologically very complicated. It would be incomprehensible to us—our notions of in and out, edge and surface would be lost, or at least very confused. Ever seen a Mobius strip?"

She shook her head, feeling awed and small before the vastness of his knowledge. Now what was he doing? His hands, brown and slender—she'd never noticed before how nice his hands were—tore a strip of paper from the long edge of the page. His eyes were alight with enthusiasm.

"Look at this strip of paper—see how I can put the ends together to form a ring?" He suited the action to the word. "Now suppose, before I do that, I twist the paper once, like this. Now I put the ends together. A ring with a twist! This is a Mobius strip."

She put a tentative finger out to touch it. He smiled.

"Go on, move your finger along the outer surface, along the length of it . . . yes, just so!" He grinned at her surprise. "You start at the outer surface and before you know it, you are inside! Except that inside and outside have lost their meaning in this case, because a Mobius strip has only one surface, not two like the ring." He was talking fast in his excitement. "People think that space-time may be a generalisation of a Mobius strip or some similar non-trivial topological object, in several dimensions . . . So also an object like the Tetrahedron could be very complex, very interesting, if we could see it in its entirety . . . "

Words failed her. She imagined a complicated structure with smoothly contoured edges and sculptured pathways curving dizzily, leading to hidden doors. She stared at him in wonder and envy.

"Hanh, I understand the idea . . . I think."

He nodded approvingly.

"If the Tetrahedron is a projection in our space of a more complicated, multi-dimensional object, it might also explain the disappearance of the people who were on the road at the time the Tetrahedron appeared. Who knows?"

"You mean they might be inside the Tetrahedron?" she said incredulously. The thought had never occurred to her. Instead she had imagined that perhaps some kind of exchange had taken place, the tetrahedron for the people. That the bus riders, the car passengers and the bicyclists were at this very moment on some other world, walking about under alien skies with their mouths open. Another world! Her mind had conjured up bizarre vistas. Yet the thought of what the inside of the tetrahedron might be like was equally mind-boggling.

Maya sat talking to Samir for another hour. He told her about current theories of the birth of the universe, the mysteries that arose with each new discovery. She liked the way he gesticulated in his excitement, the way his eyes seemed to see the wonders his words described. Now he was expounding on the eventual death of the universe.

"The solar system, of course, will die long before that," he said. "The sun will swell and swallow the earth, the moon, all the nearer planets, before collapsing into a white dwarf star."

He stopped to take a sip of his tea, and suddenly the radio started playing an old Hemant Kumar favourite: "na yeh chand hoga, na taare rahenge . . . " *The moon will be no more, nor will the stars remain . . .*

They both laughed at the same time.

"I always wondered how in Bollywood films they contrive to have a song with the right words come on at the appropriate moment," he said, smiling. "Just the other day a similar coincidence happened. There I was, wondering about what kind of star the aliens are from, if they are aliens, that is, and Ramu's radio started playing 'chand ke paas jo sitaara hai!' " *That star by the moon . . .*

"Oh yes, that is Lata Mangeshkar and Kishore Kumar," Maya said. "I love old film songs. I think Ramu's radio is tuned to the aliens' favourite station!"

It was very pleasant to be able to laugh companionably with somebody. (Maya wondered with a pang whether she and Kartik would ever have anything to laugh about.) Then she remembered fragments of a conversation she had overheard.

"It is syn . . . synchronicity," she said carefully. He looked amused.

"That's a big word. Not a scientifically valid concept, of course, but . . . wasn't it in one of the papers? Where did you come across it?"

"I heard it somewhere." She felt a slight indignation. What did he think—that she was hopelessly ignorant? Then she thought, depressingly, that it was true.

But Samir was getting up, setting his glass down on Ramu's counter with a rather awkward air.

"Got to go," he muttered. He looked shyly at her, as though seeing her for the first time. "See you tomorrow!"

She didn't understand until the radio sang the refrain again. "na yeh chand hoga, na taare rahenge, magar ham hamesha tumhaare rahenge . . . " *The moon will be no more, nor will the stars remain, yet I will always be yours . . .*

She stood staring after him, her face hot with embarrassment. She hoped he didn't think—surely he didn't?

When Maya came home one evening, her sister and mother were talking about a story on the afternoon news about a mental sickness that the tabloid press had nicknamed Tetra-fever.

"Isn't it terrible, Maya, there are these people who are obsessed with the Tetrahedron, they can't eat or sleep or function normally—they dream about it all the time," her sister said, setting a plate of hot onion pakoras before Maya. "Some of them starve themselves almost to death, there is this fellow being kept alive in a hospital, fed through a tube . . . " Maya nearly choked over her tea, then took an extra-large helping of the pakoras. Her mother nodded.

"Yes, yes, they talked on TV about a man who stopped going to work, lost his job. He spends all his time staring at the Tetrahedron. He has three children! Poor things, such a terrible thing to happen. At least your father is a sensible man. And there's this housewife, can you imagine, goes shopping at the plaza every day, has the largest collection of plastic tetrahedrons in the city, chee chee!"

Maya nodded, mouth full, and took another pakora.

"Still," said her mother, pouring herself more tea and liberally adding sugar, "it is all in God's hands." She sighed, and Maya knew what she was going to say.

"Nothing to do with us."

Her father came in at the door, stooping, tired from a long day of work and the hot, sweaty bus ride. Maya felt guilty. Maybe I am one of the crazies, she thought to herself, thinking of all the time she spent away from class, with Samir or at the Tetrahedron. Thank goodness Kartik was out of town . . . If only her brother, Manoj, was here! She had written to him some time ago but he was on a ship, and his reply would take time. Besides, letters were no substitute for seeing him face to face.

But at least she was able to talk to Samir about the Tetrahedron. Their mutual embarrassment had been short-lived; at their next meeting, they were comfortable with each other again. There was so much to talk about that she no longer paid any attention to Ramu's radio. However, Samir had not been very interested in the occupants of the white van. On a visit to Patel Chowk he had looked them over rather dismissively—they were not a fascinating astronomical phenomenon after all. He did remark on the old woman knitting away—she was like Madam Defarge, he said, a character from some famous book she'd never heard of. She found this evidence of his class and education annoying, but at least he did not think she was crazy.

They talked about the latest development in the saga of the Tetrahedron. A man had been found wandering in the Thar desert a few hundred miles west of New Delhi. He had been pushing a bicycle over the sand dunes, a strange sight indeed for the villagers who found him. They related that the man did not seem to know where he was going. Upon being questioned he had replied in what seemed to be gibberish, or another language. He seemed happy enough to be led to a villager's hut, where he had been fed and housed for several days. A social worker had come across him and, based on the contents of a bag strapped to his bicycle, had gathered that he was from New Delhi and contacted the police there. It had finally been established that he was one of the people missing when the Tetrahedron had first appeared.

As could be expected, this caused a sensation. Search teams were sent to comb the Thar desert, and there an astounding discovery had been made. The missing bus had been found in a sandy valley, with fifteen people in it—eleven of the original bus passengers, and four people who had been in cars when the Tetrahedron appeared. All fifteen were alive and well, physically that is. But two of them were in the same state as the bicyclist, and the rest kept eerily silent, reacting to nothing and nobody, confounding doctors and family members alike. Meanwhile the bicyclist's family—he was a postal clerk—appeared on TV expressing relief that he had been found, and hope that he and the others would be cured of their strange malady. The tabloid press had a field day. Headlines across the world proclaimed, "16 people kidnapped by aliens free—but what happened to them?"

Maya and Samir could only speculate. As they sat drinking tea, a thought struck Maya.

"The world is like a cracked egg," she said. "Our world, I mean, where we live. Everything we know and see and understand is in this egg. But the cracks tell us that there are things outside—a world outside our understanding . . . "

Samir gave her a startled look.

"You sound quite poetic," he said, smiling. He cleared his throat, as though to say something. Maya shook her head. An idea had been nagging her for some time, and she had suddenly found the words for it.

"What if the Tetrahedron isn't a spaceship? What if it is something we can't even imagine, something totally unknown? You know, what bothers me about all this is that there is so much talk. Just talk. You scientists seem so sure about one theory or another theory—but how can you be really know something without any experience of it?"

"That's where experiments come in," Samir said patiently, ready to expound.

"No, that's not what I mean," she said. She grinned. "The other day when you were holding your cup of tea and you told me about what the tea was made of, atoms and molecules, remember? You said if we could understand the smallest constituents of matter we would be able to know everything there is to know about tea."

"Well?"

"You forgot to drink it. Your theories can tell you a lot about tea, but not about the experience of drinking it. That is what I mean. I don't have the words to explain it, but . . . do you know what I mean?"

She was conscious of his gaze suddenly, and it seemed that there was something faintly wistful about it. He hadn't been listening to her. Embarrassed, she began to talk at once about something else that had occurred to her.

"You know, if the idea about the Tetrahedron being—what was it—a projection—of a larger object in another dimension—if that is true, then maybe this object is huge—so huge that it extends all the way to the Thar desert . . . "

He raised his eyebrows.

"Hanh, that is possible. Yes, perhaps there is another door somewhere in the Thar where they let them off. But what about the rest of the people who vanished?"

"Maybe they don't want to come back, who knows. Maybe the aliens are nicer to them than humans are to each other. Maybe this and maybe that. Samir, what I'm trying to say is, how can we know anything about the Tetrahedron without ever having been in it?"

"It isn't as though we haven't tried," he said a little defensively. "We've gone over every square centimetre . . . "

"Would you, if you could?" she interrupted. "If you found a way, would you go in? Go off on a journey through space?"

"Of course I would!"

He fell silent, rubbing his chin. He gave her an unexpectedly awkward look, then looked away.

"Listen, Maya . . . I'd like to go inside the Tetrahedron, of course, to study it. But I would have to be sure I could come back. You know," now he looked at her directly again, but it was a very different kind of look, "I am very attached to my family . . . They've been wondering why I've been spending so much time here. My friends, too. They don't always understand me, but still . . . family is family, don't you think?"

He was looking at her meaningfully, his brown eyes sorrowful, and still she did not understand. Then suddenly she realised what he was saying, what he must think of her and the direction their relationship might be going. Young men and women didn't fraternise one-on-one for weeks on end unless there was some intention, some basis for a very different kind of relationship. Through the host of confused thoughts in her mind, her pride rose like a sword unsheathed.

"I am close to my family too," she said a little too hurriedly. "In fact I am engaged to this really nice fellow, Kartik, you must meet him some day . . . "

He was staring at her, open-mouthed. She couldn't be sure whether he was angry or upset or both. Her face burned. How dare he presume? Their friendship had been strictly in the context of the Tetrahedron—she had expected no more from him than that . . . well, yes, she liked him, the way he thought about things, his generosity, the kindness in his eyes, the fact that he didn't automatically assume she was stupid, oh and his hands, how they moved when he was describing something—and yet he had assumed. How could he think her so callow, so simple, like a heroine from a third-rate movie? She wanted to tell him: Yes, my father is a clerk and my mother works in a tailoring shop, but I have a sense of dignity. And, she wanted to say, if we *were* really interested in each other in that way, so what? Coward, getting cold feet before anything had begun! She couldn't trust herself to speak. Angry tears pricked at the corners of her eyes. To hell with you and your expensively dressed-up sister and those snobbish friends you never introduce me to, she told him silently. He was getting up, looking at his watch, making some excuse. He had a class very soon. And some exams coming up . . . he was going to be very busy from now on. He gave her an uncertain, apologetic smile and walked away through the trees and down the street.

On Ramu's radio, Geeta Dutt began to sing, "na jao saiiyan, chura ke baiiyan . . . " *Don't leave, beloved, stealing my heart away.* She looked at the old man suspiciously. He winked, shrugged his shoulders and went back to scrubbing the counter, a pointless task, she thought inconsequentially, since it always seemed to be dirty.

The next day she did not go to the university. She went straight to Patel Chowk and stood watching the crowd. A crow watched Maya from the roof of souvenir stall. "What do you see," she asked it in her mind. "What do you see when you look at the Tetrahedron?" The bird cocked its head and stared at her with beady eyes. It gave a caw that sounded like raucous laughter, then took to the air, flapping its wings heavily. Maya sipped her drink and sighed. She saw the old lady in the white van, watching her in a benign sort of way. On an impulse she went up to her.

"What are you knitting?" she said in Hindi. The old woman looked puzzled. Maya asked the question again in English.

"Ah! Only a sweater for my grandson." She spoke with a peculiar accent. "I'm from Mexico," she said, smiling.

"Here to see the Tetrahedron?" Maya asked, feeling stupid. What else?

"Si . . . yes. Three times I make the trip to your country. Much like Mexico, here. Hot desert, mountain, seaside, we have them all." She smiled enigmatically. "Also old buildings. Yesterday I see the tall Minar, many tombs."

"Are you with a tourist group?" Maya asked, wondering what Ravindra Refrigeration had to do with sightseeing.

"Tourist? Tourist, yes. Like to come?"

Maya shook her head, smiling distractedly. "I have to go . . . "

"Come see us if you like to come. We here until weekend—Saturday.

What's your name? Maya? We have that name too!" She smiled with great pleasure.

Maya waved goodbye and wondered rather miserably what she should do. Go back home? Kartik had written to say he would be back next week. It had been a cold sort of letter—clearly he was expecting her to make amends for her behaviour. She could go to class, for a change. Samir could go jump in a well. With that comforting thought she took the bus to the university. Once there she could not bear the thought of dealing with the inane chatter of her friends. It was a hot day—she walked to Ramu's chai shack, thinking maybe she'd have some nimbu-pani instead of tea. The small open space in front of the shack was deserted. She watched the traffic on the road as she sipped her drink, trying not to think about whether Ramu ever washed the glasses. She tried to push away bitter thoughts of Samir. She would miss his friendship—and, she had to admit, the possibilities their relationship had contained. Lata Mangeshkar began singing on the radio: "aaj koi naheen apna, kise gham ye sunaayen . . . " *Today I have no one to call my own, to whom shall I tell my sorrow . . .*

Irritably she looked at Ramu but he had his back to her, doing something industrious with a rag. You go jump in a well too, she told him silently. Moisture beaded her glass of nimbu pani. She wiped sweat off her forehead with a handkerchief her mother had embroidered, and found a sudden lump in her throat. It's not just space and time, she thought bitterly, that are multiply connected. If she could talk to Samir now, she'd tell him: outer space, inner space, both have unknown topologies. You couldn't overlook one at the expense of the other. But he wouldn't talk to her anymore, curse him . . .

On Friday night she was unable to sleep. A pale wash of streetlight lit the room—on the other bed her sister lay sleeping, her arm about Chanchal, who stirred fitfully in a dream. Maya went up to the window and sat on the sill, leaning against the grillwork. Down on the street a watchman banged his stick on the sidewalk as he passed. There was a light on here and there among tiers of darkened windows—she wondered what was keeping those people awake. She thought about the Tetrahedron, dimensional anomalies, synchronicity. The man walking his bicycle in the middle of the Thar desert, the old woman knitting for her grandson, smiling, saying she'd be here till Saturday. Which was tomorrow. In a few days Kartik would be back in Delhi.

Abruptly, everything fell into place. She got up with sudden determination, got the flashlight from her drawer and went softly into the dark drawing room. Carefully she found a sheet of paper, sat in a chair and began to write to Kartik in the dim light of the flashlight, hoping and praying that her parents, in the next room, would not wake up. After she was done she put the letter in an envelope and put a stamp on it. She would mail it tomorrow. She felt a great relief.

Next she wrote a long, affectionate letter to Manoj. "Try to explain it to them, Bhaiya," she wrote. "I don't think I can . . . "

She went back to the bedroom. Chanchal was awake, crying to go to the bathroom.

"I'll take her," Maya told her sister, who lay back in sleepy gratitude. Chanchal did her duty and was amiable again. She climbed into bed with Maya. Maya sang to her the old children's song about Uncle Moon, about the child going up in a flying ship to play hide-and-seek among the stars. It was Chanchal's favourite song, and she always asked the same question at the end. "Will I come back?" Only this time she said, sleepily, "Will you come back, Maya Mausi?" And Maya said, through her tears, of course I will.

In the morning she rose early, cooked breakfast for everyone and washed the dishes so her mother could rest a while before going to work. She saw off her father at the bus-stop and went to the post-box where she mailed the two letters. Then she took the bus to Patel Chowk, where the white van was parked.

"I will come," she told the old lady. The woman smiled as though she had always known Maya would.

Maya's disappearance on the day the Tetrahedron left New Delhi earned only a small item in the newspapers. What was a missing girl—one of those crazies, to judge from what she had written to her family—what was her absence, compared to the most significant event of the century, the appearance and disappearance of the Tetrahedron? Her family mourned, all except Chanchal, who assured the puzzled grown-ups that Maya would be back. Kartik wrote to say he had always been afraid Maya was a little unstable, and her running away (not to mention the lack of respect in the letter she had written to him) proved it—he considered he had had a narrow escape. If she were found, he hoped the family would punish her suitably for dragging their name in mud. Although they didn't deserve it, he was sending back the little gifts her family had given him. Maya's

parents wept over the small package he sent—the final end to their dreams
for their youngest daughter. Meanwhile, Manoj took leave and came home,
torn between grief and hope.

*It was one of the hottest days of the season—the square near the
Tetrahedron was nearly empty. Even the man selling cold spiced cucumber
slices gathered his things and wandered off into the shade, where he sat
dozing. A group of bored soldiers watched Maya, the old woman and the
others as they walked up to the Tetrahedron. They just wanted to touch it,
and they were unarmed, the soldiers said later. They must have wandered
off after that, the soldiers said. We weren't really looking. But what really
happened was that Maya and her companions went all the way up to the
Tetrahedron and turned in a place where she had not known it was possible
to turn. It was a kind of narrow corridor and she could still see the soldiers,
the white van with Ravindra Refrigeration on it, the driver getting ready
to leave—she could still see the hot, dusty square under the neem trees.
But also she found herself in a large room which seemed to be made up of
walls arranged at impossible angles, like an Escher picture—and the outside
world, if it still made sense to talk of outside and inside—the outside world
was projected on a plane slanting up from her feet, making her feel giddy.
She looked up and she could see the dark of space amid spiral stairways
going towards some distant destination; she saw with a shock that there
were creatures going up on it, great beings made up of planes and angles
and curves that didn't quite fit. Some of them had human-like faces. She
turned in wonder to the old woman beside her and stopped with her mouth
hanging open.*

*For the old woman too, had changed. Her face was still the same, but her
eyes had grown large and dark, and a succession of crests and ridges rose
from her body in great arcs. There were growths dangling from her arms like
the appendages of sea-creatures. She smiled at Maya.*

Maya drew back. "You are an alien," she said.

*"No, my dear," the woman said in chaste Hindi. "I am who I am.
Remember what I told you? Do not expect to understand everything all at
once. I will be your guide. But first, take a look at yourself."*

*And the old woman took Maya gently by the shoulders and turned her to
a silver wall that was opaque and reflective. Maya saw herself. Saw her face,
mouth open in shock, her hair streaming around it, the great crenellations
and sweeping ridges that rose from her body as gracefully as the plates on
a stegosaur's back. She looked at her two hands, the familiar river-valley of*

lines and tributaries, and she saw that they were the same as before, and not the same. Other hands branched off her hands, fading off into an infinity of hands, young hands, old hands, smooth and wrinkled. She took a deep, sobbing breath.

"What has happened to me?"

"Nothing. You see yourself as you are in more than three dimensions. Now don't think about it too much. I want you to look around and tell me where you want to go first."

Around—whatever that meant—was the darkness of space, and stars caught in a thin, delicate mesh. She saw the great rings of Saturn, the shadows of three of its moons like black pimples on its bright face. She saw other planets, dead stars, worlds that drifted in space without suns. And the spiral stairways moved up and up like escalators, vanishing into the fine intricacy of the web.

"Shall we start with something close to home, like the moon?"

"I thought you said this wasn't a spaceship!"

"It is and it isn't. You will get used to not thinking in the old ways, my dear. The categories we are accustomed to on Earth have little meaning here. A square does not have the same meaning for a flat-land person as it does for a three-dimensional one. You'll see."

Maya took a deep breath. Around her the Universe beckoned. She thought she heard Lata Mangeshkar and Mohammad Rafi on Ramu's radio, singing. Chalo dildaar, chalo, chand ke paar chalo . . . Come, beloved, let us fly beyond the moon.

"Let's go further," she said.

Was that what really happened to Maya? How can we know? All she left behind was a very detailed letter to her brother, and some ideas and theories. Her story came alive from those scribbled pages, but it necessarily came to a stop when she left home. Perhaps in some dimension orthogonal to time and space, it is possible to see what came after, to follow her world-line, to see the post-script to her letter. But caught in the stream of time as we are, all her brother could do was to wait. He thought of all kinds of other scenarios, of spaceships that swept silently through space like owls through night, of aliens and alien languages, and Maya among impossible worlds, her face filled with a softness and yearning, a kind of tender curiosity. He remembered the child she had been, always straining at the barriers, being scolded and cajoled into doing whatever she was supposed to do. She had learned to replace outward defiance with a quiet raging within herself. He thought of her waiting at the bus-stop on that fateful morning before it all began, unaware of the person she would become, the person who would write so passionately in her last letter: "What if the Tetrahedron is something that is completely beyond our understanding? How can we know it without experiencing it?"

One day, some weeks after the disappearance, Samir climbed the three flights of stairs to the little flat and talked to Manoj rather incoherently about his conversations with Maya. He never doubted that she was out there somewhere in the distance between the stars. He was about to finish his Ph.D, he was going to an observatory in Chile later in the year, he would keep an eye out for her. At this, Manoj laughed a little bitterly. He guessed something from the dazed look in the young man's eyes.

"I'll be watching too," he said. "I think if she comes back it will be in the Thar desert."

"The Thar . . . why there?"

"She told me about the white van. It said Ravindra Refrigeration, Udaipur, Rajasthan. No such company, by the way, I checked. But my guess is that was where the Tetrahedron used to appear, in the middle of the desert. This time they made a mistake—or something—who knows? Although there was, I think, at least an exit door still over the Thar . . . "

Samir ran his fingers through his hair.

"But what does it all mean?" he cried.

He took his leave and returned to campus. He had an appointment with his professor in twenty minutes, and a class to attend after that. It was a hot, still, dusty sort of day, and the grit in the air burned in his throat. He stopped in front of the Physics building, then, abruptly, turned around and made his way to the tea-shack. It was deserted, except for Ramu stirring a potful of aromatic brew. Samir sat down on the bench. Ramu poured out some tea and handed him his glass wordlessly. In the background, the radio was playing an old Kishore Kumar favourite . . .

"Chalte, chalte, mere yeh geet yaad rakhana, kabhi alvida na kehena, kabhi alvida na kehena . . . " *As you go through life, remember my songs, never say goodbye forever, never say goodbye . . .*

Samir's eyes filled with tears. In the tree overhead, a crow cawed.

THE MAN

PAUL McAULEY

He came to Cho Ziyi at night, in the middle of a flux storm.

It was as dark as it ever got in the sunset zone. Low, fast-moving clouds closed off the sky. Howling winds drove waves onshore and blew horizontal streamers of snow into the forest, where the vanes of spin trees madly clattered and coronal discharges jumped and crackled. Ziyi was hunkered down in her cabin, watching an ancient movie about a gangster romance in Hong Kong's fabled Chungking Mansions. A fire breathed in the stone hearth and her huskies, Jung and Cheung, sprawled in a careless tangle on the borometz-hide rug. The dogs suddenly lifting their heads, the youngest, Cheung, scrambling to his feet and barking, something striking the door. Once, twice.

Ziyi froze the movie and sat still, listening. A slight, severe woman in her late sixties, dressed in jeans and a flannel shirt, white hair scraped back in a long ponytail, jumping just a little when there was another thump. It wouldn't be the first time that an indricothere or some other big dumb beast had trampled down a section of fence and blundered into the compound. She crossed to the window and unbolted the shutter. Pressed her cheek against the cold glass, squinted sideways, saw a dim pale figure on the raised porch. A naked man, arm raised, striking the door with the flat of his hand.

The two dogs stood behind her, alert and as anxious. Cheung whined when she looked at him.

"It's only a man," Ziyi said. "Be quiet and let me think."

He was in some kind of trouble, no question. A lost traveller, an accident on the road. But who would travel through a storm like this, and where were his clothes? She remembered the bandits who'd hit a road train a couple of years ago. Perhaps they'd come back. He had managed to escape, but he couldn't have gone far, not like that, not in weather like this. They might be here any minute. Or perhaps they were already out there, waiting for her to open the door. But she knew she couldn't leave him to die.

She fetched a blanket and lifted her short-barrelled shotgun from its wall pegs, unbolted the door, cracked it open. Snow skirled in. The naked man stared at her, dull-eyed. He was tall, pale-skinned. Snow was crusted in his shock of black hair. He didn't seem to notice the cold. Staring blankly at her, as if being confronted by an old woman armed with a shotgun was no surprise at all.

Ziyi told him to move off the porch, repeating the request in each of her half dozen languages. He seemed to understand English, and took a step backwards. Snow whirled around him and snow blew across the compound, out of darkness and back into darkness. Fat sparks snapped high in a stand of spike trees, like the apparatus in that old Frankenstein movie. Ziyi saw the gate in the fence was open, saw footprints crossing the deep snow, a single set.

"Are you hurt? What happened to you?"

His face was as blank as a mask.

She lofted the blanket towards him. It struck his chest and fell to his feet. He looked at it, looked at her. She was reminded of the cow her grandmother had kept, in the smallholding that had been swallowed by one of Shanghai's new satellite towns in the last gasp of frantic expansion before the Spasm.

"Go around the side of the cabin," she told him. "To your left. There's a shed. The door is unlocked. You can stay there. We'll talk in the morning."

The man picked up the blanket and plodded off around the corner of cabin. Ziyi bolted the door and opened the shutters at each of the cabin's four small windows and looked out and saw only blowing snow.

She sat by the fire for a long time, wondering who he was, what had happened to him. Wondering—because no ordinary man could have survived the storm for very long—if he was a thing of the Jackaroo. A kind of avatar that no one had seen before. Or perhaps he was some species of alien creature as yet undiscovered, that by an accident of evolution resembled a man. One of the Old Ones, one of the various species which had occupied Yanos before it had been gifted to the human race, woken from a sleep of a thousand centuries. Only the Jackaroo knew what the Old Ones had looked like. They had all died out or disappeared long ago.

They could have looked like anything, so why not like a man? A man who spoke, or at least understood, English . . .

At last she pulled on her parka and took her shotgun and, accompanied by Jung and Cheung, went outside. The storm was beginning to blow itself out. The snow came in gusts now and the dark was no longer uniform. To the south-east, Sauron's dull coal glimmered at the horizon.

Snow was banked up on one side of the little plastic utility shed, almost to the roof. Inside, the man lay asleep between stacks of logs and drums of diesel oil, wrapped in the blanket so that only his head showed. He did not stir when Cheung barked and nipped at the hem of Ziyi's parka, trying to drag her away.

She closed the door of the shed and went back to her cabin, and slept.

When she woke, the sky was clear of cloud and Sauron's orange light tangled long shadows across the snow. A spin tree had fallen down just outside the fence; the vanes of all the others, thousands upon thousands, spun in wind that was now no more than the usual wind, blowing from sunside to darkside. Soon, the snow would melt and she would go down to the beach and see what had been cast up. But first she had to see to her strange guest.

She took him a canister of pork hash. He was awake, sitting with the blanket fallen to his waist. After Ziyi mimed what he should do, he ate a couple of mouthfuls, although he used his fingers rather than the spoon. His feet were badly cut and there was a deep gash in his shin. Smaller cuts on his face and hands, like old knife wounds. All of them clean and pale, like little mouths. No sign of blood. She thought of him stumbling through the storm, through the lashing forest . . .

He looked up at her. Sharp blue eyes, with something odd about the pupils—they weren't round, she realised with a clear cold shock, but were edged with small triangular indentations, like cogs.

He couldn't or wouldn't answer her questions.

"Did the Jackaroo do this to you? Are you one of them? Did they make you?"

It was no good.

She brought him clothes. A sweater, jeans, an old pair of wellington boots with the toes and heels slit so they would fit his feet. He followed her about the compound as she cleared up trash that had blown in, and the two huskies followed both of them at a wary distance. When she went down to the beach, he came too.

Snow lay in long rakes on the black sand and meltwater ran in a thousand braided channels to the edge of the sea. Sea foam floated on the wind-blown waves, trembled amongst rocks. Flecks of colour flashed here and there: flotsam from the factory.

The man walked down to the water's edge. He seemed fascinated by the half-drowned ruins that stretched towards the horizon, hectares of spires and broken walls washed by waves, silhouetted against Sauron's fat disc, which sat where it always sat, just above the sea's level horizon.

Like all the worlds gifted by the Jackaroo, Yanos orbited close to the hearthfire of its M-class red dwarf sun; unlike the others, it had never been spun up. Like Earth's moon, it was tidally locked. One face warm and lighted, with a vast and permanent rainstorm at the equator, where Sauron hung directly overhead; the other a starlit icecap, and perpetual winds blowing from warm and light to cold and dark. Human settlements were scattered through the forests of the twilight belt where the weather was less extreme.

As the man stared out at the ruins, hair tangling in warm wind blowing off the sea, maybe listening, maybe not, Ziyi explained that people called it the factory, although they didn't really know what it was, or who had built it.

"Stuff comes from it, washes up here. Especially after a storm. I collect it, take it into town, sell it. Mostly base plastics, but sometimes you find nice things that are worth more. You help me, okay? You earn your keep."

But he stayed where he was, staring out at the factory ruins, while she walked along the driftline, picking up shards and fragments. While she worked, she wondered what he might be worth, and who she could sell him to. Not to Sergey Polzin, that was for damn sure. She'd have to contact one of the brokers in the capital . . . This man, he was a once-in-a-lifetime find. But how could she make any kind of deal without being cheated?

Ziyi kept checking on him, showed him the various finds. After a little while, straightening with one hand in the small of her aching back, she saw that he had taken off his clothes and stood with his arms stretched out, his skin warmly tinted in the level sunlight.

She filled her fat-tyred cart and told him it was time to put on his clothes and go. She mimed what she wanted him to do until he got the idea and dressed and helped her pull the cart back to the cabin. He watched her unload her harvest into one of the storage bins she'd built from the trimmed trunks of spike trees. She'd almost finished when he scooped up a handful of bright fragments and threw them in and looked at her as if for approval.

Ziyi remembered her little girl, in a sunlit kitchen on a faraway world. Even after all these years, the memory still pricked her heart.

"You're a quick learner," she said.

He smiled. Apart from those strange starry pupils and his pale, poreless skin, he looked entirely human.

"Come into the cabin," she said, weightless with daring. "We'll eat."

He didn't touch the food she offered; but sipped a little water, holding the tumbler in both hands. As far as she knew, he hadn't used the composting toilet. When she'd shown it to him and explained how it worked, he'd shrugged the way a small child would dismiss as unimportant something she couldn't understand.

They watched a movie together, and the two dogs watched them from a corner of the room. When it had finished, Ziyi gave the man an extra blanket and a rug and locked him in the shed for the night.

So it went the next day, and the days after that.

The man didn't eat. Sometimes he drank a little water. Once, on the beach, she found him nibbling at a shard of plastic. Shocked, she'd dashed it from his hand and he'd flinched away, clearly frightened.

Ziyi took a breath. Told herself that he was not really a man, took out a strip of dried borometz meat and took a bite and chewed and smiled and rubbed her stomach. Picked up the shard of plastic and held it out to him. "This is your food? This is what you are made of?"

He shrugged.

She talked to him, as they worked. Pointed to a flock of windskimmers skating along far out to sea, told him they were made by the factory. "Maybe like you, yes?" Named the various small shelly ticktock things that scuttled along the margins of the waves, likewise made by the factory. She told him the names of the trees that stood up beyond the tumble of boulders along the top of the beach. Told him how spin trees generated sugars from air and water and electricity. Warned him to avoid the bubbleweed that sent long scarlet runners across the black sand, told him that it was factory stuff and its tendrils moved towards him because they were heat-seeking.

"Let them touch, they stick little fibres like glass into your skin. Very bad."

He had a child's innocent curiosity, scrutinising ticktocks and scraps of plastic with the same frank intensity, watching with rapt attention a group of borometz grazing on rafts of waterweed cast up by the storm.

"The world is dangerous," Ziyi said. "Those borometz look very cute, harmless balls of fur, but they carry ticks that have poisonous bites. And there are worse things in the forest. Wargs, sasquatch. Worst of all are people. You stay away from them."

She told herself that she was keeping her find safe from people like Sergey Polzin, who would most likely try to vivisect him to find out how he worked, or keep him alive while selling him off finger by finger, limb by limb. She no longer planned to sell him to a broker, had vague plans about contacting the university in the capital. They wouldn't pay much, but they probably wouldn't cut him up, either . . .

She told him about her life. Growing up in Hong Kong. Her father the surgeon, her mother the biochemist. The big apartment, the servants, the trips abroad. Her studies in Vancouver University, her work in a biomedical company in Shanghai. Skipping over her marriage and her daughter, that terrible day when the global crisis had finally peaked in the Spasm. Seoul had been vapourised by a North Korean atomic missile; Shanghai had been hit by an Indian missile; two dozen cities around the world had been likewise devastated. Ziyi had been on a flight to Seoul; the plane had made an emergency landing at a military airbase and she'd made her way back to Shanghai by train, by truck, on foot. And discovered that her home was gone; the entire neighbourhood had been levelled. She'd spent a year working in a hospital in a refugee camp, trying and failing to find her husband and her daughter and her parents . . . It was too painful to talk about that; instead, she told the man about the day the Jackaroo made themselves known, the big ship suddenly appearing over the ruins of Shanghai, big ships appearing above all the major cities.

"The Jackaroo gave us the possibility of a new start. New worlds. Many argued against this, to begin with. Saying that we needed to fix everything on Earth. Not just the Spasm, but global warming, famines, all the rest. But many others disagreed. They won the lottery or bought tickets off winners and went up and out. Me, I went to work for the UN, the United Nations, as a translator," Ziyi said.

Thirty years, in Cape Town, in Berlin, in Brasilia. Translating for delegates at meetings and committees on the treaties and deals with the Jackaroo. She'd married again, lost her husband to cancer.

"I earned a lottery ticket because of my work, and I left the Earth and came here. I thought I could make a new start. And I ended up here, an old woman picking up alien scrap on an alien beach thousands of light years from home. Sometimes I think that I am dead. That my family survived the Spasm but I died, and all this is a dream of my last second of life. What does that make you, if it's true?"

The man listened to her, but gave no sign that he understood.

One day, she found a precious scrap of superconducting plastic. It wasn't much bigger than her thumbnail, transparent, shot through with silvery threads.

"This is worth more than ten cartloads of base plastic," she told the man. "Electronics companies use it in their smartphones and slates. No one knows how to make it, so they pay big money. We live off this for two, three weeks."

She didn't think he'd understand, but he walked up and down the tideline all that day and found two more slivers of superconductor, and the next day found five. Amazing. Like the other prospectors who mined the beach and the ruins in the forests, she'd tried and failed to train her dogs to sniff out the good stuff, but the man was like a trufflehound. Single-minded, sharp-eyed, eager to please.

"You did good," she told him. "I think I might keep you."

She tried to teach him tai chi exercises, moving him into different poses. His smooth cool skin. No heartbeat that she could find. She liked to watch him trawl along the beach, the dogs trotting alongside him. She'd sit on the spur of a tree trunk and watch until the man and the dogs disappeared from sight, watch as they came back. He'd come to her with his hands cupped in front, shyly showing her the treasures he'd found.

After ten days, the snow had melted and the muddy roads were more or less passable again, and Ziyi drove into town in her battered Suzuki jeep. She'd locked the man in the shed and left Jung and Cheung roaming the compound to guard him.

In town, she sold her load of plastic at the recycling plant, saving the trove of superconducting plastic until last. Unfolding a square of black cloth to show the little heap of silvery stuff to the plant's manager, a gruff Ukranian with radiation scars welting the left side of his face.

"You got lucky," he said.

"I work hard," she said. "How much?"

They settled on a price that was more than the rest of her earnings that year. The manager had to phone Sergey Polzin to authorise it.

Ziyi asked the manager if he'd heard of any trouble, after the storm. A missing prospector, a bandit attack, anything like that.

"Road got washed out twenty klicks to the east is all I know."

"No one is missing?"

"Sergey might know, I guess. What are you going to do with all that cash, Ziyi?"

"Maybe I buy this place one day. I'm getting old. Can't spend all my life trawling for junk on the beach."

Ziyi visited the hardware store, exchanged scraps of gossip with the store owner and a couple of women who were mining the ruins out in the forest. None of them had heard anything about a bandit attack, or an accident on the coast road. In the internet café, she bought a mug of green tea and an hour on one of the computers. Searched the local news for a bandit attack, some prospector caught in the storm, a plane crash, found nothing. No recent reports of anyone missing or vehicles found abandoned.

She sat back, thinking. So much for her theory that the man was some kind of Jackaroo spy who'd been travelling incognito and had got into trouble when the storm hit. She widened her search. Here was a child who had wandered into the forest. Here was a family, their farm discovered deserted, doors smashed down, probably by sasquatch. Here was the road train that had been attacked by bandits, two years ago. Here was a photograph of the man.

Ziyi felt cold, then hot. Looked around at the café's crowded tables. Clicked on the photo to enlarge it.

It was him. It was the man.

His name was Tony Michaels. Twenty-eight years old, a petrochemist. One of three people missing, presumed taken by the bandits after they killed everyone else. Leaving behind a wife and two children, in the capital.

A family. He'd been human, once upon a time.

Someone in the café laughed; Ziyi heard voices, the chink of cutlery, the hiss of the coffee urn, felt suddenly that everyone was watching her. She sent the photo of Tony Michaels to the printer, shut down the browser, snatched up the printout and left.

She was unlocking her jeep when Sergey Polzin called out to her. The man stepping towards her across the slick mud, dressed in his usual combat gear, his pistol at his hip. He owned the recycling plant, the internet café, and the town's only satellite dish, and acted as if he was the town's unelected mayor. Greeting visitors and showing off the place as if it was something more than a squalid street of shacks squatting amongst factory ruins. Pointing out where the water treatment plant would be, talking about plans for concreting the air strip, building a hospital, a school, that would never come to anything.

Saying to Ziyi, "Heard you hit a big find."

"The storm washed up a few things," Ziyi said, trying to show nothing while Sergey studied her. Trying not to think about the printout folded into the inside pocket of her parka, over her heart.

He said, "I also heard you wanted to report trouble."

"I was wondering how everyone was, after the storm."

He gazed at her for a few moments, then said, "Any trouble, anything unusual, you come straight to me. Understand?"

"Completely."

When Ziyi got back to the cabin she sat the man down and showed him the printout, then fetched her mirror from the wall and held it in front of him, angling it this way and that, pointing to it, pointing to the paper.

"You," she said. "Tony Michaels. You."

He looked at the paper and the mirror, looked at the paper again and ran his fingertips over his smooth face. He didn't need to shave, and his hair was exactly as long as it was in the photo.

"You," she said.

That was who he had been. But what was he now?

The next day she coaxed him into the jeep with the two dogs, and drove west along the coast road, forest on one side and the sea stretching out to the horizon on the other, until she spotted the burnt-out shells of the road train, overgrown with great red drapes of bubbleweed. The dogs jumped off and nosed around; the man slowly climbed out, looked about him, taking no especial notice of the old wreckage.

She had pictured it in her head. His slow recognition. Leading her to the place where he'd hidden or crawled away to die from grievous wounds. The place that had turned him or copied him or whatever it was the factory had done.

Instead, he wandered off to a patch of sunlight in the middle of the road and stood there until she told him they were going for a walk.

They walked a long way, slowly spiralling away from the road. There were factory ruins here, as in most parts of the forest. Stretches of broken wall. Chains of cubes heaved up and broken, half-buried, overgrown by the arched roots of spine trees, and thatches of copperberry and bubbleweed, but the man seemed no more interested in them than in the wreckage of the road train.

"You were gone two years. What happened to you?"

He shrugged.

At last, they walked back to the road. The sun stood at the horizon, as always, throwing shadows over the road. The man walked towards the patch of sunlight where he'd stood before, and kept walking.

Ziyi and the two dogs followed. Through a thin screen of trees to the edge of a sheer drop. Water far below, lapping at rocks. No, not rocks. Factory ruins.

The man stared down at patches of waterweed rising and falling on waves that broke around broken walls.

Ziyi picked up a stone and threw it out beyond the cliff edge. "Was that what happened? You were running from the bandits, it was dark, you ran straight out over the edge . . . "

The man made a humming sound. He was looking at Sauron's fat orange disc now, and after a moment he closed his eyes and stretched out his arms.

Ziyi walked along the cliff edge, looking for and failing to find a path. The black rock plunged straight down, a sheer drop cut by vertical crevices that only an experienced climber might use to pick a route down. She tried to picture it. The roadtrain stopping because fallen trees had blocked the road. Bandits appearing when the crew stepped down, shooting them, ordering the passengers out, stripping them of their clothes and belongings, shooting them one by one. Bandits didn't like to leave witnesses. One man breaking free, running into the darkness. Running through the trees, running blindly, wounded perhaps, definitely scared, panicked. Running straight out over the cliff edge. If the fall hadn't killed him, he would have drowned. And his body had washed into some active part of the factory, and it had fixed him. No, she thought. It had duplicated him. Had it taken two years? Or had he been living in some part of the factory, out at sea, until the storm had washed him away and he'd been cast up on the beach . . .

The man had taken off his clothes and stood with his arms out and his eyes closed, bathing in level orange light. She shook him until he opened his eyes and smiled at her, and she told him it was time to go.

Ziyi tried and failed to teach the man to talk. "You understand me. So why can't you tell me what happened to you?"

The man humming, smiling, shrugging.

Trying to get him to write or draw was equally pointless.

Days on the beach, picking up flotsam; nights watching movies. She had to suppose he was happy. Her constant companion. Her mystery. She had long ago given up the idea of selling him.

Once, Ziyi's neighbour, Besnik Shkelyim, came out of the forest while the man was searching the strandline. Ziyi told Besnik he was the son of an old friend in the capital, come to visit for a few weeks. Besnik seemed to accept the lie. They chatted about the weather and sasquatch sightings and the latest finds. Besnik did most of the talking. Ziyi was anxious and distracted, trying not to look towards the man, praying that he wouldn't wander over. At last, Besnik said that he could see that she was busy, he really should get back to his own work.

"Bring your friend to visit, some time. I show him where real treasure is found."

Ziyi said that she would, of course she would, watched Besnik walk away into the darkness under the trees, then ran to the man, giddy and foolish with relief, and told him how well he'd done, keeping away from the stranger.

He hummed. He shrugged.

"People are bad," Ziyi said. "Always remember that."

A few days later she went into town. She needed more food and fuel, and took with her a few of the treasures the man had found. Sergey Polzin was at the recycling plant, and fingered through the stuff she'd brought. Superconductor slivers. A variety of tinkertoys, hard little nuggets that changed shape when manipulated. A hand-sized sheet of the variety of plastic in which faint images came and went . . . It was not one-tenth of what the man had found for her—she'd buried the rest out in the forest— but she knew that she had made a mistake, knew she'd been greedy and foolish.

She tried her best to seem unconcerned as Sergey counted the silvers of superconducting plastic three times. "You've been having much luck, recently," he said, at last.

"The storm must have broken open a cache, somewhere out to sea," she said.

"Odd that no one else has been finding so much stuff."

"If we knew everything about the factory, Sergey Polzin, we would all be rich."

Sergey's smile was full of gold. "I hear you have some help. A guest worker."

Besnik had talked about her visitor. Of course he had.

Ziyi trotted out her lie.

"Bring him into town next time," Sergey said. "I'll show him around."

A few days later, Ziyi saw someone watching the compound from the edge of the forest. A flash of sunlight on a lens, a shadowy figure that faded into the shadows under the trees when she walked towards him. Ziyi ran, heard an engine start, saw a red pickup bucket out of the trees and speed off down the track.

She'd only had a glimpse of the intruder, but she was certain that it was the manager of the recycling plant.

She walked back to the compound. The man was facing the sun, naked, arms outstretched. Ziyi managed to get him to put on his clothes, but it was impossible to make him understand that he had to leave. Drive him into the forest, let him go? Yes, and sasquatch or wargs would eat him, or he'd find his way to some prospector's cabin and knock on the door . . .

She walked him down to the beach, but he followed her back to the cabin. In the end she locked him in the shed.

Early in the afternoon, Sergey Polzin's yellow Humvee came bumping down the track, followed by a UN Range Rover. Ziyi tried to be polite and cheerful, but Sergey walked straight past her, walked into the cabin, walked back out.

"Where is he?"

"My friend's son? He went back to the capital. What's wrong?" Ziyi said to the UN policewoman.

"It's a routine check," the policewoman, Aavert Enger, said.

"Do you have a warrant?"

"You're hiding dangerous technology," Sergey said. "We don't need a warrant."

"I am hiding nothing."

"There has been a report," Aavert Enger said.

Ziyi told her it was a misunderstanding, said that she'd had a visitor, yes, but he had left.

"I would know if someone came visiting from the capital," Sergey said. He was puffed up with self-righteousness. "I also know he was here today. I have a photograph that proves it. And I looked him up on the net, just like you did. You should have erased your cache, by the way. Tony

Michaels, missing for two years. Believed killed by bandits. And now he's living here."

"If I could talk to him I am sure we can clear this up," Aavert Enger said.

"He isn't here."

But it was no good. Soon enough, Sergey found the shed was locked and ordered Ziyi to hand over the keys. She refused. Sergey said he'd shoot off the padlock; the policewoman told him that there was no need for melodrama, and used a master key.

Jung and Cheung started to bark as Sergey led the man out. "Tony Michaels," he said to the policewoman. "The dead man Tony Michaels."

Ziyi said, "Look, Sergey Polzin, I'll be straight with you. I don't know who he really is or where he came from. He helps me on the beach. He helps me find things. All the good stuff I brought in, that was because of him. Don't spoil a good thing. Let me use him to find more stuff. You can take a share. For the good of the town. The school you want to build, the water treatment plant in a year, two years, we'll have enough to pay for them . . ."

But Sergey wasn't listening. He'd seen the man's eyes. "You see?" he said to Aavert Enger. "You see?"

"He is a person," Ziyi said. "Like you and me. He has a wife. He has children."

"And did you tell them you had found him?" Sergey said. "No, of course not. Because he is a dead man. No, not even that. He is a replica of a dead man, spun out in the factory somewhere."

"It is best we take him to town. Make him safe," the policewoman said.

The man was looking at Ziyi.

"How much?" Ziyi said to the policewoman. "How much did he offer you?"

"This isn't about money," Sergey said. "It's about the safety of the town."

"Yes. And the profit you'll make, selling him."

Ziyi was shaking. When Sergey started to pull the man towards the vehicles, she tried to get in his way. Sergey shoved at her, she fell down, and suddenly everything happened at once. The dogs, Jung and Cheung, ran at Sergey. He pushed the man away and fumbled for his pistol. Jung clamped his jaws around Sergey's wrist and started to shake him. Sergey sat down hard and Jung held on and Cheung darted in and seized his ankle. Sergey screaming while the dogs pulled in different directions, and Ziyi rolled to her feet and reached into the tangle of man and dogs and plucked up Sergey's pistol and snapped off the safety and turned to the policewoman and told her put up her hands.

"I am not armed," Aavert Enger said. "Do not be foolish, Ziyi."

Sergey was screaming at her, telling her to call off her dogs.

"It's good advice," Ziyi told the policewoman, "but it is too late."

The pistol was heavy, slightly greasy. The safety was off. The hammer cocked when she pressed lightly on the trigger.

The man was looking at her.

"I'm sorry," she said, and shot him.

The man's head snapped back and he lost his footing and fell in the mud, kicking and spasming. Ziyi stepped up to him and shot him twice more, and he stopped moving.

Ziyi called off the dogs, told Aavert Enger to sit down and put her hands on her head. Sergey was holding his arm. Blood seeped around his fingers. He was cursing her, but she paid him no attention.

The man was as light as a child, but she was out of breath by the time she had dragged him to her jeep. Sergey had left the keys in the ignition of his Humvee. Ziyi threw them towards the forest as hard as she could, shot out one of the tyres of Aavert Enger's Range Rover, loaded the man into the back of the jeep. Jung and Cheung jumped in, and she drove off.

Ziyi had to stop once, and threw up, and drove the rest of the way with half her attention on the rear-view mirror. When she reached the spot where the roadtrain had been ambushed, she cradled the man in her arms and carried him through the trees. The two dogs followed. When she reached the edge of the cliff her pulse was hammering in her head and she had to sit down. The man lay beside her. His head was blown open, showing layers of filmy plastics. Although his face was untouched you would not mistake him for a sleeper.

After a little while, when she was pretty certain she wasn't going to have a heart attack, she knelt beside him, and closed his eyes, and with a convulsive movement pitched him over the edge. She didn't look to see where he fell. She threw Sergey's pistol after him, and sat down to wait.

She didn't look around when the dogs began to bark. Aavert Enger said, "Where is he?"

"In the same place as Sergey's pistol."

Aavert Enger sat beside her. "You know I must arrest you, Ziyi."

"Of course."

"Actually, I am not sure what you'll be charged with. I'm not sure if we will charge you with anything. Sergey will want his day in court, but perhaps I can talk him out of it."

"How is he?"

"The bites are superficial. I think losing his prize hurt him more."

"I don't blame you," Ziyi said. "Sergey knew he was valuable, knew I would not give him up, knew that he would be in trouble if he tried to take it. So he told you. For the reward."

"Well, it's gone now. Whatever it was."

"It was a man," Ziyi said.

She had her cache of treasures, buried in the forest. She could buy lawyers. She could probably buy Sergey, if it came to it. She could leave, move back to the capital and live out her life in comfort, or buy passage to another of the worlds gifted by the Jackaroo, or even return to Earth.

But she knew that she would not leave. She would stay here and wait through the days and years until the factory returned her friend to her.

SEASONS
OF THE ANSARAC

URSULA K. LE GUIN

I talked for a long time once with an old Ansar. I met him at his Interplanary Hostel, which is on a large island far out in the Great Western Ocean, well away from the migratory routes of the Ansarac. It is the only place visitors from other planes are allowed, these days.

Kergemmeg lived there as a native host and guide, to give visitors a little whiff of local color, for otherwise the place is like a tropical island on any of a hundred planes—sunny, breezy, lazy, beautiful, with feathery trees and golden sands and great, blue-green, white-maned waves breaking on the reef out past the lagoon. Most visitors came to sail, fish, beachcomb, and drink fermented ü, and had no interest otherwise in the plane or in the sole native of it they met. They looked at him, at first, and took photos, of course, for he was a striking figure: about seven feet tall, thin, strong, angular, a little stooped by age, with a narrow head, large, round, black-and-gold eyes, and a beak. There is an all-or-nothing quality about a beak that keeps the beaked face from being as expressive as those on which the nose and mouth are separated, but Kergemmeg's eyes and eyebrows revealed his feelings very clearly. Old he might be, but he was a passionate man.

He was a little bored and lonely among the uninterested tourists, and when he found me a willing listener (surely not the first or last, but currently the only one) he took pleasure in telling me about his people, as we sat with a tall glass of iced ü in the long, soft evenings, in a purple darkness all aglow with the light of the stars, the shining of the sea-waves full of luminous creatures, and the pulsing glimmer of clouds of fireflies up in the fronds of the feather-trees.

From time immemorial, he said, the Ansarac had followed a Way. *Madan,* he called it. The way of my people, the way things are done, the way things are, the way to go, the way that is hidden in the word *always*: like ours, his word held all those meanings. "Then we strayed from our Way," he said. "For a little while. Now again we do as we have always done."

People are always telling you that "we have always done thus," and then you find that their "always" means a generation or two, or a century or two, at most a millennium or two. Cultural ways and habits are blips, compared to the ways and habits of the body, of the race. There really is very little that human beings on our plane have "always" done, except find food and drink, sleep, sing, talk, procreate, nurture the children, and probably band together to some extent. Indeed it can be seen as our human essence, how few behavioral imperatives we follow. How flexible we are in finding new things to do, new ways to go. How ingeniously, inventively, desperately we seek the right way, the true way, the Way we believe we lost long ago among the thickets of novelty and opportunity and choice . . .

The Ansarac had a somewhat different choice to make than we did, perhaps a more limited one. But it has its interest.

Their world is farther from a larger sun than ours, so, though its spin and tilt are much the same as Earth's, its year lasts about twenty-four of our years. And the seasons are correspondingly large and leisurely, each of them six of our years long.

On every plane and in every climate that has a spring, spring is the breeding time, when new life is born; and for creatures whose life is only a few seasons or a few years, early spring is mating time, too, when new life begins. So it is for the Ansarac, whose life span is, in their terms, three years.

They inhabit two continents, one on the equator and a little north of it, one that stretches up towards the north pole; the two are joined, as the Americas are, by a narrower mountainous bridge of land, though it is all on a smaller scale. The rest of the world is ocean, with a few archipelagoes and scattered large islands, none with any human population except the one used by the Interplanary Agency.

The year begins, Kergemmeg said, when, in the cities of the plains and deserts of the South, the Year Priests give the word and great crowds gather to see the sun pause at the peak of a Tower or stab through a Target with an arrow of light at dawn: the moment of solstice. Now increasing heat will parch the southern grasslands and prairies of wild grain, and in the long dry season the rivers will run low and the wells of the city will go dry. Spring follows the sun northward, melting snow from those far hills, brightening valleys with green . . . And the Ansarac will follow the sun.

"Well, I'm off," old friend says to old friend in the city street. "See you around!" And the young people, the almost-one-year-olds—to us they'd be people of twenty-one or twenty-two—drift away from their households and groups of pals, their colleges and sports clubs, and seek out, among the labyrinthine apartment-complexes and communal dwellings and hostelries of the city, one or the other of the parents from whom they parted, back in the summer. Sauntering casually in, they remark, "Hullo, Dad," or "Hullo, Mother. Seems like everybody's going back north." And the parent, careful not to insult by offering guidance over the long route they came half the young one's life ago, says, "Yes, I've been thinking about it myself. It certainly would be nice to have you with us. Your sister's in the other room, packing."

And so by ones, twos, and threes, the people abandon the city. The exodus is a long process, without any order to it. Some people leave quite soon after the solstice, and others say about them, "What a hurry they're in," or "Shennenne just has to get there first so she can grab the old homesite." But some people linger in the city till it is almost empty, and still can't make up their mind to leave the hot and silent streets, the sad, shadeless, deserted squares, that were so full of crowds and music all through the long halfyear. But first and last they all set out on the roads that lead north. And once they go, they go with speed.

Most carry with them only what they can carry in a backpack or load on a ruba (from Kergemmeg's description, rubac are something like small, feathered donkeys). Some of the traders who have become wealthy during the Desert Season start out with whole trains of rubac loaded with goods and treasures. Though most people travel alone or in a small family group, on the more popular roads they follow pretty close after one another. Larger groups form temporarily in places where the going is hard and the older and weaker people need help gathering and carrying food.

There are no children on the road north.

Kergemmeg did not know how many Ansarac there are but guessed some hundreds of thousands, perhaps a million. All of them join the migration.

As they go up into the mountainous Middle Lands, they do not bunch together, but spread out onto hundreds of different tracks, some followed by many, others by only a few, some clearly marked, others so cryptic that only people who have been on them before could ever trace the turnings. "That's when it's good to have a three-year-old along," Kergemmeg said. "Somebody who's been up the way twice." They travel very light and very fast. They live off the land except in the arid heights of the mountains, where, as he said, "They lighten their packs." And up in those passes and high canyons, the hard-driven rubac of the traders' caravans begin to stumble and tremble, perishing of exhaustion and cold. If the trader still tries to drive them on, people on the road unload them and loose them and let their own pack-beast go with them. The little animals limp and scramble back down southward, back to the desert. The goods they carried end up strewn along the wayside for anyone to take; but nobody takes anything, except a little food at need. They don't want stuff to carry, to slow them down. Spring is coming, cool spring, sweet spring, to the valleys of grass and the forests, the lakes, the bright rivers of the North, and they want to be there when it comes.

Listening to Kergemmeg, I imagined that if one could see the migration from above, see those people all threading along a thousand paths and trails, it would be like seeing our Northwest Coast in spring a century or two ago when every stream, from the mile-wide Columbia to the tiniest creek, turned red with the salmon run.

The salmon spawn and die when they reach their goal, and some of the Ansarac are going home to die, too: those on their third migration north, the three-year-olds, whom we would see as people of seventy and over. Some of them don't make it all the way. Worn out by privation and hard going, they drop behind. If people pass an old man or woman sitting by the road, they may speak a word or two, help to put up a little shelter, leave a gift of food, but they do not urge the elder to come with them. If the elder is very weak or ill they may wait a night or two, until perhaps another migrant takes their place. If they find an old person dead by the roadside, they bury the body. On its back, with the feet to the north: going home.

There are many, many graves along the roads north, Kergemmeg said. Nobody has ever made a fourth migration.

The younger people, those on their first and second migrations, hurry on, crowded together in the high passes of the mountains, then spreading out ever wider on a myriad narrow paths through the prairies as the Middle Land widens out north of the mountains. By the time they reach the Northland proper, the great rivers of people have tasseled out into thousands of rivulets, veering west and east, across the north.

Coming to a pleasant hill country where the grass is already green and the trees are leafing out, one of the little groups comes to a halt. "Well, here we are," says Mother. "Here it is." There are tears in her eyes and she laughs, the soft, clacking laugh of the Ansarac. "Shuku, do you remember this place?"

And the daughter who was less than a halfyear old when she left this place—eleven or so, in our years—stares around with amazement and incredulity, and laughs, and cries, "But it was *bigger* than this!"

Then perhaps Shuku looks across those half-familiar meadows of her birthplace to the just-visible roof of the nearest neighbor and wonders if Kimimmid and his father, who caught up to them and camped with them for a few nights and then went on ahead, were there already, living there, and if so, would Kimimmid come over to say hello?

For, though the people who lived so close-packed, in such sociable and ceaseless promiscuity in the Cities Under the Sun, sharing rooms, sharing beds, sharing work and play, doing everything together in groups and crowds, now have all gone apart, family from family, friend from friend, each to a small and separate house here in the meadowlands, or farther north in the rolling hills, or still farther north in the lakelands— even though they have all scattered out like sand from a broken hourglass, the bonds that unite them have not broken; only changed. Now they come together, not in groups and crowds, not in tens and hundreds and thousands, but by two and two.

"Well, here you are!" says Shuku's mother, as Shuku's father opens the door of the little house at the meadow's edge. "You must have been just a few days ahead of us."

"Welcome home," he says gravely. His eyes shine. The two adults take each other by the hand and slightly raise their narrow, beaked heads in a particular salute, an intimate yet formal greeting. Shuku suddenly remembers seeing them do that when she was a little girl, when they lived here, long ago. Here at the birthplace.

"Kimimmid was asking about you just yesterday," Father says to Shuku, and he softly clacks a laugh.

Spring is coming, spring is upon them. Now they will perform the ceremonies of the spring.

Kimimmid comes across the meadow to visit, and he and Shuku talk together, and walk together in the meadows and down by the stream. Presently, after a day or a week or two, he asks her if she would like to dance. "Oh, I don't know," she says, but seeing him stand tall and straight, his head thrown back a little, in the posture that begins the dance, she too stands up; at first her head is lowered, though she stands straight, arms at her sides; but then she wants to throw her head back, back, to reach her arms out wide, wide . . . to dance, to dance with him . . .

And what are Shuku's parents and Kimimmid's parents doing, in the kitchen garden or out in the old orchard, but the same thing? They face each other, they raise their proud and narrow heads, and then he leaps, arms raised above his head, a great leap and a bow, a low bow . . . and she bows too . . . And so it goes, the courtship dance. All over the northern continent, now, the people are dancing.

Nobody interferes with the older couples, recourting, refashioning their marriage. But Kimimmid had better look out. A young man comes across the meadow one evening, a young man Shuku never met before; his birthplace is some miles away. He has heard of Shuku's beauty. He sits and talks with her. He tells her that he is building a new house, in a grove of trees, a pretty spot, nearer her home than his. He would like her advice on how to build the house. He would like very much to dance with her some time. Maybe this evening, just for a little, just a step or two, before he goes away?

He is a wonderful dancer. Dancing with him on the grass in the late evening of early spring, Shuku feels that she is flying on a great wind, and she closes her eyes, her hands float out from her sides as if on that wind, and meet his hands . . .

Her parents will live together in the house by the meadow; they will have no more children, for that time is over for them, but they will make love as often as ever they did when they first were married. Shuku will choose one of her suitors, the new one, in fact. She goes to live with him and make love with him in the house they finish building together. Their building, their dancing, gardening, eating, sleeping, everything they do, turns into making love. And in due course Shuku is pregnant; and in due course she bears two babies. Each is born in a tough, white membrane or shell. Both parents tear this protective covering open with hands and beaks, freeing the tiny curled-up newborn, who lifts its infinitesimal beaklet and peeps blindly, already gaping, greedy for food, for life.

The second baby is smaller, is not greedy, does not thrive. Though

Shuku and her husband both feed her with tender care, and Shuku's mother comes to stay and feeds the little one from her own beak and rocks her endlessly when she cries, still she pines and weakens. One morning lying in her grandmother's arms the infant twists and gasps for breath, and then is still. The grandmother weeps bitterly, remembering Shuku's baby brother, who did not live even this long, and tries to comfort Shuku. The baby's father digs a small grave out back of the new house, among the budding trees of the long springtime, and the tears fall and fall from his eyes as he digs. But the other baby, the big girl, Kikirri, chirps and clacks and eats and thrives.

About the time Kikirri is hauling herself upright and shouting "Da!" at her father and "Ma!" at her mother and grandmother and "No!" when told to stop what she is doing, Shuku has another baby. Like many second conceptions, it is a singleton. A fine boy, small, but greedy. He grows fast.

LAMBING SEASON

MOLLY GLOSS

—◈—

From May to September, Delia took the Churro sheep and two dogs and went up on Joe-Johns Mountain to live. She had that country pretty much to herself all summer. Ken Owen sent one of his Mexican hands up every other week with a load of groceries, but otherwise she was alone, alone with the sheep and the dogs. She liked the solitude. Liked the silence. Some sheepherders she knew talked a blue streak to the dogs, the rocks, the porcupines, they sang songs and played the radio, read their magazines out loud, but Delia let the silence settle into her, and, by early summer, she had begun to hear the ticking of the dry grasses as a language she could almost translate. The dogs were named Jesus and Alice. "Away to me, Jesus," she said when they were moving the sheep. "Go bye, Alice." From May to September these words spoken in command of the dogs were almost the only times she heard her own voice; that, and when the Mexican brought the groceries, a polite exchange in Spanish about the weather, the health of the dogs, the fecundity of the ewes.

The Churros were a very old breed. The O-Bar Ranch had a federal allotment up on the mountain, which was all rimrock and sparse grasses well suited to the Churros, who were fiercely protective of their lambs and had a long-stapled top coat that could take the weather. They did well on the thin grass of the mountain where other sheep would lose flesh and give up their lambs to the coyotes. The Mexican was an old man. He said he remembered Churros from his childhood in the Oaxaca highlands, the rams with their four horns, two curving up, two down. "Buen' carne," he told Delia. Uncommonly fine meat.

The wind blew out of the southwest in the early part of the season, a wind that smelled of juniper and sage and pollen; in the later months, it blew straight from the east, a dry wind smelling of dust and smoke, bringing down showers of parched leaves and seedheads of yarrow and bittercress. Thunderstorms came frequently out of the east, enormous cloudscapes with hearts of livid magenta and glaucous green. At those times, if she was camped on a ridge, she'd get out of her bed and walk downhill to find a draw where she could feel safer, but if she were camped in a low place, she would stay with the sheep while a war passed over their heads, spectacular jagged flares of lightning, skull-rumbling cannonades of thunder. It was maybe bred into the bones of Churros, a knowledge and a tolerance of mountain weather, for they shifted together and waited out the thunder with surprising composure; they stood forbearingly while rain beat down in hard blinding bursts.

Sheepherding was simple work, although Delia knew some herders who made it hard, dogging the sheep every minute, keeping them in a tight group, moving all the time. She let the sheep herd themselves, do what they wanted, make their own decisions. If the band began to separate, she would whistle or yell, and often the strays would turn around and rejoin the main group. Only if they were badly scattered did she send out the dogs. Mostly she just kept an eye on the sheep, made sure they got good feed, that the band didn't split, that they stayed in the boundaries of the O-Bar allotment. She studied the sheep for the language of their bodies, and tried to handle them just as close to their nature as possible. When she put out salt for them, she scattered it on rocks and stumps as if she were hiding Easter eggs, because she saw how they enjoyed the search.

The spring grass made their manure wet, so she kept the wool cut away from the ewes' tail area with a pair of sharp, short-bladed shears. She dosed the sheep with wormer, trimmed their feet, inspected their teeth, treated ewes for mastitis. She combed the burrs from the dogs' coats and inspected them for ticks. *You're such good dogs*, she told them with her hands. *I'm very very proud of you.*

She had some old binoculars, 7 x 32s, and in the long quiet days, she watched bands of wild horses miles off in the distance, ragged looking mares with dorsal stripes and black legs. She read the back issues of the local newspapers, looking in the obits for names she recognized. She read spine-broken paperback novels and played solitaire and scoured the ground for arrowheads and rocks she would later sell to rockhounds. She studied the parched brown grass, which was full of grasshoppers and beetles and crickets and ants. But most of her day was spent just walking.

The sheep sometimes bedded quite a ways from her trailer and she had to get out to them before sunrise when the coyotes would make their kills. She was usually up by three or four and walking out to the sheep in darkness. Sometimes she returned to the camp for lunch, but always she was out with the sheep again until sundown, when the coyotes were likely to return, and then she walked home after dark to water and feed the dogs, eat supper, climb into bed.

In her first years on Joe-Johns, she had often walked three or four miles away from the band just to see what was over a hill, or to study the intricate architecture of a sheepherder's monument. Stacking up flat stones in the form of an obelisk was a common herders' pastime, their monuments all over that sheep country, and though Delia had never felt an impulse to start one herself, she admired the ones other people had built. She sometimes walked miles out of her way just to look at a rockpile up close.

She had a mental map of the allotment, divided into ten pastures. Every few days, when the sheep had moved on to a new pasture, she moved her camp. She towed the trailer with an old Dodge pickup, over the rocks and creekbeds, the sloughs and dry meadows, to the new place. For a while afterward, after the engine was shut off and while the heavy old body of the truck was settling onto its tires, she would be deaf, her head filled with a dull roaring white noise.

She had about eight hundred ewes, as well as their lambs, many of them twins or triplets. The ferocity of the Churro ewes in defending their offspring was sometimes a problem for the dogs, but in the balance of things, she knew that it kept her losses small. Many coyotes lived on Joe-Johns, and sometimes a cougar or bear would come up from the salt pan desert on the north side of the mountain, looking for better country to own. These animals considered the sheep to be fair game, which Delia understood to be their right; and also her right, hers and the dogs', to take the side of the sheep. Sheep were smarter than people commonly believed and the Churros smarter than other sheep she had tended, but by mid-summer the coyotes always passed the word among themselves, buen' carne, and Delia and the dogs then had a job to work, keeping the sheep out of harm's way.

She carried a .32 caliber Colt pistol in an old-fashioned holster worn on her belt. *If you're a coyot' you'd better be careful of this woman*, she said with her body, with the way she stood and the way she walked when she was wearing the pistol. That gun and holster had once belonged to her mother's mother, a woman who had come West on her own and homesteaded for a while, down in the Sprague River Canyon. Delia's grandmother had liked to tell the story: how a concerned neighbor, a bachelor with an interest in marriageable females, had pressed the gun upon her, back when the Klamaths were at war with the army of General Joel Palmer; and how she never had used it for anything but shooting rabbits.

In July, a coyote killed a lamb while Delia was camped no more than two hundred feet away from the bedded sheep. It was dusk, and she was sitting on the steps of the trailer reading a two-gun western, leaning close over the pages in the failing light, and the dogs were dozing at her feet. She heard the small sound, a strange high faint squeal she did not recognize and then did recognize, and she jumped up and fumbled for the gun, yelling at the coyote, at the dogs, her yell startling the entire band to its feet but the ewes making their charge too late, Delia firing too late, and none of it doing any good beyond a release of fear and anger.

A lion might well have taken the lamb entire; she had known of lion kills where the only evidence was blood on the grass and a dribble of entrails in the beam of a flashlight. But a coyote is small and will kill with a bite to the throat and then perhaps eat just the liver and heart, though a mother coyote will take all she can carry in her stomach, bolt it down and carry it home to her pups. Delia's grandmother's pistol had scared this one off before it could even take a bite, and the lamb was twitching and whole on the grass, bleeding only from its neck. The mother ewe stood over it, crying in a distraught and pitiful way, but there was nothing to be done, and, in a few minutes, the lamb was dead.

There wasn't much point in chasing after the coyote, and anyway, the whole band was now a skittish jumble of anxiety and confusion; it was hours before the mother ewe gave up her grieving, before Delia and the dogs had the band calm and bedded down again, almost midnight. By then, the dead lamb had stiffened on the ground, and she dragged it over by the truck and skinned it and let the dogs have the meat, which went against her nature, but was about the only way to keep the coyote from coming back for the carcass.

While the dogs worked on the lamb, she stood with both hands pressed to her tired back, looking out at the sheep, the mottled pattern of their whiteness almost opalescent across the black landscape, and the stars thick and bright above the faint outline of the rock ridges, stood there a moment before turning toward the trailer, toward bed, and afterward, she would think how the coyote and the sorrowing ewe and the dark of the July moon and the kink in her back, how all of that came together and was the reason that she was standing there watching the sky, was the reason that she saw the brief, brilliantly green flash in the southwest and then the sulfur yellow streak breaking across the night, southwest to due west on a descending arc onto Lame Man Bench. It was a broad bright ribbon, rainbow-wide, a cyanotic contrail. It was not a meteor, she had seen hundreds of meteors. She stood and looked at it.

Things to do with the sky, with distance, you could lose perspective, it was hard to judge even a lightning strike, whether it had touched down on a particular hill or the next hill or the valley between. So she knew this thing falling out of the sky might have come down miles to the west of Lame Man, not onto Lame Man at all, which was two miles away, at least two miles, and getting there would be all ridges and rocks, no way to cover the ground in the truck. She thought about it. She had moved camp earlier in the day, which was always troublesome work, and it had been a blistering hot day, and now the excitement with the coyote. She was very tired, the tiredness like a weight against her breastbone. She didn't know what this thing was, falling out of the sky. Maybe if she walked over there she would find just a dead satellite or a broken weather balloon and not dead or broken people. The contrail thinned slowly while she stood there looking at it, became a wide streak of yellowy cloud against the blackness, with the field of stars glimmering dimly behind it.

After a while, she went into the truck and got a water bottle and filled it, and also took the first aid kit out of the trailer and a couple of spare batteries for the flashlight and a handful of extra cartridges for the pistol, and stuffed these things into a backpack and looped her arms into the straps and started up the rise away from the dark camp, the bedded sheep. The dogs left off their gnawing of the dead lamb and trailed her anxiously, wanting to follow, or not wanting her to leave the sheep. "Stay by," she said to them sharply, and they went back and stood with the band and watched her go. *That coyot', he's done with us tonight:* This is what she told the dogs with her body, walking away, and she believed it was probably true.

Now that she'd decided to go, she walked fast. This was her sixth year on the mountain, and, by this time, she knew the country pretty well. She didn't use the flashlight. Without it, she became accustomed to the starlit darkness, able to see the stones and pick out a path. The air was cool, but full of the smell of heat rising off the rocks and the parched earth. She heard nothing but her own breathing and the gritting of her boots on the pebbly dirt. A little owl circled once in silence and then went off toward a line of cottonwood trees standing in black silhouette to the northeast.

Lame Man Bench was a great upthrust block of basalt grown over with scraggly juniper forest. As she climbed among the trees, the smell of something like ozone or sulfur grew very strong, and the air became thick, burdened with dust. Threads of the yellow contrail hung in the limbs of the trees. She went on across the top of the bench and onto slabs of shelving rock that gave a view to the west. Down in the steep-sided draw below her there was a big wing-shaped piece of metal resting on the ground, which she at first thought had been torn from an airplane, but then realized was a whole thing, not broken, and she quit looking for the rest of the wreckage. She squatted down and looked at it. Yellow dust settled slowly out of the sky, pollinating her hair, her shoulders, the toes of her boots, faintly dulling the oily black shine of the wing, the thing shaped like a wing.

While she was squatting there looking down at it, something came out from the sloped underside of it, a coyote she thought at first, and then it wasn't a coyote but a dog built like a greyhound or a whippet, deep-chested, long legged, very light-boned and frail-looking. She waited for somebody else, a man, to crawl out after his dog, but nobody did. The dog squatted to pee and then moved off a short distance and sat on its haunches and considered things. Delia considered, too. She considered that the dog might have been sent up alone. The Russians had sent up a dog in their little sputnik, she remembered. She considered that a skinny almost hairless dog with frail bones would be dead in short order if left alone in this country. And she considered that there might be a man inside the wing, dead or too hurt to climb out. She thought how much trouble it would be, getting down this steep rock bluff in the darkness to rescue a useless dog and a dead man.

After a while, she stood and started picking her way into the draw. The dog by this time was smelling the ground, making a slow and careful circuit around the black wing. Delia kept expecting the dog to look up and bark, but it went on with its intent inspection of the ground as if it was stone deaf, as if Delia's boots making a racket on the loose gravel was not an announcement that someone was coming down. She thought of the old Dodge truck, how it always left her ears ringing, and wondered if maybe it was the same with this dog and its wing-shaped sputnik, although the wing had fallen soundless across the sky.

When she had come about half way down the hill, she lost footing and slid down six or eight feet before she got her heels dug in and found a handful of willow scrub to hang onto. A glimpse of this movement—rocks sliding to the bottom, or the dust she raised—must have startled the dog, for it leaped backward suddenly and then reared up. They looked at each other in silence, Delia and the dog, Delia standing leaning into the steep slope a dozen yards above the bottom of the draw, and the dog standing next to the sputnik, standing all the way up on its hind legs like a bear or a man and no longer seeming to be a dog but a person with a long narrow muzzle and a narrow chest, turned-out knees, delicate dog-like feet. Its genitals were more cat-like than dog, a male set but very small and neat and contained. Dog's eyes, though, dark and small and shining below an anxious brow, so that she was reminded of Jesus and Alice, the way they had looked at her when she had left them alone with the sheep. She had years of acquaintance with dogs and she knew enough to look away, break off her stare. Also, after a moment, she remembered the old pistol and holster at her belt. In cowboy pictures, a man would unbuckle his gunbelt and let it down on the ground as a gesture of peaceful intent, but it seemed to her this might only bring attention to the gun, to the true intent of a gun, which is always killing. *This woman is nobody at all to be scared of,* she told the dog with her body, standing very still along the steep hillside, holding onto the scrub willow with her hands, looking vaguely to the left of him, where the smooth curve of the wing rose up and gathered a veneer of yellow dust.

The dog, the dog person, opened his jaws and yawned the way a dog will do to relieve nervousness, and then they were both silent and still for a minute. When finally he turned and stepped toward the wing, it was an unexpected, delicate movement, exactly the way a ballet dancer steps along on his toes, knees turned out, lifting his long thin legs; and then he dropped down on all-fours and seemed to become almost a dog again. He went back to his business of smelling the ground intently, though every little while he looked up to see if Delia was still standing along the rock slope. It was a steep place to stand. When her knees finally gave out, she sat down very carefully where she was, which didn't spook him. He had become used to her by then, and his brief, sliding glance just said, *That woman up there is nobody at all to be scared of.*

What he was after, or wanting to know, was a mystery to her. She kept expecting him to gather up rocks, like all those men who'd gone to the moon, but he only smelled the ground, making a wide slow circuit around the wing the way Alice always circled round the trailer every morning, nose down, reading the dirt like a book. And when he seemed satisfied with what he'd learned, he stood up again and looked back at Delia, a last look delivered across his shoulder before he dropped down and disappeared under the edge of the wing, a grave and inquiring look, the kind of look a dog or a man will give you before going off on his own business, a look that says, *You be okay if I go?* If he had been a dog, and if Delia had been close enough to do it, she'd have scratched the smooth head, felt the hard bone beneath, moved her hands around the soft ears. *Sure, okay, you go on now, Mr. Dog*: This is what she would have said with her hands. Then he crawled into the darkness under the slope of the wing, where she figured there must be a door, a hatch letting into the body of the machine, and after a while he flew off into the dark of the July moon.

In the weeks afterward, on nights when the moon had set or hadn't yet risen, she looked for the flash and streak of something breaking across the darkness out of the southwest. She saw him come and go to that draw on the west side of Lame Man Bench twice more in the first month. Both times, she left her grandmother's gun in the trailer and walked over there and sat in the dark on the rock slab above the draw and watched him for a couple of hours. He may have been waiting for her, or he knew her smell, because both times he reared up and looked at her just about as soon as she sat down. But then he went on with his business. *That woman is nobody to be scared of,* he said with his body, with the way he went on smelling the ground, widening his circle and widening it, sometimes taking a clod or a sprig into his mouth and tasting it, the way a mild-mannered dog will do when he's investigating something and not paying any attention to the person he's with.

Delia had about decided that the draw behind Lame Man Bench was one of his regular stops, like the ten campsites she used over and over again when she was herding on Joe-Johns Mountain; but after those three times in the first month, she didn't see him again.

At the end of September, she brought the sheep down to the O-Bar. After the lambs had been shipped out she took her band of dry ewes over onto the Nelson prairie for the fall, and in mid-November, when the snow had settled in, she brought them to the feed lots. That was all the work the ranch had for her until lambing season. Jesus and Alice belonged to the O-Bar. They stood in the yard and watched her go.

In town, she rented the same room as the year before, and, as before, spent most of a year's wages on getting drunk and standing other herders to rounds of drink. She gave up looking into the sky.

In March, she went back out to the ranch. In bitter weather, they built jugs and mothering-up pens, and trucked the pregnant ewes from Green, where they'd been feeding on wheat stubble. Some ewes lambed in the trailer on the way in, and after every haul, there was a surge of lambs born. Delia had the night shift, where she was paired with Roy Joyce, a fellow who raised sugar beets over in the valley and came out for the lambing season every year. In the black, freezing cold middle of the night, eight and ten ewes would be lambing at a time. Triplets, twins, big singles, a few quads, ewes with lambs born dead, ewes too sick or confused to mother. She and Roy would skin a dead lamb and feed the carcass to the ranch dogs and wrap the fleece around a bummer lamb, which was intended to fool the bereaved ewe into taking the orphan as her own, and sometimes it worked that way. All the mothering-up pens swiftly filled, and the jugs filled, and still some ewes with new lambs stood out in the cold field waiting for a room to open up.

You couldn't pull the stuck lambs with gloves on, you had to reach into the womb with your fingers to turn the lamb, or tie cord around the feet, or grasp the feet barehanded, so Delia's hands were always cold and wet, then cracked and bleeding. The ranch had brought in some old converted school buses to house the lambing crew, and she would fall into a bunk at daybreak and then not be able to sleep, shivering in the unheated bus with the gray daylight pouring in the windows and the endless daytime clamor out at the lambing sheds. All the lambers had sore throats, colds, nagging coughs. Roy Joyce looked like hell, deep bags as blue as bruises under his eyes, and Delia figured she looked about the same, though she hadn't seen a mirror, not even to draw a brush through her hair, since the start of the season.

By the end of the second week, only a handful of ewes hadn't lambed. The nights became quieter. The weather cleared, and the thin skiff of snow melted off the grass. On the dark of the moon, Delia was standing outside the mothering-up pens drinking coffee from a thermos. She put her head back and held the warmth of the coffee in her mouth a moment, and, as she was swallowing it down, lowering her chin, she caught the tail end of a green flash and a thin yellow line breaking across the sky, so far off anybody else would have thought it was a meteor, but it was bright, and dropping from southwest to due west, maybe right onto Lame Man Bench. She stood and looked at it. She was so very goddamned tired and had a sore throat that wouldn't clear, and she could barely get her fingers to fold around the thermos, they were so split and tender.

She told Roy she felt sick as a horse, and did he think he could handle things if she drove herself into town to the Urgent Care clinic, and she took one of the ranch trucks and drove up the road a short way and then turned onto the rutted track that went up to Joe-Johns.

The night was utterly clear and you could see things a long way off. She was still an hour's drive from the Churros' summer range when she began to see a yellow-orange glimmer behind the black ridgeline, a faint nimbus like the ones that marked distant range fires on summer nights.

She had to leave the truck at the bottom of the bench and climb up the last mile or so on foot, had to get a flashlight out of the glove box and try to find an uphill path with it because the fluttery reddish lightshow was finished by then, and a thick pall of smoke overcast the sky and blotted out the stars. Her eyes itched and burned, and tears ran from them, but the smoke calmed her sore throat. She went up slowly, breathing through her mouth.

The wing had burned a skid path through the scraggly junipers along the top of the bench and had come apart into about a hundred pieces. She wandered through the burnt trees and the scattered wreckage, shining her flashlight into the smoky darkness, not expecting to find what she was looking for, but there he was, lying apart from the scattered pieces of metal, out on the smooth slab rock at the edge of the draw. He was panting shallowly and his close coat of short brown hair was matted with blood. He lay in such a way that she immediately knew his back was broken. When he saw Delia coming up, his brow furrowed with worry. A sick or a wounded dog will bite, she knew that, but she squatted next to him. *It's just me*, she told him, by shining the light not in his face but in hers. Then she spoke to him. "Okay," she said. "I'm here now," without thinking too much about what the words meant, or whether they meant anything at all, and she didn't remember until afterward that he was very likely deaf anyway. He sighed and shifted his look from her to the middle distance, where she supposed he was focused on approaching death.

Near at hand, he didn't resemble a dog all that much, only in the long shape of his head, the folded-over ears, the round darkness of his eyes. He lay on the ground flat on his side like a dog that's been run over and is dying by the side of the road, but a man will lay like that too when he's dying. He had small-fingered nail-less hands where a dog would have had toes and front feet. Delia offered him a sip from her water bottle, but he didn't seem to want it, so she just sat with him quietly, holding one of his hands, which was smooth as lambskin against the cracked and roughened flesh of her palm. The batteries in the flashlight gave out, and sitting there in the cold darkness she found his head and stroked it, moving her sore fingers lightly over the bone of his skull, and around the soft ears, the loose jowls. Maybe it wasn't any particular comfort to him, but she was comforted by doing it. *Sure, okay, you can go on.*

She heard him sigh, and then sigh again, and each time wondered if it would turn out to be his death. She had used to wonder what a coyote, or especially a dog, would make of this doggish man, and now while she was listening, waiting to hear if he would breathe again, she began to wish she'd brought Alice or Jesus with her, though not out of that old curiosity. When her husband had died years before, at the very moment he took his last breath, the dog she'd had then had barked wildly and raced back and forth from the front to the rear door of the house as if he'd heard or seen something invisible to her. People said it was her husband's soul going out the door or his angel coming in. She didn't know what it was the dog had seen or heard or smelled, but she wished she knew. And now she wished she had a dog with her to bear witness.

She went on petting him even after he had died, after she was sure he was dead, went on petting him until his body was cool, and then she got up stiffly from the bloody ground and gathered rocks and piled them onto him, a couple of feet high, so that he wouldn't be found or dug up. She didn't know what to do about the wreckage, so she didn't do anything with it at all.

In May, when she brought the Churro sheep back to Joe-Johns Mountain, the pieces of the wrecked wing had already eroded, were small and smooth-edged like the bits of sea glass you find on a beach, and she figured that this must be what it was meant to do: to break apart into pieces too small for anybody to notice, and then to quickly wear away. But the stones she'd piled over his body seemed like the start of something, so she began the slow work of raising them higher into a sheepherder's monument. She gathered up all the smooth eroded bits of wing, too, and laid them in a series of widening circles around the base of the monument. She went on piling up stones through the summer and into September, until it reached fifteen feet. Mornings, standing with the sheep miles away, she would look for it through the binoculars and think about ways to raise it higher, and she would wonder what was buried under all the other monuments sheepherders had raised in that country. At night, she studied the sky, but nobody came for him.

In November, when she finished with the sheep and went into town, she asked around and found a guy who knew about star-gazing and telescopes. He loaned her some books and sent her to a certain pawnshop, and she gave most of a year's wages for a 14 x 75 telescope with a reflective lens. On clear, moonless nights, she met the astronomy guy out at the Little League baseball field, and she sat on a fold-up canvas stool with her eye against the telescope's finder while he told her what she was seeing: Jupiter's moons, the Pelican Nebula, the Andromeda Galaxy. The telescope had a tripod mount, and he showed her how to make a little jerry-built device so she could mount her old 7 x 32 binoculars on the tripod too. She used the binoculars for their wider view of star clusters and small constellations. She was indifferent to most discomforts, could sit quietly in one position for hours at a time, teeth rattling with the cold, staring into the immense vault of the sky until she became numb and stiff, barely able to stand and walk back home. Astronomy, she discovered, was a work of patience, but the sheep had taught her patience, or it was already in her nature before she ever took up with them.

CELADON

DESIRINA BOSKOVICH

———◆———

I was six years old when I shifted between worlds for the first time.

My mother and I were in our little apartment in the center of the world, the part that got built first. The world was new then and the nanites still busy about their work. The world has stretched much further now.

Our apartment was small but cozy, bathed in a vague light that spilled everywhere yet came from no particular source. Someone who had seen the first earth might have called it moonlight, or so we believed. None of us had seen earth for ourselves . . . certainly not me. Our artificial moonlight enshrined the city, slanting from every angle, drifting in a manufactured sky.

I sat at the table alone, drinking weak green tea from a chipped white teacup. Long wet hair fell around my shoulders, fresh from the bath, dampening my fuzzy robe.

I took a sip, set the teacup down, and looked at the table. A soft layer of green moss crept across it. As I watched, moss tendrils advanced toward me, trembling like slick fingers. The moss rustled as it grew, swallowing the legs of chairs.

The window had become a stained mosaic of asparagus and emerald. A small white butterfly frolicked around me, then landed on the rim of my cup.

I felt a glow of amber warmth, like the safety of cuddling into my mother's fragrant sheets, listening to her lullabies as I fell asleep.

But then I looked down. The ghostworms were poking their heads up, emerging implausibly through the concrete floor. Their slimy heads waved blindly as they wriggled and squirmed beneath the furniture.

I jumped up and knocked over my teacup, which bounced and clattered to the floor. A wash of pale green tea dribbled across my white robe. My mother rushed in.

Then the light changed, and everything resolved to normal. The table was spotless white. Suddenly, I became aware of how clean everything was: synthetic and flawless, wrapped in an artificial sheen.

"What happened, sweetheart?" my mother asked, picking up my teacup. The spill seeped into the floor and disappeared, swallowed by thirsty nanites.

"Nothing," I said, remembering the way the butterfly had landed curiously on my cup. "Can I sleep in your bed tonight?"

"Hmm," she said, which meant yes.

In my mother's bedroom, lace curtains covered the small window, shuttered to keep out the light. A flame flickered in the lamp on the desk. Her sheets were soft and smelled like lavender.

Usually she sang to me, but that night, I made her tell me the story. I knew it already, but I loved hearing it again and again. "Tell me about how it was, when you found Celadon, before I was born."

My mother loved to tell this story almost as much as I loved to hear it. Even if there were parts she skipped over. "Well," she said. She tucked a long strand of white hair behind her ears, her green eyes glistening with memories of far away days. "I was exploring with my crew on our ship, a beautiful ship. Her name was Alanis. She's retired now, but you should have seen her. Maybe someday we can go down to the docks and visit. She was so slick, so smart, so . . . gentle. You know about our home-world: it was a lovely place to live, but it was too full. It was called Tenne. So, even though we loved Tenne, we knew we'd need another world soon where we could have our children—" at this point in the story she always touched my nose—"and they could have their children. We spent years with our ship, exploring the darkness, looking for a good spot to grow another world. A planet we could make our own."

I could hardly imagine the years-long journey in that smart, gentle ship. I was only six years old, after all. Back then, I didn't understand how old my mother really was. I'm not sure if I even understand it now. "And finally you found the planet," I said.

"Yeah," she said. She looked over my head, as if she was looking out the window, though it was closed. "We descended closer and closer, and the surface of the planet was this beautiful green. So we called it Celadon. We sent the bots down to do readings, investigate the surface, see if it was safe. We had to wait for a while, but I already knew. I felt it, somehow, you know? We were home. By that time, I was already expecting you."

"And I was the very first baby born on Celadon," I interjected self-importantly.

"Yes," she said. "Yes, you were. But before that, we sent the nanites down to the surface of the planet, and they began building a new world for us, just like the cities we'd left behind on Tenne."

It was a lovely story, the beginning of a myth. And my mother was the heroine.

It was a lovely story, but it wasn't entirely true.

But no one knew that at first, except the original crew of the spaceship from Tenne. And they didn't have anything to say about it. Waves of new settlers came in every year or so, and they all viewed my mother as a heroine, too. I remember the ceremony they staged, honoring her with a medal on the steps of the newly constructed city hall. Her white hair was just as luminescent as the marble steps. They hung a glistening silver medal around her neck. She was brave and beautiful, a conqueror and a pioneer.

But when I was twelve, the anthropologists finally arrived. They were angry.

Not all of them were human. They were a motley group, a strange menagerie of feathers and wings and awkward tusks and shining cyborg limbs. This was not good. Celadon was a human planet, discovered and populated by ancient earth-stock. The others tended to be a bit resentful. They thought the humans had too many planets already.

They met in the city hall, the same one where my mother had been honored years ago. I sat in the last row of chairs, my pale hair falling in my eyes. I listened as my mother explained her case to the strange and unsympathetic panel of judges. And for the first time, I heard the whole story.

There had been life on this planet: a natural ecosystem. An endless network of worms crawled just beneath the surface. Enormous flocks of butterflies lived in the trees, roaming the oceans of moss. When they landed en masse, they could shroud a tree in shimmering snow.

The scouting bots' findings corroborated those of the few anthropologists who'd landed on this planet some years earlier. Without further intensive study—by the anthropologists, of course—it was impossible to rule out the potential that the worms and butterflies had been sentient life forms.

They no longer existed on Celadon. They had been destroyed. My mother had given the order.

Two years before the ship had arrived at the planet that would become Celadon, the travelers received the news from Tenne. Among the news, there was the gruesome story of a ship that left just before Alanis. This ship had discovered a new planet, odd but livable. There was only one possibly-sentient life form: a species of small reptiles, lizard-like creatures that traveled in swarms and packs. The settlers had already been on the ship for years, and they were determined to co-exist peacefully, while the anthropologists studied the reptiles. Somehow, the reptiles infiltrated the colony. They massacred the settlers, leaving nothing but regurgitated bones and walls smeared with blood. The nanites were already tidying the remains when the next wave of settlers arrived.

"So I did what I thought was right," my mother said, facing the panel without flinching. "I wanted this planet to be safe."

At her order, nanites swarmed the planet, pulsing the surface with brutal light. The worms and butterflies and moss that coated the surface were destroyed. The planet was scrubbed clean.

The hearings were long, the panelists long-winded. They called expert witnesses, and the settlers on the first ship called their own.

Sometime during this long proceeding, the shift happened again. I watched with interest as the windows darkened with moss and the floor disintegrated into a mass of ghostworms. I was still surrounded by people, but no panelists. Things were strangely silent in this world. No one felt the need to speak.

A man sat just ahead of me, listening intently to nothing in particular. As I watched, a ghostworm wriggled out of his left ear, explored the back of his neck with a probing tip, then slid into the right ear.

I felt the amber glow again, the numbing warmth. The bench I sat on disintegrated, then the wall beside me—whole patches consumed by a black rot, eaten wafer-thin. The moss consumed windows, and white butterflies wandered in through broken panes.

The man with worms in his ears turned around, glanced at me, and nodded kindly.

Meanwhile, in the real world, the panel was sentencing my mother for the crime of xenocide. Her sentence: life imprisonment, in a penal colony on a rock far from this world.

In a different time, there would have been riots. Blood would have run in the streets. But these people had waited too long to make this planet their home. They'd lived too long, strayed too far, sacrificed too much. They accepted her fate with penitent guilt, willing to sacrifice my mother to clear their collective conscience.

I was the only one who screamed and protested. They took her away, still calm and resolute, her hair brilliantly white around her shoulders, her eyes enigmatic emerald.

They sent me to live with a man I called "uncle"—one of the original settlers, my mother's shipmate.

The years after that were dark and ill-defined. My city that had once seemed so clean and bright felt sterile and empty. The people who I'd imagined family were strangers and betrayers.

This was when the two worlds began to diverge, no longer twinned as they once had been.

In the second world, we still lived in the old apartment. My mother was there, and we were together. Moss coated the chairs and crept across the table, blossoming thick in unexpected places like cups and plates. There were ghostworms underfoot, but they anticipated our footsteps, trailing our ankles like devoted pets. The butterflies flocked around our heads. In the second world, we rarely spoke; it no longer seemed necessary.

We followed our normal routines, setting out small meals, singing in the evenings, reading old books from my mother's library. We toured the city and the light was golden. Beneath everything shuddered a tremendous thrill: warmly it beckoned, to come ever closer, to come further in.

A snow-white butterfly landed on my fingertip, and revulsion stung through me. I pulled away, feeling sick. My mother smiled, but there was a gulf between us; she didn't understand. Butterflies wreathed her hair like garlands and the moss shifted beneath her feet, cushioning her steps. Whole sections of the city were green with its weight. Passersby wore green fingernails and heads full of worms. My mother inhabited this world, and she was content.

In this world, it was difficult for me to remember any other—my own world felt like a pallid dream. I tried to tell her, but when I opened my mouth, her world faded away.

Two decades passed. I got my own apartment. I wrote my mother letters, though they took years to reach her.

When I wrote, I felt like I was dropping my letters into an endless chasm where they would never be found.

I wrote:

Sometimes I'm in a different world. The world that would have been if we hadn't killed the butterflies. It's a green world, full of moss . . . earthworms that eat through the floors . . . butterflies that gather around heads. Walls disintegrating with black rot. It wants something. The life that was here isn't content to live and let live. It wants us, too. In that world, everything is connected. Everyone is part of it, and it wants to swallow us.

She wrote back, finally, eventually.

Love, don't think about what could have been, don't think about the past. I'm fine here. I've lived a long time, much longer than you, you know. You should find a ship, explore, see the galaxy. You'll make different choices, better ones.

She thought it was an allegory. I wrote back.

It's not a metaphor, mother. I have seen that world. Literally. I see it all the time. And I have been seeing it more and more.

Years passed, again. Finally, another letter.

Stranger things have happened. Go see Ravin. He can explain it better than I can.

Ravin had been my mother's closest friend aboard the ship. Maybe her lover, maybe even my father. I didn't know if I had one.

One image of Ravin burned white-hot for me: the way he sat silently in the back of the room as my mother was sentenced. His eyes were downcast, his cheeks pale, his lips pressed together. He'd done nothing, and I was still angry. If he was my father, I didn't want him.

But I did want answers to my questions, and it would be years before I could get another letter from my mother. So I went to find him.

His room on the other side of the city was small but comfortable. Light sparkled in the windows, glinting off the shells of blue glass bottles. Art from Tenne graced the walls. His furniture was handmade, not built by nanites.

"Sit," he said, gesturing to a small sofa. I did. I was surprised by how thin and small he seemed, even standing above me.

He'd been playing an old game from Tenne. The board was chaotic with black and white pebbles. Each pebble was black on one side, white on the other. Flipping only one could transform the board. It was a complicated game, and I didn't know how to play.

We cut through the pleasantries quickly. "My mother told me to come. She said you could explain."

"Go on," he said, his eyes penetrating blue.

"I'm in the middle of two worlds," I said. "This world that we're in right now, and another one. I don't know where it is, exactly. I tend to think it's the world that would have been if—You know. If they hadn't killed the natural life here." I said "they," though I could have said "you."

"What do you mean, you're in the middle?"

"I see both. I see this one more. But the other one, I see it too."

"What does it look like?" His interest felt cool and scientific.

I described my second world.

He thought for a while, then told me the story I already knew so well. "You know, your mother was pregnant with you when we discovered Celadon. Everyone told her she was being silly, that she had enough to worry about as captain of a pioneering ship. No one could make her change her mind. She wanted to have you, the natural way."

He gazed at me and paused, as if expecting me to say something. Silence thickened between us, and he continued.

"I still remember the way she looked, standing there on the deck. The trees crowding the edges of the window. The leaves rustling from the air in the vents. There was a red bird perched above her, and its color matched her dress. She stared out the window and all of a sudden, there was Celadon. The closer we got, the greener it became. We stayed like that until it was safe to land."

"So what are you saying?"

"I don't know, exactly. You were there from the beginning, your fate intertwined with Celadon's. You're part of this world in a way that no one else is." He was quiet for a moment. "In the second world, would you say that time works differently?"

"Yes," I said. "I didn't notice it for a while, because everything feels so brief and fragmented already. But it does. Causality seems to be missing, somehow. Things happen for no reason."

He began pacing the room. He flipped a black pebble over to reveal its white underbelly, then contemplated the ripple of results that followed. "We thought we were doing the right thing. Now I'm not so sure. There was something special here, something we should have investigated."

"You did the right thing," I said resolutely. "That world . . . well, there's just something wrong about it."

"Different, maybe," he suggested. "Special."

"Does it matter?"

"No, not really," he said. "It's gone, we'll live with the consequences."

"Some of us more than others," I said pointedly.

He looked away and cleared his throat. "It's gone, except it's not gone for you. I can't really explain what happened, or why. We made a decision, with results that changed history. And there you are, at the cusp. Caught in the middle between both paths."

There was one more thing I wanted to get clear. "So, you all decided together. You all decided to give the order to scrub the ecosystem."

"We all voted, yes. Only one person voted against."

"And who was that?" I demanded.

"Me."

For a moment, I had no words. "Why did you vote against?"

He spent a minute searching for words. "I was responsible for monitoring the bots' info-loads as they explored the planet. And I had read some of the anthropologists' texts on the surface life. I had a sense—and I wasn't the only one—that there was something at work here, something truly alive."

"But no one else on the ship felt that way," I said.

"No," he said. "Everyone else wanted to break land and start construction. They told me I had always been too mystical for my own good. Maybe it's true. Your mother was very angry at me. It was part of why we parted ways once we landed here." He fixed me with his steely blue eyes, and for a moment I knew, but I pushed the knowledge away.

I felt exhausted. "I have to go now," I said.

"Come again," he invited me, showing me to the door. "

"I will," I said. I knew I would not.

Instead, I visited the ship, Alanis.

She was retired, and lived in a special place, down at the docks. She was the most important ship on Celadon, after all. Every week, technicians came in and lovingly checked her ports, inspected her chips. The dockboys polished her hull and shined her floors. Children left flowers beneath her. Sometimes, her keepers gave tours, which she didn't enjoy very much. She did enjoy my visits, though. But they've been rare, mostly alongside my mother.

This time, I went alone, and with a mission.

"Alanis," I said, standing on her main deck, watching the dark lights that I liked to think of as her eyes.

"Yes," she answered.

"I need help. For my mother. I need logs, recordings. I need to know all the details about the weeks before they landed on Celadon. I want to know how the decisions were made. Do you have that? Do you still have the logs?"

"Of course," she said, sounding amused. "I haven't forgotten." I couldn't tell if she was teasing me or not.

"Can I have them?"

"Of course."

She painted a disk for me and gave it to me with a cup of hot chocolate. "Thank you," I said.

She couldn't make real hot chocolate anymore; her domestics were corrupted and her keepers had stopped replenishing the stores a long time ago. I didn't tell her that, just took the disk and the cup with me as I left. Why did everyone but me seem so old?

I walked through the city, clutching my disk and looking for somewhere to discard the mug of chocolate sludge.

The city alone was young, the same age as me.

You could tell. Maybe it was the effect of construction by nanites, but everything seemed youthful and energetic. The streets glowed. The stoplights inspected the traffic beneath. Houses vibrated, ever so slightly, like a picture with weak transmission.

I'd noticed that Ravin's furniture seemed solid and inert. Because it was old, or because it was built by hand?

The more I thought about it, the more his home seemed like its own kind of prison.

After visiting Alanis, I was ready. This was what I'd been waiting to do for years, and I was finally old enough. By the time the journey ended, I was even older.

I traveled to Tenne, to go before the panel. It wasn't the same panel of anthropologists who'd sentenced my mother, although I recognized a few familiar faces—if they could be called *faces*. I doubt they recognized me. It had been thirty-some years, and I was no longer the same pale and awkward girl. Slowly, falteringly, I grew into my mother's strength.

The anthropologists were clipped and impatient, glaring at me over snouts and beaks and masks. I'd traveled light-years to get here—they would have to be patient.

"I am here to speak on behalf of my mother," I said.

"State her name for the record, please."

It was a long name: new syllables garnered for every century, every experience that had marked her.

"Go on," the moderator intoned. She was a cyborg, with long synthetic limbs, metallic purple hair, and a sleek silicone shine to her skin. I couldn't interpret her inflection, nor her expression. It was a specific kind of loneliness that I'd learned to live with.

"My mother was unfairly sentenced for the crime of many. She gave the order, yes. But the whole group voted." I produced my logs from the ship. They showed my mother giving the final order; they also showed unanimous agreement.

I presented the panel with everything I had. "She should not bear the weight of this decision alone. It was a group decision. Everyone who lives on Celadon should share the responsibility, together."

The panel was brisk and disinterested. "I'm sorry," the cyborg said, "but we rarely reverse the decision of a previous court, except in notable extenuating circumstances. All this information was available at the time of the previous hearing."

"Yes. But my mother didn't bring it up. Because she wasn't like that. She was the only one who was willing to take responsibility for the actions."

"Then the responsibility clearly rests with her," the cyborg said, and I couldn't tell if she was being unkind or not. "If you'd like to appeal this to a higher court, you are within your rights as a galactic citizen to go before the High Court of Cultural Differences."

"But that's on the other side of the galaxy." It would take me longer to reach the High Court than all the years I'd been alive so far.

"Precisely," she said crisply. "Your mother has already lived for centuries. If you want to give your first years for her last, then go ahead. The next ship leaves for the High Court in a few months."

I pleaded as long as they'd allow, but their decision was final. At some level, I'd expected it all along. Only longing had made me hope for the unforeseen. After all, communication from world to world had always been hazy, and rules changed faster than space travel. I'd hoped there was a chance.

I declined their offer of transportation to the High Court. "I'll find my own ship."

I'd already decided: if I was going to the High Court, then Ravin was going with me. He would not have been my first choice of companions, but I felt he had a responsibility. I wasn't ready to make my way into the galaxy alone. And my mother had chosen him first.

Besides, what was a couple years of preparation for a fifty-year journey?

I found passage to Celadon.

Now, in transit between Tenne and Celadon, I've spent my spare hours writing this account. I've reviewed what has passed. I'm prepared for what is to come.

When I arrive on Celadon, there is a letter.

My mother has died. Peacefully, in her sleep. Perhaps she was already gone, even as I pled her case before the panel. It's so hard to calculate time.

She's been absent from my world for so long, yet death makes me feel her absence more sharply. Even worlds away, she was the force that kept my world revolving.

Heartbroken, I wander aimlessly through the city. I wish I could go to Ravin, but I can't. Too much has come between us. He will never be family.

The city feels changed, too. The change is indefinable. But the lights glare brighter; the noises are louder, more unnatural.

I sit in my apartment. I drink fragrant green tea and wait, letting my eyes drift half-closed as I watch the silver play of light in lace curtains.

Until the curtains crumble black and turn to dust, the walls are streaked with moist darkness, and the moss squelches beneath my bare feet.

I want to find my mother, but time works differently here; seeking does not always lead to finding. Instead, I wander, patient as a dream. Whole sections of the city have been reclaimed by the moss. There are few people. I glimpse them in dark corners, pale like worms, locked in tangles of arms and legs. I long to join them, but I keep walking.

Butterflies land in droves on my shoulders, sprinkling me with the sugar that dulls the sting.

In this world, all life is the same. At first, I believed there were only three life-forms here. Now I understand there is only one. The worms, the moss, the butterflies . . . all are merely manifestations of its being: spanning this world from the ground to the sky, seeing all, knowing all, devouring all.

I find my mother at the edge of a dripping forest. She sits with her back against a sturdy tree, her white hair intertwined with its roots. Her emerald-green eyes consider me, comfortably. She smiles in welcome. She opens her mouth to speak, but all that emerges is a small white butterfly, which alights gracefully on my shoulder.

I fight the urge to sleep, and struggle to speak.

"Mother," I stammer, my tongue sticky-dry. "Mother. Are you happy here?"

Her lips don't move, but I feel her voice, echoing through me. "Of course. Always."

I lie beside her, and the tree's roots shift to accommodate me. The moss drifts over my face and blinds my eyes. The butterflies weave patterns in my hair. The ghostworms caress my fingers. Finally, I understand.

This is life, eternal, everlasting. It is not good, it is not evil. It simply is. It desires to be always more. And I too desire, to be part of everything, to feel it all.

"You're here," the moss whispers into my ears as it penetrates, and it greets me with a vision: the moment on which all else depends. A moment which changes history; yet there are many histories on Celadon, and enough consciousness to hold them all.

I am a woman, strong and eager, standing on the foremost deck of a smart and gentle ship. The fans blow breezes through my hair. The leaves of trees rustle above me. Inside me, a heart beats, beautiful and unfaltering. I stroke my stomach, the swelling expanse that waits beneath my crimson dress. I stand before a window; below stretches a green and glowing planet. I've already named it, but nobody knows yet. *Celadon.*This pulsating green world and the heartbeat inside me have become the two lovers I live for.

Resolute, I turn from the window, summing up the energy to create and destroy worlds. I speak, one word:

"Now."

CARTHAGO DELENDA EST

GENEVIEVE VALENTINE

—✦—

Wren Hex-Yemenni woke early. They had to teach her everything from scratch, and there wasn't time for her to learn anything new before she hit fifty and had to be expired.

"Watch it," the other techs told me when I was starting out. "You don't want a Hex on your hands."

By then we were monitoring Wren Hepta-Yemenni. She fell into bed with Dorado ambassador 214, though I don't know what he did to deserve it and she didn't even seem sad when he expired. When they torched him she went over with the rest of the delegates, and they bowed or closed their eyes or pressed their tentacles to the floors of their glass cases, and afterwards they toasted him with champagne or liquid nitrogen.

Before we expired Hepta, later that year, she smiled at me. "Make sure Octa's not ugly, okay? Just in case—for 215."

Wren Octa-Yemenni hates him, so it's not like it matters.

It's worse early on. Octa and Dorado 215 stop short of declaring war—no warring country is allowed to meet the being from Carthage when it arrives, those are the rules—but it comes close. Every time she goes over to the Dorado ship she comes back madder. Once she got him halfway into an airlock before security arrived.

We reported it as a chem malfunction; I took the blame for improper embryonic processes (a lie—they were perfect), and the Dorado accepted the apology, no questions. Dorado 208 killed himself, way back; they know how mistakes can happen.

Octa spends nights in the tech room, scanning through footage of

Hepta-Yemmeni and Dorado 214 like she's looking for something, like she's trying to remember what Hepta felt.

I don't know why she tries. She can't; none of them can. They don't hold on to anything. That's the whole point.

The astronomers at the Institute named the planet Carthage when they discovered it floating in the Oort cloud like a wheel of garbage. They thought it was already dead.

But the message came from there. It's how they knew to look in the cloud to begin with; there was a message there, in every language, singing along the light like a phone call from home.

It was a message of peace, they say. It's confidential; most people never get to hear it. I wouldn't even believe it's real except that all the planets heard it, and agreed—every last one of them threw a ship into the sky to meet the ship from Carthage when it came.

Every year they show us the video of Wren Alpha-Yemenni—the human, the original—taking the oath. Stretched out behind her are the ten thousand civilians who signed up to go into space and not come back, to cultivate a meeting they'd never see.

"I, Wren Alpha-Yemenni, delegate of Earth, do solemnly swear to speak wisely, feel deeply, and uphold the highest values of the human race as Earth greets the ambassador of Carthage." At the end she smiles, and her eyes go bright with tears.

The speech goes on, but I just watch her face.

There's something about Alpha that's . . . more alive than the copies. They designated her with a letter just to keep track, but it suits her anyway—the Alpha, the leader, the strong first. Octa has a little of that, sometimes, but she'll probably be expired by the time Carthage comes, and who knows if it will ever manifest again.

Octa would never be Alpha, anyway. There's something in Alpha's eyes that's never been repeated—something bright and determined; excited; happy.

It makes sense, I guess. She's the only one of the Yemennis who chose to go.

Everybody sent ships. Everybody. We'd never heard of half the planets that showed up. You wonder how amazing the message must be, to get them all up off their asses.

Dorado was in place right away (that whole planet is kiss-asses), which is why they were already on iteration 200 when we got there. Doradoan machines have to pop out a new one every twenty years. (My ancestors did better work on our machines; they generate a perfect Yemenni every fifty years on the dot—except for poor Hex. There's always one dud.) Dorado spends their time trying to scrounge up faster tech or better blueprints, and we give our information away, because those were the rules in the message, but they just take—they haven't given us anything since their dictionary.

WX-16 from Sextans-A sent their royal house: an expendable younger son and his wife and a collection of nobles, to keep the bloodline active until the messenger arrived. We don't deal with them—they think it's coarse to clone.

NGC 2808 (we can't pronounce it, and sometimes it's better not to try) came out of Canis Major and surprised everyone, since we didn't even think there was life out there. They've only been around a few years; Hepta never met them. Their delegate is in stasis. Whenever that poor sucker wakes up he's going to have some unimpressed ambassadors waiting to meet him. They should never have come with only one.

Xpelhi, who booked it all the way from Cygnus, keep to themselves; their atmosphere is too heavy for people with spines. They look like jellyfish, no mouths, and it took us a hundred and ten years to figure out their language; the dictionary they sent us was just an anatomical sketch. Hepta cracked it because of something Tetra-Yemenni had recorded about the webs of their veins shifting when they were upset. The Xpelhi think we're a bunch of idiots for taking so long. Which is fine; I think they're a bunch of mouthless creeps. It evens out.

Neptune sent a think-tank themselves, like they were a real planet and not an Earth colony. They've never said how they keep things going on that tiny ship, if it's cloning or bio-reproduction or what; every generation they elect someone for the job, and I guess whenever Carthage shows up they'll put forward the elected person and hope for the best. Brave bunch, Neptune. Better them than us.

Centauri was the smartest planet. They sent an AI. You know the AI isn't sitting up nights worrying itself into early expiration. It's not bothered by a damn thing.

Octa makes rounds to all the ships. She's the only one of them who does it, and it works. Canis Major sent us help once, when we had the ventilation problem on the storage levels. She didn't ask for help; they're not obligated to share anything but information. But when she came back, an engineer was with her.

"Trust me, I know everything about refrigeration," he said, and after the computer had translated the joke everybody laughed and shook his hand.

Octa stood beside him like a mother until they had taken him into the tunnels, and then she tucked her helmet under her arm like she was satisfied.

"They're good people," she said to the shuttle pilot, who was making a face. "With no ambassador to keep them going, they must feel so alone. Give them a chance to do good."

"I've got the scan ready," I said. (I scan her every time she comes back from somewhere else. It's a precaution. You never know what's going on outside your own ship.)

"Let's be quick, then," she said, already walking down the corridor. "I have to make some notes, and then I need to talk to Centauri."

(Centauri's AI is Octa's favorite ship; she's there far more often than she needs to be. "Easier to come to decisions when it's just a matter of facts," she said.)

Octa did a lot of planning, early on, like she had a special purpose beyond what Alpha had promised—like time was short.

Of all the copies, she was the only one who ever seemed to worry that her clock was ticking down.

All the Yemennis have been different, which is unavoidable. Even though each one has all the aggregated information of previous iterations without the emotional hangover, it can get messy, like Hepta and Dorado 214. Human error in every copy. It's the reason her machines all have parameters instead of specs; some things you never can tell. (Poor Hex.)

It's hard on them, of course—after fifty years it all starts to fall apart no matter what you do, and you have to shut one down and start again— but it's the best way we have to give her a lifetime of knowledge in a few minutes, and we don't want Carthage to come when we're unprepared.

I don't know what's in the memories, what they show her each time she wakes. That's for government guys; techs mind their own business.

There's a documentary about how they picked Alpha for the job, four hundred years back. One man went on and on about "the human aesthetic," and put up a photo of what a woman would look like if every race had an influence in the facial features.

"Almost perfect. It's like they chose her for her looks!" he says, laughing.

Like Carthage is going to know if she's pretty. Carthage is probably full of big amoebas, and when they meet her they'll just think she's nasty and fragile and full of teeth.

They have a picture of Alpha up in the lab anyway, for reference. No one looks at it any more—nobody needs to. When I look in the mirror, I see a Yemenni first, and then my own face. I have my priorities straight.

Wren Yemenni is why we're here, and the reason none of us have complained in four hundred years is because she knows what she owes us. She's seen the video, too, with those ten thousand people who gave up everything because someone told them the message was beautiful.

No matter what her failings are, she tries to learn everything she can each time, to move diplomacy forward, to be kind (except to Dorado 215, but we all hate those ass-kissers so it doesn't matter). She knows what she's here to do. It's coded deeper than her IQ, than her memories, somewhere inside her we can't even reach; duty is built into their bones. Alpha passed down something wonderful, to all of them.

Octa doesn't look like Alpha. Not at all.

Just before Dorado 215 hits his twenty-year expiration, he messages a request that Octa accompany him on an official visit to the Xpelhi. There's something he wants to show them; he thinks they'll be interested.

Everyone asks her to go when they have to talk to Xpelhi. We gave everyone the code once we cracked it (we promised to exchange information, fair and square), but no one else is good at it and they need the help. The Yemmenis have a knack for language.

"I hate him," she says as I strap her into her suit. (It's new—our engineers made it to withstand the pressure in the Xpelhi ship. It's the most amazing human tech we've ever produced. Earth will be proud when they get the message.)

"If peace didn't require me to go . . ." she says, frowns. "I hope they see that what he's offering won't help anyone. It never does."

She sounds tired. I wonder if she's been up nights with the playback again.

"It's okay," I say. "You can hate him if you want. No one expected you to love him like the last one did. It's better not to carry the old feelings around. You live longer."

"He's different," she says. "It's terrible how it's changed him."

"All clones feel that way sometimes," I say. "Peril of the job. Here's your helmet."

She takes it and smiles at me, a thank-you, before she pops it over her head and activates the seal.

"I feel like a snowman," she says, which is what Hepta used to say. I wonder if anyone told Octa, of if she just remembered it from somewhere.

I stay near the bio-med readout while she's on the Xpelhi ship; if anything starts to fail, the suit tells us. If her lungs have collapsed from the pressure there's not much we can do, but at least we'll know, and we can wake up the next one.

Her heart rate speeds up, quick sharp spikes on the readout like she's having a panic attack, but that happens whenever Dorado 215 says something stupid. After a while it's just a little agitation, and soon she's safely back home.

She stands on the shuttle platform for a long time without moving, and only after I start toward her does she wake up enough to switch off the pressure in the suit and haul her helmet off.

I stop where I am. I don't want to touch her; I've worked too hard on them to handle them. "Everything all right?"

She's frowning into middle space, not really seeing me. "There's nothing on the ship we could use as a weapon?"

Strange question. "I guess we could crash the shuttle into someone," I say. "I can ask the engineers."

"No," she says. "No need."

It was part of the message, the first rule: no war before Carthage comes. We don't even have armed security— just guys who train with their hands, ready in case Octa tries to shove any more people in airlocks.

She hasn't done that in a while. She's getting worn down. It happens to them all, nearer the end.

"There's been no war for four hundred years," she says as we walk, shaking her head. "Have we ever gone that long before without fighting? Any of us?"

"Nope." I grin. "Carthage is the best thing that hasn't happened to us yet."

Her helmet is tucked under one arm, and she looks down at it like it will answer her.

• • •

The Delegate Meeting happens every decade. It wasn't mandated by Carthage; Wren Tetra-Yemenni began it as a way for delegates to have a base of reference, and to meet; no one has even seen the new Neptunian Elect since they picked her two years back, and they have to introduce Dorado 216.

We're not allowed to hear what they talk about—it's none of our business, it's government stuff—but we hang around in the hallways just to watch them filing in, the humanoids and the Xpelhis puttering past in their cases. The Centauri AI has a hologram that looks like a stick insect with wings, and it blinks in and out as the signal from his ship gets spotty. I cover my smile, though—that computer sees everything.

On the way in, Dorado 216 leans over to Octa. "You won't say anything, will you? It would be war."

"No," she says, "I won't say anything."

"It's just in case," he goes on, like she didn't already give him an answer. "There's no plan to use them. We're not like that—it's not like that. You never know what Carthage's plans are, is all." Then, more quietly, "I trusted you."

"215 trusted me," she says. "You want someone to trust you, try the next Yemenni."

"Watch it," he says. A warning.

After a second she frowns at him. "How can you want war, after all this effort?"

He makes a suspicious face before he turns and walks into the reception room with the rest of them.

Octa stands in the hall for a second before she follows him, shoulders back and head high. Yemmenis know their duties.

After the Delegate Meeting, Octa takes a trip to the Centauri AI. She's back in a few hours. She didn't tell anyone why she was going, just looks sad to have come back.

(Sometimes I think Octa's mind is more like a computer than any of them, even more than Alpha. I wonder if I made her that way by accident, wishing better for them, wishing for more.)

In the mess, the pilots grumble that it was a waste of shuttle fuel.

"That program shows up anywhere they need it to," one of them says. "Why did we have to drive her around like she's one of the queens on Sextan? They should expire these copies before they go crazy, man."

"Maybe she was trying to give us break from your ugly face," I say, and there's a little standoff at the table between the pilots and the techs until one of the language ops guys smoothes things over.

I stay angry for a long time. The pilots don't know what they're talking about.

Yemennis do nothing by mistake.

Alpha was the most skilled diplomat on the planet.

They don't say so in the documentary; they talk about how kind she is and how smart she is and how she looks like a mix of everyone, and if you just listened to what they were saying you'd think she hardly deserved to go. There were a lot of people in line; astronauts and prime ministers and bishops all clamoring for the privilege.

And she got herself picked—she got picked above every one of them; she was the most skilled diplomat who ever lived. She could work out anything, I bet.

There's an engineer down five levels who looks good to me, is smart enough, and we get married. We have two kids. (Someone will have to watch over the Yemennis when I'm gone, someone with my grandfathers' talents for calibrating a needle; we've been six generations at Wren Yemmeni's side.)

We celebrate four hundred years of peace. All the delegates put a message together, to be played in every ship, for the civilians. For some of them, it's the first they've heard of the other languages. Everyone on the ship, twelve thousand strong, watches raptly from the big hangar and the gymnasium level, from the tech room and the bridge.

They go one by one, and I recognize our reception room as the camera pans from one face to another. They talk about peace, about their home planets, about how much they look forward to all of us knowing the message, when Carthage comes.

Wren Octa-Yemenni goes last.

"I hope that, as we today are wiser today than we were, so tomorrow we will be wiser than we are," she says. Dorado 216 looks like he wants to slap her.

She says, "I hope that when our time comes to meet Carthage, we may say that we have fulfilled the letter and spirit of its great message, and we stand ready for a bright new age."

Everyone in the tech room roars applause (Yemennis know how to talk to a crowd). Just before the video shuts off, it shows all the delegates side by side; Octa is looking out the window, towards something none of us can see.

One night, a year before she's due to be expired, I find Octa in the development room. She's watching the tube where Ennea is gestating. Ennea's almost grown, and it looks like Octa's staring at her own reflection.

"Four hundred years without a war," she says. "All of us at a truce, talking and learning. Waiting for Carthage."

"Carthage will come," I promise, glancing at Ennea's pH readout.

"I hope we don't see it," she says, frowns into the glass. "I hope, when it comes, all of us are long dead, and better ones have taken their places. Some people twist on themselves if you give them any time at all."

Deka and Hendeka are in tubes behind us, smaller and reserved, eyes closed; they're not ready. We won't even need them until I'm dead. Though it shouldn't matter, I care less for them than I do for Ennea, less than I do for Octa, who's watching me.

Octa, who seems to think none of them are worthy of Carthage at all. She's been losing faith for years.

None of these copies are like Alpha. They all do their duty, but she *believed*.

At the fifty-year mark, Octa comes in to be expired.

She hands over the recording device, and the government guys disappear to their level to put together the memory flux for Ennea, who will wake up tonight and need to know.

"You shouldn't keep doing this," she tells me as we help her onto the table and adjust the IV.

There are no restraints. The Yemennis don't balk at what they have to do; duty is in their bones. But Octa looks sad, even sadder than when she found out that the one before her had loved someone who was already dead.

"It's fine," I say. "It's the best way—one session of information, and she's ready to face Carthage."

"But she won't remember something if I don't record it? She won't know?"

Octa's always been a little edgy—I try to sound reassuring. "No, she won't feel a thing. Forget Dorado. There's nothing to worry about."

Octa looks like she's going to cry. "What if there's something she needs to know?"

"I'll get you a recorder," I say, and start to hold up my hand for the sound tech, but she shakes her head and grabs my sleeve.

I drop my arm, surprised. No one else has even noticed; they're already starting the machines to wake up the next one, and Octa and I might as well be alone in the room.

After a second she frowns, drops my hand, makes fists at her sides like she's holding back.

The IV drips steadily, and around us everyone is laughing and talking, excited. They seem miles away.

Octa hasn't stopped watching me; her eyes are bright, her mouth drawn. "Have you seen the message?"

She must know I haven't. I shake my head; I hold my breath, wondering if she's going to tell me. I've dreamed about it my whole life, wondering what Alpha knew that made her cry with joy, four hundred years ago.

"It's beautiful," she says, and her eyes are mostly closed, and I can't tell if she's talking to me or just talking. The IV is working; sometimes they say things.

She says, "I don't know how anyone could take up a weapon again, after seeing the message."

Without thinking, I put my hand over her hand.

She sighs. Then, so quietly that no one else hears, Octa says, "I hope that ship never comes."

Her face gets tight and determined—she looks like Alpha, exactly like, and I almost call out for them to stop—it's so uncanny, something must be wrong.

But nothing is wrong. She closes her eyes, and the bio-feed flatlines; the tech across the room turns off the alarm on the main bank, and it's over.

We flip on the antigrav, and one of the techs takes her down to the incinerator. He comes back, says the other delegates have lined up in the little audience hall outside the incinerator, waiting to clap and drink champagne.

It's always a long night after an expiration, but it's what we're here to do, and it's good solid work, moving and monitoring and setting up the influx for Yemenni's first night. Nobody wants a delay between delegates. You never know when the Carthage is going to show up. We think another four hundred years, but it could be tomorrow. Stranger things have happened.

Wren Ennea-Yemenni needs to be awake, just in case; she'll have things to do, when Carthage comes.

I AM THE ABYSS, I AM THE LIGHT

CAITLÍN R. KIERNAN

━━◆━━

1.

There is only a passing, brief glint of panic when the process has reached the point that cognitive integrity is finally, and almost irrevocably, compromised. During all the interminable months of psychological prep and antemorphic therapy, Ttisa was repeatedly trained for this moment, against this moment, and both the *shhakizsa* midwives and her human counselors have taught her meditation techniques for making the transition with as little trauma as possible. But, most importantly, as her mind and the mind of the surrogate suddenly bleed one into the other, a carefully constructed series of posthypnotic images is triggered. And Ttisa finds herself staring down from suborbit at a living planet that might be Earth, and a muddy, winding river that might be the Mississippi, or perhaps the Nile, or the Ganges, or no river that has ever flowed anywhere but across the floodplains of her imagination. She sees that the river has reached the sea, as rivers do, and here is the place where sediment-laden freshwater collides with the brine, where an opaque torrent the color of almonds interfaces with blue-green saltwater. The confluence, and there is nothing here to fear, for gravity drags all rivers oceanward, just as it drags all raindrops from the sky, and then hauls water vapor up again.

The confluence, she thinks. *The meeting of the waters. Encontro das Águas.* And so the surrogate echoes, *The confluence, the meeting of the waters.* It continues, then, finding thoughts that are no longer only Ttisa's thoughts, before she has had time to find them herself. *Or it is only one river meeting another,* they each think *almost* in unison. *In Brazil, they call it Encontro das Águas, where the Rio Negro joins with the upper Amazon. Brown water and black water,* but then, linked thus, they come to the next bead on this chain. Ttisa sits at a table, and having just added cream to a cup of coffee, she watches while the cold white swirls like a tiny galaxy, its spiral arms starting to blend with the steaming void. *Soon,* they think (for now there is near-perfect synchronization) *the coffee will be cooler, or the milk will be warmer. The milk will be darker, or the coffee will have brightened. It can hardly matter which.*

Across the breakfast table, a teacher that Ttisa never actually had says, "Now, Ttisa, tell me, where, exactly, does the galaxy begin and intergalactic space end? Likewise, where does each of this galaxy's constituent solar systems begin and end?"

And the new coconsciousness that is neither precisely Ttisa nor her *shhakizsa* surrogate, but which fully accommodates them both, begins to answer. It very nearly offers the teacher facts and theories from dutifully recollected lectures on the heliopause and solar winds, hydrogen walls and the interstellar medium. But then it stops itself and glances back down at the muted caramel-colored liquid inside the cup, and the mind can no longer distinguish milk from coffee, nor coffee from milk. Strictly speaking, both have ceased to exist in the creation of a third and novel substance.

"In any objective sense, the question you've asked is meaningless," the woman seated at the table across from the teacher construct replies. The woman wears the face that Ttisa once wore, when Ttisa was only herself. It speaks with the same voice Ttisa spoke with, and the coconscious entity immediately recognizes the face's residual utility as a cushion avatar—a useful tool, so long as that likeness is not mistaken for anything possessed of singularity.

"Well said," the teacher smiles. "You're doing much better than anticipated. Shall we continue?"

The avatar thoughtfully sips her coffee, and then she nods to the teacher. "Please," she replies, and the teacher returns her nod and glances back down at his notes, displayed in the flickering tabletop.

"You're doing so well, in fact, there's quite a bit here we can skip over—heterogeneous mixtures, including suspensions and colloids, for example."

"Which brings us to compounds," the avatar says.

"Indeed, it does."

From its vantage point in geospace, the new mind goes back to watching the nameless river as it empties into that unknown marine gulf, and it marvels at the memory of the taste of milk and coffee, simultaneously familiar and exotic. There is a line of dark clouds moving in from the northwest, and soon they will hide the landscape below from view. Lightning sparks and arcs, belying the violence inside those thunderheads, and Ttisa shivers, despite the temperature of the amnion, which is identical to her own. Here, there is a slip, a misstep, and in *this* instant, she *is* almost Ttisa again. Identity and discreteness threaten to reassert themselves, dissolving the compound back into its constituent parts; there is a second (and stronger) flare of panic before the surrogate can react.

Without hesitation, it points to the next bead on the chain. And the teacher looks up from his notes and clears his throat.

"We might call it binary fusion," he says, "taking care to distinguish this bonding process from the binary *fission* commonly witnessed in the prokaryotic organisms of the Sol system. Nothing here of either partner is split away, but only combined to create a third, which mentally subsumes the parents, in a sense, even though the end product does retain two functionally independent bodies."

"Am I dying?" Ttisa asks him. The man scowls and furrows his eyebrows, but she continues. "Is it like Theodore said? Is the surrogate devouring me alive?"

"You already have the requisite knowledge to answer those questions for yourself," the teacher tells her. "I'm not here to cater to a lazy pupil."

The confluence, her surrogate whispers wordlessly, in silent tones as soothing as the sight of that primeval, earthly river, flowing fifty kilometers below. *The meeting of the waters. Encontro das Águas, as they say in Brazil.*

"Encontro das Águas," she says, and sips her coffee. The teacher smiles, satisfied, and, once again, there is only a single mind, and once again, the face and voice of the woman at the table is only an avatar to ease the crossing, and nothing that is being lost.

2.

Four months earlier, and Ttisa Fitzgerald opens her eyes again, because Theodore is still talking to her. Talking at her. Ttisa wants to sleep, not talk. Lately, it seems that *all* she wants to do is sleep, and she knows it's mostly a side effect of the drugs and dendrimer serums, her antemorphic regimen combined with the demands of her psych conditioning schedule. The doctors told her to expect the grogginess, but it still annoys her. Right now, Theodore is also annoying her. He's sitting naked at the foot of the bed, talking. He's turned away from her, facing the wall, which is currently displaying a realtime image of the north polar region of the planet below. Seventy years before Ttisa was born, a team of Mars-based astronomers christened it Iota Draconis c. If she were not so tired, and beginning to feel nauseous again, she might find the sight moving—the vast boreal icecaps hiding an arctic sea, a wide desert of frozen water which, even from orbit, is more blue than white. The light of an alien star reflected off a swirl of high-latitude clouds. The network of lights marking the ancient *shhakizsa* city, waiting to receive her in only a few more weeks. It is all surely still as wondrous as the day her transport dropped out of sublight, more than thirty parsecs from Earth, and Ttisa first laid eyes on this new world circling a third-magnitude star. But she's sleepy. And nauseous. And her head is beginning to ache.

"Maybe it would be easier," Theodore says, "if you expected me to stay. It would be easier, I think, if you'd not seemed so . . . indifferent . . . when I said I wanted to rotate back next quarter."

"I don't know what you want me to say," Ttisa tells him, because she doesn't, and she's too tired and feels to bad to make something up.

"Do you really think you'll even remember me, after?" he asks ruefully, and yes, she says, trying harder than she wants to sound reassuring.

"Of course, I'll remember you, Theo," and she's said this a hundred times now, if she's said it once. "No memories are lost. None at all."

"And you believe that?"

"I believe the data, yes."

She asks the ship to extinguish the lights in the room, and, immediately, they dim and wink out. Then Ttisa closes her eyes again, because even the soft glow from the image on the wall is painful.

"Memory isn't the same as feeling," Theodore says.

"No, it isn't," she agrees.

"Even if you *do* remember me, there's no reason to think that you'll still want to *be* with me."

"There's no guarantee," she admits. Passing across her lips, the words seem unnaturally heavy, and she imagines them tumbling off her chin and scattering across the sheets. "But you've known that for months now."

"You didn't even ask me to stay," Theodore says.

"It would have been selfish of me to do something like that. It would have been greedy and hypocritical."

Theodore makes a doubtful sort of noise, a scoffing noise. "It *might* have helped me believe that you haven't stopped caring about me, about us," he says.

"Yes, it might have," she says, her heavy, tumbling words sounding impatient with him. "But it would also have been cruel, and I'm *trying*, Theo—"

"You think *this* is kindness?" he asks, interrupting her, and if Ttisa's words have begun to seem heavy, Theo's fall like lead weights. "It would have been kinder if you'd *told* me to go. It would have been kinder if you'd said we were done and gotten it over."

Neither of them says anything more for a moment, and Ttisa opens her eyes partway, squinting and trying not to flinch. Theodore is silhouetted against the monitor, the lines of his muscular body eclipsing the planet on the wall. He's five years younger than her, and was born Theodora, but that was simple enough to fix when he was still a teenager and started figuring out that the inside wasn't suited to the outside. He was born on one of the Mars colonies, in the shadow of Ascraeus Mons, and has never set foot on Earth.

"I don't want it to be like this"," she says, hardly speaking above of whisper. "I've tried so hard, to make sure that it wouldn't go this way."

"You might have asked me to stay," he replies, and she sighs, wishing she'd managed to get to sleep before Theo came back to their quarters after finishing his shift in Telemetry and Comms. He wouldn't have awakened her. He never does. "If you had, perhaps I would be more convinced of your sincerity."

"Theo, *you* said that you wanted to go home, remember? I assumed, when you said that, you were telling me the truth. If you *were*, it would have been wrong of me to try to manipulate you into staying out here with me. I couldn't do that." The words topple from her lips and roll across the bed; even she doesn't find them particularly convincing.

"When I dream, I see all the others," he says, losing her for a second or two. "I dream of them all the time now. I dream of you, with them."

"You've never *seen* the others, Theo. Neither of us has seen the others."

"Yeah, but that doesn't mean that I don't dream about them, almost every time I sleep. *You* could wind up like that, Ttisa, and you know it."

"It's been almost a decade," she tells him. "Almost ten years since the last attempt, and the advances since then . . . " but she trails off, feeling sicker and wondering if she's going to vomit.

"No guarantees," Theo says. "Your own words. So let's not pretend, okay? Let's not fucking lie to ourselves or each other about all the ways this thing could go wrong. For all we know, it's going wrong already, all that shit they're pumping into you day after day."

"Theo," she whispers, "I'm sorry, but I *need* to sleep. We'll talk later. I finished with the second-tier posthyps today, and I just need to sleep for a few hours. Please."

"I'm going for a walk," he says, and then tells the ship to close down the image feed. Ttisa opens her eyes, and the wall is only a wall again, and the compartment is much darker than before.

"I'm going for a walk," Theodore tells her a second time. "I need some air. I'll be down in the garden, maybe, if you need me."

"Well, put some clothes on first," she says, and Theo mutters something angry that she can't quite make out. He quickly dresses while she stares into the darkness, and soon she's alone with her torpid, muddled thoughts and the nausea and exhaustion. She rolls over, looking for the fast-fading warm spot Theo left on the mattress. She asks the ship to resume the video feed, same coordinates as before, and Ttisa watches the blue-white planet far below until she drifts down to a fitful, haunted sleep.

3.

In the present life there are two impediments which prevent us from seeing each other's thoughts: the grossness of the body and the inscrutable secrecy of the will. The first impediment will be removed by the Resurrection, but the second will remain, and it is in the angels now. Nevertheless the brightness of the risen body will correspond to the degree of grace and glory in the mind; and so will serve as a medium for one mind to know another.

Thomas Aquinas, *Summa Theologiae*, (1265-1274)

4.

Ttisa asks the ship to provide her with a mirror, and so a moment later it does. She stands alone in the cramped lavatory, gazing back at herself with those bloodshot green eyes squinched half-shut against the light. She's dressed in nothing but the short, drab station-issued smocks. No one can ever seem to agree if they're meant to be a very orange shade of yellow, or a rather yellowish shade of orange. The woman in the mirror looks as though she hasn't slept in days, a week, maybe. Her skin is sallow, and there are perpetual shadows beneath her eyes, like matching bruises.

Her lips are pale and badly chapped, and there's still a dark smudge across her septum and upper lip from the latest nose bleed.

"You are a liar, Miss Fitzgerald," she says, and yes, the woman in the mirror agrees.

"You are, indeed, a liar."

"And a very poor liar, at that," her reflection sighs.

"I'm not sure that it matters any longer," Ttisa says very softly. "I honestly don't know why I even bother to lie to him."

"Old habits," the woman in the mirror suggests, and Ttisa nods.

"I *am* leaving him," she says. "I'm leaving everyone and everything, in a sense. Most times, it's all I can manage to remember why."

"Being alone is unbearable," the woman in the mirror reminds her, using Ttisa's mouth and tongue to make the words.

"Yes, it is, isn't it?"

"For those who realize that they're alone, and how completely they are alone, very much so."

"*Only* for those who've realized how completely alone they are."

"Yes," the woman in the mirror concedes. "Ignorance is the best defense."

Ttisa stops talking to herself and watches the mirror in silence for a time. Anyone could be forgiven for thinking that she was sick, sick and likely dying, anyone who got a good look at her. Maybe, that hypothetical anyone might suppose, there'd been a malfunction in her slot on the sleeper during the long trip from Sol, or maybe it was only something prosaic, some humdrum malady she'd picked up before leaving Earth. Either way, they would surmise, the outcome will likely be the same. Medicine can only do so much, after all.

"It's nothing that wasn't expected," she whispers, as though she might be overheard.

"No. Nothing yet," the sickly looking woman in the mirror says, qualifying the observation.

Ttisa asks the ship to please get rid of the mirror, and soon the lavatory wall is the same dull, non-reflective gray as any other wall. She sits down on the toilet, because her legs feel weak, and she wonders if Theo came back while she was sleeping. There's no evidence that he did, but it's not impossible. Maybe he stood near the bed and watched while she slept. Perhaps, he sat on the padded bench near the bed and kept an eye on her while she dreamed of a meeting that she's told him repeatedly never took place. Officially, it never did. There's no record of it anywhere in her files, and news of the meeting certainly was not included in any of the press packs. She has often wondered why they took the chance, and has never yet arrived at an entirely satisfactory answer. It might have been the doing of one of the project leaders, one of the dissenters, trying to prove a pet point. Or it might have been the *shhakizsa* who saw to it that the meeting took place, leaving the agency with little choice but to acquiesce. In the end, though, *why* and *how* it happened don't seem particularly important. Only that it did. Whatever doubts Ttisa had before she met the sixth attempt were undone by that encounter.

She stares down at the floor between her bare feet. Her toenails look as if they have each been struck smartly with a mallet or hammer, and she thinks about polishing them to hide the discoloration. Again, it's nothing that wasn't anticipated by the pharmacokinetic profile. Nothing to be worried about.

"Being alone is unbearable," she says again. When she asked the sixth why it had proceeded with the process, even after being presented with evidence that there was insufficient momentum to clear all the requisite psychosomatic barriers, that's the reply that Ttisa received. *Being alone is unbearable.*

The answer had not been spoken, of course, because the sixth was no longer capable of speech, any more than it was able to hear. But it was able to communicate with Ttisa, and with its caretakers, by way of a wetware transference matrix incorporated into the sixth's artificial womb. The vox program possessed a very distinct PanAsian mech accent—a giveaway in the enunciation—hinting at its provenance.

"Yes," Ttisa replied, peering into the murky tank, straining to see clearly through the gelatinous support medium and into the sunken black slits that were the vestigial eyes of the sixth. "I think I understand."

"I had thought that you would," the sixth replied. "I had *hoped* that you would."

And later, one of the project psychiatrists wanted to talk about that part of the exchange. Specifically, he wanted a clearer definition of what the two of them had meant by *alone*. At first, Ttisa was at a loss to explain, and then a rather obvious analogy occurred to her.

"I'm in a bubble," she told the man. "And you are in a bubble, as well. We are each in our own perfectly transparent bubble. I can see you, and you can see me. We can even hear each other perfectly well. In fact, the physics of our bubbles even allow us to touch one another. We could even fuck, if we wished. The bubbles are that flexible. But, regardless, we are *still* trapped inside our respective, inviolable bubbles, and no matter how hard we may try, we can never truly touch one another. We cannot ever fully *know* one another. In my thoughts, I am alone, Doctor, isolated, and so are you. And being alone is unbearable."

Ttisa heard a rumor the psychiatrist resigned from the project, shortly after that interview, and that he was rotated back to Sol following a board inquiry. Whether or not the rumor was true, she never saw him again. And no one else on the project has ever asked about her conversation with the sixth.

"I'm sorry, Theo," Ttisa says. "I'm a goddamn liar." And then she realizes how late it's getting, that she's going to be late for her morning conditioning session if she doesn't stop moping about the lavatory and get dressed. She tugs the drab smock off over her head, lets it slip from her fingers, and then leaves it lying on the floor. There will be time to pick it up later. Later, there will be time to worry about Theo.

5.

"Has it begun?" Ttisa asks. "Has it started?" But then she realizes that she's hasn't actually asked the question aloud, and so she doesn't expect an answer. She tries to open her eyes, but finds that she's unable to, and so thinks that she might only be dreaming and struggling to wake up.

And struggling to breath.

A dream, then, of drowning, perhaps. But, if so, the dream would be little more than hazy, disarranged recollection, proceeding from a childhood mishap. She was not quite five years old, and had gone with her mother to a public natatorium. There was an artificial waterfall at one end of the pool, and, also, a hidden machine that generated artificial waves, so that swimmers might know what it had been like to swim in the sea, when swimming in the sea was still an option. There was a sandy beach, and plastic sea shells.

Hold it up to your ear and listen, her mother said. *Tell me what you hear.*

"I hear a roaring, mother. I hear a terrible endless roaring, like a wind blowing between the stars."

There is the sense that she is floating, weightless, but it's not the sickening weightlessness of space travel. Which is, in truth, the sensation of always *falling*. Ttisa knows that she is not falling, though she may well have *fallen*, in some archaic, mythic denotation of the word. Having fallen, then, she floats.

Fiery the Angels rose, & as they rose deep thunder roll'd
Around their shores: indignant burning with the fires of Orc

The dim memory of her feet kicking out and not finding bottom, and indeed there is no bottom now to be found. *And when they pulled you from the pool,* her mother once told her, *you were so pale. I thought that we had lost you.*

I am lost now, mother. I am lost forever and always.

They've found me, and I am lost.

The half dream whirls, like cream in coffee, or muddy freshwater meeting a clear tropical sea.

One of the project biologists is talking, though his voice is muted and seems to be reaching her from some place or some time far away from now and here. It is one of her first sessions, an introduction to *shhakizsa* physiology. In particular, digestion and reproduction, two processes inextricably linked in the life cycle of the aliens. She wants the woman to stop lecturing her. Wants only to drift in this silent nowhere that is not falling, and is not drowning, and is neither cold nor warm.

"Direct comparison with humans, or any other mammal, or, for that matter, with any animal species, is problematic. For example, we can refer to this orifice as a mouth, but it also functions as a vagina and anus. We could call this muscular tube here the esophagus, or cervix, or the colon, but we would not be quite correct in doing so, for their functions are not truly analogous. Is *that* organ there a stomach? A womb? How, you'll ask, could it function as both?"

"They're great ugly brutes, you ask me," Theodore says, then goes back to picking at the meal he's only pretending to eat.

"I don't recall asking you," she replies, and he shrugs. "And I don't see where such a subjective matter as 'beauty' is even relevant here."

Theo stops rearranging the food on his plate and glares at her a moment, and his expression is so complex an interweave of contempt, concern, fear, confusion, and anger, that she could not hope to *begin* to separate one emotion from the others.

"When this thing is over," he says, then pauses to take a deep breath, flaring his nostrils slightly. "*If* you survive it, then you'll be as much one of them as human, yeah?"

"Yes," she replies.

Theo lays his fork down and wipes at his mouth with a napkin. "And I'll say, 'She was a woman, once. She was the most beautiful woman I ever saw, and I loved her.' I'll say, 'You might find that hard to believe, but she *was* a woman, once.' "

"And to whom would you say such things?"

"Who do you think would bother to ask? Anyway, they'll take me for a liar, or a madman, if I dare."

Her mother laughs and shows her how to hold the plastic conch shell to her ear. "Now, dear," she says, "don't you hear the sea inside? Don't you hear the waves against the beach?"

I won't tell her what I hear. This time, I'll keep it all to myself.

The biologist draws Ttisa's attention back to the faintly quivering holographic diagram, a generalized cross section of a *shhakizsa*'s radially symmetric anatomy.

"We can make very rough parallels with some Sol taxa," she says. "Among the Eumetazoa of Earth, for example, I might mention the Ctenophora and Cnidaria, and, to a lesser degree, the echinoderms, especially crinoids. If we look to the hydrothermal biomes of Europa, there is a superficial similarity with the parahydroids and the more familiar Gorgonophores. In all these instances, though, if we look closely enough, the parallels break down, and only serve to demonstrate how truly foreign to our concepts of biophysics and morphology these beings are. They—and most other organisms we've seen from the *shhakizsa* homeworld—are without precedent, in our experience, which is presently too bound to a single perspective."

"Ugly fuckers," Theo mutters, and gets up from the table. "You ask me—and I *know* that you never bothered to ask me, Ttisa—this whole goddamn affair is an abomination. It is abominable."

Now the project's chief anthropologist is talking, and Ttisa remembers his name, John Grant, because he was one of the few people selected for the panel that she found likeable. His voice is firm and, yet, somehow lyrical.

"It is imperative," he says, "to understand that, for *shhakizsa* society, this process is nothing short of sacred. It's marriage, copulation, and parent-hood combined. It is the most intimate communion between two persons imaginable. There are fifteen different words their priests commonly used when referring to the process, and they all translate, more or less, the same: *unification*."

"Did he actually call them *persons*?" Theo scoffs, and he turns away from her.

She is floating, and the feeling of suffocation has passed. Her lungs have filled with fluid, and there is no longer any need to breathe. The oxygen she requires will be transferred directly to her bloodstream now. There is no pain, despite the corrosively low pH environment surrounding her, and despite that, by now, various enzymes will have triggered the early stages of epidermal transformation and horizontal gene transfer. The digestive, amniotic fluid is filled with powerful analgesics, and the serums and months of conditioning have insured that her human neurology is receptive to them.

"Doesn't it sound like the sea?" her mother asks, and Ttisa, not yet five years old, shakes her head and sets the conch back down on the white, white sand of the natatorium's fabricated beach.

The six umbilical cords begin to wrap themselves tightly about her, each one attaching to a critical, predetermined site on Ttisa's body by means of razor-sharp beaks composed primarily of chitin and complex cross-linked proteins. One for her throat (entering by way of her mouth), another through her sex, her belly, her rectum and the base of her spine, and yet another penetrating the medulla oblongata via the foramen magnum.

I am not drowning, she thinks. *I could never drown. I am held fast. Embraced, as I have never been embraced before, and I will not fall again.*

"Has it started?"

"Yes," whispers a voice that is not a voice. "It has started. Rest now. You will need it, farther along."

Theo puts down his tab and squeezes his eyes shut. He rubs at his temples, as though his head aches. "It sounds like rape to me," he says. "No, it sounds much *worse* than rape."

"I wish I could make you understand," she tells him. "I would, if I could."

And around Ttisa, all the wide world has shrunken to this golden lagoon of kindly, flesh-filtered light and transmuting fluids and the gentle, voiceless reassurances in a tongue she understands without having learned.

And, for the first time in her life, she is sure that she not falling.

6.

Though she didn't go down to the departure bay in time to say goodbye to Theo (and, for that matter, he didn't come to say goodbye to her), Ttisa did watch him leave. She stood alone on the observation deck, and, with an index finger pressed to the wall, traced the steady, silent path of the ungainly, multi-hulled sleeper as it exited the station and moved away towards the pulsing scarlet ring of the starboard ftl portal. She looked away before the embarkation flash, and when she looked back, the ship that would ferry him home was gone. He was gone. And she knew that she'd never see him again.

She knew that she *should* feel remorse.

And she knew, too, that there should be a profound emptiness inside her, an ache that she would carry for a long time to come. But there was nothing of the sort, and it seemed very silly to counterfeit, or to worry over the absence of emotions that would have only caused her pain.

They've changed me this much already, she thought, still watching the ftl portal as the lateral vector array stopped flashing while the entire circuit powered down. The plasma stream had dissipated, and there was nothing visible through the portal now but stars. She picked out the yellow speck of Arcturus, then pulled her hand back from the wall and stared at her fingertip, instead.

That's it, then. He's away. It is for the best, really. He was so unhappy.

"Sleep tight, my love," she said aloud. "Sleep tight and dream." Then, wondering if this was possibly only another part of the experiment, and, if so, how she'd scored, Ttisa turned and left the observation deck.

7.

This far along in the process, three Sol days and counting, there is no longer any meaningful distinction between her memory and that of the surrogate. "It" clearly recalls kneeling on a white beach and holding a plastic conch to its ear, listening for a phantom sea. "She" remembers, with equal clarity, the towering, crystalline spires buried miles deep, beneath the *shhakizsas'* sprawling polar megalopolis, the quartz lattice of temples erected to long-forgotten gods and demons. "It" recalls a day at the beach, and "she" relives a pilgrimage to an archeological wonder. The rapidly mutating body that was Ttisa Fitzgerald drifts, not falling, safe within the sanctuary that has grown around it, the amniotic cyst that cradles what it has become and what it is still becoming.

The confluence, this new, compounded consciousness thinks again. *The meeting of the waters. Encontro das Águas.*

Milk in coffee.

The cold swirl of stars in near vacuum.

All but one of the surrogate's umbilici has withdrawn, completely resorbed into the host's endometrium. The one that remains is there for no other reason than the carnal pleasure of contact. It has swollen to completely fill the thorny, cilia-lined slit that can longer be described as a human vagina. The enormous body of the surrogate and the far smaller body of the reborn shiver is unison.

We are whole, it thinks, as the latest in a seemingly ceaseless series of orgasms fades. *This is our gift, the gift we have given to ourself. This wholeness, unfettered by the jail of individuality. Our minds are laid bare, and there can be no mental isolation here, and no secrets.*

Being alone is unbearable, it thinks.

We will never be alone again, it replies. *Even when the cyst ruptures and we divide, we will remain as one.*

Is she still here, watching from somewhere within us? The one who was named Ttisa Fitzgerald? but it knows the answer even before the question has been fully articulated. Nothing has been lost, save the abyss between one consciousness and another.

Hold it up to your ear and listen. Tell me what you hear.

You might have asked me to stay.

And I'll say, "She was a woman, once. She was the most beautiful woman I ever saw, and I loved her." I'll say, "You might find that hard to believe, but she was a woman, once."

And, if not woman, and if not shhakizsa, *what are we now?* it asks itself. *What is this beast we have become?*

There are many words available with which to answer that question, but they all, each and every one, signify unification. It pauses in the flow of questioning and revelry to examine what has been fashioned from the willing offering of Ttisa Fitzgerald—the reborn child, the holy feast, the marriage consummated. In combined lifetimes, it has beheld precious few things so singular in their loveliness, so unlikely in their realization. That impatient daughter tugs roughly at the remaining umbilicus, snared between her legs. And, pleased at the unprecedented fruits of so painful and perilous a labor—a labor that failed six times previously—the amalgam resumes its ministrations.

7.

It is not from space that I must seek my dignity, but from the government of my thought. I shall have no more if I possess worlds. By space the universe encompasses and swallows me up like an atom; by thought I comprehend the world.

Blaise Pascal (1623-1662), *Pensées*

THE BEEKEEPER

JAMIE BARRAS

———⟨⟩———

I was born in freefall on a boneship of the Stro. My parents named me Elena, *after my mother's mother, but to the Hila I am* Andalian, *orphan of the storm and keeper of Kimonayev's bees.*

We made planetfall one hundred kilometres east of the candidate garden. My father had timed our arrival to coincide with local dusk, and we spent the rest of the night unloading our equipment. By daybreak, we were finally ready to break camp and start for the garden. But we had one last thing to do before we could set off: we had to kill the boneship. Antonov drew the short straw. We all said our goodbyes to the ship and then Antonov fired the safety charges. With a crick-crack of splintering bulkheads and the hiss of released respiratory gases, the ship shuddered and died. We watched the outer shell began to warp and bubble as the accelerated processes of decay began. By the time that they finished, all that would be left of the ship would be a quarter-tonne of cellulose and a few hundred grammes of long-chain hydrocarbons, alcohols and esters. Even the most iterated of Melzemi hunters would be unable to distinguish the remains from the indigenous flora. It was a sad end to an old friend, but it was something that we had to do just to survive.

We turned away at last and climbed the valley side to watch the sunrise. We were none of us planetborn—this was the first real sunrise for us all. We stood in silence with our faces to the sun and drank in the heat, the light, the depth and breadth of it all. Kimonayev's bees buzzed lazily about our heads seemingly just as mesmerised.

"We're here," Antonov said at length. "We're finally here."

Sylvain laughed derisively. "We're stuck here, you mean." She gestured back down towards the valley floor. "We just blew the brains out our ride."

My mother hugged me close and shook her head. "Have a heart, Marie." Sylvain ignored her.

"We can express our reserve ship once we get to the garden," Kimonayev said. Every search team carried a spare copy of the boneship expression licensed from the Stro.

"If we can make the garden bloom," Sylvain said, rounding on Kimonayev—she didn't need reminding what we could or couldn't do. "And what chance of that? A Class D, on the edge of Melzemi territory? The last time that I was awake, the *Veche* would never have wasted a search team on a prospect as poor as this."

Sylvain appeared young in years—not more than forty. In fact she was the second oldest on the team in terms of time spent. Thanks to the vagaries of *Acheron*'s coldsleep lottery the last time that she had been awake had been over two hundred fixed years earlier. Back then, the *Veche*—*Acheron*'s governing committee—had not been even a third of the way through the list of abandoned gardens that they had bought from the Stro. These were different days: only a quarter of the list remained, and *Acheron*'s search teams had still not found so much as a single uncorrupted copy of the faster-than-light expression. These days, the *Veche* sent teams to anywhere within range.

"We'll make do," Kimonayev insisted. He looked at least thirty years older than Sylvain, but he was far younger in terms of time spent, with only a single, two-decade-long spell in coldsleep behind him. The things that he knew about how things currently stood with *Acheron* made him much more stoical.

Sylvain started to respond but my father cut her off. "We're wasting daylight."

Sylvain cursed.

My father looked to her. "Are you done?" After a long moment, Sylvain nodded her head. "Good." my father looked to Kimonayev. "How are your little pets doing, Alexandr Simonovitch—they ready to travel?" Kimonayev's bees were only a couple of hours out of coldsleep, but they were typed for quick recovery and rapid orientation. Kimonayev watched them sketch patterns in the air for a few moments then turned to my father. "Yes, Grigori Pietrovitch."

"Then let's go."

• • •

Early on the first day of our march, we cut the trail of some local animal life. My mother and Antonov broke out a couple of dumb guns and set off to follow the trail. They returned half an hour later carrying the carcase of a small, grey-haired quadruped: binocular, binaural, warm-blooded. Sylvain ran its DNA: it was indigenous—not a child of the garden. She extracted and then strained its stomach contents. The juices went into one of her vats. To survive on this world we would need to eat what the local animal life ate. The contents of the dead quadruped's stomach would provide the source code for the retyping of our own intestinal flora and fauna. At dusk, Sylvain dosed us with a cocktail of laxatives and oral antibiotics followed a couple of hours later by helpings from the contents of the vat. By dawn the next day, we were ready for our first breakfast of locally grown food: fruits and legumes chased down with unfiltered local water.

We were adapting, getting ready for the physical challenges ahead. By the third day, even I was finding the going easier. The first two days, I had struggled. My mother had taught me to swim in the boneship's bladder, developing my muscles by making me push and pull myself through the water, but, even so, supporting my own weight had not come easily to me after an infancy spent in freefall. And yet by that third day, I was able to walk unassisted—and even run for short distances. It felt good.

We reached the lower slopes of the garden's outer rim on the afternoon of the fourth day. A short reconnoitre showed that we were less than three kilometres south of the spot that the survey from orbit had fixed as our point of entry into the garden. This was a broken line of ridges streaked with waterfalls, and stacked one above and behind the other like a crumbling staircase. Although it was impossible to tell from the ground—clouds shrouded the rim's upper reaches—the survey from orbit had revealed that this staircase led all the way up and over the top. But the top was a full kilometre above the level of the surrounding forestland— even taking it in stages, it wouldn't be an easy ascent, especially with all the gear that we had with us.

"If things go smoothly, we should make it to the top in two days," Antonov said confidently. Like Sylvain, he was of athletic build and a young physiological age. He sounded as if he was looking forward to the challenge.

Kimonayev shook his head and laughed. "What I wouldn't give for a floater right now. Or even just a pallet or two."

There couldn't be any of those things, not this close to Melzemi territory. This was by necessity a largely technology-free expedition. My mother, my father and the other adults would have to carry the team's gear up on their backs.

"We'll rest up for what's left of today," my father said. "And start our ascent bright and early tomorrow. Alexandr Simonovitch: you better start packing up your little pets. It's going to be windy up there."

We made camp.

The next morning, while we were still at breakfast, the beyonders appeared.

They were three-metre tall bipeds, bimanous, binocular, binaural, furry-backed, bare-bellied—unmistakably children of the garden. There were six of them, all dressed in the simple animal-skin garments of temperate pre-trade peoples, and carrying rudimentary throwing weapons.

My father went forward to greet them, his hands empty and his face dressed in a smile. They started to close on him, slowly, but surely. I hid behind my mother's legs.

"Worker-type three eighty-seven," Kimonayev said, keeping his own lips fixed in a smile, but speaking loudly enough for my father to hear. "Low mil. capability, minimal aggression—and zero exchange value."

"What's their trigger?" my father asked.

There was a pause while Kimonayev searched for the answer amongst the masses of information that the boneship's smart engine had fed into his brain during the long journey to the target world. At length he said, "Asbal Command Language—any tone."

The garden-builders had typed their children for obedience—and language comprehension.

My father took another step forward. The beyonders kept coming on. "Stop where you are," my father said, in pitch-perfect ACL—more smart-engine-delivered knowledge. The beyonders came to an immediate halt. "We are no threat to you. Ground your weapons." The beyonders rested the butts of their spears on the ground. My father fixed his gaze on the closest of the beyonders—a redback with a paint-daubed face. "Tell the rest of your group to join us."

There were shadows moving through the trees beyond the clearing's edge—more beyonders; the redback and its five companions were scouts sent to assess the situation. The garden-builders might not have typed the 387s for combat or tactics, but the 387s were smart enough to know not to take any chances.

Nothing happened for a long moment. "Could they be functionally mute?" Sylvain said, speaking Ruslac.

With no master to bring them on, many children of abandoned gardens failed to develop normally, no matter what skills the garden-builders had hardwired into them. There was no reason to suppose that these 387s would express their language skills in the absence of anyone ever having talked to them. But for all that, after a few moments, the redback threw back its head and called out, "Rest your arms, and come here!"

It pitched its voice high—the sound didn't seem to fit with its massive frame. "That was Child Common," Kimonayev said. He laughed. "Actual Child Common. From the mouth of a child."

The boneship's smart engine had fed us all the sound of children's voices many times across the boneship's three-year fall towards the target world. But that had been on microdat—and mostly simulated speech. This was live—sounds generated within organic voice boxes, given their timbre by a planetary atmosphere.

The redback looked to my father when it had finished. "They are coming, speaker-of-commands," it said.

My father shook his head. "My name is 'Rahmatov.' This replaces 'speaker-of-commands.' And these are—" he went around the rest of the team "—Seremnova, Kimonayev, Sylvain, and Antonov—and the little one there is Elena." He looked again to the beyonder. "Do you have a name?"

Another long pause. Then: "I am the 83rd to be called 'Beyonder Who Starts At The Tall Rock Then Goes Towards The Sun Three Days Before Turning North And Moving . . .'"

It carried on in that vein for half a minute or more, describing what sounded like a search pattern through the forest that surrounded the garden. Eventually, it reached the end—back at the "Tall Rock" where it had started.

"I think we'll go with '83'," my father said, looking to the rest of us for agreement.

More beyonders started appearing from the trees. Within a few minutes, almost twenty had crowded into the small clearing. The shortest was perhaps two-metres twenty, the tallest three-metres ten; fur colours ranged from golden-brown through russet-red to black, and skin tones showed a similar degree of variation. One of the newcomers had lost its arm below the elbow, something that excited some comment and speculation from my mother, Sylvain and Kimonayev—the team's organics specialists. Ofttimes, societies established by the children of abandoned gardens were intolerant of physical impairment. The garden-builders had been interested in only the best produce; they had equipped many child types with an inbuilt drive to attack the weak and the damaged.

"Rahmatov," the redback—83—said. "Every member of this party of beyonders is now here." Task completed. Awaiting further commands.

"We going to let them haul our gear for us?" Antonov asked.

"First things first," my father said. He looked to 83 and then pointed to the garden rim. "We need to get to the other side of that. Can the . . . the 'beyonders' take us there?"

As one, the beyonders all turned towards the garden rim. Then they just stood there looking up at it. Seconds ticked by.

"How sure are we that these are typed for minimal aggression?" Antonov asked quietly. "Because it looks like we have just come up against a local taboo."

"The trigger's stronger than any cultural artefact," Kimonayev said. Some abandoned children came to regard their birthplaces as something like holy ground—closed not only to outsiders, but also to themselves once they were fully-grown. It was an offshoot of their wired-in drive to both protect the garden from damage and to travel beyond its bounds—to deliver themselves up to the harvest. But the garden-builders had placed obedience at every child type's core. That remained a major selling point.

One by one, the beyonders turned back around to face the team once more. 83 dipped its head at my father. "Yes, the beyonders can take you there, Rahmatov."

My mother stepped forward. She looked to my father. He nodded to her: *go ahead*. She turned to 83. "Can you remember the last time that you were there?"

"Yes, Seremnova."

"When was that?"

Another long pause; then, "When I was a child, Seremnova. I was last there when I was a child."

Antonov and Sylvain shared a smile. My mother ignored them and pressed on with her next question. "Do you have a name for it?"

"Yes, Seremnova. It is called 'The Place Bound On All Sides By A Wall That Rises, Not Ten Times The Height Of The Tallest Tree, Nor Twenty Times, Nor Thirty Times, Nor . . . ' "

With the beyonders to help us, it took us less than a day to scale the outer rim. Moving slowly through the mist and rain, we crossed over to the other side and started down. We camped that evening just below the cloud base. At sunrise the following morning, the whole team gathered on a ledge overlooking the garden.

A ring of clouds had settled like a halo over the garden rim—where air from the interior met air of the world beyond—but the sky over the garden itself was entirely clear. As the morning progressed, we watched as the light of the rising sun drove back the shadows and revealed more and more of the garden below. The impact crater was almost forty kilometres across at its widest point, and thirty-five at its narrowest—a testament to the steep angle of descent sketched out by the asteroid that the garden-builders had thrown at the planet. It was perhaps fifteen hundred metres from the summit down to the garden floor—and the floor sloped downwards from there to the crater centre: a measure of the force of that impact.

This was the artificial bowl that the garden-builders had created; the place where they had seeded their garden, safe from contamination by indigenous flora and fauna. There was only light vegetation on the steep slopes at the foot of the rim—grasses and scrub, stands of long-stemmed, flat-capped fungi, and patches of surface mould interspersed with water-courses. Towards the centre of the crater, the vegetation grew denser and more varied; however, grasses, scrub and outcroppings of mould and fungi still predominated. The few stands of trees and tall ferns that we could see stood isolated from one another. The largest was only a few kilometres in length and less than a kilometre in width—a band of woodland crowded into a narrow land bridge between two large lakes just east of the centre of the crater, its trees furred with more fungi and cross-threaded with epiphytes.

More *veldt* than rainforest: this was not how things were supposed to be. The whole scene spoke of serious biomass depletion. And that meant repeated mass emigrations—the sort of thing that had brought our own beyonders to the world beyond the garden. And we could see that the garden was still turning out children even now. The trees and ferns, fungi and moulds, were the factories that produced the seeds from which the children grew, but it was in the lakes and rivers that those children started to develop, and where they spent the first part of their lives. All the watercourses that we could see were dark with organic matter: humus and vegetation, yes, but also neonatal children spawned from seeds carried into the water by the wind.

At the same time, there was precious little evidence of there being mature children still within the garden. They were still obeying that drive to leave the garden—to self-harvest. But each mass emigration was supposed to trigger a balancing event—a "bloom": the process whereby the garden replaced its lost biomass. We were looking down on a garden that had stopped blooming but kept right on producing children, a garden that was slowly, but surely, bleeding itself dry. Was there enough life left in the garden for us to make it bloom again? That wasn't part of our mission. We weren't there to rejuvenate the garden; we were there to search for an uncorrupted copy of the faster-than-light expression. However, making the garden bloom *was* our one chance of getting off the planet afterwards. In its current state, it didn't contain nearly enough biomass to feed a growing boneship.

"303 K," my mother said. "Perhaps . . . 7 degrees above local ambient."

"Pretty much what the survey showed," Antonov put in. "It's still hot."

"That's a good sign," Kimonayev said.

Sylvain shrugged. "Perhaps."

My mother turned to my father. "What do you want to do, Grigor Pietrovitch?"

My father responded by calling forward 83. He gestured down into the garden. "Do any of your people live here?"

"We are beyonders, Rahmatov. We live beyond." It gestured back the way that we had come the day before.

"The clue was in the name, Grigor Pietrovitch," Antonov said with a smile.

My father ignored him. Looking to 83 still, he said, "But you do remember being here—" he turned to face the rest of the children "—you all do?"

Not all children were born sapient; many infant children got by on hardwired instinct alone. And many of those children retained no memory of their infancy.

"Yes, Rahmatov," the beyonders responded, in a ragged chorus.

My father turned back to 83. "Is it a dangerous place?"

It was a question that needed to be asked—anything in the garden big enough or poisonous enough, to worry the beyonders would be big enough or poisonous enough, to worry us too.

"No, Rahmatov."

"Fond memories, do you think?" said Antonov in Ruslac. 83's tone did seem lighter whenever it talked about the garden.

Sylvain laughed. "If ignorance is bliss," she said, "then pre-sapience must be ecstasy."

"Okay," put in my father. "I'm satisfied. Secure your gear. We start our descent in half an hour."

The paths on the garden-side of the crater rim were just as worn as were those on the outside. For a hundred thousand fixed years or more, the children's genes had driven them to try to climb up out of the garden. Every one of our beyonders had trodden those paths in their youth without knowing why or what was waiting for them on the other side of the crater rim. As we climbed down, my mother quizzed 83 and the rest of the beyonders about their memories of leaving the garden. Her efforts brought forth the story of the society that the beyonders had developed in the millennia since the garden-builders stopped coming back. We had arrived outside the candidate garden at a time of heightened activity. 83 and the rest of his group were there because, after a three-year lull, they were expecting a new wave of adolescent 387s to merge from the garden sometime in the next half-year or so. Beyonder society had ceremonies of reception for emerging children, coupled with traditions of sending out colonies when the local population grew too great. A new equilibrium.

Predictably, Sylvain didn't see it that way. To her, beyonder society's traditions spoke of stagnation. It was a favourite theme of hers: just because some child types hit all the marks for sapience, did not mean that they *were* sapient. "The garden-born lack any innate ability to innovate," Sylvain said, "to break out of the box. So why do we persist in describing them as sapient?"

"You don't regard them as sapient just because they can talk?" Antonov said.

"No. No, I don't. It's all wet-wired responses."

"You eat meat, right?"

"Pavel Mikhailovitch . . . ?" my mother asked warily. *Where are you going with this?*

Antonov held up his hand: *it's okay.*

Sylvain shook her head. "Don't."

"No, come on: you eat meat, yes?"

Sylvain rolled her eyes and shook her head—she, at least, knew where Antonov was going with this. "Yes," she said with a sigh. "Yes, I eat meat."

"So you would have no problem eating 83, then, being as how, as far as you're concerned, it isn't sapient."

Sylvain kept shaking her head. "The two don't connect."

Antonov just shrugged: he considered his point made.

A short while later, we reached the garden floor.

"They're all distinct cultures," my mother said. She threw away the last of the mould scrapings that she had taken and climbed back to her feet. She wiped her brow with the back of her hand, leaving a trail in the sweat that had gathered there. There was a slight breeze blowing but the air was heavy with heat and humidity. The atmosphere inside the garden smelled like crushed citrus fruit: at once acrid and overly sweet. My mother turned to the rest of the team. "We're not looking at a stalled bloom."

A bloom was a cataclysmic event. It began with a single mould culture, one amongst many in the garden, suddenly starting to grow at an exponential rate, consuming every piece of vegetation in the garden, stripping the garden bare. Fuelled by this feast, it would then spill out over the crater rim and consume every piece of indigenous flora within reach, before channelling all of this new biomass back into the garden. This process completed, the mould culture would then retreat over the crater rim, before finally dying. In time, the garden vegetation would spring reborn from the mould's rotting remains, ready to begin anew the process of seeding children for the harvest. At least, that was how the process was supposed to work.

"So it could still be just a trigger fault?" Antonov asked. "The bloom never got started?"

"Or the bloom stalled somewhere else in the garden," my mother said. "Somewhere closer to the centre." She rocked her head from side to side and shrugged. "Still too early to tell."

The question was a critical one: we could correct a trigger fault by replacing the corrupted expression for triggering the bloom—an uncorrupted copy of the bloom trigger came bundled with the boneship expression. However, if the bloom had started only to stall sometime later, this would suggest that the problem was with the whole garden—

something lacking, a more widespread corruption. Trying to trigger a fresh bloom would be a waste of time in that scenario.

"I'll have to conduct a wider search," my mother said, looking to my father. Then she paused as the air thickened suddenly with a cloud of spores. When the cloud had passed, she sneezed, clearing her nasal passages. Then she concluded: "And run a lot more tests."

My father nodded. "We can all get involved in that—the beyonders too, if you think you can use them?" My mother nodded. "Good." He turned to Kimonayev. "Meanwhile: time to release your little pets, Alexandr Simonovitch, and set *them* to work."

The whole team stopped to watch Kimonayev set free his bees from their little prison. Whatever slim chance we had of successfully completing our mission rested with Kimonayev's bees. The faster-than-light expression was one small part of a longer expression, the blueprint for a star-faring vessel built on a much grander scale that the boneship that the *Veche* had licensed from the Stro. Either by accident or by design, seeds for this particular child type were very rare. Only half a dozen or so species were known to possess an intact example—the Stro, the eternally-hostile Melzemi, a few others—and none of them was willing to license the faster-than-light expression to humanity at a price that the *Veche* could afford to pay. So, instead, the *Veche* had chanced everything on buying a list of abandoned gardens from the Stro. *Acheron*'s search teams had been working through that list for over three hundred years searching, without success, for a seed that humanity could call its own.

That was where Kimonayev's bees came in. Every child type carried an identifying genetic marker. But we couldn't hope to search the whole garden by hand, sampling every seed on every piece of vegetation. We just couldn't do it. But the bees could. *Acheron*'s geneticists had programmed them to "taste" everything in the garden in search of the marker for the FTL-equipped child type; and, if they found it, to return then to their handlers and "dance" out the location to them. We were too close to Melzemi territory to use a machine-based search method, but even if that had not been the case, the bees would still have been just about the best way to conduct the search.

Kimonayev released them. They took a few moments to orientate themselves. Then they went to work.

My father turned to my mother. "How do you want to work our own search?" *For the answer to the mystery of why the garden had failed to bloom.*

My mother pursed her lips and thought for a moment. Then she said, "Let's start at one of the watercourses."

"What about the local childlife?" Antonov said.

"Stomach contents?" Antonov nodded. My mother looked to my father. "That might be something to set the beyonders to doing."

The "local childlife" was Antonov's name for children—pre-sapient infant or non-sapient mature—abroad in the garden. We had already seen a few rodents running through the scrub and fungi bushes and some amphibians feeding on the aquatic neonates, but we could expect to find many more, and varied child types much closer to the centre, where the thicker vegetation and deeper rivers and lakes lay. There would be carnivores amongst these child types, but many, including most of the very youngest, would be getting by on a diet of moulds and fungi. And the beyonders were dressed in animal skins, so they clearly weren't averse to killing other living things.

My father gestured to 83. He explained to him what he wanted from the beyonders. "I'd like to go with them," Antonov put in. "If you don't need me at the river." My father assented. Antonov drew a dumb gun then turned to the beyonders. "Come on then." They started to move off, spreading out through the fields of grass and fungi. Kimonayev's bees were already out of sight.

"Pavel Mikhailovitch!" Antonov turned back around. "Tell the beyonders to choose for themselves the animals that they want to kill," my mother told him.

"Why?"

"You don't want to end up ordering them to kill one of their own infant young by mistake. That would be testing a 'local taboo' to the limit, I think."

Just as with some natural-born animal species, there wasn't any great resemblance between an infant child of the garden and that same child in its mature form—or, for that matter, between the child in its infant and neonatal forms. As my mother was reminding Antonov, metamorphosis was a defining characteristic of the life paths of all child types. Antonov smiled and raised his hand in a gesture of surrender: *okay: you win*. He started to address the beyonders a second time.

The breeze picked up, triggering another cloud of spores. "Let's find a river," my father said, gruffly.

• • •

By sunset, Antonov and the beyonders had still not returned.

"Damn the Melzemi," Sylvain said. We had the gear to build a transmitter if ever we found what we were looking for, but we weren't carrying any other comm. equipment—not even line-of-sight optics. That would have been too dangerous. "And damn the *Veche*."

"I should have made one of the beyonders stay with us to act as a runner," my father said with a curse.

My mother patted him on the shoulder. "It's not your fault, Grigor Pietrovitch: they seemed so certain that this place wasn't dangerous."

"Perhaps it is safe for them," Kimonayev put in. His bees were not back yet, either—but that was to be expected: they would keep searching until either they found the faster-than-light child type marker or else had covered the whole garden. That could take fixed weeks or even months. "We're out of place here. That could have triggered an attack response that the beyonders would never have had to worry about themselves. And if Pavel Mikhailovitch told the beyonders to defend him . . . ?"

They would have stayed. They would have died alongside him.

But Sylvain wasn't having any of it. "The beyonders said that this place wasn't dangerous," she reminded him. "If there's nothing here big enough to worry the beyonders . . . ?"

Kimonayev shrugged. He had just been trying to come up with a theory that fitted the facts.

"Right now we have no way of knowing what has happened," my father put in. "But we're not going to take any chances. There's nothing we can sensibly do about Pavel Mikhailovitch tonight. So, we'll make for the rim and camp somewhere above the vegetation layer—somewhere defensible— then tomorrow morning we'll come back down and start a search." He turned to my mother. "You and the little one had better stay up on the rim." He laid his hand on my head. I tried to catch hold of it as he pulled it back, but missed.

My mother shook her head. "Without you—"

"You'll live a long and happy life out there in the wider world." My father gestured up over the crater rim. "You won't have much trouble finding more beyonders."

There were already beyonder groups out there waiting for the next 387 mass migration.

"Light sticks?" Sylvain said.

My father shook his head. "Let's not draw attention to ourselves. We'll

pack up our gear, and when we're done, we'll follow the river bank all the
way back to the rim."

Night descended; and the air filled with the sound of crying children: calls
of warning, calls of challenge, calls to bring the rest of the pride or pack
or herd to the feast.

"It's all wrong," my mother said. "If this place is so safe, why have all
these children waited until dark to emerge?"

It had been quiet during the day, but we had thought nothing of it.
Many child types didn't vocalise, especially when young—the garden-
builders had evidently liked the quiet. But now the garden behind us—
closer to the centre—was filled with noise.

We kept moving back towards the crater rim. Kimonayev was in the
lead, my mother and I walked close behind. My father brought up the rear,
while Sylvain moved parallel to us about ten metres further back from the
riverbank. I was the only one not carrying a dumb gun.

It started to rain. The setting of the sun had cooled the air over the
garden to such a degree that clouds now covered nearly two thirds of the
sky, leaving a hole centred over the middle of the garden through which
we could see the stars. They were bright and thickly clustered, and theirs
was the only light that we had to guide us. The breeze picked up, then
started to gust, causing the sound of crying children to wax and wane like
a pneumatic siren.

"It's all wrong," my mother repeated.

We kept moving.

The Hila caught up with us just short of the foot of the crater rim.

Up until that moment, we had been making good progress. Then, suddenly,
my father called out, drawing everyone's attention his way. He had drawn
to a halt and was looking back down the low slope—back the way that we
had just come. "Stop!" he shouted. "Stand still!" Long moments passed. He
cursed, brought his dumb gun to his shoulder and took aim.

"They might have trouble hearing us in the wind and rain, Rahmatov!"
Sylvain called out from off to the side. I glanced across at her: she too was
aiming her dumb gun back down the slope.

My father tried again. "Stop! Stand still!"

My mother moved to one side, coming out from behind my father to
get a clear view back down the slope.

I saw them then, the Hila: a mass of dark shapes running through the grass and scrub up the slope towards us. Taller and thinner than even the beyonders, they were moving quickly across the ground, drawing closer and closer. Five hundred metres. Four hundred and fifty. Four hundred. They started to spread out across the slope, forming a line. Those furthest from the riverbank began to outpace the others. The wind and rain grew heavier.

"They're trying to surround us," Kimonayev said, as he took up a position between my father and Sylvain. "They're definitely predators of one type or another."

"I don't understand," my mother said. "What are they doing here?"

Her voice sounded strained. My father came over and placed his hand on her shoulder, but only for a moment. Then he turned back to Kimonayev. "We'll take cover," he said. "The riverbank." He looked to Sylvain. "Marie! Over here!"

We moved quickly, retreating towards the riverbank, and then lying down in whatever folds in the terrain we could find.

The Hila came on. Two hundred metres. We could see them a little more clearly now. Their features were still a blur, but we could see that they were bimanous bipeds—unmistakably children of the garden—and they were carrying what looked like spears and short propelling sticks.

"I count thirty eight," Sylvain said.

"Same here," Kimonayev put in.

"Stop!" my father called out once more. "Stand still."

They were close enough now that they had to be able to hear him, even in the wind and the rain, but still they came on.

My father cursed. "Marie: give them a warning shot. Negative baffle."

The dumb guns were ultra low-tech—EM-emission free; little more than a means of launching solid-fuel projectiles down a ceramic barrel. Sylvain took hold of the end of the barrel of her gun and twisted it around, retracting the internal baffles that acted as a silencer. My father wanted her to make some noise.

"That won't work, Grigor Pietrovitch," Kimonayev put in. "They're running on a closed command set—that's why they're ignoring your orders. It won't work."

Events very quickly proved him right. Sylvain fired, thunder rolled down the slope, but the Hila kept coming on. One hundred and fifty metres. One hundred.

"Rahmatov . . . ?" Kimonayev prompted.

My father looked to him. Then, without a word, he climbed back to his feet and started to walk back towards the advancing children. My mother cried out and started to rise, but Sylvain took hold of her by the shoulders and pressed her back to the ground. She saw what my mother didn't: we needed to know if the Hila's closed command set said "kill" or "capture." My father didn't want to start a fight if he could avoid it. He advanced at a fast walking pace towards the Hila, his dumb gun held in one hand down by his side.

Within moments, the lead Hila had reached him. My mother stiffened. And then the lead Hila went right past him and continued towards the riverbank. Sylvain cursed. "They saw right through it!"

She didn't doubt the sapience of these children, at least. The lead Hila had left my father for the Hila coming up behind them. And they had done it to keep us guessing about their intentions as they closed on the rest of us. Hila flowed around my father and closed on the riverbank, five, a dozen, still more. They were only metres away now.

I started to cry then.

"Rahmatov!" Kimonayev called out. *Time to decide.*

My mother turned away from the Hila. She laid down her dumb gun and gathered me up in her arms, bringing my face close to hers. Tears mingled with raindrops on her cheeks, just as they did on mine. "I'm sorry," she said.

Then she spoke my trigger word and threw me into the river.

The Hila, military type 5150: the Melzemi—the eternally hostile Melzemi—owned the rights to that expression. *Acheron* had flown too close to the borders of their territory, putting them on the alert. They had sent out more hunters, and, as an added precaution, seeded the abandoned gardens nearest to *Acheron*'s flight path with Hila. This was all in the past couple of fixed years—after the last beyonder emigration. That was why 83 and the other beyonders had not known how dangerous their garden had become. It wasn't their fault. The *Veche* had miscalculated. They had taken too great a risk in their desire to make the most of the list that they had sold everything to buy. That miscalculation cost my parents and Kimonayev, Sylvain, Antonov and twenty or so beyonders their lives. The Hila killed them, just as their closed command set required of them. And I swam away—just as my closed command set required of me—seeking deeper water, chasing the need to eat, grow, and change.

I was born in freefall on a boneship of the Stro, expressed and nurtured through my neonatal and early infancy by Rahmatov and Seremnova. Seremnova named me "Elena," after her mother, and the whole team called me their little one—*their* child. And my infant form *was* so like that of a human child: bipedal, bimanous, binocular, and binaural—the garden-builders favoured design. But I was always, only ever, a boneship-in-waiting: an infant ship type 32, licensed from the Stro. A life-raft on legs. And when my mother spoke my trigger word, moments before the Hila killed her, she began the process designed to drive me towards maturity.

Now. I swim in the deep waters of the lakes and larger rivers, I eat—children, young and old; and Hila when I can catch them—and I grow. None of this has escaped the Hila's attention. They quickly came to call me Andalian—"orphan of the storm"—because of that night and what they did; although they have added new names for me since. They try to kill me from time to time, as their closed command set demands, but I am quick through the water, and they cannot reach me in the depths of the lakes. I am safe from them. They are not safe from me.

I eat and I grow. But the garden is depleted—it hasn't food enough to help me reach critical mass and begin my final metamorphosis, to harden into bone, to hollow out, become airtight and express a drive system. To escape. And, so, I am in limbo, trapped in adolescence, for as long as there is no hope of the garden blooming. But the trigger for the bloom is within me, and I could release it. My mother found nothing to suggest that it wouldn't work, that it wouldn't trigger a new bloom. And I would lose nothing by trying.

But I don't try. Instead, I wait; because, more than once, I have swum back up river and returned to the place where my parents, and Sylvain and Kimonayev died. I have seen their bodies there, carpeted in moulds and other fungi, slowly merging with the garden. And I have seen Kimonayev's bees. The Hila have learned to their cost not to interfere with Kimonayev's bees, because they are special to me, special because I have seen them circling over his body, landing on it. And dancing.

I eat and I grow, and I wait. And all the while, I am studying Kimonayev's bees and slowly, but surely, learning the language of their dance.

NOUMENON

ROBERT REED

━◈━

The signal was feeble but intriguing—a twenty-hertz radio source tied to an ice-clad world orbiting an M-class star. A xeno-researcher named Mere was dispatched to investigate a deep warm ocean full of vibrant life. But what looked intriguing at a distance proved tragic. The cold white crust of the world hid nothing but cold acid and sluggish bacteria. An alien species once tried to colonize the planet but failed miserably and subsequently went extinct. All that remained was an automated station broadcasting bold, impossible plans. Yet the human remained upbeat: In her final transmission, Mere reminded her superiors—the lordly captains—that she still had plenty of time to wander. The native hydrogen had replenished her fuel stocks. A million sweet vectors were ready to lead her home. The Great Ship was steady-quick, but streakships like hers were swifter and far more nimble, and to give her meanderings that veneer of respectability, she claimed that a nearby belt of sunless worlds was teasing her with signs of activity—odd heat signatures and odder cold sinks that only she could see and that might, just might signal a civilization or two fighting to avoid detection.

This was only Mere's third mission, yet she had already proved herself capable. Nobody was concerned when she stopped broadcasting—stealth was a powerful ally when chasing secretive species—and no alarms were raised when she was past due. Captains worried about quite a lot, but not about that tiny woman with legendary independence and endless reserves of what could only be regarded as exceptional good luck.

Washen was one of the waiting captains. Born inside the Great Ship, she was an ambitious and talented and perpetually optimistic human rising steadily through the endless ranks. The missing xeno-researcher was more than a colleague: Mere was a good friend and trusted confidante, and Washen missed their long conversations about humans and aliens and how to trick ten thousand species to coexist peacefully inside one enormous starship.

Thirty years after the due date, Washen sent a few words back along her friend's most likely course, asking for a whisper to prove her existence.

No whisper came.

Fifty years of silence triggered a longer message. Washen begged for the recipe to cook grief for a pack of windells—an embarrassing story known only to the captain and Mere, and of course to the giggling windells.

No punch lines arrived and no giant telescope saw her engine burning, but Washen kept her worries small, waiting for the stories to come.

Higher captains moved Mere from the active roster to the missing, and at the fifty-nine-year-late mark, her small, sophisticated ship was logged as unavailable.

Seventy-one years behind schedule, her accumulated pay was funneled into a trust reserved for the beneficiaries mentioned in a sealed will.

At the one hundred-and-nine year mark, the Master Captain's office declared the streakship lost in the course of duty and began training of a new xeno-researcher selected from the candidate pool—mostly miscreants with just enough imagination to believe they would find happiness in the void far removed from comfort and normalcy.

A century and a half of silence earned genuine concern. Mere was later than any normal late. Even if she were healthy, vast distances had to be covered, while wandering comets and gravity wells never stopped accumulating. Worst of all, the Great Ship was approaching what was dubbed an omega burn, where its course would be significantly tweaked. The burn was scheduled long before Mere embarked, but its duration and precise trajectory weren't known until today. No matter how swift the streakship was or how lucky Mere might be, there was a moment looming when she would find herself out of fuel, racing toward a rendezvous with nothing but empty space.

Washen planned a simple funeral—not to mark her friend's death, which probably would never be known for sure, but to celebrate a friendship that had proved mortal and all the richer because of it.

Then at the one-hundred-and-sixty-seven year mark, seven months shy of the omega burn, telescopes identified an exhausted streakship making a rapid approach. Every spare gram had been jettisoned from the craft. There was no com-system and minimal life support, and the only remaining fuel tanks were drained dry by one final inadequate burn. Deep-space grit had battered the exposed hull, but someone had skillfully reconfigured the ship's hyperfiber armor, shrouding a substantial cargo hold that didn't match the original schematics. Coming in too fast, the streakship avoided Alpha Port and every other official docking station, striking the hull like a flat stone and then skipping, pieces scattering wildly while the cargo hold rolled like a ball out into the middle of the wreckage field.

Washen was third on the scene.

A fortune in high technology was destroyed. Attempts to contact the pilot were unanswered, but from the cargo hold came a coded light that warned everyone to stand aside, some undefined hazard lurking in its interior.

Washen stood two steps inside the quarantine zone. A tall woman, more stately than beautiful, she was wearing a borrowed lifesuit and a captain's cap. Glancing back at the support staff, she asked what was happening onboard.

The lead engineer eased forward. "There's too much stealth," she complained. "A lot more shielding than the girl left with, that's for sure."

Washen urged the engineer to approach. "Hello, Aasleen."

"Madam."

"Do you know the pilot?"

"By reputation," Aasleen said. "And we've had a handful of conversations over the last thousand years. So I don't know her, madam."

"Tell me about the shielding," the captain said.

"Metametals slathered inside that hyperfiber blister. And no, I won't guess what that could possibly mean."

Standing on the bare gray plain—the largest expanse of pure hyperfiber anywhere in the universe—the two officers watched the warning light pulse on and on, and they studied the mystery that didn't move and the stars that moved very slowly. Then Washen turned to the engineer, who happened to be another one of her good friends, and being nothing but honest, she smiled and halfway laughed as she said, "This couldn't be any more fun. Now could it?"

Instinct shouted at her to flee and she went fast fast fast to put herself in that sweet place where she could not be caught. Just once she looked back, beholding what had no right to exist, and not knowing her foe, she felt such perfect terror that her body was suddenly filled with power. She launched herself from the ground and landed and launched again and then fell back again to the wide graveled beach. Then she imagined her new enemy bearing down on little her, and for the first time since childhood she leaped high and beat the air furiously with her adolescent wings, the half-grown body carried impossibly high into the bright sky.

Then her wings lost their rhythm.

Flapping wildly and with little purpose, she fell. The smooth lovely shoreline seemed remote now. She was tumbling toward a rocky knoll, watching the knoll with two eyes and the beach with the other eyes, fighting for the courage to look farther. The sea stretched out as it should, flat and calm, reflecting the glory of the sky's light. Despite every hope, the intruder that terrified her was still there—a stubborn round object of undetermined size, though it seemed fantastically large. Floating motionless on the endless sea, it was silent and unwelcome and cold to the eye and deeply, wickedly wrong, and what unnerved her most was the sense that the intruder, impassive as it seemed, was watching her.

She dropped hard on the knoll's crest, on the whitest rock in the world. Exhausted wings begged for rest, but first she had to show her power, her bold and considerable will. Elegant wing waves and thunderous flaps proved that she was no small thing. She screamed and leaped a little and then leaped higher, and was the intruder impressed? Nothing changed in its appearance, but wasn't that the mark of real fear? The enemy was stunned, maybe. Maybe she had the mysterious thing ready to flee. Perhaps another few artful flaps would make it abandon Creation for good.

But her exhaustion was too much. Lowering her wings, she breathed and quivered and watched what refused to change, and she wondered if perhaps she was an ignorant, silly fool.

This was one of her defining traits: A wicked capacity for doubt. Her first-mother said it was a weakness and would eventually be the source of her doom. But that quality was what her second-mother loved best about her, and reading signs nobody else could see, the woman promised her child that there would be a time and a circumstance when nobody but she would be able to appreciate what was happening.

Eventually the girl felt rested. Still perched on the white knoll, she was ready to flee by whatever means seemed best, and that's why she stood again, watching the intruder while listening to a thousand neighbors leaving by flight and by foot—save for the rich ones who rode fancy wagons into the interior.

The world was fleeing, but she was not.

Not yet, at least.

She turned her full attention on the impossibility riding the mirrored sea. Where had it come from? What did this mean? Then she eventually heard new voices approaching from behind, voices from those who heard stories of an apparition, and despite fear and good sense, they had come down to the edge of the world to see what shouldn't be.

These were souls like her, the girl realized.

And just like that, she felt as if she weighed nothing, but instead of fear, this time she was buoyed up by an unexpected and luscious happiness.

Rich emptiness stretched out before Mere. Sunless worlds of many ages, many constitutions, had assembled themselves into a ribbon-like cluster perfectly aligned for a long careful flyby. Some of those worlds were large and naturally warm in their hearts, nourishing oceans of methane or water as well as vigorous life forms. Colder places might conceal little colonies of hermits and refugees and other tall-technology oddballs. And there was always the promise of some full civilization struggling not to be found. But the hot and frigid signatures that she mentioned to the captains were lies. Mere had seen nothing interesting while looking up from the disappointing first world, and she didn't even bother synthesizing data to give her fable a spine. This was her mission. This was her ship, if not by title then at least by every measure that mattered. A steady watchful journey along the dark ribbon would give her hundreds of large targets and millions of comets. The odds of success—some good, worthwhile, and profitable triumph—seemed just short of inevitable.

By some measures, Mere was any modern human: She had a tough body ready to heal from all but the most grievous wounds and a tougher, nearly immortal mind that could hold thousands of years of experience and small wisdoms. Except for the tiny body and the waif face, she was immediately recognizable as human. But her history was as peculiar as any great ape could ever claim. She was an embryo when her family and entire crew were killed in deep space. Born in poverty and pure isolation, she was raised by the battered, voiceless ship. Eventually the ship dropped the orphan on a living world, and she was raised by natives who worshipped her as a god and despised her for being a god. As their world was dying, the aliens sent Mere on her way to complete her journey, which was why she was thousands of years old and deeply peculiar before ever laying eyes on another human being.

Mere was barely human, and she was barely anything else. Boredom was an affliction for other people. Loneliness was for souls profoundly different from her own. She was curious and resourceful, and like the extinct creatures that raised her, Mere understood that she was insignificant—another whisper in the multiverse, freed by her tininess, and as inevitable as the stars.

As a xeno-researcher, she sneaked up on these orphaned worlds, telescopes watching for EM signals and heat signals while neutrino detectors sniffed for signs of fusion reactors burning inside hidden cities. But nothing earned her affections. She studied and recorded and sometimes tossed a few tiny probes overboard, impacting on the frozen atmospheres at a fat fraction of light speed. But the probes found nothing amazing, and with a third of her journey done, Mere started to plan excuses for her long delay.

Then one cold terrestrial world gave a strong signal.

Bright and hot and very beautiful, the display might well be a city floating on a frozen sea. Mere began to cheer while her AI pilot calculated courses. If she maneuvered now and made a hard burn now or in the next nine hours, she would reach that world at a manageable pace. Unfortunately the world was turning, the interesting face invisible for now. For ten hours she studied the inadequate data, and then she fell asleep and dreamed, waking without clear direction from intuition or her fellow gods. But after flipping a mental coin, she ordered the pilot to make the tardy burn, ignoring the safety margins on her main engine. Eleven minutes into the bone-smashing deceleration, the target world finally turned its intriguing heat source back into view, and what seemed fascinating before proved to be nothing. The brightness was the splash mark where a comet recently hit a pocket of salty dead water.

The rocket burn had to be finished regardless; how else could she make up the spent fuel?

Coming in too fast, she damaged the streakship when she splashed down inside the slushy fresh crater. Systems had to be repaired, and Mere was as good with tools as any of the mouse-sized robots that helped maintain her ship. She was still reworking the main pumps when one of her resident telescopes noticed a far sun flickering. Looking harder, it found a shielded and cold and not particularly large body moving on a separate but roughly parallel trajectory.

Mere used every telescope, measuring the object.

Ten billion kilometers separated her and it, which was nothing. It was a jump done easily and without much fuel lost, and she soon placed herself close to an object that was as artificial as anything in the universe. She knew quite a lot about machines, particularly alien machines, but this was something rarer—a dark, sleek, deeply engineered collection of sophisticated devices bearing little resemblance to anything waiting inside any of her onboard texts or familiar to her resident AIs.

No standard markers defined an owner.

As far as every sensor could tell, nobody was onboard.

Mere could have sent word of her discovery. But there was no telling who might notice her voice, and worse, who might come here to interrupt her fun.

Mere went onboard. Tenaciously cautious about what she touched and what she did, she recorded everything, and after several weeks she finally slipped inside the belly of this unexpected, undoubtedly lost machine, finding an object that made the rest of it seem almost ordinary.

The world stood behind her, behind all of them. They numbered in the thousands, perhaps more than ten thousand, and the last of them towed in rumors of multitudes marching from the ends of the world.

Perhaps that was so, perhaps not. What mattered was the impossible object floating on the once-perfect sea. Questions about what it was and what it couldn't be were offered and debated, resulting in contests of will and reason, flapping wings and occasionally ugly fights. But the greatest question, at least for some, was deciding what they should do about this object floating at the edge of existence.

Inevitably the conversation turned to boats. But not the narrow paper boats built for children and child-like adults, or the little skiffs that rode the world's rivers and lakes. They needed sturdier craft, magnificent in scope and able to bear considerable weight while crossing the slick sea, and since distance was never easy to measure at sea, they would need supplies and bravery and the strength to use paddles and enough conviction to bear up while carrying every abuse.

Three groups coalesced around a trio of plans. Leaders were named, talents were claimed, and the countryside was scoured for mature blue-shafts and paper-growth and living waxes that would seal gaps and help keep the boats riding high.

The largest group pulled up an entire forest before setting to work on a quickly built vessel. Their ship was gigantic enough to carry forty bodies out to where the ship looked tiny, and that was where the hull was breached—

far enough away that nobody could hear the panicked shouts as everyone sank and died.

The girl belonged to the second largest group. They were the slowest workers, as it happened, led by a guild engineer who seemed to have considerable knowledge about the other fine sciences. The engineer advocated caution and careful pacing. He grew even more certain after the third group launched their boat. While there was room for ten, he claimed that a crew of five would be much better, and after studying everyone's strength and everyone's will, he named his five—small and young, all of them, one of them being the girl who once flew away from the sudden marvel.

Others would have complained if he named the crew earlier. But their competition had left, riding swiftly out into the glare of sea and sky where they were soon lost. The race was lost, and who cared who went chasing after the winners?

But the girl was happy, even if she was in the losing party.

Beating her wings happily, she promised her strength and her scarce courage too, and then she thought to ask the leader what he believed that the marvel was.

"It is another world," he said calmly, as if nothing could be more obvious.

But there was only one world and it was theirs. Maybe she knew little about history and the sciences, but she would recall any story about a second world cast out onto the eternal sea.

"There are no stories like that," he replied. "When I was your age, I made a careful study of this very issue. None of our old writers speak of second worlds, and to my mind that signals that this is a truly unique event."

She enjoyed being in agreement with this learned fellow.

"But any answer leaves other questions," he continued. "For instance, where did this new world come from? And even more important, what caused our world and our sea to come to this Creation?"

About the first question, she knew nothing. But she immediately started to recite the story about the Creation.

"Yes, I know the legend," he said, shriveled adult wings beating with authority.

"And outside imbeciles and perhaps the dead, everyone knows that story by heart."

"Of course so," she said.

"Everyone," he repeated. Then he listed the world's nations and its cities, including remote places that she had never heard of. And once the enormity

of the world was established, he concluded by saying, "Each of us is born with that story in his heart and her head, and as a man of science, that is a mystery onto itself: Why do we know that so well?

"That is a wonder at least equal to the puzzle floating off our perfect shore."

Knowing enough was never possible. Even knowing half-enough was unlikely. Ten thousand years of training, memorization, and diligent practice couldn't prepare the xeno-researcher to meet every situation with suitable expertise. The better solution was to stow as much knowledge as possible, carrying AIs and encyclopedias and other forms of bottled brilliance into the wilderness, and hope that gave the lone soul resources enough to make sense of every conundrum.

Mere had a battalion of sleeping AIs waited to be called. They consumed room and power—two assets that she didn't like to share—but after five months poking around inside the alien vessel, it was time for a companion.

"Hello, Aasleen."

Floating eyes and sinuses and a standard mechanical mouth were surrounded by a facsimile of the famous Ship officer. Eyes blinked and the nostrils inhaled the dry cold air. The AI paid enough attention to the living person to realize that Mere wasn't worth a second glance. But the room was fascinating. Hyperfiber cabling and superconductive arteries were woven around technological conundrums. Every machine was deeply, wonderfully unexpected. Mere had resurrected ten of the resident readout screens, but they were filled with coded symbols and jumbled, unhelpful images that only heightened that delicious sense of understanding almost nothing.

"I don't recognize anybody's fingerprints," Aasleen said. "Where are we?"

Mere explained.

The facsimile pointed and pointed. "Well, that could be a plasma router, and those could be—probably are—antimatter genies. But of course everything is richly alien, and since the facility is so strange, I assume that it's ancient and lost."

"That's what I am assuming, yes."

"Have you sent word home?"

"I would have, but this facility might not be old and misplaced. Someone might notice my signal, and maybe that someone has a rightful claim."

"More likely, he would just rip the prize from your grip."

"Exactly," she said.

"Show me your maps and diagrams," said the engineer. "Show me."

The next day was filled with silence and hard study. Wearing a personality made the AI slower than a machine or a human. That was one nagging limitation of this trickery. But progress was made, and meanwhile Mere had time to invest in the routine maintenance of her streakship—a dozen little jobs that didn't require the help of a Ship engineer.

Aasleen called her back to the alien ship. "This is all fascinating," she said.

"It is, yes."

"This big place was just one piece of something much bigger." She pointed to clean old breaks on the exterior, adding, "Something very bad happened. Maybe it was a million years ago, or maybe a thousand times farther back."

"A sobering concept," Mere said.

"Thank you for showing me. But really, you should dredge up a historian or your xeno-archaeo AI. They could tell you a lot more."

"Good advice. Thank you."

Aasleen nodded, distracted by every machine in view. "I would love to have this old wreck inside my machine shop."

"I would love to bring it to you," Mere said.

"But it's too massive."

"By a long ways."

"Scans," said the engineer. "Make them and keep them."

"I have been."

Then the expert offered suggestions about key junctures and counter-intuitive techniques.

Mere memorized every slip of advice.

The next long pause ended with laughter. Then Aasleen said, "You are testing me. From the beginning, this has been an examination of me."

"Maybe."

"Well, I noticed the chamber. Of course."

"Good."

"A hyperfiber sphere wrapped around a perfect vacuum, and something important suspended in its center."

Mere waited.

"The object is tiny. That's obvious. And its mass is very, very high."

"Enormously so."

"Yet if it was a black hole, you'd know so. You wouldn't have to bother me."

"I didn't think I was bothering you."

"But I am ruining your peace and solitude. Isn't that right?" Aasleen offered a wise appreciative wink.

"That's perceptive. Are you certain that you're an engineer?"

Both of them laughed for a long while.

"So it isn't a black hole," Aasleen said. "And I don't think it's stabilized neutronium or some kind of strangelet stew either. The signatures are wrong."

"What else is there?" Mere asked.

"Theory," Aasleen said.

The living woman drifted closer to the round chamber. It wasn't large, almost unnoticed in the jumbled mass of greater machines, and if the chamber was once attached to any of them, those links were long since erased.

"I'm not an expert in this business," Aasleen said.

"Who knows hyperfiber better?"

"Few do."

"But I think that's what it is," Mere said.

"Do you even know what hyperfiber is?"

Mere shrugged. "Obviously, I don't."

"Hyperfiber is a miracle. To an engineer, it is the only miracle in the universe. Baryonic elements are woven into precise metacrystal patterns, and for the higher grades, dark matter splicing helps to tease out even greater strength."

"I know that hyperfiber is strong."

"Like nothing else," Aasleen said. "And do you know where the strength comes from?"

"No," Mere lied.

"Yes, you do," Aasleen said. "But it's just theory to you. Abstractions pulled from a text. I doubt that you truly appreciate the principle at work here."

"Tell me."

"The hyperfiber in your hand isn't especially strong. But quantum effects are always in play. The invisible, unreachable multiverse influences every shard of the stuff. Even the smallest splinter of the poorest grade fiber exists in millions of parallel realms, and those millions and billions of shards occupy the same position in their space and time. Their strength leaks into our realm and ours into theirs. Take a hammer or a laser to that splinter, and you aren't just fighting one bit of sour gray gristle . . . you are waging war against a mountain of sisters."

"It is a miracle," said Mere.

"Better grades, better miracles."

Mere pointed. "Inside that chamber . . . is what?"

"Something else," Aasleen said. "Because it's too dense and far too massive to be hyperfiber."

"But there is a theory—"

"Shut up. I need to think."

That was an engineer talking. Blunt, focused.

After a long spell, Aasleen finally said, "I will concede to a point, yes. If you began with the very best grade of hyperfiber—the sort that forms the Great Ship's hull, for example—and then you took some very powerful hammers and beat the bloody hell out of that raw material . . .

"Okay."

"By 'hammers,' I mean shaped matter-antimatter charges, and by 'beat the bloody hell,' I mean that you'd have to use absolute precision while minimizing chaotic flows and quantum vagaries. And that doesn't solve the biggest problem of them all."

"Multiverse effects."

With a brittle tone, Aasleen asked, "Do you really need help from me? Because you seem to know this quite well."

"We're discussing ultimate hyperfiber," Mere said. "In principle, the maximum-density variety can be manufactured, particularly in tiny quantities. But the work has to be successful in many, many multiverses. Otherwise the compressed materials will lose their grip and explode."

"Exactly," Aasleen said. "In fact, most estimates demand that factories in a billion quadrillion universes have to do the magic inside the same picosecond, and the chance of a large enough fraction of that multitude doing its work correctly is . . . well, it's a fool's hope, if you ask me."

"What we see is impossible," said Mere. "Thank you for that."

Aasleen said nothing for an hour, and then another. The silence ended with joyous disgust, and she said, "All right. I don't know what else it could be."

"Ultimate hyperfiber."

"Bring it home to me," Aasleen said. "I want to see it for myself."

"I plan to do just that. But I want to know how."

The engineer crossed her nonexistent arms. "If you're right, then there is no problem. The Ship's hyperfiber hull is nothing but fog and steel next to its theoretical strength. Just put that magic inside a bag and come home. Today, if you can."

"But whoever built it—" she began.

Aasleen interrupted. "Someone with boundless energy built it, and they had a helluva lot of patience too, by the looks of it."

"They bottled it inside a vacuum."

"You want to know why."

"Don't you?"

The two women fell silent. Then at last, Aasleen said, "All right. If we're going to talk theory, I know a whopper."

"Tell me."

The engineer explained the possibility in the barest, least sympathetic fashion.

"Suppose that's so," Mere said. "Can I move the ultimate hyperfiber safely? Can I protect its cargo well enough? Using just what I have onboard my ship and this facility, can I manage all that work soon enough to make my last open window home?"

The facsimile looked at the schematics again, and with confidence, she said, "You're starting too late. You cannot make it."

"Even with your help?"

"I accounted for that, and no. It is impossible."

"Well then," Mere said. "That just means we should start our work this minute, isn't that so?"

Each paddle stroke carried the boat forward. Yet even as the new world grew taller and broader, it stubbornly refused to come close. The crew of five worked as heroes, without pause or complaint, but eventually one soft voice mentioned his aches and then another felt obligated to describe her deep fatigue, and soon everyone was cursing the relentless, withering boredom. Rations shrank, and bodies shrank, and the colors of dread edged toward outright panic. As a result the crew found themselves stabbing the water with long sloppy strokes, precious energy bleeding away while they barely moved faster. There was the bright gray bulk of the world, featureless and cold, yet the sea between was as vast as always. It was easy to believe that they were chasing an illusion, some awful lost dream sent to prey on the gullible, and it was inevitable that the bravest, strongest among them would be the first to curse this pathetic effort and beg for them to turn around and hurry home.

Except while no one was watching, their home and its millions of lives had vanished, stolen by the distance or engulfed by the flat boundless sea.

Grief ripped them open. They wept hard and ate double-shares from what little was left. But misery at least gave them a little rest before they

set to work again. Soon they came upon the wreckage of the second ship—
scattered water-soaked pieces of hull and one living man clinging to an
empty cask. He lay on his back, wearing the largest, oddest, and most joyous
expression. They asked him what had happened. He said that every seam in
their ship failed. He said that there was an awful fight among the starving
crew, and violence destroyed his ship. Then he claimed that nothing went
wrong and there was no way to know how he had ended up here.

The girl felt sorry for him, regardless of the truth, but in the same instant
she hoped they wouldn't drag him onboard. The man was big and obviously
spent, and they were down to their last mouthfuls of food.

The crew thought as she did. Up came the five paddles, everyone ready to
work hard, at least until they had won some distance.

Each of the man's eyes stared at the girl's face. She braced herself for
pleading. If he tried to grab the boat, she would strike him. But no, he said
only, "Good. Go now, go." Then after a long mad laugh, he said, "You have to
complete the journey. Do you see? We will keep coming and dying until one
of us succeeds. So finish the voyage now and save the rest of us. Do you see?"

Sensors and reactors and portable armored habitats were brought to
the Ship's hull and assembled into a ring-shaped city with one narrow
purpose: Contemplating mysteries too shy or too awful to show themselves.
Specialists arrived to give uninformed opinions. Engineering units were
reinforced, working efficiently until there was nothing left to accomplish.
Then an army of genius machines was plugged into the available
telemetry, and everyone waited for insights. But the shielded cargo
proved extraordinarily stubborn. Without offering reasons, the warning
signal continued begging for distance and time, and despite mounting
pressures from higher captains, Washen honored the request. That's why
only passive instruments were wakened and calibrated and unleashed.
Big mirrors mapped the blister's slick gray exterior. Radio whispers and
other EM noise gave confusing clues about composition and internal
heat patterns. Sometimes a distant chunk of comet would strike the hull,
rattling the wreckage in meaningful ways. But the best telemetry came
from neutrinos—ghostly particles generated by the surrounding reactors,
piercing the hyperfiber blister and whatever was inside before coming out
the other side with a fresh trajectory, or sometimes not emerging at all.

"Where is Mere?" Washen asked.

"I see no trace of her, madam."

"But she has to be onboard," the captain said stubbornly. "Anywhere else means she's lost."

A few lockboxes had survived the impact, and maybe that's where a piece of bioceramic hardware was hiding—the basis of a modern brain. But before offering that slender hope, Aasleen gave the telemetry a long glance. The newest model of the hold's interior was finished moments ago, incorporating all of the neutrino data.

"A black hole's lurking," she said.

Space was littered with tiny black holes, and they were rarely problems. Washen began ordering the standard machinery necessary to contain a fleck of infinite density, even as she wondered why Mere had gone to so much bother for an item they already had in their inventory, in substantial quantities.

"Wait," Aasleen said. "No, I was wrong. Wait."

"What do you see?"

The engineer was hunched over a wide screen, dozens of overlapping feeds competing for her full attention. "Inside the hyperfiber is a second blister. What I see . . . the picture's getting clearer . . . what I see is a hyperfiber sphere holding a vacuum, and it's surrounded by contraptions and more contraptions, plus some crap that actually looks familiar."

"What crap?"

"Biosynthesis hardware."

Washen pulled up Mere's equipment roster.

But Aasleen had anticipated as much. "No, this is just her simple galley gear. What we'd use to synthesize escargot for lunch."

"What about the contraptions?"

"Deeply, stubbornly alien."

"And the black hole?"

"There isn't any," said Aasleen.

Washen offered a few candidates.

But the engineer stopped her halfway through the standard list. "Look at this face," she said. "What does this face tell you?"

Aasleen had purple-black skin and wide bright eyes. She was a master of all mechanicals—an engineer famous among engineers for her poise and practical genius—yet her usual reserve was gone. Simple nervous wonder made her body shake. Quick breaths grew quicker and shallower. She looked ready to scream for joy yet held herself back because she had no experience with so much pleasure. The moment deserved hard figures. But all that she could manage to say was, "The neutrino diffraction is critical, and it looks right. It looks perfect."

"What are you saying?"

She didn't hear the question. "And if the contraptions, those other features . . . if they accomplish what I think they're meant to accomplish . . . " Her voice slipped away. More rapid breathing helped nothing. Aasleen looked ready to crumble or break into song, and then she rubbed at her mouth with both hands, working the lips hard before naming the marvel that was floating in the midst of a small perfect vacuum.

"Infinite-strength hyperfiber," the captain said skeptically.

"Which should not be," the engineer said.

"Who would make it, and how?"

"I would, and I don't have any idea how," Aasleen said.

"What would you do with it?"

"Quite a lot," she said. "Black holes can't be shaped. But in theory, ultimate hyperfiber can hold any shape. And it could be handled fairly easily, even if you had it in huge quantities. That's why it would provide a wondrous armor or a reaction chamber for some farfetched reactor, or it could be the business end of some fabulous chisel."

"How big a piece do we have?"

"A few gigatons, which is nothing. It's a fleck of a fleck, and I can't even guess its shape yet."

"But if you had a small piece like that," Washen began.

"What would I do?" Aasleen shrugged, and then out from some deep old reserve of youth, she let loose a girl's wild giggle.

"Give me a guess," Washen said.

"A competent guess, or a hopeful, dreamy guess?"

"Pick one and don't tell me."

The engineer's face shone, and she wiped at her face and closed her eyes, diving into her own imagination. "A black hole serves as a huge data sink. The trouble is that teasing out useful information, at least inside the lifespan of a universe, is pretty unlikely. But a slip of ultimate hyperfiber retains its internal structure. If laid down properly, that structure could serve as a computer or some variation on that theme. What's sitting out there could hold as much or more data than a black hole—nobody knows if either answer is true—but I've seen estimates where there's enough sheer memory that an entire world could be modeled, right down to the atomic level, and all of that could ride inside a very small human hand."

Washen said nothing.

Her colleague wiped her face again, and then something on her display panel changed, or moved, or otherwise grabbed her attention.

"What is it?" the captain asked.

"The galley biosynthesizer was busy."

"Is it operating now?"

"Not now, madam." Aasleen crossed her arms, her body rigid as her legs impulsively began to shake. "No, no. The machine stopped working just now. Whatever it was making is ready. Our lunch is finished." And she laughed, adding, "Which is good, because I could use a little something."

The sea was not the sea anymore, more vapor than fluid. She felt as if she were flying across the surface, wings helping the kicking legs as she drove on with the last dregs of her strength.

The rest of the crew was gone. The finest boat ever built by her species was scattered and drowned, and she was clinging to an empty box that smelled like the dried fat it had once carried. She kicked and flapped and whenever she looked up the new world appeared no closer. Looking up was a hazard, so she focused on the lid of the box and her skinny dying hands, and then she would forget about both worlds. It felt as if she was born in the sea, alone forever, and her home world was a dream while the other was a separate, equally misleading dream, and her doom was to fight forever between two realms, each as unreal as the other.

The shoreline grabbed her without warning.

Startled, her first instinct was to flee. If she were stronger and better prepared, she might have succeeded in kicking her way back into the gaseous realm. But she was too weak. She lay where she would die and wished for blackness and peace. She tried to breathe and found nothing but vacuum, and then a machine that was always above her suddenly spat out a great wet mass that splashed over her, grabbing hold of a body that had barely survived her most unlikely creation.

Fluids burrowed into her flesh, into every orifice.

She struggled until exhausted, and only then did she breathe. The liquid inside her lungs wasn't water and it wasn't quite air either, but it brought her oxygen as well as a peculiar menu of rare sugars and simple lipids that clawed their way into her cells, into her baby-new blood.

A tiny ocean covered her as a skin, protecting its sole inhabitant from space and the killing cold.

Grams mattered. In the end, single atoms mattered. It was impossible to carry even the basic thoughts of an invaluable AI, and Mere didn't pretend to be happy with that limitation or to consider doing otherwise.

Her Aasleen would be left behind. So long as the machine functioned, she could fill her days with study and thought, and perhaps some later survey party would come to tour the facility, finding a qualified tour guide on duty.

Mere was hours away from leaving, and in a very different fashion, she was also close to death.

"I pity you," the AI said.

Mere's body was another indulgence. It would be stripped from her mind and left in space, frozen and empty and everlasting. She would make the journey home as a brain tucked inside the strongest lockbox, minimally fed and almost devoid of thought.

"I pity me too," she admitted.

"Thank you," Aasleen told her. "For letting me out, letting me play, I can't thank you enough."

The two women looked at each other's hands. Years spent together, and they had never touched. Then Mere asked once more, "Do you think these machines can pull someone or something free of that data sink?"

"Since I don't understand half of the principles at work . . . " Aasleen shrugged. "I'll say, 'Yes.' But that's only because I'm ignorant, and who's going to blame me for being wrong?"

Mere removed her clothes, making ready for a greater disrobing.

The engineer began to talk and then hesitated.

"What's wrong?"

"There is a signature on the ultimate," Aasleen said. "Something distinct, something busy. It could be a library or a self-absorbed computer. But maybe it's a substantial population and who knows how long a history, which leads me to wonder where they came from."

Mere mentioned the first world that she visited. Technological species often tried to make a dead world live, and the work was difficult and the results often tragic. But what if a much more advanced species decided that the safer, sober route was to boil itself down to a series of elaborate computer programs?

"Noumenon," said Aasleen.

"What is that?"

"I think it's an ancient word," she said. "I don't know where I first heard it, and I don't remember all of the meanings. But the definition that always impresses me: Noumenon is the triumph of the abstract over the flesh, ideas and memes stripped away from their mortal bonds."

"That's a mystical attitude," Mere said. "You don't sound like yourself, friend."

With a strange smile and measured voice, she agreed. "New ideas can take root, even in this old head of mine."

The girl breathed and rolled onto her back. The new world was an astonishingly ugly place. A forest of machines stood about her. One of them was dripping a thick fluid that covered her while the other machines did nothing. In the middle of the mechanical forest was a gray sphere that somehow looked both bland and important, while a larger ball of gray defined the ends of this tiny new world.

She sat up and then tried to stand, and she fell down again. But her next attempt was successful, and she learned that she could walk slowly and dared herself to touch the machinery and her own wet body. Then the wall of the world cracked and split wide—a piece of the grayness fell away—and through the hole she saw a barren plain that dwarfed her lost world, and a line of small structures standing in the distance, everything beneath a blackness marred by tiny points of cold light.

The girl climbed onto the Ship's hull.

Two gray-clad figures were moving closer, apparently coming toward her. Instinct told her to run, to fly.

But the time had come not to trust instincts, and with the sweetness powering her new flesh, she stood tall and flapped her wings against the vacuum, and with a voice that still couldn't be heard, she sang hard about the End of All and the Creation.

This was supposed to be a celebration.

But the strong drinks hadn't been touched. Flies from a dozen worlds stole tastes from the cold dinners. The three officers sat quietly, and then one would talk about the latest news while the others listened or at least pretended to listen. Even Washen—the unabashed optimist—was shaken by what the linguists' and physicists' wild theories were claiming. The captain was smart and endlessly competent, but that didn't stop her from waging war against this unwelcome news.

"We only think that she's a new species," Washen said. "A hundred years from today, we'll find her cousins hiding inside a dyson bulb or some other hard-to-spot high-technology enclave. She's their child, and she got lost."

"Except that's not what her song claims," Mere said.

"Creation songs are legends," Aasleen said, pushing a stern finger into the air between them. "Legends are muddy, and you can't take them seriously."

Mere sat quietly, saying nothing.

"The creature has to be from the Milky Way," Washen said. "She couldn't have come from some thin belt of stars and planets out between the galaxies. That isn't remotely possible."

"We found her inside a piece of derelict technology," said Aasleen. "The machine was moving slowly, as far from the intergalactic as you can be."

In the legend, galaxies and space began to collapse. There was no warning. The event was catastrophic and nearly instantaneous, and every piece of the universe came close to every other piece.

Mere knew the saga by heart, and unknown to her companions she secretly sang portions of it to herself.

"I don't care what the physicists claim," said Aasleen. "Nothing about that story makes sense to me."

"Her old world died," the captain said. "That's what the creature remembers."

Mere looked at the two women, and then she considered her own tiny hands. With a calm sorry voice, she said, "You mentioned something to me, Aasleen. We were onboard the derelict together."

"My AI told you something. That's what you mean to say."

"You were talking about the ultimate," Mere said. "That hyperfiber is unbreakably strong because it reaches deeper into the multiverse. Infinite connections give it the phenomenal strength and the rich capacity to soak up information, and souls, and entire civilizations, and that leads to other possibilities. Possibilities that you found intriguing."

Washen looked at Mere.

The engineer preferred to watch the tip of her finger.

"Moving between universes," Aasleen said. "Even when the craziest theoreticians throw out their most optimistic calculations, jumping to another universe is a brutally unlikely event."

Washen moved a little nearer to Mere, extending one hand as if ready to make amends.

The tiny woman closed her eyes, and in a near-whisper, she said, "You are missing the point. Both of you are being fooled, and so is everyone else too."

They waited.

"Someone did build a tiny piece of perfect hyperfiber. They did what we can't do, and then somehow they lost control of their work. Maybe that means that their trick is relatively easy and its products aren't worth the trouble to keep. But then if that's so, why isn't the universe littered with stuff?"

Washen retrieved her hand.

"So maybe it isn't easy to make," Mere said. "But that implies that someone or something went to a lot of trouble to build what I found, and its misplacing that treasure is about the last event you would expect. So maybe it wasn't lost. Maybe it isn't lost now. Perhaps its makers were hoping that I would find it."

The others had to laugh, but they did it secretly, only a little doubt showing in their eyes.

"No," said Mere. "My mission was planned in advance. I went where I went and found nothing, and then I traveled on an obvious trajectory that found nothing useful. And then because of an apparent comet impact, I landed on still another disappointing world. Every step of my path could have been part of someone's scheme. Intention could be at work here, some purpose beyond what I ever envisioned, and I only wish that I had an idea who could have dreamed this up and carried it off."

Washen still could not accept that crazy tale. The blood-and-bone Aasleen was even less agreeable to the idea. But everyone remained polite, stifling their doubts in the presence of a true hero. And eventually the three of them brushed the flies off the chicken legs and filled their mouths with the splendid tastes.

Often Mere felt like an alien among humans.

But today she was the human animal—the bold blessed creature that leaped into the stars and beyond.

Against long odds, she felt supremely gifted.

Someone had thought to warn her that a universe can collapse and die.

And even better, that same benefactor had given her a clear sign, proving that under certain conditions, in the most critical times, it was possible to escape even that ultimate End.

THE DEATH OF TERRESTRIAL RADIO

ELIZABETH BEAR

The first word was meant to be spoken quietly, if it should ever be spoken at all. A dribble of signal. An echo. A ghost. A coded trickle, something some PC running SETI-at-home would pick out of the background noise, flag, and return silently to the great database in the sky, the machine's owner innocent of her role in making history.

I am one of the few who is old enough to remember what we *got*. Something as subtle as a solid whack across the nose with a cricket bat. We couldn't believe it at first, but there it was, interfering with transmissions on all frequencies, cluttering our signals with static ghosts.

Television had largely abandoned the airwaves by then, so the transmissions that came to houses and offices over fiber optic cable were unperturbed. Dueling experts opined with telegenic confidence that the suggestive sequence of blips was some natural, cosmological phenomenon—and not somebody broadcasting to the whole world, simultaneously, intentionally.

That lasted all of about three hours before the first cable news channel produced an elderly man, liver-spotted scalp clearly visible between the thinning strands of his hair. He was a ham radio operator, a lifetime wireless hobbyist who folded his hands before his chest and closed his eyes to listen to those noises straight out of an old movie—exactly like the chatter of a wireless telegraph.

He let his lids crack open again, "It's Morse code; of course I recognize it. It might be the most famous Marconi transmission in history."

He quoted, as if reciting a familiar poem, "*CQD CQD SOS* Titanic *Position 41.44 N 50.24 W. Require immediate assistance. Come at once. We struck an iceberg. Sinking.*"

I was in my office at the ALMA site, surrounded by coworkers, and you could have heard a pin drop. We hadn't exactly gotten the jump on this one—not when the signal was interfering with people's baby monitors. But we had been engaged in trying to track it.

A simple task, given the strength of the signal. It originated in Taurus, and exhibited measurable parallax over the course of a couple of days. Not only was it loud, in other words—but it was close, and moving fast.

A few weeks later, we found the second one. Suddenly, radio signals were blossoming all over the sky. Our own dead signals, our own dead voices— ham radio, *The Shadow*, coded signals from World War I—spoken back to us.

And then they stopped.

When I was fifteen years old, other girls wanted to be doctors and actors and politicians. They played soccer and softball, went to Girls State, marched in band.

I ran SETI and stayed late at school for Math League and Physics Club. Almost nobody really believed in aliens, but I wanted to talk to them so badly I didn't even have words for the feeling, the cravings that welled up inside me.

Other girls and boys—even other geeks—dated. And I guess I tried, sort of. But the people around me never seemed as entrancing as the numbers in my head. I *wanted* to like them—loneliness was certainly an issue—but the gap between wanting and being able seemed unbridgeable.

In retrospect, what I sought refuge in was not too dissimilar from the age-old fantasy that one is adopted, that one's real family will come along someday and rescue one from these weirdos one's been left with. Except I felt so weird I turned to aliens. Maybe someone out there would be like me. Certainly, it seemed like I had nothing in common with anybody else on *this* planet.

Sooner or later, you put aside childish things—or risk being labeled a crackpot. By the time I turned twenty-seven, I had two grad degrees and a tenure-track job at a major research university. I'd gotten time on the VLA and was mining the research for my dis towards further publications.

Radio astronomers get drunk and speculate about extraterrestrial life . . . I'd say "like anybody else," but I guess most people don't actually do that. The difference is, we know on a visceral level how prohibitive the distances and timescales are, how cold the math.

We really *didn't* expect to hear from anybody.

Maybe it's like falling in love. You have to truly stop expecting something to happen before it will.

You talk about things that change the world. Usually, it's in hindsight. Usually you don't notice them when they're happening.

Ah, but sometimes. Sometimes there's no way you could have missed it unless you were in a vegetative state.

It's hard to remember now, but we didn't know, then, what the Echoes were or what they wanted. It could have been a passing alien ship, psychological warfare from inbound would-be conquerors (Stephen Hawking would have been vindicated!), or some previously unsuspected cosmological phenomena.

There were new cults; a few suicides. The occasional marriage self-destructed, and I confess I was naively surprised at the number of people who joined or left religions, apparently at random.

I'd never been much of a joiner, myself.

Six months later, our own voices echoed back to us again. This time it was *War of the Worlds* and Radio Free Europe.

With those two datapoints, we could figure out where they were, and how far away, and how fast they were moving.

By the third round, nobody was surprised to receive the signals of early broadcast television—and some clever souls even filtered the signals and recovered fragments of our own lost history: early live episodes of *The Avengers* and destroyed episodes of *Doctor Who*. So *much* entertainment used to be broadcast, carried over public airwaves now mostly used for cellular calls and more practical things—where great swaths of them are not simply abandoned.

The idea of a cosmological explanation had always been farfetched. Now it seemed laughable. Somebody was bouncing our own words back to us. A means of communication, certainly . . . but a threat or a reassurance? Psychological warfare or reaching out?

How do you know for sure?

It's a little disconcerting to have your cell calls to your place of business interrupted by Jackie Gleason threatening his fictional wife with domestic violence.

Suddenly, after decades of neglect, a new space race rose, phoenix-like, from the ashes of exploration. Except this time we weren't racing other nation-states, but rather the slow motion tumble of what might turn out to be a hammer from the sky.

They were slowing down. And by the fourth round, we managed to spot their lightsails—their parachutes—and now we could watch as well as hear them come. Hailing them produced more echoes, and as we sent them new, specific signals they stopped reproducing our old ones.

The sources further away from Earth were braking harder; some had paused entirely (not that anything really pauses in space, but allow me the conceit) and at least one—the initial signal, the strongest Echo—seemed likely to pass very close indeed. We had a betting pool. My money had it making orbit.

I figured they weren't here to blow up the planet, enslave us, or kidnap our nubile young men away to Mercury. For one thing, if they were hostile, the easiest thing in the world—*out* of the world—would have been for them to sneak up on us and drop a rock on our heads from orbit, which would pretty much soften up any useful resistance right then and there. Alien invasion movies aren't usually written by physicists. For another thing, sending back our own voices . . . it seemed kind of friendly, somehow.

My work friend Carl pointed out that it was something bullies did, too, mocking what you said by repeating it. I looked across a plate of gyros at him and replied, "They do it in funny voices."

The constellation of radio sources strung out against the sky seemed to me to be relay stations, signal boosters. I guessed they were sending messages home.

I won the betting pool, which was a strange sensation. Carl, who shares my office and sits at the desk next to mine, knew better than to tease me about it. He'd tried when we were first thrown together, but I think he caught on that I was faking engagement with his jokes.

Rather than being offended, though, he just backed off of them.

Carl was a good guy, even if he wasn't funny. I was so young then; it was so amazingly long ago. Sixty-three years: a human's productive lifetime, under pretty good circumstances.

He was also the guy who thought enough of me to forward me the links to the breaking news articles on China's emergency manned mission to the Echo.

"Crap," I said.

"Easy, Courtney," he responded, without looking up from the rows of numbers scrolling his desktop. "We've still got their trail to chase back up the sky."

I was still frowning. He was still looking at me.

He said, "Look, it's seven. Let's get some dinner and you can vent all you want."

"Thanks," I said. "But I need to work tonight."

The U.S.A. was outraged, and loudly said so to everyone, whether they would listen or not. But there wasn't much America could do about it, having sacrificed our space program on the altars of economic necessity and eternal war. I found the prospect of China getting first crack at the Echo frustrating mostly because it meant that my odds of getting near it were exponentially smaller. And if I could have itched—I mean physically *itched*—with desire . . .

But as it turned out, we didn't have to go to the Echo.

The Echo came to us.

It separated into a dozen identical—we later learned—components, which settled themselves near population centers scattered around the globe. China got one; so did India.

It will surprise no one that I read a lot of science fiction. Read and read—one spelling, two pronunciations, two tenses. There's a subset of the genre that fans call the "big dumb object" plot: basically, *2001*. Intrepid human explorers meet up with an abandoned alien artifact—a probe, a relic—and have to decide what to make of it.

This wasn't a single big dumb object so much as a web of little ones. I spent some time thinking about it—well, who didn't?—and what I realized was that whoever built it had allowed for the fact that it might make landfall at a world where the sentient life forms had not yet achieved space flight. If we couldn't come to them, they would have to come to us.

The component that drifted down in New York City wound up at JPL, and a number of xenologists—a new specialty pretty much as of that morning—were invited to examine it.

● ● ●

And so I became one of the vanishingly small percentage of humans privileged to hold in my hands a disc of metal originated on another world. It was pristine, a perfect circle electroplated with gold, the surface etched with symbols and diagrams I forced myself not to try to interpret, just yet.

Carl leaned over my shoulder. He put his hand on it and gave me an excited squeeze. "Damn," he said. "It's just like Voyager."

"I guess good ideas tend to reoccur." Through the nitrile gloves, I felt the slight irregularities of its surface. "You don't suppose this one is a phonograph record too?"

To human ears, their voices sound like the layered keening of gulls.

You know who I am because I'm the one who found their star. It's a small, cool red sun about 31.5 light years away.

If you can name something that already belongs to someone else, I named it Hui Zhong, for my grandmother.

We've never actually seen Hui Zhong—it's too small, too cool, and washed out behind a brighter neighbor—but we know where it has to be. Hui Zhong burns at about 3000 degrees Kelvin—half the temperature of Earth's own sun. It's a Population II star, and poor in heavy elements. Its spectrum is recorded on the discs, and so we know that it is a first generation star, one of the early citizens of the thirteen-and-three-quarters billion-year-old universe.

Hui Zhong is nearly immortal. The convective structure of such dwarf stars offers them stability, constant luminosity, and a lifespan in the hundreds of billions of years. Our own Sun, by contrast, is only some four and a half billion years old—and in about that same amount of time, will become a red giant as its nuclear furnaces inevitably begin to fail.

We'll die with it, unless we find someplace else to go.

One of the tracks on the record the Echoes sent us is a voice counting, and one of the diagrams on its surface is of a planet and primary—so we have a sense of their homeworld's orbital period—a mere fourteen Earth days or so . . .

The Echoes, in other words, could have been planning their approach to other civilizations and sending out probes in likely directions for a very, very long time. The probe was a sublight vehicle; we couldn't know exactly how long it had taken us to reach us . . . but "millennia" wasn't out of the question.

We returned the call.

Not as one strong, unified signal, but as an erratic series of blips and dashes—governments and corporations and research institutions. There was an X-Prize. Groups and mavericks, answering the stars.

And we kept answering. We've been answering for almost seventy years now. I've gone from hot young Turk to eminence gris in that time, from sought-after expert to forgotten emeritus. For sixty-five of those years, I think I must have been holding my breath. Waiting for the word across the void. Waiting for these people who reached out from their ancient world, circling their ancient, stable star, to hear our reply and start a slow, painstaking dialogue.

On Turnaround Day they dusted me off. I found myself standing at a cocktail party next to the President of East America, wondering how I'd gotten there, wondering what was in the brown paste on the glorified cracker in my hand.

I turned around to say something to that effect to Carl before I remembered he'd died eighteen months before, predeceased by his wife of forty years. After she died, he used to call me every week, like clockwork.

His jokes still weren't that funny. But I could feel him waiting, lonely, on the other end of the line. As waiting and as lonely as me.

The world really did hold its breath. And our silence was met by an answering silence . . . and after a pause the world moved on.

It's not just Carl. Most of my other colleagues are gone. I live alone, and the work I can still do goes frustratingly slowly now.

Sometimes I think waiting to hear the answer was what kept me going this long.

I don't expect to hear an answer anymore.

Maybe the Echoes forgot they'd called out to us. Maybe they never really expected an answer. Maybe they moved beyond radio waves, the same way we have. Maybe—even more so than us—they no longer listen to the stars.

Maybe, despite their safe old world and their safe old star, something horrible happened to them. Maybe Fermi was right, and they blew themselves up.

Maybe we'll blow ourselves up someday really soon, too.

But they reached out once. They let us know we weren't alone. We heard them and reached back, and they haven't answered—or they haven't answered *yet*.

Maybe they live a lot longer than we do. Maybe they don't have the same sense of urgency.

We do keep trying. And maybe someday they'll send an answer.

But it will be a slow conversation and I won't be here to hear it. (Two words; one pronunciation.)

Too late, I think I figured something out. It's everybody, isn't it? It was Carl, too, and that's what he was trying to tell me. That we could be lonely together, and it might help somehow.

The silence stretches loud across the space between us. And I can't decide if knowing they were out there and that they reached out in friendship, with a map and the sound of their voices, is worse than imagining they were never there at all.

HONEY BEAR

SOFIA SAMATAR

───◆───

We've decided to take a trip, to see the ocean. I want Honey to see it while she's still a child. That way, it'll be magical. I tell her about it in the car: how big it is, and green, like a sky you can wade in.

"Even you?" she asks.

"Even me."

I duck my head to her hair. She smells fresh, but not sweet at all, like parsley or tea. She's wearing a little white dress. It's almost too short. She pushes her bare toes against the seat in front of her, knuckling it like a cat.

"Can you not do that, Hon?" says Dave.

"Sorry, Dad."

She says "Dad" now. She used to say "Da-Da."

Dave grips the wheel. I can see the tension in his shoulders. Threads of gray wink softly in his dark curls. He still wears his hair long, covering his ears, and I think he's secretly a little bit vain about it. A little bit proud of still having all his hair. I think there's something in this, something valuable, something he could use to get back. You don't cling to personal vanities if you've given up all hope of a normal life. At least, I don't think you do.

"Shit," he says.

"Sweetheart . . . "

He doesn't apologize for swearing in front of Honey. The highway's blocked by a clearance area, gloved hands waving us around. He turns the car so sharply the bags in the passenger seat beside him almost fall off the cooler. In the back seat, I lean into Honey Bear.

"It's okay," I tell Dave.

"No, Karen, it is not okay. The temp in the cooler is going to last until exactly four o'clock. At four o'clock, we need a fridge, which means we need a hotel. If we are five minutes late, it is not going to be okay."

"It looks like a pretty short detour."

"It is impossible for you to see how long it is."

"I'm just thinking, it doesn't look like they've got that much to clear."

"Fine, you can think that. Think what you want. But don't tell me the detour's not long, or give me any other information you don't actually have, okay?"

He's driving faster. I rest my cheek on the top of Honey's head. The clearance area rolls by outside the window. Cranes, loading trucks, figures in orange jumpsuits. Some of the slick has dried: they're peeling it up in transparent sheets, like plate glass.

Honey presses a fingertip to the window. "Poo-poo," she says softly.

I tell her about the time I spent a weekend at the beach. My best friend got so sunburned, her back blistered.

We play the clapping game, "A Sailor Went to Sea-Sea-Sea." It's our favorite.

Dave drives too fast, but we don't get stopped, and we reach the hotel in time. I take my meds, and we put the extra in the hotel fridge. Dave's shirt is dark with sweat, and I wish he'd relax, but he goes straight out to buy ice, and stores it in the freezer so we can fill the cooler tomorrow. Then he takes a shower and lies on the bed and watches the news. I sit on the floor with Honey, looking at books. I read to her every evening before bed; I've never missed a night. Right now, we're reading *The Meadow Fairies* by Dorothy Elizabeth Clark.

This is something I've looked forward to my whole adult life: reading the books I loved as a child with a child of my own. Honey adores *The Meadow Fairies*. She snuggles up to me and traces the pretty winged children with her finger. Daffodil, poppy, pink. When I first brought the book home, and Dave saw us reading it, he asked what the point was, since Honey would never see those flowers. I laughed because I'd never seen them either. "It's about fairies," I told him, "not botany." I don't think I've ever seen a poppy in my life.

Smiling, though half-asleep,
The Poppy Fairy passes,
Scarlet, like the sunrise,
Among the meadow grasses.

Honey chants the words with me. She's so smart, she learns so fast. She can pick up anything that rhymes in minutes. Her hair glints in the lamplight. There's the mysterious, slightly abrasive smell of hotel sheets, a particular hotel darkness between the blinds.

"I love this place," says Honey. "Can we stay here?"

"It's an adventure," I tell her. "Just wait till tomorrow."

On the news, helicopters hover over the sea. It's far away, the Pacific. There's been a huge dump there, over thirty square miles of slick. The effects on marine life are not yet known.

"Will it be fairyland?" Honey asks suddenly.

"What, sweetie?"

"Will it be fairyland, when I'm grown up?"

"Yes," I tell her. My firmest tone.

"Will you be there?"

No hesitation. "Yes."

The camera zooms in on the slick-white sea.

By the time I've given Honey Bear a drink and put her to bed, Dave's eyes are closed. I turn off the TV and the lights and get into bed. Like Honey, I love the hotel. I love the hard, tight sheets and the unfamiliar shapes that emerge around me once I've gotten used to the dark. It's been ages since I slept away from home. The last time was long before Honey. Dave and I visited some college friends in Oregon. They couldn't believe we'd driven all that way. We posed in their driveway, leaning on the car and making the victory sign.

I want the Dave from that photo. That deep suntan, that wide grin.

Maybe he'll come back to me here, away from home and our neighbors, the Simkos. He spends far too much time at their place.

For a moment, I think he's back already.

Then he starts shaking. He does it every night. He's crying in his sleep.

"Ready for the beach?"

"Yes!"

We drive through town to a parking lot dusted with sand. When I step out of the car the warm sea air rolls over me in waves. There's something lively in it, something electric.

Honey jumps up and down. "Is that it? Is that it?"

"You got it, Honey Bear."

The beach is deserted. Far to the left, an empty boardwalk whitens in the sun. I kick off my sandals and scoop them up in my hand. The gray sand sticks to my feet. We lumber down to a spot a few yards from some boulders, lugging bags and towels.

"Can I take my shoes off too? Can I go in the ocean?"

"Sure, but let me take your dress off."

I pull it off over her head, and her lithe, golden body slips free. She's so beautiful, my Bear. I call her Honey because she's my sweetheart, my little love, and I call her Bear for the wildness I dream she will keep always. Honey suits her now, but when she's older she might want us to call her Bear. I would've loved to be named Bear when I was in high school.

"Don't go too deep," I tell her, "just up to your tummy, okay?"

"Okay," she says, and streaks off, kicking up sand behind her.

Dave has laid out the towels. He's weighted the corners with shoes and the cooler so they won't blow away. He's set up the two folding chairs and the umbrella. Now, with nothing to organize or prepare, he's sitting on a chair with his bare feet resting on a towel. He looks lost.

"Not going in?" I ask.

I think for a moment he's going to ignore me, but then he makes an effort. "Not right away," he says.

I slip off my shorts and my halter top and sit in the chair beside him in my suit. Down in the water, Honey jumps up and down and shrieks.

"Look at that."

"Yeah," he says.

"She loves it."

"Yeah."

"I'm so glad we brought her. Thank you." I reach out and give his wrist a squeeze.

"Look at that fucked-up clown on the boardwalk," he says. "It looks like it used to be part of an arcade entrance or something. Probably been there for fifty years."

The clown towers over the boardwalk. It's almost white, but you can see traces of red on the nose and lips, traces of blue on the hair.

"Looks pretty old," I agree.

"Black rocks, filthy gray sand, and a fucked-up arcade clown. That's what we've got. That's the beach."

It comes out before I can stop it: "Okay, Mr. Simko."

Dave looks at me.

"I'm sorry," I say.

He looks at his watch. "I don't want to stay here for more than an hour. I want us to take a break, go back to the hotel and rest for a bit. Then we'll have lunch, and you can take your medication."

"I said I'm sorry."

"You know what?" He looks gray, worn out, beaten down, like something left out in the rain. His eyes wince away from the light. I can't stand it, I can't stand it if he never comes back. "I think," he tells me, "that Mr. Simko is a pretty fucking sensible guy."

I lean back in the chair, watching Honey Bear in the water. I hate the Simkos. Mr. Simko's bent over and never takes off his bathrobe. He sits on his porch drinking highballs all day, and he gets Dave to go over there and drink too. I can hear them when I've got the kitchen window open. Mr. Simko says things like *Après nous le déluge* and "Keep your powder dry and your pecker wet." He tells Dave he wishes he and Mrs. Simko didn't have Mandy. I've heard him say that. "I wish we'd never gone in for it. Broke Linda's heart." Who does he think brings him the whiskey to make his highballs?

Mrs. Simko never comes out of the house except when Mandy comes home. Then she appears on the porch, banging the door behind her. She's bent over like her husband and wears a flowered housedress. Her hair is black fluff, with thin patches here and there, as if she's burned it. "Mandy, Mandy," she croons, while Mandy puts the stuff down on the porch: liquor, chocolate, clothes, all the luxury goods you can't get at the Center. Stuff you can only get from a child who's left home. Mandy never looks at her mother. She hasn't let either of the Simkos touch her since she moved out.

"I'm going down in the water with Honey," I say, but Dave grabs my arm.

"Wait. Look."

I turn my head, and there are Fair Folk on the rocks. Six of them, huge and dazzling. Some crouch on the boulders; others swing over the sea on their flexible wings, dipping their toes in the water.

"Honey!" Dave shouts. "Honey! Come here!"

"C'mon, Hon," I call, reassuring.

Honey splashes toward us, glittering in the sun.

"Come *here!*" barks Dave.

"She's coming," I tell him.

He clutches the arms of his chair. I know he's afraid because of the clearance area we passed on the highway, the slick.

"Come here," he repeats as Honey runs up panting. He glances at the Fair Folk. They're looking at us now, lazy and curious.

I get up and dry Honey off with a towel. "What?" she says.

"Just come over here," says Dave, holding out his arms. "Come and sit with Daddy."

Honey walks over and curls up in his lap. I sit in the chair next to them and Dave puts his hand on my shoulder. He's got us. He's holding everyone.

Two of the Fair Folk lift and ripple toward us through the light. There seems to be more light wherever they go. They're fifteen, twenty feet tall, so tall they look slender, attenuated, almost insect-like. You forget how strong they are.

They bend and dip in the air: so close I can see the reds of their eyes.

"It's okay," Dave whispers.

And it is, of course. We've got each other. We're safe.

They gaze at us for a moment, impassive, then turn and glide back to their comrades.

Honey waves at them with both hands. "Bye, fairies!"

On my first visit to the clinic, I went through all the usual drills, the same stuff I go in for every two weeks. Step here, pee here, spit here, breathe in, breathe out, give me your arm. The only difference the first time was the questions.

Are you aware of the gravity of the commitment? I said yes. Have you been informed of the risks, both physical and psychological? Yes. The side effects of the medication? Blood transfusions? Yes. Yes. The decrease in life expectancy? Everything: yes.

That's what you say to life. *Yes.*

"They chose us," I told Dave. Rain lashed the darkened windows. I cradled tiny Honey in my lap. I'd dried her off and wrapped her in a towel, and she was quiet now, exhausted. I'd already named her in my head.

"We can't go back," Dave whispered. "If we say yes, we can't go back."

"I know."

His eyes were wet. "We could run out and put her on somebody else's porch."

He looked ashamed after he'd said it, the way he'd looked when I'd asked him not to introduce me as "my wife, Karen, the children's literature major." When we first moved into the neighborhood he'd introduce me that way and then laugh, as if there was nothing more ridiculous in the world. Children, when almost nobody could have them anymore; literature when all the schools were closed. I told him it bothered me, and he was sorry, but only for hurting me. He wasn't sorry for what he really meant. What he meant was: *No.*

That's wrong. It's like the Simkos, hateful and worn out with saying *No* to Mandy, saying *No* to life.

So many people say no from the beginning. They make it a virtue: "I can't be bought." As if it were all a matter of protection and fancy goods. Of course, most of those who say yes pretend to be heroes: saving the world, if only for a season. That's always struck me as equally wrong, in its own way. Cheap.

I can't help thinking the absence of children has something to do with this withering of the spirit—this pale new way of seeing the world. Children knew better. You always say yes. If you don't, there's no adventure, and you grow old in your ignorance, bitter, bereft of magic. You say yes to what comes, because you belong to the future, whatever it is, and you're sure as hell not going to be left behind in the past. *Do you hear the fairies sing?* You always get up and open the door. You always answer. You always let them in.

The Fair Folk are gone. I'm in the ocean with Honey. I bounce her on my knee. She's so light in the water: soap bubble, floating seed. She clings to my neck and squeals. I think she'll remember this, this morning at the beach, and the memory will be almost exactly like my own memory of childhood. The water, the sun. Even the cooler, the crumpled maps in the car. So many things now are the way they were when I was small. Simpler, in lots of ways. The things that have disappeared—air travel, wireless communication—seem dreamlike, ludicrous, almost not worth thinking about.

I toss Honey up in the air and catch her, getting a mouthful of saltwater in the process. I shoot the water onto her shoulder. "Mama!" she yells. She bends her head to the water and burbles, trying to copy me, but I lift her up again. I don't want her to choke.

"My Bear, my Bear," I murmur against the damp, wet side of her head. "My Honey Bear."

Dave is waving us in. He's pointing at his watch.

I don't know if it's the excitement, or maybe something about the salt water, but as soon as I get Honey up on the beach, she voids.

"Christ," says Dave. "Oh, Christ."

He pulls me away from her. In seconds he's kneeling on our towels, whipping the gloves and aprons out of the bag. He gets his on fast; I fumble with mine. He rips open a packet of wipes with his teeth, tosses it to me, and pulls out a can of spray.

"I thought you said it wasn't time yet," he says.

"I thought it wasn't. It's really early."

Honey stands naked on the sand, slick pouring down her legs. Already she looks hesitant, confused. "Mama?"

"It's okay, Hon. Just let it come. Do you want to lie down?"

"Yes," she says, and crumples.

"Fuck," says Dave. "It's going to hit the water. I have to go make a call. Take this."

He hands me the spray, yanks his loafers on and dashes up the beach. There's a phone in the parking lot, he can call the Service. He's headed for the fence, not the gate, but it doesn't stop him, he seizes the bar and vaults over.

The slick is still coming. So much, it's incredible, as if she's losing her whole body. It astounds me, it frightens me every time. Her eyes are still open, but dazed. Her fine hair is starting to dry in the sun. The slick pours, undulant, catching the light, like molten plastic.

I touch her face with a gloved hand. "Honey Bear."

"Mm," she grunts.

"You're doing a good job, Hon. Just relax, okay? Mama's here."

Dave was right, it's going to reach the water. I scramble down to the waves and spray the sand and even the water in the path of the slick. Probably won't do anything, probably stupid. I run back to Honey just as Dave comes pelting back from the parking lot.

"On their way," he gasps. "Shit! It's almost in the water!"

"Mama," says Honey.

"I know. I tried to spray."

"You sprayed? That's not going to do anything!"

I'm kneeling beside her. "Yes, Honey."

"Help me!" yells Dave. He runs down past the slick and starts digging wildly, hurling gobs of wet sand.

Honey curls her hand around my finger.

"Karen! Get down here! We can dig a trench, we can keep it from hitting the water!"

"This is scary," Honey whispers.

"I know. I know, Hon. I'm sorry. But you don't need to be scared. It's just like when we're at home, okay?"

But it's not, it's not like when we're at home. At home, I usually know when it's going to happen. I've got a chart. I set up buckets, a plastic sheet. I notify the Service of the approximate date. They come right away. We keep the lights down, and I play Honey's favorite CD.

This isn't like that at all. Harsh sunlight, Dave screaming behind us. Then the Service. They're angry: one of them says, "You ought to be fucking fined." They spray Honey, right on her skin. She squeezes my finger. I don't know what to do, except sing to her, a song from her CD.

A sailor went to sea-sea-sea
To see what he could see-see-see
But all that he could see-see-see
Was the bottom of the deep blue sea-sea-sea.

At last, it stops. The Service workers clean Honey up and wrap her in sterile sheets. They take our gloves and aprons away to be cleaned at the local Center. Dave and I wipe ourselves down and bag the dirty wipes for disposal. We're both shaking. He says: "We are not doing this again."

"It was an accident," I tell him. "It's just life."

He turns to face me. "This is not life, Karen," he snarls. "This is *not life*."

"Yes. It is."

I think he sees, then. I think he sees that even though he's the practical one, the realist, I'm the strong one.

I carry Honey up to the car. Dave takes the rest of the stuff. He makes two trips. He gives me an energy bar and then my medication. After that, there's the injection, painkillers and nutrients, because Honey's voided, and she'll be hungry. She'll need more than a quick drink.

He slips the needle out of my arm. He's fast, and gentle, even like this, kneeling in the car in a beach parking lot. He presses the cotton down firmly, puts on a strip of medical tape. He looks up and meets my eyes. His are full of tears.

"Jesus, Karen," he says.

Just like that, in that moment, he's back. He covers his mouth with his fist, holding in laughter. "Did you hear the Service guy?"

"You mean 'You ought to be fucking fined'?"

He bends over, wheezing and crowing. "Christ! I really thought the slick was going in the water."

"But it didn't go in the water?"

"No."

He sits up, wipes his eyes on the back of his hand, then reaches out to smooth my hair away from my face.

"No. It didn't go in. It was fine. Not that it matters, with that giant dump floating in the Pacific."

He reads my face, and raises his hands, palms out. "Okay, okay. No Mr. Simko."

He backs out, shuts the door gently, and gets in the driver's seat. The white clown on the boardwalk watches our car pull out of the lot. We're almost at the hotel when Honey wakes up.

"Mama?" she mumbles. "I'm hungry."

"Okay, sweetie."

I untie the top piece of my suit and pull it down. "Dave? I'm going to feed her in the car."

"Okay. I'll park in the shade. I'll bring you something to eat from inside."

"Thanks."

Honey's wriggling on my lap, fighting the sheets. "Mama, I'm *hungry*."

"Hush. Hush. Here."

She nuzzles at me, quick and greedy, and latches on. Not at the nipple, but in the soft area under the arm. She grips me lightly with her teeth, and then there's the almost electric jolt as her longer, hollow teeth come down and sink in.

"There," I whisper. "There."

Dave gets out and shuts the door. We're alone in the car.

A breeze stirs the leaves outside. Their reflections move in the windows.

I don't know what the future is going to bring. I don't think about it much. It does seem like there won't be a particularly lengthy future, for us. Not with so few human children being born, and the Fair Folk eating all the animals, and so many plant species dying out from the slick. And once we're gone, what will the Fair Folk do? They don't seem able to raise their own children. It's why they came here in the first place. I don't know if they feel sorry for us, but I know they want us to live as long as possible: they're not pure predators, as some people claim. The abductions of the early days, the bodies discovered in caves—that's all over. The terror, too. That was just to show us what they could do. Now they only kill us as punishment, or after they've voided, when they're crazy with hunger. They rarely hurt anyone in the company of a winged child.

Still, even with all their precautions, we won't last forever. I remember the artist in the park, when I took Honey there one day. All of his paintings were white. He said that was the future, a white planet, nothing but slick, and Honey said it looked like fairyland.

Her breathing has slowed. Mine, too. It's partly the meds, and partly some chemical that comes down through the teeth. It makes you drowsy.

Here's what I know about the future. Honey Bear will grow bigger. Her wings will expand. One day she'll take to the sky, and go live with her own kind. Maybe she'll forget human language, the way the Simko's Mandy has, but she'll still bring us presents. She'll still be our piece of the future.

And maybe she won't forget. She might remember. She might remember this day at the beach.

She's still awake. Her eyes glisten, heavy with bliss. Large, slightly protuberant eyes, perfectly black in the centers, and scarlet, like the sunrise, at the edges.

THE FORGOTTEN ONES

KARIN LOWACHEE

In the twilight, my brother Hava's eyes glow red. Before the old women of Rumi village were washed from this life, they said it was the spirit of blood in him, my twin. I do not have such spirit. I am the silent breath, the old women said, she who walks behind the blood and is last in the sand before death. Death is the final hand that smooths your tracks beneath the waves. And before death there is the silent breath, and before the silent breath there is the blood. And my brother's eyes glow red with it.

In the twilight, hidden by broad leaves that bend over the shore and give shadow, we wait. We lie on our stomachs, Hava and I and all of our twenty soldiers, chins to the dark earth, smelling the spring richness of new growth. The wind plays a song above us in the trees. The scampering feet of the little animals up and down the trunks and across the floor of the forest are a low drumbeat, a thudding of tiny hearts. I could go to sleep here, like I used to do with Hava on the fallen trunks of lightning-struck trees. Before the Lopo came and killed our parents. Lopo from across the waters.

When I first saw them with their guns and their tall hats, I was afraid. But now I have seen them without their hats. I have taken their guns and felt the power of their shouts like a storm come in from the sea. The power in my hands, from their guns. And though the Lopo sit in our villages and sharpen their knives on our stone and rest their boots on our tables, I have seen them at my feet, in blood, and it flows as dark and thick as what runs out of me in that week of womanhood.

The Lopo keep coming from across the waters, and though we are half their size, barely thirteen strides along the sands of life, we drive them back. We, Hava and I and our twenty soldiers, have forced the Lopo to huddle in our villages, to sharpen their knives on our stone and beat their boots on our tables in frustration. Eventually, Hava says, their blood will flow to the waters and become one, until nothing will be left but the waters. And us, the children of the dead ones. We who have been here for as long as the old women remembered. We who were here first.

"Sister," Hava whispers to me. "Go tell Umeneni to climb the father tree. I think I see them on the waters."

I slither backward, deeper into the forest, until the glow of moonlight on the water disappears. The earth is damp beneath my knees as I scamper to the left, where Umeneni waits on his belly, chin to the ground. Broad chair-leaves arc over his back and narrow shoulders. The black mud in his deep red hair smells like starberries. We crush the sour buds into the earth until their juices create the paste. For a moment I think of our morning together and the feel of his coarse hair through my fingers when I twisted them with mud. He sat on a rock and cleaned his killing knife and the sun was strong on his brown shoulders and the back of my neck. His eyes are not spirit red, but blue like the waters. My father would have liked Umeneni. We would have had a child by now, if not for the Lopo.

Tonight he might die and I hate the Lopo. When I look at Umeneni and think of the children we do not have, I can kill the Lopo as viciously as Hava. I can slice their skin from their sinew and throw them to the sharks. My bones are tired with the feeling of it.

"Ara," Umeneni whispers, his breath against my cheek.

"Hava says to climb the father tree. The Lopo might be on the waters now. You must count how many, and where."

I see his mud-locks bob up and down in shadow, and then he is gone, leaving nothing behind but the twitch of a sheltering leaf and the scent of starberries.

We do not know why the Lopo came. We do not know why we were forced to flee our homes as children and hide among the trees, prey for the big cats and the Lopo alike. One morning when Hava and I were only ten strides across the sands of life the Lopo landed on our shores with their long boats and their guns and their tall hats. Their shiny booted feet left deep imprints in the ground that filled up with rain but never washed away. The old women in our village, the ones who were there to remember and to carve, cursed at the Lopo and called them by names I had never heard. And the Lopo said, "That was long before our time and the agreement means nothing." Somehow they knew our language. And I understood them perfectly, though their words made no sense.

But it did not matter. Their weapons were their words.

I wait beside Hava. The waves roll into shore like a mother's gentle breath, rippling the skin of the earth. Moonlight flitters on the waters as if it is calling for the fish to surface. Yet it calls the Lopo and when the Lopo come they bring only ruin. They row in as silent as the forest when a hunter is on the prowl. And all the world knows that death sits among it.

"Something is wrong," Hava says. I see the moon line of his profile in the near-dark. The corners of his eyes are red as though he bleeds tears. But it is only the glow of his blood spirit.

A hand touches my heel and I look back over my shoulder. Umeneni crawls up between us and lays down on his belly. His shoulder touches mine and it is warm from his climb on the father tree. Mine is cool from the night.

"There are lights," he whispers. "Far out along the horizon. But they come closer and they are fast."

"How many?" Hava asks. "How fast?"

Umeneni's voice is a shudder. "Too many and too fast."

Umeneni has the best sight among us. He has always spied far and wide. Once he saw a line of five Lopo hunters winding furtive and silent through the path of the big cats, covered in leaves and soil. Yet Umeneni saw them.

My brother says, "Maybe they come in different boats. Maybe they have new boats."

"Maybe," Umeneni says.

Hava knows the Lopo. He's tasted their golden blood.

"We will wait," Hava says. "And hide."

Umeneni says nothing, but I feel his gaze in the dark just as close as his skin. The disturbance in my brother's voice wafts through me like a shiver.

Before our attacks on the Lopo, Hava would always draw our positions in the sand, in the earth. We and our soldiers, fifty strong as they once were, and even now when they are twenty, we all gathered around this map of our close futures and Hava would take his finger and trace patterns in the ground. His touch glided through the fine grains like the gods must sift our lives, separating some, pushing others together. We knew at some time the waters or the rain would wipe these marks away, but we never stayed long enough to see it. And so the lines of life that Hava traced in the earth would remain in our minds, marked deep and true. And we took them with us into battle. Lines like the grooves on the skin of our palms. Lines like the veins that run beneath our skin.

Blood paths.

And I would think, always, Is this the path of my children, if ever I should have them? Would their feet ever imprint on sand that does not wash away after two turnings of the moon?

The lights scud toward us like falling stars, rolling through the surface of the waves. Impossibly fast. Faster than any Lopo boat. The closer they come, the clearer we see. Not just Umeneni and his far sight. We all see.

The lights do not touch the waters. They fly above it.

"Not the Lopo," Umeneni whispers, in fear. Umeneni who has killed a hundred Lopo and yet with me his touch is gentle. He fears little. He doesn't even fear my brother.

I feel our soldiers shifting behind us. What do we do? Run? Scatter?

"Stay," Hava says, loud enough so it branches through the trees and quiets the others.

The lights come silent. They pour day onto the shore, the trees, our hidden forms among the forest floor. White day. The lights bring wind and heat like a summer breeze, and the shake and growl of a thunderstorm, but only in passing. Only in nearness, like you hear someone breathe in sleep if you are the only one awake.

The lights sweep over our heads like birds and disappear.

And in a flash, my brother chases the beat of their windless wings through the feet of the bowing trees.

I run, Umeneni by my side, our soldiers around us. We follow Hava and the storm of the lights as they skate the top of the forest. If these are Lopo, we must track them. We must get to them before they join the Lopo in our villages and become one.

The ground stabs my feet. The forest is alive with the snap and crack of our fiery path, cut by my brother.

These Lopo fly.

The three words beat a rhythm in my breath. The loud drumming of a death dance.

I want to grab Hava back and keep him still. I want to hold Umeneni to my breasts and say, Wait.

The blood can wait.

These Lopo fly.

Yet if the Lopo had such ability to fly among the clouds like birds, surely we would have known it. Surely you cannot go from water to sky in just a few turnings of the moon. The Lopo are not gods. They bleed, though their blood is golden like honey. But their spirits are not red like my brother's.

"Hava!" I shout. I don't care. The lights drown all but the closest noise.

But he doesn't stop. In his hand flashes the silver of his killing knife. He hunts the lights.

"Rumi village," Umeneni says, on a gasp. Running as I run.

I recognize the path, even in moonlight and the dying blaze of the beasts overhead.

We are going home.

My brother stops on the edge of our village. What was once our village, where the old women sat outside their homes and braided long leaves into mats for our beds. Now the Lopo lie on our mats, still stained by the blood of our mothers.

Hava crouches at the feet of the trees. Our soldiers gather around in a line of attack, the positions of habit. I barely gather breath enough to speak before Hava turns to me, the red now so vibrant in his eyes that I barely see the white.

"They are friends of the Lopo," Umeneni says, his voice harsh, his teeth bared.

The lights touched ground in the clear spaces of the village. They are shaped almost like boats, almost like birds. Strange inbetween creatures that bellow the white of bright day over all the scattered homes. Yet the mud roofs don't melt and the grass of the walls do not burn.

"But the Lopo do not come out," I say. "Where are their brothers, if it's true they are friends?"

"The Lopo hide," Hava says, resting the tip of his killing knife in the earth. "See the shadows move inside that house? They do not come out. They are afraid."

There is no fear in Hava's voice. He stares at the inbetween creatures.

A door opens on the belly of one of the creatures. We wait, silent, but no Lopo emerge from the homes to greet the open door. Not a stirring.

A tall figure walks from the creature's belly, but it isn't clad in tattered Lopo grey. It wears stitchless black. And it is the shape of us, with arms and legs. But big like our mothers and fathers had been.

Hava sheaths his knife and reaches to his other hip. Soon he holds a Lopo gun and aims it through the trees. Tracking. Umeneni does the same, but I don't move.

Things that travel inside a flying creature. How will guns help? Better to sneak up on them. Better to jump on their backs and bring them down one by one, and then use the knife.

More figures emerge from the creature's belly. I lose the count at fifty. Soon the entire village is filled by these black-clad people. They are beetle-shaped on the head and about the eyes, as though they come from insect kin.

A voice calls out. It sounds like language, but not ours. Lopo words. Calling to the Lopo who hide in our houses.

But the Lopo do not come out. They are cowards.

So the beetle people swarm into the houses. Noise erupts, shouting, gunfire, flashes of light and the shake of violence. Some of the beetle people wait outside, not speaking. Not helping. They stand like trees.

Soon the rest of them reappear. The lights from their inbetween creatures reflect on their insect heads.

They hold the Lopo by their long spindly arms. Lopo warriors, men and women, some of them bleeding. They are ugly clean, and uglier in blood. They make a sticky yellow visage and their too-long legs bend deeper than normal, driven to kneel by these beetle people. The beetle people set the Lopo in the middle of our village, like the Lopo had once done to us, and make them sit on the earth. They hold the Lopo guns and they do not say a word. Yet they all move in agreement as though they can read one another's minds.

Enemies of the Lopo, yet Hava does not twitch or give us a command. Are these beetle people here to return our villages to us? Or will they push us to the ground, smoothing it with our blood?

My hands are cold with the thought. I touch Umeneni's back to feel his warmth. We must hide. We must pretend we are not here and when these beetle people leave with the Lopo, we will have our villages back. And we will grow old under the sun like the women who weaved and carved and remembered.

But my brother does not move.

One of the beetle people walks away from the others. The insect head faces the trees, turns toward us. It raises an arm. I see now that it has five fingers on its hand. On both hands. It is very much in the shape of our people. Except for the insect head.

But then it removes its insect head, like you would remove a hat. The black eyes go with it too and beneath it all is a face much like Umeneni's. Like mine.

A woman.

"Come out," it says, toward the trees. To us. Somehow it speaks our language even though the lilt and sigh of the words are unfamiliar, like when the Lopo speak. Yet we understand. It says, "Come out now, children."

I want to grip Umeneni's hand, and my brother's, but instead we hold our weapons. Hava stands and looks over his shoulder at me.

"Stay," he says. "All of you."

"No, Hava." I try to catch his arm, but he walks out alone toward the beetle people. Toward the one who has a face like mine, and speaks our language, though she flew to us like a bird.

Umeneni tries to touch my shoulder, but I run out after my brother.

The beetle people swivel to face me. I stop, planting my feet, feeling the night air breathe cold up my bare legs. Hava turns.

"Ara!" He gestures sharply. "Go back!"

"No," the beetle woman says. Closer and I see she is like my mother was, beneath the smooth clothing. She has a woman's breasts and she is tall like one, broader than me about the hips. Her voice, free of the insect head, is the gentle trickle of river water. "Let her come too. Both of you."

Hava frowns at me. But he offers his hand. So I take my brother's hand and we approach.

"You look so much alike," the woman says. "You must be brother and sister."

Up close, they don't smell like Lopo. They smell like our knives after the rain has washed them clean.

The Lopo on the ground watch us with hatred in their small white eyes. We have killed many of them. They recognize us.

Hava looks at them once, then up at the woman. "What are you?"

They haven't taken our weapons. They called us children, though we have been without parents since our tenth stride across the sands of life.

Maybe they have come to steal our forest from us, to steal our beaches and our near waters, like the Lopo stole our villages.

"What are you?" Hava asks again, louder.

"We are your fathers and mothers," the woman says.

"Our fathers and mothers are dead," Hava says. He points to the Lopo. "They killed them. They came from across the waters and wiped the shores of our homes. They let our parents' blood run with the waters and the rain. Is that what you are here to do?"

My brother's voice is a kitten mew compared to the smooth strength of the woman's. She is tall enough to pick him up by the back of his neck like the big cats do with their little ones. Yet Hava doesn't waver. And I grip his hand to feel him, not for him to feel me.

"No," the woman says. "You were lost for too long. Now we've remembered."

"How is it that you speak our language?" I ask. "How do your boats fly? Where do you come from, if not from across the waters?"

"There is too much to say," the woman says, like a sigh. She holds her beetle head in her hand. It is hollow inside, and padded with a strange cloth, one that shines like the moon on the waves. She says, "You must come with us now, children."

"Come?" Hava says. He lets go of my hand.

"Yes," the woman says, and lifts her chin.

The other beetle people start to move in, silent like a footstep on the sand.

I see the Lopo sitting on the ground, weaponless. Overtaken. So swiftly, like we have never been able to do for all our attacks and killings. The Lopo just kept coming from across the waters, like fishes spawned from an endless egg.

But now they sit, and can do nothing.

The beetle people are many. Soon they will block our sight of the forest's edge, where Umeneni and the others wait.

But now Hava raises his gun and that is the signal, and all of our twenty soldiers attack.

Though we fire our guns and stab with our knives, the beetle people do not bleed. There are enough of them to keep the Lopo encircled and still bat us away. They flick us away as though their arms are tails and we are nothing but rodents on their backs.

Soon we are all on the ground beneath the daylight of the inbetween creatures. I ache but I don't know how I was hit. I remember lightning, though there is no storm, and the sound of it was louder than a summer-shock. Beside me, Umeneni cradles his wrist in his other hand. It is broken. Some of us cry, little voices in the silence.

But not my brother. He kneels on the ground looking up at the woman. And the lines of his spirit make marks down his cheeks, in red.

The woman's eyes glow like stars.

"You must understand," she says. "You cannot stay here. This world now belongs to the mothers and fathers of these people." She points to the Lopo.

"You say you are our mothers and fathers," Hava spits out. "Then you should help us kill the Lopo. This is *our* village. This is *our* forest. The sands are *our* sands." He drives his fist into the earth. It leaves a mark.

"No," the woman says. "You never should've been here."

She speaks our language, yet I cannot understand her words as they are pressed side by side.

"Where else would we be?" my brother asks.

They have taken our weapons. There is nothing to do but sit.

"You need to be with us," the woman says. "We are of the same blood. Look in my face. The fathers and mothers of the Lopo will come. This is their world now. We were fighting, and had forgotten, but now the fighting is over and we have found you. And you cannot stay here anymore."

"Why not?" Hava says. Almost shouts. For this woman's words are like the wind. As it passes our ears, it makes a noise and yet we cannot hold it.

"We have given this world to the fathers and mothers of the Lopo," the woman says. Her face pinches as if she tastes something bitter, and she looks to the side, toward another beetle person. Not one of them has removed their insect heads. Only her. "The Lopo will never destroy any more of our villages. I come from a village too, but one that sits among the stars. My brothers and sisters—" She motions to the other beetle people who stand so still, and do not bleed or speak. "They were born among the stars. You were not meant to be born here. Your ancestors and the ancestors of these Lopo fought, and fell to this world, and were forgotten amidst the fighting. We fought as well, as you fight them here. But now it is over and now the Lopo are ours. Here they will all be kept."

"But this is *our* village," Hava insists. I can see in the woman's unblinking eyes that somehow she does not understand us either, though we speak the same words. "You talk nonsense!" Hava says. "How are we to believe these words? They are written in the air."

"It's impossible to sit among the stars," I say. "Our blood is of the sand. We walk upon the sand and when we can no longer walk, the waters will wash us away."

But our words fall like crystal grains through our fingers, weightless against these insect kin and their daylight boats.

Another beetle figure steps up and removes the shell of its head. Underneath he is a man with the strong bones of my father. His hair is the dark red of a sunset, like Umeneni's. His face is bare and there is a scar above his right eye that shines like a blade, not like the puckered pink of healing skin.

And his eyes are Hava's eyes. Under the bright lights that push back the night, I can see the spirit of blood in his gaze.

This man says to my brother, "There are more years on this world than what passes when we are among the stars. Do you understand?"

"We will understand if you speak with words that stay together," my brother says. He points to the man's face. "How is it that you have the eyes of blood?"

I do not know why, but I begin to shake.

The man looks down at Hava. He reaches to his hip and I see a knife there, but it is long and glowing, like his eyes. Like Hava's eyes. Red.

He pulls it from his side and I am too far from my brother to warn him, or protect him, and Hava does not move. He watches the blade. I want to cry out. Umeneni lets go of his broken wrist and grabs my hand. He won't let me run ahead again. There is nothing in my grasp but the earth, nothing to fling at these beetle people but my words which they do not understand.

The red-haired man crouches in front of my brother. His black body shines with the light of the false day. He turns his knife blade down and sticks it in the ground. The red glow pools on the brown, as though the earth did bleed.

"You lead your warriors," he says to Hava, "like I lead mine. So now you must lead them to their true home. It is my home too."

My brother is silent for a long moment, looking at the ground. His hair falls forward like a wing and covers his eyes. He has led us through so many battles with the Lopo and never feared. Now he puts his finger into the earth and draws. I step closer to see, but only as far as Umeneni's grip allows. I will not let go. My brother draws a familiar pattern in the earth. It is our forest, the edges of the trees, our shore and the waters.

"This is our home," Hava says, looking up now. Red with strength. "We will not leave it."

I feel Umeneni's hand, how warm it is, surrounding mine.

I feel all the blood of our children, the children we may yet have, waiting to be born but afraid to be spilled. I feel it as though it is growing from the roots of the trees and twining through my bones from the planting of my heels on the ground.

Then the red-eyed man takes the flat of his blade and wipes it across the lines my brother made.

Once.

The blood path of our close futures, gone.

I cannot breathe. There is nothing but silence. Nothing but the smooth step that treads behind the blood. Not even Hava speaks. He is a small body beside the large black shell of this beetle man. He never looked small beside the Lopo.

Around us, blazing with light, the inbetween creatures open up their bellies. Some of the other beetle people begin to walk inside. Most of them surround us and the woman behind the red-eyed man points into the belly, where it shines an unnatural blue.

And I feel it as I feel Umeneni's hand around mine.

My children will never know the warmth of sand beneath their feet.

"Enough of this," the beetle man says. "You are children of our ancestors and you are coming home."

And with the tip of his red knife, he carves it deep into the earth.

THE GODFALL'S CHEMSONG

JEREMIAH TOLBERT

—◆—

The dead expedition member floats on the surface of Kharybdis for days before enough corpse gas escapes that the currents drag him down. His corpse drifts from the shallow reefs into deeper water where he sinks ever downward. He is lost to the total darkness of the abyssal plains. The corpse ends its fall with a gentle splash in the thick benthic sediments.

The body blooms like a flower, releasing an irresistible smell of fresh rot. Life awakens. Strange polychaetes burrow into the body from the benthos, confused at the unusual taste, but the chemistry of life is analogous enough. Skitterlings nervously dart from their burrows and clip away at his wetsuit to get at the flesh inside.

These are only the first to feast. It is not long before even larger scavengers are drawn in.

Muskblue does not *see* the godfall, as it gives off no light. She instead tastes its rot with her filterstalks, feathery organs sensitive to minute changes in chemistry in the water. Muskblue tastes the seascape, the presence of her sisters and their clouds of feisty broodlings. Always and loudest, she tastes the protective chemsong of Mother in the center of their pod, picking over the remains of their last captured godfall.

Muskblue cannot remember the last food she was allowed. The scent of this godfall meat is overwhelming.

She has drifted as far away from the pod as she can bring herself, so far that she risks her life in waters where Mother's chemsong is weak enough that predators might catch Muskblue's own scent or see the subtle flash of her chromatophores. Her transluscent skin provides some protection against the creatures that hunted with reflections of light, but some hunt by taste as she does. The foulness of the chemsong is the only defense against such monsters.

Muskblue has been praying to the Gods for a quick death. Life within the pod is no longer bearable. There can be no life outside the pod. But she will not give her flesh to the pod. Instead, let one of the beasts take her, she decided. Until tasting the godfall.

Muskblue drifts on the low currents, ever closer to the limits of Mother's chemsong, away from her sisters and the clouds of irritating brood, but closer now to the food.

A small cluster of broodlings brush past, taking bites from her without fear. She shudders in pain. Even the stupid broodlings know her lowly status. Muskblue has no broodlings of her own to protect her, no joined mate with which to create them. She is too weak from hunger to even form a small protective chem in the cellular factories that run along her long, emaciated flanks.

Muskblue is always last of the sisters Mother allows to feed. Little but gristle and bone remains, usually. Muskblue has searched her memories of youth, wondering what offense she could have given, but finds none. The pod is large, and someone must be weakest. The Gods have decreed that to be her role.

Now, she tastes for her sisters, waiting to learn if they have sensed this odd new godfall. They are caught up in their gossip and stories. Their flashes of bioluminescent lightspeak are bright and fearless, deep within Mother's chemsong cloud.

She finds more confidence now. Muskblue follows the new taste further away from the chemsong than she has ever risked before. Hunger overrides her fear and suicidal thoughts. There is godfall near! Muskblue greedily grasps for the source of the taste/smell resting on the world's floor.

She runs her four broad, flat arms over the godfall, coiling around it, probing, flushing the taste to her stalks. The godfall is small and shaped differently from every other she has found. It is thin, straight, only three times as long as Muskblue, with two narrow limbs at each end. The meat could feed two of the pod at most—most godfalls could feed the pod for many shifts before Mother led them away in search for another.

She should not eat this meat, even if it is not normal. It tastes edible, delicious, but to feed without Mother's permission is to sin against the Gods. If Mother learns that she has found food and not signalled its location to the pod, Muskblue will be punished severely.

This would make a substantial feast for a solitary individual, she thinks, if she could get past the bad taste. The godfall is stiff and the outside tastes unpalatable, but here and there, she finds holes in the outer surface where the rich taste of meat spills out.

Such an unusual shape, not like the familiar, bulky bodies of godfall. It has no filterstalks, although other scavengers may have picked them away. She thinks the spherical object at one end might be the sense organ—they flesh is more delicate there, like the feathery stalks.

As she tugs at the outer surface, pulling the foul-tasting parts away to expose the meat, a piece slips away, hard, cold, and sharp-tasting. It edge cuts her arm. For a moment, Muskblue panics, releasing a small and weak cloud of chem to mask the blood.

Muskblue leaves the meat aside to inspect the object—it is like the knives that the godfalls sometimes carry. Muskblue hurriedly hides the object in her pouch, coating the hard blade with a protective layer of mucus.

The greatest sin in the eyes of the Gods is to withhold food from one's sisters. The pod will strip her to nothing, cut off her arms and filterstalks and leave her to drift blind in the silent dark. Senseless, unable to control her direction.

But still . . .

No one else has smelled the meat. *Just a little,* she thinks. Enough so she can make chem to protect her from the brood clouds. Just a little, so that perhaps her chem will attract a mindless male from the quiet dark.

She feels a thrill sweep through her at the thought. She imagines tasting his presence as he darts forth, a bright and shining beacon. The sharp sweet pain of him biting her lateral vein and feeding. Just one male, not dozens of mates like Mother—it's all she wants. She could never dream of more stature, but one would be enough for her to give birth to her own brood. Even if they never matured, she could at least feed on them in the lean times as her sisters did.

Muskblue's filterstalks fan out to taste for approaching sisters as she devours the meat. She doesn't mean to eat it all, but it tastes so strange and new that she loses track of time in the sensation. Some parts of the meat are inedible, and she disgorges them. The pieces drift to the Bottom and vanish in the muck. She stirs the muck, hoping the smell will cover the taste of meat.

After a rest to allow digestion, she nervously sprays fresh chem. It is not nearly strong enough to protect from the predators, but its bitterness will shield her from the hungry mouths of the brood clouds. She hurries back into the heart of the pod, before her absence is noted.

She speaks little to her sisters, and they ignore her presence—all except for Tangred, a sister from her own brood, but favored by Mother. Tangred lightspeaks a greeting from a gathering of older sisters, then swims away to meet Muskblue.

"We missed you at the Telling," Tangred says.

"I'm sorry." Muskblue's colors dim with obedient shame. She knows her place, even if the forbidden meat has restored her energy. Tangred's status is greater. "I was too hungry to focus on the stories."

"Sweetviolet told the Banishing tale," Tangred says. "The taste of it was like never before. Such vividness. You would have liked it. It made me ache to understand the Gods."

It does sound like something Muskblue would have liked. She has always loved the sad stories that explain the why of pods, how their ancestors had once lived in the heavens. The Gods had become angry and cast them out from grace and into the Deep Banishment. What Muskblue especially loves are the descriptions of heaven's food. There is meat to be taken everywhere. No Mother could stop a daughter from feeding. No mother needs to, in such bounty.

"Mother noticed your absence and commented on it. You will never rise in status if you continue to catch her attention this way."

"I cannot catch her attention in any other way," Muskblue angrily flashes. "What would you have me do?"

"Such vehemence." Tangred's colors are vibrant and thoughtful. "You seem stronger since last speaking to me. Why/how?"

Muskblue thinks quickly. "It is only my disappointment in not pleasing Mother. There is strength is shame."

"Perhaps. But then what is that unusual taste about you?"

"I don't know what you mean," Muskblue says.

"It is like meat!" Tangred flashes excitedly. "Before, you said you were hungry. Are you hungry no longer?"

"No, no, no," Muskblue flashes more brightly than appropriate.

"The Gods' gifts are for the pod, not one sister," Tangred scolds, but her colors are sympathetic. "If you share your find with me, I will not tell the others."

"There is no more." Muskblue wishes she had not been so greedy. Tangred will not hesitate to use her knowledge of Muskblue's sin to advance in the pod. Mother might reward her with a choice bit of the next godfall for this, enough to make her strong enough to draw another mate.

"I knew it! Your chem is too strong, and my brood does not sting you like usual." Tangred's flash is rapid and dim so the others cannot see. "Where did you find it?"

"At the edge of Mother's chemsong, out near the silence," Muskblue said.

"Are you sure there is nothing left?" Hopeful colors.

Muskblue hesitated. The godfall meat was like no other that she had tasted. She couldn't be sure that some morsel remained. It was much smaller than any other godfall their pod had ever found.

"I don't know," she says.

"Let's search." Tangred swims away from the pod. Muskblue follows obediently. The rush of energy from the meat is already fading, and her despair begins to return.

They drift away as far as they can dare and taste the silence. Once, Muskblue thinks that she senses the flavor of the strange meat again, but it is only an echo. It was unique, and she had kept it all for herself. Guilt at this, but pleasure too. There are few ways to rebel within the pod. Even if Mother never knows what she has done, as she hopes, her sin gives her secret pleasure.

Tangred makes no attempt to hide her disappointment. As they return to the safety of the heavier chemsong, she threatens to reveal Muskblue's sin to the others.

"Have mercy," Muskblue pleads. "I was weak and as thoughtless as a male. I was mad with hunger, sister."

"Perhaps you could give me some trinket to ensure my silence," Tangred says. A jolt of fear strikes as Muskblue wonders if Tangred somehow knows of the knife. Muskblue is relieved that her sister does not ask for it. "A skitterling shell would please me."

Muskblue pretends to reluctantly give over a smooth skitterling carapace from her pouch. Inwardly, she feels triumphant.

As she transfers the shell to Tangred's eager arms, the chemsong suddenly grows loud and sour around them.

"Where have you been, Muskblue?" Mother flashes brightly. Muskblue hurts at the intensity of it. Mother's brood cloud swarms around them, ignoring Muskblue's protective chem to nip her skin. No chem protects against Mother's brood except her own.

"Tasting at the quiet dark," Muskblue lies. "Seeking for godfalls for you."

"Is this true?" Mother asks Tangred. Tangred pauses just long enough to compose her answer—a mistake that Muskblue realizes too late. Mother lashes out with a god's knife, cutting Tangred deeply. Tangred curls up on herself in agony.

"No," Tangred flashes weakly. "Muskblue has sinned."

Suddenly, everything churns and Muskblue is blinded by the activity of so many bodies moving at once. The sisters gather tightly around, called by Mother's furious chemsong.

Mother prods Tangred with her blade again, not yet enough to break her skin. "Tell us more," she demands.

Muskblue thinks to flee. She still has enough food in her that she might survive the effort of escape. But she will not last long alone. There is no leaving the pod. There never has been. A calm descends upon her as she accepts this fate. She knew the risk she took by eating the meat.

Tangred tells the pod in loud flashes of Muskblue's secret feeding. The angry, aghast responses of the sisters choke the water and send the brood clouds scattering in fear. They call for her death.

"Show me your shame," Mother demands. She grasps Muskblue with a massive arm, holding her firmly. Muskblue, flashing colors of absolute obedience, leads Mother and the sisters to the indigestible bits in the mud.

Mother's chemsong becomes thoughtful. She too recognizes the strangeness. For a brief moment, Muskblue hopes that she will declare the meat to not be proper godfall, and except from sinning.

Now her sisters demand to be allowed to devour Muskblue alive, piece by piece, a punishment from the Tellings meant only for those who brought great misfortune to their pods. Muskblue remains silent.

Mother listens to the demands a while. Her chemsong forces silence. She drifts without light, deep in thought for many pulses of current before pronouncing Muskblue's punishment.

"Exile," she says. "For sinning against the pod, Muskblue shall know no chemsong for four shifts. Afterward, she will be accepted back to the pod and forgiven." It is no different from a death sentence, Muskblue knows.

Without the protection of the chemsong, she will not live one shift, let alone four. Her anger flashes bright and into the infrared.

"You would kill me without striking a blow," she says with all the luminescence she can muster. "Bring your god knives at me and do the deed yourself."

Shocked darkness. The chemsong alters to amusement. "A little strange meat and you become interesting, Muskblue. If I had known you had it within you, I might have fed you better. The punishment stands."

Mother glides away, and the sisters follow, filterstalks pointed back to taste if Muskblue attempts to follow. She considers it. It would force them to fight, and perhaps she might tear an arm or two away from a sister. It could give her something to feed upon before the predators descend from above. But what is the point?

Mother's chemsong grows quieter until, for the first time in her life, Muskblue cannot taste it at all. She is alone in the dark quiet. A great shuddering overtakes her. She floats to the muck below, waiting for the end to come. Her mind blanks in the absence of stimulus. No light, no chem, only emptiness.

She thinks of how Tangred betrayed her, despite demanding to share in the sin. It is this memory, this injustice, that stirs Muskblue.

She pours her remaining energy into the strongest chem she can manage, composing elements to formulate notes of toxic structure like Mother's song. It is a basic melody, but beautiful in its simplicity. Muskblue admires her work with awe. Perhaps it will protect her long enough that she can to return to the pod, but only if she does not starve to death first. She must find more food, she realizes.

Muskblue draws the strange, cold knife from her pouch, brushing away the mucus on her filterstalks and recycling the precious protein strings. She wields the knife in her arm and begins to swim just above the plain. In the quiet dark, it is easy to taste even the smallest things.

She hunts skitters. Their hard shells make getting at their meat difficult, but it is something. She feels some strength return after capturing and devouring three.

Some time later, she tastes the presence looming above. The scent drifts down, faint, but in the quiet dark, it is unmistakable. It tastes of death and sharpness and digesting acid. It is unimaginably huge, putting off taste everywhere as it draws near.

Instinctively, Muskblue flares her arms, attempting to increase her size. The beast rushes downward, flashes of incoherent light blazing to disorient her.

Sharp teeth close around an arm. With a jerk, the predator tears away. Simultaneously, Muskblue lashes out with the blade, striking something soft, and feels the blade cut deep. She has wielded knives before in disputes with other pods over godfall. This knife is sharper than any other she has held.

A rush of rich meat juice flares across her filterstalks. She knows that this one blow is all that she will deal—the predator is too fast and it blinds her to its movements with the intense pulses of light.

Another attack does not come. The taste of Muskblue's would-be killer fades into the distance. Perhaps this predator is not accustomed to prey that fights back. She finds grim satisfaction in this.

The stump of her arm trickles blood. The taste disorients her and brings back memories of a young Sourgreen. Sourgreen had been the weakest, before. Mother let her starve until she could no longer swim against the current. She was carried up into the heavens where lightning eels struck. They showered bits of Sourgreen down upon the pod. Muskblue sucked greedily for flesh, as did all her sisters. Little was wasted in the pod.

Muskblue pushes down to the muck and rubs the stump into it. Lancing pain shoots through her body, but the stump grows cold and numb. *This should mask the taste,* she thinks.

She pulls herself along the muck floor like a skitter, moving in the direction of the pod. Her stalks are oriented to the heavens to taste for another attack. She loses track of the time, drifts in and out of memories. The quiet dark calms her now.

She wanders for a shift, tasting faint traces of Mother's chem and little else. A flash in the darkness sends her sprawling flat against the mud. Something small and bright zoomed by, tasting so familiar she cannot believe it.

It is a trick of the quiet dark, she thinks.

When the tiny male darts back and circles her, flashing a pattern of courtship, she chems a more beautiful song than she ever thought she could make. More beautiful even than Mother's. She strings together the organic notes in harmonies never tasted before.

The little male, driven by her chemsong, latches on beneath her arms and bites, just a small jolt of pain, and then they are one. In an explosion of ecstasy, they release sperm and egg all around them.

Muskblue struggles not to devour the eggs, instead following ancient instinct. She draws the eggs one after another into her pouch. Contentment at this, despite her exhaustion.

A mate. A brood, soon too. She never truly believed these things would ever happen for her. The odd godfall has brought a mixture of fortune—she cannot help but feel that it was a message from the Gods, in answer to her prayers.

Later, after the bliss fades, she tastes an unfamiliar chemsong. Another pod swims nearby. It is not one that she recognizes, and she can only guess at the pods strength. She considers approaching and making an offering of peace—there is an ancient Telling regarding the Adopted Daughter. Things did not end well for her in the Telling, but still some pods considered loners a sign of good luck and would accept them. Many others would devour them and move on.

Muskblue grips her god knife and huddles low. She feels the male's body press against her belly. It is a reason to continue, to avoid unnecessary risk. She waits until the chem fades before she continues.

Two more shifts pass without any sight of food. With the male sapping her strength, and so much lost to the birth of the eggs, Muskblue comes to rest in the muck and contemplates the cruel fate the Gods have given her.

To survive, she will have to eat her unhatched young. It will be many, many shifts before she can make more eggs. But if she does not live, she will never make more. The decision should not trouble her as much as it does. It feels like giving in to failure after struggling so long.

Muskblue expels the eggs from her pouch. They float, luminescing softly, tiny sisters and little males growing within already. Sisters do not feel sentiment for their broods. That the strong survive is all that matters in the pod.

Something lands with a soft swoosh in the muck nearby, ruffling her stalks and kicking up a swirl of familiar flavor. The strange godfall taste is thick as chemsong.

Another and another, she can taste the falls. Godfall rains down all around her; the strange new type of meat now mixed with the old gods. Wounded bodies, torn and mutilated, spilling their taste. Lightning eels and other shapes flashing light dart above, in and out of detection among the bulks of meat.

Muskblue imagines what must be happening in the heavens.

The old gods and the new are at war with one another. Perhaps over a godfall from a higher heaven? Waves of new gods strike with their cold blades—the old gods lash with tails, strangle with arms. The battle is surrounded in a glow of light that comes from everywhere at once, illuminating the *shapes* of things, not their tastes. The image comes from some deep recess of her mind.

The Tellings teach that pods came from the heavens. The Gods made the pods and cast them into Banishment to wait for their message. The Gods have never spoken, not in taste or chem or light.

Now they speak with bounty. Muskblue cannot count the number of godfalls around her. It seems as if the meat will never end. What is the message? What are the Gods saying?

Come to us, she thinks. *Here is the strength. Rise to heaven and join us.* The thought does not seem as if it is her own.

Muskblue retrieves her eggs. She feeds ravenously upon the bounty, swelling with fresh gore. As she feeds, she crafts a new chemsong. It tastes of the new meat, of richness and wealth. It is the chemsong of the new godfalls. It speaks of the future and of purpose.

Satiated for the first time, she is ready. She will find her pod and lead her sisters to this feast. And then, they will climb to Heaven and answer the call of the Gods.

FOR THE AGES

ALASTAIR REYNOLDS

It's a terrible and beautiful thing I've done.

I suppose I already had it in mind, when the last uplink came in. Not that I'd come close to voicing the possibility to myself. If I'd been honest about the course I was on, I might well have requested immediate committal to stasis.

The right thing to do, in hindsight. And maybe we'd be on our way home now, back to the gratitude of a thousand worlds. Our house would have crumbled into the sea by the time we got back. But we could always have built a new one, a little further from the headland.

Let me tell you something about myself, while there's still time. These words are being recorded. Even as I speak, my suit's mouse-sized repair robot is engraving them onto the suit's exterior armour. Isolated in this cavern, the suit should be buffeted against the worst excesses of cosmic ray and micro-particle damage. Whether the inscriptions will remain legible, however, or whether in some sense *you've already read them*, I won't begin to speculate. There's been enough of that already, and I'm a little burned out by it all. Deep futurity, billions of years—the ultimate futility of any action, any deed, enduring for the smallest fraction of eternity—it's enough to shrivel the soul. Vashka could handle that kind of thing, but I'm made of less stern stuff.

I am—let's be honest, *was*—a human being, a woman named Nysa. I was born on Pellucid, a world of the Commonwealth. After a happy childhood I had dreams of being a dancer or choreographer. In my teens, however, I showed a striking aptitude for physics. Not many people have the right mental architecture to fully understand momentum trading, but I grasped the slippery fundamentals with a quick, intuitive ease. Rapidly it was made clear to me that I had a duty, an obligation, to the Commonwealth. The encouragement to study propulsion physics was fierce, and I duly submitted.

In truth, it wasn't a hard decision. I would have been one dancer among thousands, struggling for recognition. But as a physicist I was already a singular, bright-burning talent.

It was at the academy that I fell into Vashka's orbit, and eventually in love. Like me, she'd been plucked from obscurity on the basis of a talent. Vashka's brilliance lay in nothing so mundane as the mechanics of space travel, though. She was drawn to the grandest and oldest of the physical disciplines: the study of the origin, structure and destiny of our universe. This project, this entire mission—sponsored by the economies of hundreds of planets, across dozens of solar systems—was her brainchild.

I think of Vashka now, when her hate for me had reached its bitter zenith. We were in Sculptor's conference room, all twelve of the vivified crew, debating the impact of the latest uplink. Through the upsweeping radiation-proof glass of the windows, the pulsar's optical pulses strobe-lit the glittering face of Pebble five times a second. Each pulse sapped angular momentum from the pulsar's rotation. In ten billion years, that little city-sized nugget of degenerate matter would have exhausted its capacity to pulse at all. But it would still be out here, a softly radiating neutron star. In a hundred billion years, much the same would still be true.

"It's not a question of whether we do this," Vashka said, looking at each of us in turn with that peculiar steely gaze of hers. "We have no choice in the matter. It's what we were sent out here to accomplish; what the entire Commonwealth is depending on us to get done. If we turn back now, we may as well not have bothered."

"Even allowing for this latest uplink," Captain Reusel said carefully, "the majority of the symbol chains won't need significant modification. There'll be a few mistakes, a few incorrect assertions. But the overall picture won't be drastically different." Reusel spoke with judicial equanimity, committing herself to neither side until she'd heard all the arguments and had time to weigh them.

"If we knowingly leave errors in the Pebble engravings," Vashka replied, "we'll be doing more harm than if we'd never started."

I coughed by way of interjection. "That's an exaggeration. Our cosmological descendants—the downstream aliens, whoever they are—

will be at least as smart as us, if not more so. They'll be aware that we weren't infallible, and they'll be alert to mistakes. We don't have to get this absolutely, one-hundred per cent correct. We just have to give them a shove in the right direction."

Vashka couldn't mask her disgust. "Or they may be so inflexible in their thinking that they tie themselves in knots trying to reconcile our errors, or decide to throw Pebble away as a lost cause. The point is we don't have to take a chance either way. All we have to do is *get this right*, before we leave. Then we can go home with a clear conscience."

In the run-up to the decision about the latest draft the tension had opened a cleft neither of us was willing to bridge. Vashka, rightly, saw me as the one thing standing between her and the satisfactory completion of the project. In my instinct to caution, my willingness to accept compromise over perfection, I'd shifted from ally to adversary.

We'd stopped sleeping together, restricting our interactions to acrimonious exchanges in the conference room. Beyond that, we had nothing worth saying.

"You won't have a conscience to keep clear, if the cores go critical," I said.

Vashka shot back a look of unbridled spite. "Now who's exaggerating, Nysa?"

Reusel sighed. She hated bickering among her crew, and I knew ours caused her particular hurt. "Estimated time to engrave the new modifications, Loimaa?" The question was directed at the willowy senior technician in matters of planetary sculpture.

"Based on the last round of modifications," Loimaa said, glancing down at hidden numbers, "with both grasers at maximum output . . . thirty thousand orbits, give or take. Around a thousand days."

"Forget it," I said. "That'll take us much too far into the red. I'm already uncomfortable with the existing over-stay."

"Home wouldn't have uplinked the modifications if they didn't mean us to implement them," Vashka said.

"Home don't have realtime data on our engine stability," I countered. "If they did, they'd know that we can't delay our return much longer."

"Things are that critical?" Reusel asked, skepticism and suspicion mingling in her narrowed eyes. "If they were, I trust you'd have let me know by now . . . "

"Of course," I said. "And for the moment things are nominal. We're probably good for another hundred days. But a thousand . . . that's completely out of the question."

By accident or design, *Sculptor*'s starboard engine pod was visible through the conference room windows. I didn't have to ask any of the others to glance at it—their attention was drawn anyway. I imagined what they were thinking. The light spilling from the radiator grids—was it hotter, whiter, than it had been a week ago, a month?

Of course. It couldn't be otherwise, with the momentum debt we'd incurred reaching Pebble. A debt that the universe sought to claw back like a grubby-fingered pawnbroker.

It would, too: one way or the other.

"We could begin the resculpting," Loimaa proposed, looking hesitantly at Vashka for affirmation. "Stop it the moment Nysa gave the word. It wouldn't take more than a few days to clear up shop and begin our return home."

"A few days might still be too much, if the instabilities begin to mount," I said.

"Abandoning the work half-unfinished isn't an option either," Vashka declared. "The corrections are too complex and inter-dependent. We either implement them fully, or not at all."

"I see your point," Reusel said. "At the moment, the Pebble engravings embody errors, incorrect premises and false deductions. But at least there's a degree of internal consistency, however flawed it might be. The sense of an argument, with a beginning, middle and end."

Vashka's nod was cautious. "That's correct. It offends me that we might leave these errors in place, but it's still better than tearing up half the logic chains and leaving before we've restored a coherent narrative."

"Then it's simple," I said, trying hard not to let my satisfaction break through. "The lesser of two evils. Better to leave now, knowing we've left something self-consistent in place, than be forced to bail out halfway through the next draft."

The captain was thoughtful. Her heavy-lidded eyes suggested a fight against profound weariness. "But it would be unfortunate," she said, "to let our sponsors down, if there was a fighting chance of completing this work. Never mind the downstreamers." Alertness snapped into her again. Her attention was on me. "Nysa: I can't take this decision without a comprehensive overview of our engine status. I want to know how the real odds lie." She paused. "We all accepted risks when we volunteered for this mission. *Sculptor* has brought us thousands of light years from home, thousands of years of travel from the friends and loved ones we left behind on our homeworlds."

We nodded. We'd all heard this speech before—it was nothing we didn't know for ourselves—but sometimes the captain felt the need to drill it into us again. As if reminding herself of what we'd already sacrificed.

"Even if we were to commence our return mission now," she went on, "at this moment, it would be to homes, worlds, most of us won't recognise. Yes, they'll reward our return. Yes, they'll do all that they can to make us feel welcome and appreciated. But it will still be a kind of death, for most of us. And we knew that before we stepped aboard." She knitted her fingers together on the table's mirror-black surface. "What I mean to say is, we have already taken the hardest decision, and here we are, still alive, chasing a neutron star out of the galaxy, falling further from the Commonwealth with every passing second. Any decisions we make now must be seen in that light. And I think we must be ready to shoulder further risks."

"Then you've already made up your mind?" I asked, dismayed.

"No, I still want that report. But if the odds are no worse than ninety percent in our favour, we will stay. We will stay and finish Vashka's work. And then we will go home with heads high, knowing we did not shirk this burden."

I nodded. She would have her report. And I hoped very much that the numbers would persuade her against staying.

The neighbourhood of a pulsar, a whirling magnetic neutron star, is no place for anything as fragile as a human being. We should have sent robots, I thought, as I went out for a visual inspection in one of our ridiculously armoured suits. Robots could have completed this work and then self-destructed, instead of worrying about getting back home again. But once Vashka had implanted the idea in their minds, the collective leaders of the Commonwealth had demanded that this grand gesture, this preposterous stab at posterity, be shaped under the guidance of human minds, in close proximity. Ultimately, the Pebble structures might be the last imprint that the human species left on the cosmos. The last forensic trace that we ever existed.

But even this wouldn't last forever.

Why had we come?

It was simple, really. We knew something, a single cosmic truth, one that we had discovered through patient scientific observation. It was one of the oldest pieces of information known to the species, something so elementary, so easily grasped, so familiar to any child, that it seemed self-evidential.

Before the Commonwealth, before our emergence into space, our ancestors had peered into the night sky. They mapped the starry whirlpools of other galaxies, at first mistaking them for nearby nebulae, formations of spiralling gas. Later, their instruments had shown them that galaxies were in fact very distant assemblages of stars, countless billions of them. And these galaxies were located far beyond our own Milky Way, out to the horizon of observations, out to the very edge of the visible universe. They were also receding. Their light was shifted into red, evidence of a universal cosmic expansion.

Backtracking this expansion, our ancestors deduced that the universe must have emerged from a single dimensionless point of spacetime, less than fourteen billion years ago. With a singular absence of poetry they labelled this birth event the Big Bang.

Quite a lot has happened since that discovery. We have settled interstellar space and spread our influence through a wide swathe of the galaxy. Our science is vastly more sophisticated. We don't think of the birth event as a "bang" at all, or even an "event" in the accepted sense. But we continue to preserve the notion that our universe was once infinitely small, infinitely dense, infinitely hot, and that there is no sense in which anything can be said to have happened "before" this eyeblink epoch.

Our Earthbound ancestors made this discovery using telescopes of glass and metal, recording spectral light onto silvery plates activated by crude photochemistry. That they were able to do it at all is a kind of miracle. Of course, it's much, much simpler now. A child, with the right demands, could reveal this truth of cosmic expansion in a single lazy afternoon. The night sky is still aspray with galaxies, and each and every one of them still feels that tug of cosmic expansion.

There's a catch, though. The galaxies aren't just rushing away from each other, like the blasted fragments of a bomb. If they were, then their mutual self-gravity would eventually retard the expansion, perhaps even bring the galaxies crashing in on each other again.

Instead, they're speeding up. Eight billion years into the universe's life, something began to accelerate its expansion. Our ancestors called this influence "dark energy." They measured it long before they had even the sketchiest understanding of what might be motivating it. Our understanding of the underlying physics would be unrecognisable to them, but we still honour their name. And dark energy changes everything. It's the reason we came to this miserable and desolate point in space, around a dense dead star that will soon leave the galaxy altogether.

It's the reason we came to leave Vashka's message, engraved into the crust of a world made of star-fired diamonds.

I circled *Sculptor*, taking care to keep away from the banks of gamma-ray lasers that were even now etching Vashka's patterns. The ship's orange peel orbit brought it over every part of Pebble eventually, the lasers sweeping like spotlights, and when we were done there would be no part of the planet's surface that hadn't been touched. The lasers took the raw diamond of her crust, melting and incinerating it to leave elegant chains of symbolic reasoning, scribed from the sky in canyon-wide lines. The chains of argument formed a winding spiral, quite distinct from the surface track of our orbit. That spiral converged on a single spot on the planetary surface, the entry point to a cavern where the entire statement had been duplicated for safekeeping.

In truth we were finished; had been so for many orbital cycles. What *Sculptor* was doing now was completing the tidying-up exercise after another uplink from home. We were finishing off the ninth draft, and now home wanted us to begin again on the tenth.

We'd left the Commonwealth with what appeared to be a complete, self-consistent statement of physics and cosmology, encoded in terms that ought to be decipherable by any starfaring intelligence. But by the time *Sculptor* arrived, the eager minds back home had had second thoughts. A tweak here, an edit there. The first and second drafts had been simple enough, and there'd been no cause for concern. But by the time we were on the fifth and sixth edits, some of us were having qualms. The changes were progressively more sweeping. We'd had to begin almost completely from scratch—lasering the planet back to a blank canvas before starting over, changing our story. As fluent with physics as I was, the level of encoding had long ago slipped beyond my ready comprehension. I had to take Vashka's word that this was all worthwhile. She seemed to think it was.

But then she would, wouldn't she? This entire project was Vashka's idea. Always a perfectionist, she wasn't going to settle for second best.

The problem was that we couldn't stay here forever. Which was where my own narrow expertise came in.

For thousands of years we've been crossing interstellar space using momentum-exchange drives—long enough that it's easy to think that the technology is routine and safe. For the most part, that's exactly what it is. Give or take a few tens of kilometres per second, the stars and planets of the Commonwealth are all co-moving in the same spiral arm, travelling at the same speed with respect to the galactic core. Interstellar transits proceed without incident. We steal momentum from the universe, but we give it back before the universe gets irritated. The net momentum deficit between a ship starting its journey around one star, and the same ship ending its journey around another, is close enough to zero to make no difference. Momentum—and by extension kinetic energy—has neither been created nor destroyed.

But that's not true here. Because the Pebble and its pulsar are hurtling away from the galaxy at twelve thousand kilometres per second, we haven't actually *stopped*. We started off at zero relative to the Commonwealth, and we're still travelling at a good clip away from it.

Which means that a momentum debt is still waiting to be repaid.

The engines were a dull red when we arrived, but with each day that we *delay* paying that debt, they glow a little more intensely. That's the universe reminding us, in an accumulation of microscopic thermal fluctuations, that we owe it something.

Leave it long enough, and the antimomentum cores will undergo catastrophic implosion.

But that wasn't going to happen today, or tomorrow, or for months in the future. As much as I'd hoped to find some problem or trend that could be used to justify our early departure, nothing was amiss. The cores were progressing according to expectations. Loimaa's thousand days might be a stretch too far, but I had to admit that we were good for at least the next two or three hundred. And if and when the cores started deviating, I'd be able to give Captain Reusel plenty of warning.

That didn't mean I felt easy about it.

Yet I'd turned things over in my head long enough, and knew that twisting the facts, over-stressing the hazards, wasn't an option. Reusel would see through that in a flash.

As would Vashka.

My suit picked up a proximity signal. I used the thrusters to spin around, in time to see another suit looping out from behind *Sculptor*. Like mine, it was an upright armoured bottle with manipulators and steering gear. The ident tag told me exactly who it was.

"Come to talk me into lying?" I asked.

"Not at all. I know you better than that, Nysa. You'd never lie, or read anything into the data that wasn't really there. That would take . . . " Vashka seemed to trail off, as if her thoughts had carried her in a direction she now regretted.

"Imagination?"

"I was going to say, a streak of unprofessionalism that you don't have."

"Yes. I always was the diligent plodder, while you made the wild, intuitive leaps."

"I didn't mean it that way."

"But it's not too far off the mark. Oh, don't worry. I'm not offended. It's basically the truth, after all. I'm very good with fixing engines and making them work a bit better. That's a rare skill, one worth cherishing. But it can't be compared with what you've done, what you've brought into being. No one had ever thought of anything like this before you did, Vashka. It's all yours."

"It was a shared enterprise, Nysa."

"Which wouldn't have happened without your force of will, your imagination."

Vashka took her time in answering. "Until it's done, and we're on our way home, there are more important things to think about than credit and glory."

"Well, I've good news for you. My report will conclude that proceeding with the tenth draft is an acceptable risk. And you're right. It never occurred to me to bend the facts."

"I'm . . . happy," Vashka said, as if she feared a trap in my words.

"It won't be perfection," I added. "It'll be a step in that direction. But don't delude yourself that this is the end. As soon as we're back on Pellucid, you'll be wishing you changed this or deleted that. It's human nature. Or yours, anyway."

"Then perhaps I'll program my stasis berth so that I never wake up."

It was a flip response, something that—had it come from anyone else—I'd have been more than willing to dismiss as bravado. But with Vashka, I was prepared to believe quite the opposite. She would easily choose death over living with the knowledge of irreversible failure.

Always and forever.

"I'd best get back inside," I told her.

The day she first explained it to me we were in our old house, the one we bought together during our time at the academy, the one that overlooked the bay, with the ground floor patio windows flung open to salt-tang sea breezes and hazy morning sunshine. I was doing dance exercises, going through the old motions of stretching and limbering, but still listening to what she said. I'd made the mistake of only half-listening before, nodding in the right places, but from bitter experience I knew that Vashka would always catch me out.

It wasn't that I didn't care. But I had my area of obsession and she had hers, and it was increasingly clear that the two only slightly intersected.

"Dark energy is the killer," she said. "Right now we hardly feel it. It's making all the galaxies accelerate away from each other, but the effect is small enough that people argued over it for a long time before convincing themselves it was real." Vashka was standing at the door, doing stretching exercises of her own. Whereas mine were in the service of art, hers served no higher purpose other than the toning of her body, a maintenance routine to keep the machine in working order.

I knew enough about cosmology to ask the easy questions. "The Milky Way's just one galaxy in the Local Group. Won't the gravitational pull of nearby galaxies always outweigh the repulsion caused by dark energy?"

Her nod was businesslike, as if this objection was no more than she'd anticipated. "That's true enough, and most galaxies are also bound into small groups and clusters. But the gravitational pull *between* groups and clusters is much too weak to resist dark energy over cosmological time. At the moment we can see galaxies and galaxy clusters all the way out to the redshift horizon, but dark energy will keep pushing them over that edge. They'll be redshifted out of our range of view. Nothing in physics can stop that, and there's nothing we can ever do to observe them, once they've passed over the horizon."

"Which won't happen for a hundred billion years."

"So what? That only seems like a long time if you're not thinking cosmologically. The universe is *already* thirteen billion years old, and there are stars now shining that will still be burning nuclear fuel in a hundred billion years."

"Not ours."

"We don't matter. What does is the message we leave to our descendants."

She didn't mean descendants of humanity. She meant the alien beings who would one day supplant us, in whatever remained of the galaxy that far downstream. Carriers of the flame of sentience, if that doesn't sound insufferably pompous.

"Fine," I said. "The dark energy pushes all those galaxies out of sight. But the local group galaxies are still bound."

"That's irrelevant. For a start, they can't be used to detect the expansion of the universe, for the same reason that dark energy doesn't disrupt them—their short range attraction predominates over long range cosmological effects. But it's worse than that. In six or seven billion years, the local group galaxies will have merged with each other, pulled together by gravity. There'll just be a single super-galaxy, where once there was the Milky Way, Andromeda, the Clouds of Magellan, all the other galaxies in our group. This isn't speculation. We've seen galactic mergers across all epochs. We know that this is our fate, and we know that the mixing process will erase the prior histories of all the involved galaxies."

"I accept this," I said. "But if aliens arise in that super-galaxy, tens of billions years from now, they'll have billions of years to consider their situation. Our technological science is a few thousand years old. Isn't it presumptuous of us to assume that they won't be capable of making the same discoveries, given time?"

"Physics says otherwise. There'll be no observable galaxies, other than the one they're inside. They may not even retain the *concept* of a galaxy. All they'll see around their own island universe will be a perfect starless black. And there won't be any easy way for them to measure the expansion of spacetime by other means. The cosmic microwave background will have been redshifted far into the radio frequency, and it'll be a trillion times fainter than it is now. They could send out probes to gauge the effects of expansion, if it even occurred to them, but it would take billions more years for those probes to get far enough out to feel measurable effects." Vashka paused in her work-out. "An unpalatable truth, but truth is what it is. We happen to exist inside a window, a brief moment in the universe's history, in which intelligent creatures have the means to determine that the universe was born, that it has a finite age, that it is expanding. To not know these things is to not know the universe at all. And yet the downstreamers will be unable to determine these absolute fundamentals!

That is why it is our duty, our moral imperative, to send a message from our epoch to theirs."

"This monument you've been talking about."

"I've submitted my ideas to the Legislation. And it'll have to be more than a monument. We can't leave a message on Pellucid, or any other planet orbiting a solar-type star: it'll be incinerated when the star goes red giant. And even if that didn't happen, the galactic merger event will play havoc with stellar dynamics. The best place would be around a star bound to the local group, but on an orbit that will take it far enough out to avoid the convulsions. A bystander. I think I might even have found a candidate."

"You're getting ahead of yourself, if you've only just submitted that proposal."

"There's no point counting on failure, Nysa. If I'm going to see this through to completion, I might as well start working on the details. It's a pulsar, with a planetary companion, on a high-velocity trajectory that will take it far from the Milky Way."

I hardly dared ask the next question. "If we were to go out there, how long would it take to get home again?"

Vashka looked out through the open patio windows, to the headland and the wide sweep of the bay. "If we left now? The fastest ship could get us home again in just under five thousand years. Four, if we could get a little closer to the speed of light. To do that, though—and to make rendezvous with such a fast moving object—we'd need a number of radical breakthroughs in engine design." She shrugged, now that she'd delivered her lure, the hook that would sink its way into me. "Whatever happens, this house will have crumbled into the sea by then. We'll just have to get a new one."

"We?" I asked.

"You'd come with me, Nysa." Vashka closed her eyes, resumed her stretching. "You know you would."

Sculptor swung around Pebble in its endless winding orange peel. Loimaa's gamma-ray lasers were scribing constantly. They scissored and whisked like knitting needles. From the inspection cupola we'd watch their furious industry, mesmerised as the landscape was reshaped to our latest whim. It wasn't simply a question of ablation, boiling diamond away in plumes of atomised carbon. Loimaa's methods were so skilled that she could literally *move mountains*—slicing chunks of diamond here, pushing them there—

and then allowing their interlattice bonds to reform again. She could melt diamond and use shockwaves to compress it back to solidity in a dozen different allotropes. She was carving a world with light.

Days passed. *Sculptor* completed hundreds of orbits. The engines glowed a little hotter from day to day, but the thermal progression was entirely within expectations. To her credit, Captain Reusel still demanded a constant supply of updates, keeping a nervous eye on our status. The ritual was always the same. I'd tell her that nothing untoward had happened, but that I was still uncomfortable with the overstay.

"Objection duly noted," Reusel would say. "But until we've something better to go on than your natural tendency toward pessimism, Nysa, then we keep cutting. You have my word that we'll break orbit the moment things change."

"I hope we have sufficient warning, in that case."

"I'm sorry, Nysa. But we're doing this for the ages. We can't leave it as a botched job, not when there's a chance of getting it right. No one's going to come out here again and correct our mistakes."

I accepted this. I might have not liked it, but I wasn't so self-centred that I couldn't see things from Reusel's viewpoint. She'd been a good and kind-mannered captain and I knew she wasn't one to make snap decisions. In her shoes, I'd probably have done exactly the same thing.

Things thawed between me and Vashka.

Now that she'd got her way, Reusel on her side, she admitted that she'd always understood my position, sympathised with my professional concern for the engines, but felt she had an equally pressing duty to fight her corner over the engravings.

I feigned understanding and forgiveness. It was almost like old times.

"I didn't mean it to turn so bitter," Vashka told me, the last time we slept together. "But you know how it is. We've both given up so much to make it here. It's worth spilling some blood, if that's the difference between perfection and good enough."

"I just wish some of that blood hadn't been mine."

"You know I still love you." She stroked the side of my face with a tenderness that snapped me back to our first days together on Pellucid. "Besides, it's all water under the bridge now. We're well into the tenth draft. It'll be done before you know it."

"Unless another update arrives."

"They wouldn't dare." Vashka declared this with the flat certainty of a believer, not a scientist. "I've studied this iteration, and it really is beautifully self-consistent. There's no scope for improvement. If they sent another draft . . . I'd reject it."

I smiled, although I didn't really believe her.

"Daring of you."

"This one is right. I know it's right. I know when *I'm* right."

"It's always good to have self-belief. I wish I had more of it myself. Perhaps I should have stayed a dancer."

"As a dancer, you died a thousand years ago," Vashka said. "Forgotten and obscure, just another middlingly talented artist on a little blue planet in the Commonwealth. As you, as Nysa the engineer, you're still alive. Still out here. Doing something magnificent. Participating in an act of altruism that will endure across cosmological time."

At that moment I found Captain Reusel's choice of words springing to mind. "For the ages."

"Precisely," Vashka said, pulling me closer, as if everything was and always would be all right. "For the ages."

And for a while it was right, too. Until it hit me what I needed to do.

I'd been outside, making another engine inspection. After dispensing with my suit, I travelled through *Sculptor* to what we still referred to as the "engine room," a name that conjured an archaic, sweating furnace of boilers and pistons, but which was in fact merely a cool, calm control node, isolated far from the fearsome, transgressive physics of the engines themselves. The room was empty when I arrived, as I had expected it to be.

My hands summoned the control interfaces. They sprang into obliging solidity under my touch. My fingers danced, caressing rainbow-coloured keys and sliders. Around me, status graphics swelled for attention. To anyone not schooled in momentum-trading, these squirming, intertwining, multi-dimensional figures would have seemed as strange and unfathomable as deep-sea organisms, engaged in courtship and combat. To my eyes, they signalled chains of branching probability, tangled meshes of counter-intuitive cause and effect. Thermal-kinetic tradeoff matrices, momentum-event spinors, clustered braids of twistor-impulse covariance. Lucid to my eyes, but only just. It still took tremendous concentration to make sense of the entirety. That I could do it at all was the wonder.

Sweat prickled my skin, drying instantly in the room's cool. A necessary wrong was still a wrong. For a moment, I quailed. Perhaps Vashka really was right, and we should see this through.

But no.

There was a mode, a faculty, to push the engines out of their stable operating regime. It was a test function, nothing more. It was meant to be used only in those rare instances when we might want reassurance that the automated safety cut-ins were functioning normally.

The mode could be misused.

I meant only to nudge the engines, to push them a little more into the danger regime. Not enough to endanger us, but enough to be able to demonstrate the glitch to Reusel, to make her think that we were better off cutting our losses now. "Look at that spike," I might say, all plausibility and professional concern. "It's a warning sign. I thought we could hold back the debt longer than this, but the stochastic coupling's evidently running away from us. There was always a chance . . . "

"It's understood," she might say, with a regretful nod, trusting my professional judgement implicitly. "Prep *Sculptor* for immediate departure."

I'd echo the same grave nod. "It's a pity," I'd say, "that Vashka's work won't be finished."

"Vashka will just have to live with imperfection, like the rest of us."

That's not the way it happened, though.

I knew my error as soon as I'd made it. There are no simple mistakes in momentum-trading, but I'd come as close as possible to making one. A slip of inattention, a failure to consider all repercussions. We were in one stability mode, and I'd neglected to remember that the test function would, by default, assume a slightly different one. Much earlier, as part of another, entirely innocent test exercise, I had disabled the safety overrides that would have prevented this mismatch. I could have corrected matters, had I remembered, and still perpetrated my lie. But by the time I did, it was far too late to do anything about it.

Sculptor was going to die. It was going to give back to the universe all the energy it had stolen to get here. The antimomentum cores would surrender their debt in a lightless eruption of transient exotics, imparting a barely measurable kink into the local dark energy distribution. An obligation discharged.

But just as the inward collapse of a denegerate stellar core results in an outward pulse of energy and matter—a supernova—so the failure of the antimomentum cores would have a vastly more visible effect on the rest of *Sculptor* and its contents.

When panic hit me, it was as novel and unanticipated as the kiss from a new lover. All the exercises, all the simulations, had failed to prepare me for this moment. My routines deserted me. As much as it shames me to admit it, I had no instinct other than my immediate self-preservation.

I still had enough presence of mind to warn the crew. "Engine overload!" I shouted, pushing my voice throughout *Sculptor*, using emergency privilege to override any other business, even that of the captain. "Repeat, engine overload! Abandon ship! This is not a drill!"

Even as I knew it wouldn't do any of them the slightest good.

It was different for me. I'd just come back in from outside, and I didn't have far to go to reach the suit I'd only recently vacated. The suit was still warm, and it welcomed me back into its armoured embrace.

Then I left.

With the suit's thrusters on maximum power, I aimed myself at Pebble. With the criticality event in progress, *Sculptor* had automatically shut down its scribing operations, so I didn't have to worry about falling into the path of the gamma-ray lasers. Not, of course, that that would have been a bad way to go. Instantaneous annihilation, as painless as non-existence. A kiss from eternity, then nothing.

But then I wouldn't be here, thinking these thoughts, leaving this testimony.

To survive the death of *Sculptor*—the momentary energy pulse would exceed the neutron star's emissions by a factor of a thousand—I'd need a lot of shielding between me and the ship. There wasn't time to get around the other side of Pebble, to use the planet itself as cover. But there was time to reach the cavern.

I knew even then it wasn't to save me—just buy me enough time for self-reflection. The panic didn't care, though. All that mattered to the panic was the next five minutes.

I followed the spiralling logic-chain to its dark epicentre. With a tap of thruster controls I fell into the hole in the world's crust. Down through the glittering, symbol-lined throat, until the shaft widened and I could finally bring the suit to rest. I aligned myself with the local vertical, and settled down to the floor, taking care that my arrival should not damage any of our finely graven inscriptions. This was our backup policy: a reiteration of the entire external statement, on a much smaller scale. If some unforeseen cosmic process scrubbed Pebble's crust back to a blank canvas, there was still a chance that the engravings in this chamber might endure. Here, in duplicate, was Vashka's cosmological statement. It began near the top of the cavern and wound its way around and down in gorgeous glittering intricacy. Squandering suit power, I drenched it in artificial radiance.

I had to admit that it was quite an achievement. And it would last, too. I didn't doubt that. Whether anyone would ever find it . . . well, that was a different question.

Sometimes, though, you just had to take a gamble.

I've said nearly all that needs to be said, I think. I've been truthful with you, or as truthful as I can be with myself. We came here to do something glorious, and it would be unfair to say that we failed. The ninth draft is complete, after all. You, whoever you might be—however far downstream you may be from us, a hundred or a thousand billion years—will, I'm confident, be able to make absolute sense of our primitive cave-wall scribblings. Because (I'm certain) you'll have been around for a very, very long time, and by the time you stumble on this little diamond cinder, spinning through the dark galactic void, you'll be infinitely cleverer than us. The mistakes we fret about, the errors and inconsistencies, won't trip you up at all. You'll have the wisdom to grasp the shining truth behind our fumblings, and in doing so you'll look on us with a sublime combination of gratitude and pity. Gratitude that we committed this deed, in order to reveal unto you this one cosmological truth that lies forever beyond the reach of even your science.

Pity because you'll see us for what we truly were. Dragonflies who lived and died in the first few heartbeats of creation, leaving no more than a scratch on time.

Vashka's gone now, along with everyone else. But I think she can rest easy. As much as it would have pained her to think that we left the project riddled with mistakes, it was still sufficient for its intended purpose. Vashka was just too close to her work. She always had been, from the moment we met. Always reaching for the unattainable. Me, I'm much more of a pragmatist.

That doesn't mean I'm not open to possibilities, though.

This suit was never designed to keep me alive this long, so I can't be sure that what I'm about to say isn't the result of some gradual neurodegenerative breakdown, caused by the starvation of oxygen to my brain. But the mere fact that I'm able to frame that doubt . . . doesn't that speak to my higher faculties still being more or less intact?

I don't know.

But I can be certain of this much: since I've been in this place, in the chamber, surrounded by Vashka's symbols, I've felt something. Not all the time. Just occasionally. Like a searchlight sweeping through me. A sense of presence, of the numinous. I don't believe in God, so that's not the answer. But I'm prepared to believe in you.

Downstream, however many billions of years that might be, you find this place. You find this cavern, and you find what's left of me, bottled in my suit. A creature you don't recognise, dead so long that generations of stars have come and gone since my demise. I doubt that there's much of me left. Unlike diamond, I'm prone to decay.

On the other hand, I'll be in vacuum, in the cold between the galaxies. So who knows?

These moments of presence, these numinous interludes . . . a skin-crawling sensation of being watched, studied, scrutinised . . . could it really be *you*, at the end of time? Running some kind of scan, for want of a better word, on the relics you find? And the effects of that scan, rippling back in time to me, here, in my suit?

And how do you feel about me, exactly?

I can't imagine that you'll have had much difficulty unravelling the symbols scribed on my suit, and then stitching them into language you understand. Allowing for the gulf of species and time separating us, I'm certain you'll have been able to comprehend the shape of my account. Why we came here, what happened when we arrived. The sordid outline of my crime.

I hope you won't judge me too harshly. I acted out of fear, not malice. I had our best intentions at heart. I just got things slightly wrong, that's all.

The point is, if I'm the only one of us you ever find, please don't taint us all with the flaws that were mine alone. I'll take responsibility for what I was, what I did.

But then the thought occurs.

Why would you need to know at all? These markings aren't indelible. My little mouse-sized robot still has power, and while I'm under no illusions that I'll be dead soon enough, for now I still have some air and life-support, and presumably sufficient intact brain cells to maintain some kind of lucidity.

I wonder if there's time to change my story?

SUN DOGS

BROOKE BOLANDER

Floating through endless night in a tiny silver ball, surrounded by noise and confusion and the overpowering scents of metal and her own push-stink, the dog Laika dreams.

Snow crunches under the pads of her feet, biting at them with tiny unseen fangs. She is running with a pack of others through the cold and the city-smell, claws skittering on slippery hard water. They are all shaggy and long-toothed and their breath makes little clouds in the air. Frost grows a fur coat over Brother's whiskers and nose, like a pup's first layer of down. The cat they are pursuing is just strides ahead, a leap and a shake away from being warm meat between Laika's jaws, when people appear at the mouth of the alleyway holding nooses and sticks.

In the real world, the catch-men had taken everything. In dreams, they are fooled as easily as rabbits. Laika is a smart dog. She grows brown-and-white wings, like a pigeon or a seagull. The other members of her pack follow—Brother's feathers are as black and tangled as the rest of him—and together they fly away, leaving the catch-men empty-handed far below. The cool air lifts Laika up and up. She can smell garbage and fish-gutting places and the sting of salty water, all the wonderful reeks of home. Cat water-stink. The less pleasant odors of tar-coated poles and burning dead things, harsh enough to dull the best nose. They all go to a park with grass and trees and lots of cat push-stink to roll in. The puddles here aren't hard. Laika drinks until her stomach sloshes and water dribbles from the corners of her mouth.

She wakes from the dream needing to make water-stink herself and whines softly when she realizes where she is. The padded ball is her den now, and everything inside her whispers that making stink in one's den is not a thing smart dogs do. But eventually she has to. Nothing else remains. The world through the window is black and empty, marked with tiny faraway gleams that might be the eyes of unknown animals. All the trees and grasses and even the whitecoats have long since vanished in a blur of heat and tumbling, fearful movement.

There's a rubber bag strapped to her hind end, a net of harnesses holding her tightly in place, and a feeling of floating that never disappears no matter how many times she scrabbles at the floor for purchase. It makes her dizzy and sick. Beneath the straps her skin itches, so warm and close it feels like it might split open. She cannot turn around or even circle to make a proper bed.

Laika re-adjusts herself as best she can, closes her eyes, and wishes for brown-and-white wings.

There is no trusting the ball and no understanding it, no more than one can understand the intentions of a whitecoat. Like them, it is neither good nor bad. It emits a constant howl, dispenses food slime, and shakes so terrifyingly that Laika trembles and makes water-stink without thinking. She would curl into a tiny invisible ball if she could, but the chains and the harness hold her in place. All she can do is bark to let the panic out, over and over until her throat hurts and the metal walls echo like she is many.

Her coat reeks of the whiteplace-smells they rubbed her down with before fastening her in the metal ball, painful and numbing to sensitive nostrils. Little bits of plastic are taped here and there, attached to long tails of rubber that hum quietly with strange energy. They make her nervous. *Everything* makes her nervous; she's been scared and panic-bitten almost since the day the catch-men put the noose around her neck. There's always some new terror crouched just beyond her reckoning, waiting to spring in an unseen way.

It had begun with shining crates, slippery and cold-smelling. The whitecoats spoke kindly to her, far gentler than the rough-handed catch-men, and Laika wagged her tail politely, resisting the urge to snap and bite at their hands even when they shaved her fur and poked the bare spots with stinging needles. The loss of Brother gnawed all the fight from Laika. She let them drag her from cage to progressively smaller cage without resistance, and they patted her head and gave her a name and called her good dog. She ignored the other crate-dwellers, even when they screamed and wailed and flew at the bars as she was tugged past, and the whitecoats said she was steady, ignoring the way her limbs shivered and twitched.

Cages and spinning, noise and noise and noise. The whirl-crate had been the worst, like being picked up by the scruff and twirled around by a giant unseen hand. Old food and stinks flew from both of her ends. The whitecoats would pull her out, wash her off, scrabble scratches onto their ever-present papers, and push her back inside the thing to go again. It happened forever, for what seemed like many forevers. The streets and breezes and Brother vanished into the foggy places inside Laika's head, shadowlands where she couldn't smell them to follow.

She does not miss the whitecoats, the whirl-crate, or the noises. She misses the blue blanket from her first cage. She misses chasing pigeons with Brother, the feeling of meat and bone crunching gristle-thick between her teeth.

She dreams about the week one of the whitecoats took her home to stay with his family, grass and blue sky and not a cage in sight. The children scratched her ears and threw sticks for her to bring back—it took her a while to understand what they wanted—and at night she slept on a towel in the kitchen-place beside the stove, breathing in the smells of vegetables and stew. Laika knew it wouldn't last—she had snuffled the treachery before it even rounded the corner—but a part of her yearned for it to go on for as many forevers as it could. Like a puppy she pretended it actually might, right up until they loaded her back into the truck and drove to the waiting metal ball.

In her dreaming, the week never ends. On and on it goes, and Brother is there too, to share the sticks and the stew and the warm fingers scratching just so behind a cocked ear.

The sun is bright against her face. The light chews the tether of her sleep apart and then she's suddenly awake again. Realization creeps in like a mouse stealing kibble, a slow prickling that moves in a wave from the tip of her snout to her rising hackles. Confused as her senses are in this place, Laika understands the feeling. It's a familiar one, an old packmate from her days at the whiteplace.

She is being watched.

The inside of the ball is filled with Laika and the things that hold her down. If so much as a flea was hiding within the tangle of wires and chains she would smell it, sense the movement and the hunger and the tiny pulsing life. When she left the world, nothing rode with her. Now there is a definite *something*. A faint scent of burning that does not come from the ball. Invisible eyes resting on her head, taking in every sneeze and pant.

Laika cannot see whatever it is, but she has no need to. It's there, waiting in the shadows, content for now to merely observe.

Laika and Brother had occasionally come across human-shapes with no smell, usually in abandoned buildings or other forgotten corners of the city. Dogs, too. Like echoes they were nothing but memories of memory, old thoughts drifting smoke-thin through the damp hallways and streets until a gust of wind blew them away. Taking one's scent seemed a cruel thing, for how could one truly *be* without it? This is much the same, but not. It has a smell. She can feel its thoughts bouncing through the walls, *plink-plink-plink*, like the chirps of fluttering bats.

The sensation grows. It gets bigger, and bigger, until Laika's head is pulsing with confusing ideas that are not her own. Pictures of flame and white-hot light flash behind her blinking eyelids. They drive everything else out: Brother, the fear, all her memories of streets and cages and needles and whitecoat-men shoving her roughly into a tiny silver ball. Nothing remains but fire, licking tongues of fire lapping at the darkness like thirsty dogs. It consumes all that Laika is. She throws back her head and lets out a howl, but to her ears it sounds like the crackle and roar of a great blaze. The world is heat and orange glow. Long-legged, four-legged shadows dance and gallop through it, snapping and growling.

All at once, it pulls away. Laika is Laika again, alone in the nothing. Her howl drops to a whimper. The feeling withdraws, leaving her bewildered and mournful and somehow even lonelier than before. She raises her muzzle for a final cry, calling out to a pack that does not exist. It comes from the very bottom of her, the she that resides in her stomach and scent glands.

And from somewhere outside, there is an answer, and a blossoming of white fire in the dark.

Light streams through the bubble-window. Laika finally sees the watcher.

It's a ball of dog-sized, dog-shaped flame and headlamp-glare. Heat ripple crawls along its coat. Rays of light jut ear-and-snout fashion from the place where a head might be. Shadow-rimmed legs stretch down and down into the nothing sky, paddling at the emptiness. It flicks its fiery tail and swims closer to the box, so bright Laika has to squint against the shine.

The hairs on her shoulders and neck bristle again, and a challenge-bark tickles the back of her throat. Is it a predator? Some new whitecoat-trick?

Who are you? her bark asks. *What pack do you run with? Friend or foe? Come closer and I will bite you!* Even the stupidest puppy knows that snapping at fire is foolish, but it's the only defense Laika has. *Speak! Speak speak! Why are you here?*

There's a flash that leaves little dots of darkness skimming across her eyes. When they clear, the dog-thing has fled. The air smells like a fire, crackling somewhere out of sight.

It's almost too hot to breathe. The air burns Laika's insides and dries out her nose. She pants constantly, even in her sleep. No summer she has ever known has been this warm.

Her dreams mix with the awake-time. Noiseless, scentless shapes appear and vanish, looking like great leaping rats or fluttering birds or drifting blue lights. Sometimes the walls of the ball fall away and she's back in the whitecoat's kitchen with a dish of water that fades to fog just as she bends her head to lap. Brother comes to see her once—she knows it's not really Brother, this hollow-eyed, smell-less shadow, but she wants so much to believe—and after that a whitecoat with the head of a dead dog, flies buzzing around its dried gums. She crouches and curls her lip and rattles a warning deep in her throat until it goes again. Knowing the thing is a not-creature makes it no less terrifying. If anything, that simply makes it more wrong.

When green fire blossoms across the ceiling and walls, panic finally overwhelms sense, and Laika screams. The harness pinches clumps of hair from her shoulders. Tubes rip free and float around her like weeds in a river. The flames roll into balls that skitter and spark across her coat, bouncing without scorching, crawling all over her in that same horrible way. She thrashes, froths at the mouth, shrieks and howls and claws at her restraints, a cloud of spittle and loose fur forming around her head. Laika's energy is blazing now, the urge to live tugging at her muscles. Death is a lean and tireless wolf. If she stops for a second it will catch her and tear the meat from her flanks and belly.

Laika fights. She is braver than the whitecoats could have ever guessed.

Two of the sun dogs now, peering through the window at her with whitecoat curiosity. Laika can no longer focus. Her brain is full of heat and humming insects, chewing and scraping and buzz buzz buzzing. Thoughts drift by like soap bubbles, impossible to hold onto. Each breath flutters stale and shallow beneath her ribs. Lifting her lip for a snarl would use more strength than she has left.

They are so bright, full of flickering life that ebbs and flows and throbs. The warmth burning beneath her skin is nothing compared to their glow. An idea cuts through her fever: If she can touch them, reach them, communicate with them somehow, maybe they will pull the heat away, like a big fire pulling a little one within. Slowly, painfully, against the crying out of her energy-sapped body, Laika raises her head. She stretches her muzzle and touches the glass with her nose.

And the brightness sucks her up, sight and hearing and smell, and Laika knows nothing at all.

Everything she has grown accustomed to has vanished. The wires and bags, the harnesses, even the silver ball itself. All have gone in the nervous flick of a tongue. Laika floats in a world of liquid fire, the heart of a great orange sun. Her thoughts are clear now. The fear that buried itself in her skin and fur like a fat burrowing tick is dried up and dead, fallen off somewhere with the rest of the whitecoat things.

She can smell heat, and burning, but it's like paddling through warm water, not uncomfortable at all. A low-pitched sound like many throats singing to the moon hums just within reach of her hearing, endless variations on a harmonious theme. It vibrates deep inside her bones and makes her want to sing along. She wonders what sort of pack lives here to create such songs.

The sun dogs appear in flashes of white and yellow to either side of her. Laika barely has time to yelp before images flood over her, playing through her head like awake-dreams. Suns with pointed muzzles howling a joyful welcome, spewing great flames into the dark. Fields of glowing lights, singing songs of the beginning of the world. The sound she hears is the sun itself baying, accompanied by its many brothers and sisters.

The two are speaking to her, not in the muttered groans of humans, but in the language of her own kind, pictures and thoughts and bits of sense-memory. They send polite images of sniffing and tail-wagging, simple things she can understand. Laika hesitantly returns the gesture and the sun dogs act pleased, jumping about and play-bowing like sunbeams on a wall.

A mystery: How, one asks, did Laika arrive where they found her, drifting alone in a silver ball no bigger than a rock? Was there some purpose to it, some motive she had in mind when first starting out into the nothing? Can they help her reach the place she was going? The worlds the sun dog shows her are confusing jumbles that make no sense to her. The colors and sounds are all wrong, the creatures that live on them fearful and strange beyond smell or any other sensation Laika knows. She shrinks away and the pictures stop. The sun dogs pause courteously, waiting for her to gather the strewn bits of her own memory into something she can exchange.

Laika answers as best she can. City streets: wet, gray, bursting with smells and the noises of gulls and pigeons and people. Brother: shaggy black warmth and the gleam of long white fangs, big and solid and curled around her like a mother protecting a pup. The whiteplace: clean reek, fear reek, cold reek, as close to a nothing-smell as the whitecoats could manage. The whitecoats themselves, difficult to understand as any other world the sun dog showed her.

Tiny, cramped spaces. Shaking and roaring, pressure building in her ears until she cried out in pain and panic. No more grass, no more sun, no more blue sky. If there is a why to any of this, Laika cannot understand it. She gives the sun dogs everything she knows and waits to see if they have answers.

Long moments pad by. Reading the body language of the strangers is difficult, but their sudden silence and stillness make Laika afraid she has offended them somehow. Is something wrong? Will they open their bright teeth and toss her like she's shaken so many rats? She tries to send apologetic pictures of bared bellies and tucked tails. They quickly reassure her that it is not her own actions that bother them, but the ones who sent her there in the first place. Their thoughts now are black and red bursts of confusion and anger, smoldering like coals. Something like a conversation passes between the two, and a decision is made.

The sun dogs present Laika with something she has not had in many forevers. They offer her *choice*.

If revenge is what she wishes, they will punish the whitecoats for their misdeeds. They will take everything from the humans—sight, hearing, even their smell—and leave them stumbling alone in darkness, scentless nothings not even a sharp-nosed hound could track. The marrow they gnaw from bones will taste like fog. The chirping of birds and mice and the trickle of clear water will go unheard. If they roll in carrion, the smell will drift right off their hairless skins. All Laika has to do is ask.

They can give her freedom, too. She will sing the forever-songs alongside them, endless and happy, bright as the sun that once hung in the sky. Her old body will burst into cinders like a log exploding in a blaze, all flame-crackle and burn smell, and the new one that emerges will be fiery, with great flaming wings to carry her wherever she pleases. Laika will have a pack. Brother is lost to her, but she need never be lonely again. There are new trails to follow, new sights to see and sniff and chase, new worlds she needn't be afraid of. All she has to do is wish it so and it will be, as sudden as weeds burning.

Or they could simply send her home. Alone, of course, but back in her world, some place the whitecoats will never find her. Dirt between her toes, frost on her whiskers, and all of this nothing more than a terrible nightmare. All Laika has to do is think the thought.

She considers each in its turn, rolling them over inside her head like a crow with a nut. She gnaws at the marrow of them. But what Laika finally chooses is none of these things. Instead, she sends back an old dream: green grass, a warm kitchen smelling of stew and root vegetables, and Brother stretched out beside her, happy and safe on a battered blue blanket.

HONORARY EARTHLING

NISI SHAWL

Yes, they are cute, *very* cute. And you better believe they know it, too. Who's in charge? Yes, that's Corgis for you. Aren't we lucky Seattle lets dogs ride the bus? I don't think they'd understand if someone were to tell them they couldn't. Probably they would blame me.

Thank you, but you don't need to move anything—well, thank you! I surely do appreciate a chance to sit down. Mighty white of you, as they used to say. . . .

Go ahead; they won't bite. There you—Now, Cookie! You don't mind? Okay, if you're sure—I *have* heard that dog spit's hygienic, that it can kill most germs. You're sure? Awww, looky there! Pattycake, she's usually a bit more standoffish, but she likes you, too. Evidently. Well all righty then!

That's probably why. It may sound silly, but I'll *bet* they can smell them on you, which makes you pretty interesting to their noses. How long since you were with—Years? Light years? Oh, you're making a *funny*! I bet you wish you'd brought them along, especially now you've found out that Metro's set up so they could be riding all around town right with you.

Oh, it's an excellent system! I've lived here most of my life, but I often ride the bus in other towns, when I'm visiting relatives or on a vacation. We have the nicest, most polite bus conductors.

No, of course you didn't have to pay when you got on. When you're coming out of the Ride Free Area, you pay as you're getting out of the bus. Some people say it's so complicated, but that's how I remember it. Oh, are you? Nothing much out here, this late at night, but if those are your directions. Well, certainly, I don't mind holding it for you while you find your change, but let me just switch Cookie's and Pattycake's leads to the other hand—There.

This is it? Here, I'll pull the cord for—Ma'am? Where'd she—Ma'am, you forgot your paper!

Yes, Driver, that was me. But I didn't want this stop—No, nor the next one. I was doing it for that other lady. Well, you must have; she was sitting up here right next to me.

The Vanishing Hitchhiker

Legend: A man bidding his unusual hitchhiker goodbye discovers that she has disappeared. He later learns his mysterious passenger died in that exact location a year earlier.

Variations: Sometimes the ghost is identified through a personal item left behind in the car, or the sweater or coat the driver lent his spectral passenger is found draped over her tombstone. Very rarely, the passenger is identified as an extraterrestrial or a visitor from the future by an obscure joke or pun, or by some otherworldly artifact.

—*www.snopes.com/horrors/ghost/vanish.asp*

Findeverthinyouneeded? Oh. Guess you did. What you tryna say? You change your mind? Okay. Okay, maybe I can answer your—No, I don't. No, I didn't. I—I didn't realize that. You positive they's only on the things for black folks? No, I don't use none a these products myself. Yeah, I do get a discount, but see, but my Big Mama, she's a beautician, so she give me the good stuff, salon formula and all like that.

Well, yeah, I agree. I mean, obviously. I mean, what, white people don't steal nothin? Sure. Ridiculous. Right. Either they oughta put them security tags on *everything*, for whites *and* blacks, or on nothin at all. Uh-huh. I'll tell 'im.

No he ain't. 'Cause it's a Sunday. Sunday night, he got better things to do than hang around in here. Sorry, I don't mean to sound like that. Wartells' all right.

I will. Only, you know. How it is. Yeah, you know.

Be about half an hour. No, I ain't doin nothin after. Goin home; kids gonna be expectin me. Uhhh, no, I rather not. I—Nothin against gays— my younger sister one—but—

Oh. Sorry.

Sorry. I just sorta assumed.... Anyway, that's the genuine gospel truth bout my kids waitin up for me. Little Shinel, she think I can help do her trigonometry.

You could? Well, maybe, then, if you don't have nothin else better to do. And you don't mind waitin? There some chairs for people on the wall by the pharmacy. . . .

. . . Ready? I'ma start turnin out the lights now. Ready? Where you— you still in here? Hey?

Last Days
"The Week in Review"

Sunday, September 20: The week kicks off with a Close Encounter of the Clueful Kind. **Hot Tipper Jacquetta** writes that while finishing her shift at Wartell's on Broadway she was approached by a "ghost woman" who looked "just like me." The spectral twin raised a special spectral fuss about black hair care products tagged with security devices while equivalent products for white folks were apparently available to anyone who felt like a little shoplifting. The ghost woman then offered to help Jacquetta's daughter **Shinel** with her math homework, but disappeared before the harried Wartell's worker could lock up and take her twin home to make good on the offer. "She vanished without a trace," Jacquetta informed *Last Days*, "and I was by the one door the whole time. She couldn't have sneaked out past me—Not possible. It's really weird." Even weirder: later in the week Shinel will ace her trig test, scoring 95 of a possible 100.

'Course I stopped for you. I could tell you were all right. I could just tell. I'm a good judge of character. Car break down? Yeah. Mighta happened to anyone.

You have to watch out, though, around here. Some of the ones that live in this neighborhood, I don't even like to think myself of what they get up to, let alone talk about it. Vainness thy name is woman. Dyein their hair's the least of it. They put holes in themselves, holes right through their bodies in places Jesus never meant 'em to go. How do I—please. I mean, come on, they make certain, they come on out and *tell* you about it, seems as if they *want* you to, you know. . . .

Thanks. 97 Toyota. They made some pretty good vans. Had to paint it white myself. Yeah, I fixed it up nice. Messy back there now, though, can't let you see it. No, don't—no, I said—I'm not hiding *anything*, I—

Sure. Next offramp. We'll get some gas, a bite to eat, stretch our legs a bit, you can lay down a while on—I got a mattress, but I need to kinda straighten things up a minute first—

Meanwhile, what say we listen to some tunes? That box on the floor between us has my tapes. You dig Pink Floyd? The radio works all right but the only thing they have is that rap on most stations. No, the knob next to—no, that's the flashers—Damn! The police are right behind us! Turn it off! You just push the same button you—Right there! Right—No, *push* it! It ain't supposed to come off like that. Try stickin i—Hellfire! They're gonna want us to pull over. I gotta—Gimme that! You—where'd you—Hey! Where'd you go—Where'd he—Oh my God! My God! My—

[BASED ON A TRUE STORY]

FADE IN:

EXT. HIGHWAY—NIGHT

Two dirty white high top sneakers stagger unsteadily along the road's shoulder. Tracked by camera for several steps, they soon exit frame to right.

DISSOLVE TO:

Medium long shot of wrecked white Toyota van lying on its side, presumably on same highway.

FADE TO BLACK:

(No visuals—sirens only)

FAST FADE IN:

EXT. HIGHWAY—NIGHT

Tight focus on wrecked van reflecting flashing lights. Pull back to reveal police and plainclothes examining interior.

OFFICER TOBIAS peers over flashlight beam.

OFFICER TOBIAS
Nope, no sign of any passenger. Maybe they got away same as the driver?

OFFICER RICE
(From off screen) Only one set of tracks, and not much blood....

Sounds of hammering, screech of wrenching metal.

OFFICER ALVAREZ
Awww, no, ugh, god, I—

Sounds of retching, groans, splattering.

OFFICER TOBIAS

What? Alvarez, you okay?

Looking up from his examination of the van's forward compartment, Tobias walks quickly to the van's rear. Camera follows. Head and shoulders shot of him as he views sight that made Alvarez lose her lunch, but we don't see what he does.

Hey, Rice, honey, you wanted blood? Back here.

Rice appears in frame.

OFFICER RICE

Oh Jeezus. Jeezus.

Several short flashes of seminude female form colored in various reds from lights and spilled blood, splayed unnaturally on side-slumped mattress.

No way an accident did this.

OFFICER TOBIAS

Well, it's not a secret now how come the driver fled the scene. . . .

China. Shooting a documentary on global warming and adaptations in aquatic insects. . . . Yes, quite interesting, actually. Because we seem to be living in one of those moments, those junctures in punctuated evolution when the paradigm doesn't just shift, it leaps some chasm formerly supposed to be unbridgeable, or at least only by long eons. And yet—you know, I believe I've come to expect the unexpected. An open mind and all that.

Well, my grandmother, for instance. She was an exceptional woman. Only had a grade-school education, formally speaking, but a special mind, great powers of memorization. Yet, what could she, a black woman, do with mental gifts like that? Whereas I graduated from one Ivy League university and I teach, I'm a tenured professor here at another. Yes, and a black man is president of the United States, let's not forget that.

My point being, who could have foreseen such a set of circumstances? Not she. On the other hand, she never entirely ruled them out. Open-minded. It only shows you.

So, why don't you tell me a little about yourself, then? New here, I take it—I flatter myself that I know all the other academic brothers in this neck of the woods. What's your area? Rather not say? This is a small town; no privacy to speak of, so you might as well—

Really? Cultural anthropology as opposed to forensic or anything like that, I take it. Of course. What was your thesis, then?

Not precisely original—Oh, I don't mean to be rude. Sorry, I shouldn't let my mouth run ahead of my thoughts that way. I don't usually—my excuse, I guess, is that you somehow make me feel as if I could say anything. Almost like talking to myself; that's how I'd put it if anyone pressed me.

What I meant was, the idea that mimicry is pedagogical is merely an outgrowth of the whole "learning-by-doing" philosophy everyone was embracing during the 70s. And its roots are even further in the past, apprenticeships and so on—But you're right, it's always possible to place a new spin on an old idea, and it's certainly not my field . . . .

Oh, "ontology of embeddedness," I like that. Bet your advisors did, too.

Well, it's been a pleasure, but this is my block here, and—Oh, I'll be fine. Don't let the cane fool you. Besides, I'm sure the shuttle driver is perfectly capable of helping me, and after all, it's what she's paid for. Well, if you insist. . . .

Yes, just the two, that black one with the wheels and the duffle bag with the dragon embroidered on the side . . . Anywhere there on the porch will do, thanks.

Hey! Wait! Hey! Can you believe that? She simply drove off and left you here! Must think because we're both African American we live in the same house, like we're related or—Racism, pure racism. All it is. Can't say it's anything else. Well.

Well, now what? Why don't you come on in, use my phone, call a cab? No, no trouble. Honestly.

It—it seems to be stuck. No, this is the right key, turns in the lock. It's the damn door. Pardon my French. Frame must've warped in the heat—I've been away all summer and, well, I apologize. I don't know what to say, I'm so embarrassed. I was only attempting to help you and—but I'm sorry. No, you don't need to stay any longer, though how you're going to get home, I have no idea—and your luggage—Well, you could *try* it. If you want a running start, I'll—let me stand back here and—all right. Have at it!

Thank goodness! I don't mind telling you, it's been a long day. A long trip. I've really, really been looking forward to sitting down in my kitchen with a nice cold beer. Come on in. You're welcome to share.

• • •

http://theangryblackwoman.com/chipgate
No comment needed, but be my guest

Posted by: Great Joukoujou
Category: Angry at the Police
September 27, 2009

8 comments

A man's home is his castle. Unless you're black.

If you haven't heard about this one yet, [link] here's a fairly objective account[end link]. Basically, Harvard Professor Harold Woolrich was arrested for breaking into his own home. Chip, as his friends call him, is 60 years old and walks with a cane, but they had the nerve to **handcuff** the man. And lock him in a cell.

Like the Cambridge cops would do that to any **white** professor.

Tags: Woolrich arrest, Harold Woolrich, racial profiling
8 comments
Share, Save, or Send

Lady Dane: Sometimes I am ashamed of my people.

browbomber: Man, I heard of driving while black, but this is the first time I know of someone got arrested for drinking a beer in their own kitchen while black. What next, watching Saturday morning cartoons while black? They gonna start draggin off little black boys and girls?

Priorities: Profiling is okay when it's scary neegrows with imaginary friends.

Parallax: Right, what was that about that second beer sitting across the table from him? And the neighbor who called the cops in the first place, she said there were two African American men breaking and entering. Scarier in groups than by theyselves.

FanFan: Lucky they didn't put him in a straight jacket.

currious: [link]Charges have been dropped[end link]. Not that this isn't still completely appalling.

FanFan: Specially since the idiot that arrested Chip [link]refuses to apologize[end link]!

Parallax: Yeah, the cop claims Chip was tryin to weasel out of the charges by pleadin insanity.

Leave a Reply
Submit Comment

'Course I stopped for you. That's one of the best parts of having a car: getting to give people rides. Not so long since I was out there thumbing myself. Don't you think it's kinda dangerous for a woman at night all by herself? Yeah, and I did have some close calls.

A musician. That's what all the equipment back there is about: keyboard—a Clavinet, actually; bass guitar—

Oh, you mean, "What *am* I?" Adopted. Not sure.

That right? You kidding? You too? That's crazy!

Well, I do sort of see a resemblance, now you mention it. Have you ever figured out what *your* background is? Absolutely no clue, but, well I used to have all these wild theories. Indians: Sioux? Kiowa? Cree? Or I always wondered about maybe some of the Alaska tribes. Or Chinese, Japanese . . . .

Wow. What were the chances we'd run into each other this way, I'd see you hitching and pick you up? Just, wow.

We might even have the same parents. Hey, you ever, you know, gotten into music? Singing, or you play an instrument maybe? That box down by your feet has a bunch of harmonicas in it, if you wanna—Well even if you haven't before, they're fairly easy to get the hang of.

Take your pick. Okay, hand me one, I'll show you a couple tricks. Aw, come on, you gotta at least try. Put it in your mouth like this—right—and breathe. In is one note and out is another—each of those little holes—Good!

Awright, here we go. I'll lead, and you follow and copy me:

"You get a line, I'll get a pole, honey;

You get a line, I'll get a pole, babe;"

Nice! You catch on fast! Next chorus we'll have to institute us some harmonies.

"You get a line, I'll get a pole;

We'll go down to the crawdad hole;

Honey, sugar baby mine."

SHALLOT

SAMANTHA HENDERSON

"Oh—the Lady!"

Little-Ghu stared dreamily across the water at the small, triangular islet with its queer castle, and Michael laughed, chunks of green apple falling from his mouth. The three boys lay on the stubble of the newly-mown barley field, watching the river twinkle.

"I saw her fall," offered Cam, although he could not be sure.

"Ha! 'Twas long before your dam was bred that *she* fell. A hundred year ago."

Cam scratched his head. Michael usually had the right of it, but he did have the dim impression of a streak of green like the stories the Friar told of a comet, and the taint of burning air, and the island flaring emerald for a day, and all the sheep dead. But maybe it was the stories the old men told.

"My Da said she's always been here," Michael continued, "and the star an angel falling to her. He said the King's Men should burn all down, burn all black, and send her back to Hell."

Little-Ghu had not stopped staring across the water. "I saw her eyes, once."

Michael stopped. Little-Ghu was crazy enough to be telling the truth. Little-Ghu could toss fifty bales without sweat and lift a fallen log to rescue a kitten. He was slow to anger and slower of thought; he liked to taste the goat cheese before it was ripe, although his belly hurt each time; he never lied.

"Summer, when the river were low," he went on. "There's a bar down o'er, in the narrows where the boats don' go, and I waded across."

"Strewth!" They were entranced and horrified. They say that those who touch the isle will die of sores and the wasting-sickness. And Big-Ghu would beat his son, no doubt.

"Was she fair as the Queen?" said Cam. It mattered not that none had seen the Queen. They all knew a Queen must, by definition, be fair. Little-Ghu shuddered.

"Her eyes were all I saw, and that was enough. And hair, I think, black and long. I crept to that window, yonder, and looked inside, and she was there. She looked at me, straight on. Huge yes, they were, black as sloes. I think I should go mad if I should see the rest."

"Will ye be her knight then, and go her service?" teased Michael. But Little-Ghu was beyond him, staring at the wall, the parapets.

"The Lady, the Lady," he muttered, all entranced.

Her eyes indeed were large, and dark, and shiny. Little-Ghu was mistaken quite about the hair, for she had none, nor needed none, nor gave it any thought. And she had done more than look at him through the bubbled windows of her chamber, although Little-Ghu remembered it not. He was her man indeed.

Call him back.

They were open, this race, their minds open and smooth, ready to be planted. As the boy crept about the hive she'd sensed him and waited. His face, white and startled and doughy; his mind, white and startled and doughy. It was little effort to hold him there and probe within. How strange that their minds were all in one place, inside their brainmeat, and in no other time but the present. He stared at her, unresisting, as she prodded.

Castle, she understood; she learned it from the brainmeats that foraged about the fields to either side. *Castle* meant stone, and fighting, and the storage of *grain*. Curious, she unraveled the word where it lived inside this boy, and found more—towers, and flags snapping in the breeze, jewels and velvets, proud men on horses. He'd watched it all go by with the taste of green apple on his tongue and the print of his father's belt warm on his back, for malingering. Inside the tangle of *Castle* she found another, *Lady*, and there was a song with this one. Crude and crippled, but a song nonetheless, that wove so deeply within the word *Lady* that she couldn't tease them apart. Here's where the jewels and the velvets lived, and the smell of spice and oranges, and a hand lain for an instant on an armored shoulder. She didn't understand, but the song gave it a form and sense she could taste and ponder.

The boy outside the rough glass was shaking. She searched behind his eye and found the nerve, found the little image of herself, delicate as a wax bubble and tucked it into the word *Lady*. And then she sent him home, primed for her call.

Time to call him back.

All sterile, all. The egg-cradles she had woven in careful tiers from floor to ceiling of her high tower, useless. Their heavy round burdens, naught but shell and fluid. Nothing quickened there. Almost useless to try, anyway, but all she could do, without the Intersect to tup her there; the yolk would rarely quicken without, strange and charmed, another's matter. And the Intersect had failed to meet her here, had diverged so slight, so deadly on the path and as she/shem blazed, safe but lonely, onto the blessed isle he/hem crashed, imploded, out-then-in, toppling *pines, they were, fair tall pines of Russia* in a fragrant burst of balsam, somewhere else entirely, sometime else entirely. Somewhere out of the blossoming river of time, a cry, implosion, then silence. The Intersect was bound to her—they would not send another. They would dismiss this place, this time as flawed and invest resource and breeders elsewhere, only checking here and there to see if she, against odds, had succeeded.

She crashed alone, and while her nets embraced her, the ship that was her/she that was the ship blossomed like a flower and plunged its petals deep into the strange soils, tasting it and grain by grain building her hive, high and hollow, ready for eggs doomed never to quicken, while the four brief seasons of this world faded one to other, green to gold to white to pale green eleven, twenty-two, thirty-three times round.

There was a bare chance they'd ripe on their own, although the offspring were headblind and crippled the line might continue and strengthen. And there were other ways, born of desperation. She would not quit now.

So she called Little-Ghu back to her, and in cooling autumn night he went through the shorn fields, waded-then-swam the swollen waters and dragged himself on her shores, half-drowned. Doors opened for him and closed behind, and the spirits of the air whispered in the frigid air of the castle while he knelt before his Lady.

A hand that was not a hand snaked down to stroke Little-Ghu's cheek. Delicate claws shredded away his tattered shirt and teased away the epidermis, raveled apart the muscle fibers underneath. All the while he was still, drowning in a song of cinnamon and clove, eyes shut tight.

It does not hurt. It does not hurt. I am your Lady.

Planted, one by one, like peas in a hole, tucked between the red and white, fiber and fascia, grain in the furrow, spores on the mud. Naught to do but wait, now, and pray that her germ cells would find something in his to batten on.

Over the hill they rode, following the riverbank, Bedwyr and Cai and Gwalchmai and Caradoc—Lance du Lac brightest of them all, down the river to Camelot, while the autumn sun spilled like a broken yoke over the trees and fields and touched their shoulders with gold. Michael and Cam watched them from the crotch of an ash; Little-Ghu was home, sick. His back was a nightmare of sores and pustules, his sister said, and midwife and priest were called regardless of cost.

"Bedwyr fought the giants of Wales," said Cam. "And killed a dozen. I'm going to run and 'prentice to a squire, I am."

"Will he die?" said Michael, still thinking on Little-Ghu.

"Oh, aye," said Cam, still staring and dreaming of horse and giants and the rolling hills of Wales.

It was the secret pleasure and sin of Padre Thomas to walk past the rim of the green fields, where the wheat blackened sometimes where the island curved: the demon's isle, they called it sometimes. The Demon of Shallot, that some called the Lady, and some *la Belle*. He knew she didn't fall from Heaven. He knew she must be devil-spawn. But she'd been there since he was in bum-rags, and was part of the land's inheritance, was she not? And he must admit, when he walked beside Shallot, he grew accustomed, even desirous of the tickle in his brain, the curious, questing inquiry from that presence.

What strange songs you sing, it—she, perhaps—had said once, halting him in his tracks. *Alpha, and omega, and three-no-four, three-no-four.*

And he'd smiled, then frowned and turned aside, hurrying home, but returned to the path the next day, and let the mind move in his, longing for that strong-thewed tickle.

Three things are never satisfied, she echoed at him. *And one is Sheol, the empty womb.*

The grave, he echoed back, *Sheol is the grave. The grave, the womb, the earth for water, the fire for everything. There are four.*

Three, the demon returned. *Your own song says three.*

• • •

From the island, she watched them too, her webs rent about her. The last eggs, those she'd planted with some of the boy's queer proteins, lay with their tops sheared off, their contents inert.

She did not despair. Her race did not despair.

Sheol.

The empty womb.

Years since a boat spun about from upstream and beached at the island, moving up and down with the tides, never enough to break free. She watched it, sometimes, when the waters were high and rain fell and no brainmeats came for days.

Now she gathered a crook-ful of the torn webbing-material and wet it, and spun it, and caressed it, and molded it, and took of herself within it, and presently it was glass-thick and glass-solid, opaque and delicately colored, a mask in the shape of a woman's face, framed by the song in Lance du Lac's head.

The waters were medium-low and calm. Without looking back at the destroyed nest, the dead eggs, she clutched the mask to her and broke her seals; the wall shivered and fell open, and she breathed the outside air at last, heavy and thick with pollen, with the chaff of wheat fields, with the mold of the stream, with the microbes that already were eagerly feeding on her. Quick, quick, there was no time to lose, and she loosened the little boat from its place and spread her silks upon it and, as it bobbed dangerously, lay down with the mask over her face-tendrils, her large gleaming eyes.

The craft bobbed uncertainly, as if reluctant to leave its longtime home, then nosed out into the stream until a current caught it, and it arrowed downstream, and she lay and watched the sky and felt herself decay.

Little-Ghu felt no pain as he lay on his belly on the rough blankets, as Padre Thomas and witch-Mary picked at the boils on his back, which burst open one by one. Small headless creatures coiled within each one, mostly still but some stirred, and these the priest and the midwife crushed, quickly between their thumbs, and dropped into a bucket of vinegar-wine. They had looked at each other, priest and witch, bonded in horror as the little parasites burst forth from the flesh beneath their hands, dozens of little demons.

The islet shall burn, thought Thomas as he tried not to listen to the boys tuneless, blissful humming as he lay under their hands. *Tomorrow, it will burn, and the Sheol-thing with it.*

Outside Big-Ghu stood by a great gnarled oak, half-live and half-rotted out. As he heard the priest exclaim once, involuntarily, he struck the pulpy wood with his ham-fist, filling the air with wood-dust and fracturing one of his fingers.

The little boat was caught on the rushes midstream; Lance watched, frowning as it rotated and broke free. It was leaky and floated half-submerged under its burden.

The Court had spilled out, in the warm twilight, to the decking where the water lapped beneath, the women trailing rich fabrics on the rough wood, the men sleepy with wine. Some joined him in watching the derelict bump along the piers, until it came to rest on a snag beneath them and all gasped in wonder at the woman inside, dead and fair as glass. Some of the women, too, came to see, and a dozen songs were hatched in their brainmeats, could but She, Sheol hear them.

Lance crouched low and fit two fingers under the edge of the mask, thinking as he did that he shouldn't, trying to stop his own impulsive movement but he couldn't; he pulled it back as one would tear a scab away from a half-healed wound. He rose and stood, staring, the mask dangling from his hand and it seemed to those who stood a ways back that Lance du Lac, the perfect knight, had torn the very face from a beautiful lady. And then the mask fell from his fingers and shattered on the decking.

One fragment spun away and came to rest at the feet of the Queen where she stood at the lip of the doorway—a staring glass eye and the start of the curve of the bridge of the nose. The broken edge glinted sharp and harsh, the surface was matte and crushed with something clear and viscous. The Queen shuddered and stepped back. Most rare, puissant, noble, false-called the perfect knight. Love turned fetid in her throat—she hated him now. A horrid kind of pity, a sister-feeling blossomed in her for a moment, and then she kicked the fragment away with an embroidered slipper and fled inside.

Lance looked down into liquid horror; what remained of features that had never been human were rapidly dissolving into a pool that settled in the bottom of the sinking boat. As the bilge overcame there was a tiny *pop*, a burst of spores that blossomed over the surface, and never reached the decking—ineffective, they fell back against the water, speckling it like pollen. Far away, Padre Thomas wept and did not know why, and the small slimy thing in his palm convulsed and moved no more.

Later, when the boat had sunk to bottom and only a rotted plank and a greasy swirl remained on the surface, none was left to see: inside the hall there was dancing and the blaze of candles to make the women's gowns more golden than before, and the gems to shine like fire.

THE BOY WHO LEARNED HOW TO SHUDDER

SONYA TAAFFE

✦

She doesn't say, *Hold still.* She doesn't say, *This won't hurt a bit.* She says, "You must be very careful," and you can hear how much even that single sentence costs her to say. Her armor is not her silence, but her mouth was never fashioned for this unwieldy, spoken speech.

All her vowels are hollow, windy as bone flutes; arid clicks for consonants, tooth-clacks, twig-cracks; the unstrung skeletons of words. Her claws resettle at your temples, trace needlepoint into your hair, and you remember for the fifth or fifteenth or five hundredth time that you didn't have to come here. Because who was it decided xenofolklore was a hitherto unexploited field of study in which a fearless woman's name could be made? Who was it determined that to collect love-riddles from the Askiothe and the untold epics from the Hannenerenti was too uncomplicated—not difficult, not alien enough? *No, of course I don't know their stories,* Haskif had said. His face was invisible behind his winter mask, but he spoke with the same blank disbelief as if you had propositioned his mother; his hinged, snake-spined hands moved restlessly on the tabletop, some courteous gesture you had never bothered to pick up. Then, as resignedly cosmopolitan as a proper student of Eswith, he had explained, *They don't . . . tell stories. Not even to the xenolings. They've been literate since before the Settlement, but they only use it for economics, politics, legal documents. Not for narrative, not as you'd define it. It's supposed to be a cult. Or a form of sex,* and the uncharacteristically prudish twist of his shoulders surprised you. *Some of the phils are supposed to like it . . . And* whether you understood the fine reverberation beneath your skin, ice and brandy, the clench of adrenaline low in your belly, or whether you only imagined that curiosity and ambition leaped up in your story-hunter's veins, you answered, *Well, it's worth checking out, isn't it?*

So you never came to her ice-locked, sulfur-geysered homeworld, beneath the crisscross orbits of its cold, asteroidal satellites and the distant light of its double sun, nor to a diplomatic enclave on some warmer, more cordial world, where an academic might mingle respectably with artists and ombudsmen, but to this small room in a district so bristling and bizarre that its first glimpse through the flyer's windshield looked to you like a medieval hellscape, an industrial transcension. *She'll turn you to stone*, clattered the Tkikst man who took your money, the transfer whose secure anonymity had cost more than its newmarket worth; up the stairs in their geofluorescent glimmer, dry-mouthed, notepod in your shirt pocket like a talisman. There once was a boy who did not know how to shudder, so he went to the gates of hell itself to see if the Devil could frighten him. So you sit cross-legged on the platformed corner where she sleeps within these walls of streaked and fibrous metal, that might replicate the comforts of home and might only serve to keep out the wind and the rain that always smells like iron filings, and the shadows sting your eyes. And not once have you reached for your notepod since she let you open her door; since you saw her for the first time, the storyteller, the priestess, the whore.

Because she does look like Medusa, if Medusa had been stripped out of volcanic rock with teeth and fingernails, unpolished and abandoned to weather for millennia until some unmerciful god's hand stirred her to life again, but she moves as fluently and serpentine as oil sheened on the skin of water. Even after all the research, so much about her still canceled out your expectations: the sweatless warmth of her skin, high-summer asphalt and heavy latex, so lean and resilient where you anticipated fossilized bone; the thousand facets of her eyes, where this ammoniac light splinters and splits to recognizable colors. The stiletto thorns at wrist and heel and elbow are each tipped with iridescence now. And like a fallen halo around her face that could never be mistaken for human, so incomprehensible that it ceases to terrify, or so terrifying that it becomes remote, drift the tendrils that make up her species' nickname: the radulae budded at each end do not look, after all, so different from snakes' heads.

Where her forehead presses against yours, pain seeps in slow sparks; but the toxins injected by the fine spines above her brows, brittle as hairs, hook-tipped like burrs or stingers, are already pulling the pain into vague strands and haze and you would remember all their names, which are biochemical and which are retroviral, if you were not so distracted. *I know the risks,* you told Haskif. *I understand,* you told her, *I consent.* One basalt-black dewclaw brushes your cheek, as she shifts her hands; the shiver that chills down your spine is enough to catch the unprotected flesh on its scalpel tip, and now you are bleeding. Almost, you pull from her grasp, stumble drunkenly down the stairs and out through the boil of neon where the Tkikst doorkeeper waits, hail a flyer or a diesel in the rain-ruined night and someone else can make their reputation on perversions and rumors and sacramental profanities. You'll toss and burn in bloody fevers and sleepless delirium for weeks, but you have waited out worse addictions before.

You lift your hands from your lap, and gently place your palms to either side of her unreal face. And now the blood laces down the insides of your wrists, from barb-nipped fingers and spur-pricked palms, and the toxins have begun to take your dreams apart.

She doesn't say, *It's okay,* because it's not. She doesn't say, *This is what you asked for,* because it's not. She is in a place where words are not spoken, and all her instruction would not avail you, either way. But you make your numbed lips move, your deadweight tongue, and through drowning prisms and saliva, you whisper, "I'm always careful with stories." And you imagine this amuses her, as the tendrils nudge against your skull, twining through your hair and rasping at your scalp, as gentle as cat's tongues, as inexorable as erosion; as the stories that she tells start to burrow their way inside.

Out of the maelstrom at whose still center she crouches, while the world rounds off its corners turning always toward the day, always toward the dark, and she straddles dawn and twilight as one: the drum-rattle of rain and caustic shadow, and once a year the ghosts come up to smell the incense. Your last semester at Eswith, you transcribed ten variants of a morality joke from Taih in which a woman attends her own funeral only to find that the coffin was empty all along. *Because she couldn't wait,* you explained to Haskif, thumbing in annotations as you talked, *her dead self wasn't there to be reclaimed. There's a version in which now she'll never die, and another where her children put her into the coffin while still she's alive, instead, and sink it in nVehya Bay. Then her name can be spoken.* Beneath summer's split-reed fretwork, his face shifted wryly. *Are you sure? I always thought it meant, you never die when you expect to . . .* You blink grit-sticky lashes, the sourness of consciousness and this buzz and staggered blur inside your skull that would be a sledgehammer if not for some guardian poison of hers: slumped like a ragdoll where she sleeps, hard and comfortless to your thinly-clothed bones; and one night you fancied that she curled beside you, thorned and plated like a chitinous dragon around its maiden prize, but you are no longer innocent of her. All these days and hours you paid for, whose full value she will not withhold. By now, the blood has dreadlocked into your hair.

So you lapse and float in her paralytic dreams, drowned in the telling to which all your memories lead. Fragments and scenes snagged past in the abyss, and sometimes it's polluted oxygen in your lungs and sometimes methane snow, and sometimes the molten earth itself tumbles over you, geological undertow, dragged down to an underworld of shadow faces, white-lipped, sewn-eyed, whose bones build their own lintels and roofs. These alleywalks through cities whose architecture clambers up into desert-colored skies, bruised off into haze and daystars half-glimpsed like peeks through a keyhole; the moist, acrid scent of cloverleafed catacombs, rubble-walled, arches crusted with niter and minerals that shimmer in traceries like a peacock's throat. Volcanism coughs up ropes of white-hot lava and the frostbitten dunes convulse underfoot. Your bones dissolve in fire. And she whispers, or she sings, or her words are written inside your eyelids in the copperplate of galaxies and crystal proliferation: down the helices of metamorphosis, she draws you deeper in. Once you struggled awake, sweat-drenched, strychnine-muscled, sicker than hangover and still clinging to those last siren strands, to find her kneeling before the little niche dented into the wall that even a thoughtful ethnologist might have taken for a household shrine—but now you know what she prays to, and it's not those shapeless keepsakes. You know her pack-ice wastes and a midnight sky glittering with sickle moons. You have seen the world-belt of the launch docks and sunrises like a conjurer's coin trick. The oceans move slow, and black, and endlessly freeze to the stars.

"If I tilt my head," you murmur up to her, slurred like a swirl down the drain, mouth too slipshod for a smile, nerveless fingers, "it'll all spill out . . . " And you mean planets dropped like pearls of blood from your ear, marbles rolled noisily across the scratched pie-plate floor, but the game that comes first to mind is played with counters of razor-edged keratin incised in a base twelve system, and if you too were made from obsidian and nematocysts, you could recite the name and lineage of the hero who once staked her life and her lover's mind on the fall of those tetrahedral dice. But their firstborn died in fire and airless cold, betrayed by his dearest companions and the mothers of his child, and his vacuum-dried skull still drifts elliptically between the moons named for the grave-washer and the bone-eater: himself an unmoored satellite, an exile in the underworld that lies between planets and systems and galactic rims . . .

On the bitten tip of your tongue are their names you don't repeat: neither blasphemy nor unpronounceable, but futile. Echoes and travesty; potsherds and ash. And the small, faded voice of reason, like a wraith of distant Haskif, practical, professional, reminding you that if you can't reproduce the stories outside their original medium, published and analyzed and pinned down for comparison, ten different versions of a ta'nTaib joke, the scansion of oracles in Collective Ciriir, then your whole rationale is up in flames. *Call me, please, if* anything *happens,* and not because of the way his willowbark hair gathered over his mask-ties, not because you had heard your first love-riddles from him, but because he loved stories too, you did promise. But you reach up with a shaky, blood-flecked hand, stare for a moment at her spiny face framed where the ceiling and the wall come together at odd, rusted angles: the slipped-gear laws of geometry on this hall, or the unremarkable world only looks askew after all that time in the landscapes of her tales. When the young fisherman opened the chest, all the years that he had spent in the otherworld leaped out onto him, and in that moment his hair withered white and his face fell into wrinkles and he was an old, old, dying man in the house of his great-grandchildren: a century had passed in a night. The minute you found out where she was, when the Praznish tagger handed back the address and grinned liplessly in the screenlight and you snapped, hot-faced, *It's not like that*—maybe all stories are lies, but you should have known that if you ever came home, you'd have changed in more than years.

She doesn't make a sound as your sting-blistered fingertips touch her chin, but she bends forward and the whipsnake coils of her tendrils slide restlessly on the air. With a delicacy that still amazes you, neither clinical nor casual, she parts your matted hair with the claws of one hand and closes the other lightly around your throat. Slivers of light break on her shoulders, the ridge and hollow of tendons beneath her sun-and-stone skin. Your bloodstream must be filled up with her already, saturated stiff;

her dreams are crystallizing from your pores and you whisper, "Tell me another."

She poured cold water down his back, as he slept by her side in their royal marriage-bed, because who else should a princess marry but a hero so brave he does not know how to shudder? Who can look the Devil in the eye, unafraid, because he doesn't yet know how much there is to fear, whom hanged men cannot unsettle nor churchyards unnerve, and all the retinue of hell are no more than ghost stories and shadow tricks to him. But when she dumped a bucketful of brook water onto him, he jerked upright amid the pillows, spluttering and shivering, with little minnows thrashing in the satin sheets and underneath his embroidered nightshirt, and our hero yelled out loud in surprise—*and now,* his clever young wife said, *now you know how to shudder.*

You think she would appreciate this story, if you could tell it to her, but you are even less capable of speech than she: perhaps she will unreel it from your hindbrain, uncoil its fine wires and tease them loose from your spark and sputter, until she can pull herself hand over needle-clawed hand into the maze that is all the tales you once wrote down. Ariadne's thread leads into darkness forward and back. But the flagstones underfoot are the spine-plates of the monster out of whose scalded blood was made the bright nebulae, whose charred marrow was scattered for the dark, the shield of heaven is the interlock of its rictus teeth and its flesh fell like viral strikes and piled up into the earth. Down the unfamiliar corridors of its viscera, the minotaur staggers in a daze, and bellows, and somewhere up in the chartless stars the first voice in days that is not hers says, "Oh, tearing Jesus."

Your eyes are open, you have never closed them, not to see all the wonders and terrors she has planted inside you, have you never closed them? Cold ceramic metal underneath your cheek and the human woman in the cut-down labcoat, rice-pale skin laced with metal, dark hair stripped white in arbitrary slashes, towers into the fractured sun; raised up monolithic to deities whose constellations time picked and pushed apart eons before your homeworld spun down out of dust, before she kneels and diminishes and becomes a palm that smokes like dry ice against your forehead, pulse-points of winter at your wrist. The woman inside the blizzard, who takes up children in her frost-sleek arms and kisses them breathless and blue, and the splice doctor mutters, "No, forget it, I don't want to know. Did she leave a contact?" Behind her, black and wooden white, the bird-mask clappers its beak: hell's doorman, whom you threatened with the dead. He took your eyes and handed you a mirror instead. But the dead ravened up in you, millenial ash and darkness-capped dust, and the reddened gill-cuts of uplinks at the doctor's temples could never tell her their histories or their erosion. Her rewoven eyes are chatoyant, but her voice is rasped thin as any mortal's; her hands on your collarbones are soft. "Get staved, *itsiikip!* How long has she been here? Do you *want* me to jibe Tauwhahi in on this? Fucking phils and their specialities—"

But *her* arms are close around you, no matter that you bleed wherever she touches; she cradles you against her warmth, like the spat-out heart of a star, tektite, meteorite, burned to nickel and charcoal in her fall, because it is not yet done. The doctor and the doorkeeper and your absent lover pass their single smudged eyeball hand to hand, grey ghost-washes on the harsh light and the smell of damp iron, unable to see more than one flat face of things. The hero who peeled himself out of his own skin to rumple it carefully into a mountain range, who stamped into the sea and its canyons were made for the lightless, depthless waters to fill, recites rockslides and riptides for you alone. A husband and wife walked beneath the gas-glim sprawl of nebulae and each bargained their hearts to darkness that the other might never die alone. Perseus only ever looked into the mirror. In her arms, you shudder, and her dreams open up beneath you. How she will tell you, in time, to the next suppliant at her feet, is the last unspoken story you take with you into the dark.

KNACKSACK POEMS

ELEANOR ARNASON

Within this person of eight bodies, thirty-two eyes, and the usual number of orifices and limbs, resides a spirit as restless as gossamer on wind. In youth, I dreamed of fame as a merchant-traveler. In later years, realizing that many of my parts were prone to motion sickness, I thought of scholarship or accounting. But I lacked the Great Determination that is necessary for both trades. My abilities are spontaneous and brief, flaring and vanishing like a falling star. For me to spend my life adding numbers or looking through dusty documents would be like "lighting a great hall with a single lantern bug" or "watering a great garden with a drop of dew."

Finally, after consulting the care-givers in my crèche, I decided to become a traveling poet. It's a strenuous living and does not pay well, but it suits me.

Climbing through the mountains west of Ibri, I heard a *wishik* call, then saw the animal, its wings like white petals, perched on a bare branch.

> "Is that tree flowering
> So late in autumn?
> Ridiculous idea!
> I long for dinner."

One of my bodies recited the poem. Another wrote it down, while still others ranged ahead, looking for signs of habitation. As a precaution, I carried cudgels as well as pens and paper. One can never be sure what will appear in the country west of Ibri. The great poet Raging Fountain died there of a combination of diarrhea and malicious ghosts. Other writers, hardly less famous, have been killed by monsters or bandits, or, surviving these, met their end at the hands of dissatisfied patrons.

The Bane of Poets died before my birth. Its[1] ghost or ghosts offered Raging Fountain the fatal bowl of porridge. But other patrons still remain "on steep slopes and in stony dales."

> "Dire the telling
> Of patrons in Ibri:
> Bone-breaker lurks
> High on a mountain.
> Skull-smasher waits
> In a shadowy valley.
> Better than these
> The country has only
> Grasper, Bad-bargain,
> And Hoarder-of-Food."

Why go to such a place, you may be wondering? Beyond Ibri's spiny mountains lie the wide fields of Greater and Lesser Ib, prosperous lands well-known for patronage of the arts.

Late in the afternoon, I realized I would find no refuge for the night. Dark snow-clouds hid the hills in front of me. Behind me, low in the south, the sun shed pale light. My shadows, long and many-limbed, danced ahead of me on the rutted road.

My most poetic self spoke:
"The north is blocked
By clouds like boulders.
A winter sun
Casts shadows in my way."

Several of my other selves frowned. My scribe wrote the poem down with evident reluctance.

"Too obvious," muttered a cudgel-carrier.

Another self agreed. "Too much like Raging Fountain in his/her mode of melancholy complaint."

---

[1]   Goxhat units, or "persons" as the goxhat say, comprise four to sixteen bodies and two or three sexes. The Bane of Poets was unusual in being entirely neuter, which meant it could not reproduce. According to legend, it was reproductive frustration and fear of death that made The Bane so dangerous to poets.

Why poets? They produce two kinds of children, those of body and those of mind, and grasp in their pincers the gift of undying fame.

Far ahead, a part of me cried alarm. I suspended the critical discussion and hurried forward in a clump, my clubs raised and ready for use.

Soon, not even breathless, I stopped at a place I knew by reputation: the Tooth River. Wide and shallow, it ran around pointed stones, well-exposed this time of year and as sharp as the teeth of predators. On the far side of the river were bare slopes that led toward cloudy mountains. On the near side of the river, low cliffs cast their shadows over a broad shore. My best scout was there, next to a bundle of cloth. The scout glanced up, saw the rest of me, and—with deft fingers—undid the blanket folds.

Two tiny forms lay curled at the blanket's center. A child of one year, holding itself in its arms.

"Alive?" I asked myself.

The scout crouched closer. "One body is and looks robust. The other body—" my scout touched it gently "—is cold."

Standing among myself, I groaned and sighed. There was no problem understanding what had happened. A person had given birth. Either the child had been unusually small, or the other parts had died. For some reason, the parent had been traveling alone. Maybe he/she/it had been a petty merchant or a farmer driven off the land by poverty. If not these, then a wandering thief or someone outlawed for heinous crimes. A person with few resources. In any case, he/she/it had carried the child to this bitter place, where the child's next-to-last part expired.

Imagine standing on the river's icy edge, holding a child who had become a single body. The parent could not bear to raise an infant so incomplete! What parent could? One did no kindness by raising such a cripple to be a monster among ordinary people.

Setting the painful burden down, the parent crossed the river.

I groaned a second time. My most poetic self said:

> "Two bodies are not enough;
> One body is nothing."

The rest of me hummed agreement. The poet added a second piece of ancient wisdom:

> "Live in a group
> Or die."

I hummed a second time.

The scout lifted the child from its blanket. "It's female."

The baby woke and cried, waving her four arms, kicking her four legs, and urinating. My scout held her as far away as possible. Beyond doubt, she was a fine, loud, active mite! But incomplete. "Why did you wake her?" asked a cudgel-carrier. "She should be left to die in peace."

"No," said the scout. "She will come with me."

"Me! What do you mean by me?" my other parts cried.

There is neither art nor wisdom in a noisy argument. Therefore, I will not describe the discussion that followed as night fell. Snowflakes drifted from the sky—slowly at first, then more and more thickly. I spoke with the rudeness people reserve for themselves in privacy; and the answers I gave myself were sharp indeed. Words like pointed stones, like the boulders in Tooth River, flew back and forth. Ah! The wounds I inflicted and suffered! Is anything worse than internal dispute?

The scout would not back down. She had fallen in love with the baby, as defective as it was. The cudgel-bearers, sturdy males, were outraged. The poet and the scribe, refined neuters, were repulsed. The rest of me was female and a bit more tender.

I had reached the age when fertile eggs were increasingly unlikely. In spite of my best efforts, I had gained neither fame nor money. What respectable goxhat would mate with a vagabond like me? What crèche would offer to care for my offspring? Surely this fragment of a child was better than nothing.

"No!" said my males and neuters. "This is not a person! One body alone can never know togetherness or integration!"

But my female selves edged slowly toward the scout's opinion. Defective the child certainly was. Still, she was alive and goxhat, her darling little limbs waving fiercely and her darling mouth making noises that would shame a monster.

Most likely, she would die. The rest of her had. Better that she die in someone's arms, warm and comfortable, than in the toothy mouth of a prowling predator. The scout rewrapped the child in the blanket.

It was too late to ford the river. I made camp under a cliff, huddling together for warmth, my arms around myself, the baby in the middle of the heap I made.

When morning came, the sky was clear. Snow sparkled everywhere. I rose, brushed myself off, gathered my gear, and crossed the river. The water was low, as I expected this time of year, but ice-cold. My feet were numb by the time I reached the far side. My teeth chattered on every side like castanets. The baby, awakened by the noise, began to cry. The scout gave her a sweet cake. That stopped the crying for a while.

At mid-day, I came in sight of a keep. My hearts lifted with hope. Alas! Approaching it, I saw the walls were broken.

The ruination was recent. I walked through one of the gaps and found a courtyard, full of snowy heaps. My scouts spread out and investigated. The snow hid bodies, as I expected. Their eyes were gone, but most of the rest remained, preserved by cold and the season's lack of bugs.

"This happened a day or two ago," my scouts said. "Before the last snow, but not by much. *Wishik* found them and took what they could, but didn't have time—before the storm—to find other predators and lead them here. This is why the bodies are still intact. The *wishik* can pluck out eyes, but skin is too thick for them to penetrate. They need the help of other animals, such as *hirg*." One of the scouts crouched by a body and brushed its rusty back hair. "I won't be able to bury these. There are too many."

"How many goxhat are here?" asked my scribe, taking notes.

"It's difficult to say for certain. Three or four, I suspect, all good-sized. A parent and children would be my guess."

I entered the keep building and found more bodies. Not many. Most of the inhabitants had fallen in the courtyard. There was a nursery with scattered toys, but no children.

"Ah! Ah!" I cried, reflecting on the briefness of life and the frequency with which one encounters violence and sorrow.

My poet said:

> "Broken halls
> and scattered wooden words.
> How will the children
> learn to read and write?"[2]

Finally I found a room with no bodies or toys, nothing to remind me of mortality. I lit a fire and settled for the night. The baby fussed. My scout

---

[2] This translation is approximate. Like humans, goxhat use wooden blocks to teach their children writing. However, their languages are ideogrammic, and the blocks are inscribed with entire words. Their children build sentences shaped like walls, towers, barns and other buildings. Another translation of the poem would be:

> Broken walls.
> Broken sentences.
> Ignorant offspring.
> Alas!

cleaned her, then held her against a nursing bud—for comfort only; the scout had no milk. The baby sucked. I ate my meager rations. Darkness fell. My thirty-two eyes reflected firelight. After a while, a ghost arrived. Glancing up, I saw it in the doorway. It looked quite ordinary: three goxhat bodies with rusty hair.

"Who are you?" one of my scouts asked.

"The former owner of this keep, or parts of her. My name was Content-in-Solitude; and I lived here with three children, all lusty and numerous.—Don't worry."

My cudgel-carriers had risen, cudgels in hand.

"I'm a good ghost. I'm still in this world because my death was so recent and traumatic. As soon as I've gathered myself together, and my children have done the same, we'll be off to a better place.[3]

"I stopped here to tell you our names, so they will be remembered."

"Content-in-Solitude," muttered my scribe, writing.

"My children were Virtue, Vigor, and Ferric Oxide. Fine offspring! They should have outlived me. Our killer is Bent Foot, a bandit in these mountains. He took my grandchildren to raise as his own, since his female parts—all dead now—produced nothing satisfactory. Mutant children with twisted feet and nasty dispositions! No good will come of them; and their ghosts will make these mountains worse than ever. Tell my story, so others may be warned."

"Yes," my poet said in agreement. The rest of me hummed.

For a moment, the three bodies remained in the doorway. Then they drew together and merged into one. "You see! It's happening! I am becoming a single ghost! Well, then. I'd better be off to find the rest of me, and my children, and a better home for all of us."

The rest of the night was uneventful. I slept well, gathered around the fire, warmed by its embers and my bodies' heat. If I had dreams, I don't remember them. At dawn, I woke. By sunrise, I was ready to leave. Going out of the building, I discovered three *hirg* in the courtyard: huge predators with shaggy, dull-brown fur. *Wishik* fluttered around them as they tore into the bodies of Content and her children. I took one look, then retreated, leaving the keep by another route.

---

[3] According to the goxhat, when a person dies, his/her/its goodness becomes a single ghost known as "The Harmonious Breath" or "The Collective Spirit." This departs the world for a better place. But a person's badness remains as a turbulent and malicious mob, attacking itself and anyone else who happens along.

That day passed in quiet travel. My poet spoke no poetry. The rest of me was equally silent, brooding on the ruined keep and its ghost.

I found no keep to shelter me that night or the next or the next. Instead, I camped out. My scout fed the baby on thin porridge. It ate and kept the food down, but was becoming increasingly fretful and would not sleep unless the scout held it to a nursing bud. Sucking on the dry knob of flesh, it fell asleep.

"I don't mind," said the scout. "Though I'm beginning to worry. The child needs proper food."

"Better to leave it by the way," a male said. "Death by cold isn't a bad ending."

"Nor death by dehydration," my other male added.

The scout looked stubborn and held the child close.

Four days after I left the ruined keep, I came to another building, this one solid and undamaged.

My scribe said, "I know the lord here by reputation. She is entirely female and friendly to the womanly aspects of a person. The neuter parts she tolerates. But she doesn't like males. Her name is The Testicle Straightener."

My cudgel-carriers shuddered. The scribe and poet looked aloof, as they inevitably did in such situations. Clear-eyed and rational, free from sexual urges, they found the rest of me a bit odd.

The scout carrying the baby said, "The child needs good food and warmth and a bath. For that matter, so do I."

Gathering myself together, I strode to the gate and knocked. After several moments, it swung open. Soldiers looked out. There were two of them: one tall and grey, the other squat and brown. Their bodies filled the entrance, holding spears and axes. Their eyes gleamed green and yellow.

"I am a wandering poet, seeking shelter for the night. I bring news from the south, which your lord might find useful."

The eyes peered closely, then the soldiers parted—grey to the left, brown to the right—and let me in.

Beyond the gate was a snowy courtyard. This one held no bodies. Instead, the snow was trampled and urine-marked. A living place! Though empty at the moment, except for the two soldiers who guarded the gate.

I waited in an anxious cluster. At length, a servant arrived and looked me over. "You need a bath and clean clothes. Our lord is fastidious and dislikes guests who stink. Come with me."

I followed the servant into the keep and down a flight of stairs. Metal lamps were fastened to the walls. Most were dark, but a few shone, casting a dim light. The servant had three sturdy bodies, all covered with black hair.

Down and down. The air grew warm and moist. A faint, distinctive aroma filled it.

"There are hot springs in this part of Ibri," the servant said. "This keep was built on top of one; and there is a pool in the basement, which always steams and smells."

Now I recognized the aroma: rotten eggs.

We came to a large room, paved with stone and covered by a broad, barrel vault. Metal lanterns hung from the ceiling on chains. As was the case with the lamps on the stairway, most were dark. But a few flickered dimly. I could see the bathing pool: round and carved from bedrock. Steps went down into it. Wisps of steam rose.

"Undress," said the servant. "I'll bring soap and towels."

I complied eagerly. Only my scout hesitated, holding the baby.

"I'll help you with the mite," said my scribe, standing knee-deep in hot water.

The scout handed the baby over and undressed.

Soon I was frolicking in the pool, diving and spouting. Cries of joy rang in the damp, warm room. Is anything better than a hot bath after a journey?

The scout took the baby back and moved to the far side of the pool. When the servant returned, the scout sank down, holding the baby closely, hiding it in shadow. Wise mite, it did not cry!

The rest of me got busy, scrubbing shoulders and backs. Ah, the pleasure of warm lather!

Now and then, I gave a little yip of happiness. The servant watched with satisfaction, his/her/its arms piled high with towels.

On the far side of the pool, my best scout crouched, nursing the babe on a dry bud and watching the servant with hooded eyes.

At last, I climbed out, dried off, and dressed. In the confusion—there was a lot of me—the scout managed to keep the baby concealed. Why, I did not know, but the scout was prudent and usually had a good reason for every action, though parts of me still doubted the wisdom of keeping the baby. There would be time to talk all of this over, when the servant was gone.

He/she/it led me up a new set of stairs. The climb was long. The servant entertained me with the following story.

The keep had a pulley system, which had been built by an ingenious traveling plumber. This lifted buckets of hot water from the spring to a tank on top of the keep. From there the water descended through metal pipes, carried by the downward propensity that is innate in water. The pipes heated every room.

"What powers the pulley system?" my scribe asked, notebook in hand.

"A treadmill," said the servant.

"And what powers the treadmill?"

"Criminals and other people who have offended the lord. No keep in Ibri is more comfortable," the servant continued with pride. "This is what happens when a lord is largely or entirely female. As the old proverb says, male bodies give a person forcefulness. Neuter bodies give thoughtfulness and clarity of vision. But nurture and comfort come from a person's female selves."

Maybe, I thought. But were the people in the treadmill comfortable?

The servant continued the story. The plumber had gone east to Ib and built other heated buildings: palaces, public baths, hotels, hospitals, and crèches. In payment for this work, several of the local lords mated with the plumber; and the local crèches vied to raise the plumber's children, who were numerous and healthy.

"A fine story, with a happy ending," I said, thinking of my fragment of a child, nursing on the scout's dry bud. Envy, the curse of all artists and artisans, roiled in my hearts. Why had I never won the right to lay fertile eggs? Why were my purses empty? Why did I have to struggle to protect my testes and to stay off treadmills, while this plumber—surely not a better person than I—enjoyed fame, honor, and fertility?

The guest room was large and handsome, with a modern wonder next to it: a defecating closet. Inside the closet, water came from the wall in two metal pipes, which ended in faucets. "Hot and cold," said the servant, pointing. Below the faucets was a metal basin, decorated with reliefs of frolicking goxhat. Two empty buckets stood next to the basin.

The servant said, "If you need to wash something, your hands or feet or any other part, fill the basin with water. Use the buckets to empty the basin; and after you use the defecating throne, empty the buckets down it. This reduces the smell and gets rid of the dirty water. As I said, our lord is fastidious; and we have learned from her example. The plumber helped, by providing us with so much water.

"I'll wait in the hall. When you're ready to meet the lord, I'll guide you to her."

'Thank you," said my scribe, always courteous.

I changed into clean clothing, the last I had, and put bardic crowns on my heads[4]. Each crown came from a different contest, though all were minor. I had never won a really big contest. Woven of fine wool, with brightly colored tassels hanging down, the crowns gave me an appearance of dignity. My nimble-fingered scouts unpacked my instruments: a set of chimes, a pair of castanets and a bagpipe. Now I was ready to meet the lord.

All except my best scout, who climbed into the middle of a wide soft bed, child in arms.

"Why did you hide the mite?" asked my scholar.

"This keep seems full of rigid thinkers, overly satisfied with themselves and their behavior. If they saw the child they would demand an explanation. 'Why do you keep it? Can't you see how fragmentary it is? Can't you see that it's barely alive? Don't you know how to cut your losses?' I don't want to argue or explain."

"What is meant by 'I'?" my male parts asked. "What is meant by 'my' reasons?"

"This is no time for an argument," said the poet.

All of me except the scout went to meet the keep's famous lord.

The Straightener sat at one end of large hall: an elderly goxhat with frosted hair. Four parts of her remained, all sturdy, though missing a few pieces here and there: a foot, a hand, an eye or finger. Along the edges of the hall sat her retainers on long benches: powerful males, females, and neuters, adorned with iron and gold.

"Great your fame,
Gold-despoiler,
Bold straightener of scrota,
Wise lord of Ibri.
"Hearing of it,
I've crossed high mountains,
Anxious to praise
Your princely virtues."

---

[4] Actually, cerebral bulges. The goxhat don't have heads as humans understand the word.

My poet stopped. Straightener leaned forward. "Well? Go on! I want to hear about my princely virtues."

"Give me a day to speak with your retainers and get exact details of your many achievements," the poet said. "Then I will be able to praise you properly."

The goxhat leaned back. "Never heard of me, have you? Drat! I was hoping for undying fame."

"I will give it to you," my poet said calmly.

"Very well," the lord said. "I'll give you a day, and if I like what you compose, I'll leave your male parts alone."

All of me thanked her. Then I told the hall about my stay at the ruined keep. The retainers listened intently. When I had finished, the lord said, "My long-time neighbor! Dead by murder! Well, death comes to all of us. When I was born, I had twenty parts. A truly large number! That is what I'm famous for, as well as my dislike of men, which is mere envy. My male bodies died in childhood, and my neuter parts did not survive early adulthood. By thirty, I was down to ten bodies, all female. The neuters were not much of a loss. Supercilious twits, I always thought. But I miss my male parts. They were so feisty and full of piss! When travelers come here, I set them difficult tasks. If they fail, I have my soldiers hold them, while I unfold their delicate, coiled testicles. No permanent damage is done, but the screaming makes me briefly happy."

My male bodies looked uneasy and shifted back and forth on their feet, as if ready to run. But the two neuters remained calm. My poet thanked the lord a second time, sounding confident. Then I split up and went in all directions through the hall, seeking information.

The drinking went on till dawn, and the lord's retainers were happy to tell me stories about the Straightener. She had a female love of comfort and fondness for children, but could not be called tender in any other way. Rather, she was a fierce leader in battle and a strict ruler, as exact as a balance or a straight-edge.

"She'll lead us against Bent Foot," one drunk soldier said. "We'll kill him and bring the children here. The stolen children, at least. I don't know about Bent Foot's spawn. It might be better for them to die. Not my problem. I let the lord make all the decisions, except whether or not I'm going to fart."

Finally, I went up to my room. My scout lay asleep, the baby in her arms. My male parts began to pace nervously. The rest of me settled to compose a poem.

As the sky brightened, the world outside began to wake and make noise. Most of the noise could be ignored, but there was a *wishik* under the eaves directly outside my room's window. Its shrill, repeating cry drove my poet to distraction. I could not concentrate on the poem.

Desperate, I threw things at the animal: buttons from my sewing kit, spare pens, an antique paperweight I found in the room. Nothing worked. The *wishik* fluttered away briefly, then returned and resumed its irritating cry.

At last my scout woke. I explained the problem. She nodded and listened to the *wishik* for a while. Then she fastened a string to an arrow and shot the arrow out the window. It hit the *wishik*. The animal gave a final cry. Grabbing the string, my scout pulled the beast inside.

"Why did I do that?" I asked.

"Because I didn't want the body to fall in the courtyard."

"Why not?"

Before she could answer, the body at her feet expanded and changed its shape. Instead of the body of a dead *wishik,* I saw a grey goxhat body, pierced by the scout's arrow, dead.

My males swore. The rest of me exclaimed in surprise.

My scout said, "This is part of a wizard, no doubt employed by the keep's lord, who must really want to unroll my testicles, since she is willing to be unfair and play tricks. The *wishik* cry was magical, designed to bother me so much than I could not concentrate on my composition. If this body had fallen to the ground, the rest of the wizard would have seen it and known the trick had failed. As things are, I may have time to finish the poem." The scout looked at the rest of me severely. "Get to work."

My poet went back to composing, my scribe to writing. The poem went smoothly now. As the stanzas grew in number, I grew increasingly happy and pleased. Soon I noticed the pleasure was sexual. This sometimes happened, though usually when a poem was erotic. The god of poetry and the god of sex are siblings, though they share only one parent, who is called the All-Mother-Father.

Even though the poem was not erotic, my male and female parts became increasingly excited. Ah! I was rubbing against myself. Ah! I was making soft noises! The poet and scribe could not feel this sexual pleasure, of course, but the sight of the rest of me tumbling on the rug was distracting. Yes, neuters are clear-eyed and rational, but they are also curious; and nothing arouses their curiosity more than sex. They stopped working on the poem and watched as I fondled myself.[5]

Only the scout remained detached from sensuality and went into the defecating closet. Coming out with a bucket of cold water, the scout poured it over my amorous bodies.

I sprang apart, yelling with shock.

"This is more magic," the scout said. "I did not know a spell inciting lust could be worked at such a distance, but evidently it can. Every part of me that is male or female, go in the bathroom! Wash in cold water till the idea of sex becomes uninteresting! As for my neuter parts—" The scout glared. "Get back to the poem!"

"Why has one part of me escaped the spell?" I asked the scout.

"I did not think I could lactate without laying an egg first, but the child's attempts to nurse have caused my body to produce milk. As a rule, nursing mothers are not interested in sex, and this has proved true of me. Because of this, and the child's stubborn nursing, there is a chance of finishing the poem. I owe this child a debt of gratitude."

"Maybe," grumbled my male parts. The poet and scribe said, "I shall see."

The poem was done by sunset. That evening I recited it in the lord's hall. If I do say so myself, it was a splendid achievement. The *wishik's* cry was in it, as was the rocking up-and-down rhythm of a sexually excited goxhat. The second gave the poem energy and an emphatic beat. As for the first, every line ended with one of the two sounds in the *wishik's* ever-repeating, irritating cry. Nowadays, we call this repetition of sound "rhyming." But it had no name when I invented it.

When I was done, the lord ordered several retainers to memorize the poem. "I want to hear it over and over," she said. "What a splendid idea it is to make words ring against each other in this fashion! How striking the sound! How memorable! Between you and the traveling plumber, I will certainly be famous."

That night was spent like the first one, everyone except me feasting. I feigned indigestion and poured my drinks on the floor under the feasting table. The lord was tricky and liked winning. Who could say what she might order put in my cup or bowl, now that she had my poem?

---

5   The goxhat believe masturbation is natural and ordinary. But reproduction within a person—inbreeding, as they call it—is unnatural and a horrible disgrace. It rarely happens. Most goxhat are not intrafertile, for reasons too complicated to explain here.

When the last retainer fell over and began to snore, I got up and walked to the hall's main door. Sometime in the next day or so, the lord would discover that her wizard had lost a part to death and that one of her paperweights was missing. I did not want to be around when these discoveries were made.

Standing in the doorway, I considered looking for the treadmill. Maybe I could free the prisoners. They might be travelers like me, innocent victims of the lord's malice and envy and her desire for hot water on every floor. But there were likely to be guards around the treadmill, and the guards might be sober. I was only one goxhat. I could not save everyone. And the servant had said they were criminals.

I climbed the stairs quietly, gathered my belongings and the baby, and left through a window down a rope made of knotted sheets.

The sky was clear; the brilliant star we call Beacon stood above the high peaks, shedding so much light I had no trouble seeing my way. I set a rapid pace eastward. Toward morning, clouds moved in. The Beacon vanished. Snow began to fall, concealing my trail. The baby, nursing on the scout, made happy noises.

Two days later, I was out of the mountains, camped in a forest by an unfrozen stream. Water made a gentle sound, purling over pebbles. The trees on the banks were changers, a local variety that is blue in summer and yellow in winter. At the moment, their leaves were thick with snow. "Silver and gold," my poet murmured, looking up.

The scribe made a note.

A *wishik* clung to a branch above the poet and licked its wings. Whenever it shifted position, snow came down.

> "The *wishik* cleans wings
> As white as snow.
> Snow falls on me, white
> As a *wishik*,"

the poet said.

My scribe scribbled.

One of my cudgel-carriers began the discussion. "The Bane of Poets was entirely neuter. Fear of death made it crazy. Bent Foot was entirely male. Giving in to violence, he stole children from his neighbor. The last lord I encountered, the ruler of the heated keep, was female, malicious and unfair. Surely something can be learned from these encounters. A person should not be one sex entirely, but rather—as I am—a harmonious mixture of male, female, and neuter. But this child can't help but be a single sex."

"I owe the child a debt of gratitude," said my best scout firmly. "Without her, I would have had pain and humiliation, when the lord—a kind of lunatic—unrolled my testes, as she clearly planned to do. At best, I would have limped away from the keep in pain. At worst, I might have ended in the lord's treadmill, raising water from the depths to make her comfortable."

"The question is a good one," said my scribe. "How can a person who is only one sex avoid becoming a monster? The best combination is the one I have: male, female, and both kinds of neuter. But even two sexes provide a balance."

"Other people—besides these three—have consisted of one sex," my scout said stubbornly. "Not all became monsters. It isn't sex that has influenced these lords, but the stony fields and spiny mountains of Ibri, the land's cold winters and ferocious wildlife. My various parts can teach the child my different qualities: the valor of the cudgel-carriers, the coolness of poet and scribe, the female tenderness that the rest of me has. Then she will become a single harmony."

The scout paused. The rest of me looked dubious. The scout continued.

"Many people lose parts of themselves through illness, accident, and war; and some of these live for years in a reduced condition. Yes, it's sad and disturbing, but it can't be called unnatural. Consider aging and the end of life. The old die body by body, till a single body remains. Granted, in many cases, the final body dies quickly. But not always. Every town of good size has a Gram or Gaffer who hobbles around in a single self.

"I will not give up an infant I have nursed with my own milk. Do I wish to be known as ungrateful or callous? I, who have pinned all my hope on honor and fame?"

I looked at myself with uncertain expressions. The *wishik* shook down more snow.

"Well, then," said my poet, who began to look preoccupied. Another poem coming, most likely. "I will take the child to a crèche and leave her there."

My scout scowled. "How well will she be cared for there, among healthy children, by tenders who are almost certain to be prejudiced against a mite so partial and incomplete? I will not give her up."

"Think of how much I travel," a cudgel-carrier said. "How can I take a child on my journeys?"

"Carefully and tenderly," the scout replied. "The way my ancestors who were nomads did. Remember the old stories! When they traveled, they took everything, even the washing pot. Surely their children were not left behind."

"I have bonded excessively to this child," said my scribe to the scout.

"Yes, I have. It's done and can't be undone. I love her soft baby-down, her four blue eyes, her feisty spirit. I will not give her up."

I conversed this way for some time. I didn't become angry at myself, maybe because I had been through so much danger recently. There is nothing like serious fear to put life into perspective. Now and then, when the conversation became especially difficult, a part of me got up and went into the darkness to kick the snow or to piss. When the part came back, he or she or it seemed better.

Finally I came to an agreement. I would keep the child and carry it on my journeys, though half of me remained unhappy with this decision.

How difficult it is to be of two minds! Still, it happens; and all but the insane survive such divisions. Only they forget the essential unity that underlies differences of opinion. Only they begin to believe in individuality.

The next morning, I continued into Ib.

The poem I composed for the lord of the warm keep became famous. Its form, known as "ringing praise," was taken up by other poets. From it, I gained some fame, enough to quiet my envy; and the fame led to some money, which provided for my later years.

Did I ever return to Ibri? No. The land was too bitter and dangerous; and I didn't want to meet the lord of the warm keep a second time. Instead, I settled in Lesser Ib, buying a house on a bank of a river named It-Could-Be-Worse. This turned out to be an auspicious name. The house was cozy and my neighbors pleasant. The child played in my fenced-in garden, tended by my female parts. As for my neighbors, they watched with interest and refrained from mentioning the child's obvious disability.

> "Lip-presser on one side.
> Tongue-biter on t'other.
> Happy I live,
> Praising good neighbors."

I traveled less than previously, because of the child and increasing age. But I did make the festivals in Greater and Lesser Ib. This was easy traveling on level roads across wide plains. The Ibian lords, though sometimes eccentric, were nowhere near as crazy as the ones in Ibri and no danger to me or other poets. At one of the festivals, I met the famous plumber, who turned out to be a large and handsome, male and neuter goxhat. I won the festival crown for poetry, and he/it won the crown for ingenuity. Celebrating with egg wine, we became amorous and fell into each other's many arms.

It was a fine romance and ended without regret, as did all my other romances. As a group, we goxhat are happiest with ourselves. In addition, I could not forget the prisoners in the treadmill. Whether the plumber planned it or not, he/it had caused pain for others. Surely it was wrong— unjust—for some to toil in darkness, so that others had a warm bed and hot water from a pipe?

I have to say, at times I dreamed of that keep: the warm halls, the pipes of water, the heated bathing pool and the defecating throne that had— have I forgotten to mention this?—a padded seat.

"Better to be here
In my cozy cottage.
Some comforts"
Have too high a cost.

I never laid any fertile eggs. My only child is Ap the Foundling, who is also known as Ap of One Body and Ap the Many-talented. As the last nickname suggests, the mite turned out well.

As for me, I became known as The Clanger and The *Wishit*, because of my famous rhyming poem. Other names were given to me as well: The Child Collector, The Nurturer, and The Poet Who Is Odd.

NULLIPARA

GITTE CHRISTENSEN

—◆—

Alone and static on a shifting landscape, the dome stoically bears the ceaseless bombardment.

Returning Daughter crosses the battlefield, her whole being focused on the task ahead, Beloved Son at her side. Winds whistle past bearing particles for the assault. Regular application of zeal and purpose once made short shrift of these specks of the desert, but now sand has piled so high that Dilmun's dome is half buried. In a war won by microscopic increments, the scales have tipped. Soon the dome will be just another dune.

Returning Daughter marvels at the stubbornness of the colonists. The desert tries each day and every night to grind their community from existence, yet despite the inevitability of defeat, and as tired and forlorn as it is, Dilmun endures. The achievement inspires a certain pride even though Returning Daughter knows the settlement is an abomination. Already she is changing. She reminds herself that she must be wary and constantly monitor her character.

When they reach the dome, Comical Son dances with excitement. He is fascinated by the construct and dashes about searching for a way in. Returning Daughter firmly reminds Restless Son that he cannot accompany her but must wait outside. Naughty Son sulks and the space about him crackles with displeasure. Mere moments later, a whirly wind of shimmering heat comes spinning by, pauses and twinkles, flicks a teasing tendril of glistening air at Moping Son and flits off. Amused Son is distracted. He laughs and chases after the bright toy. Returning Daughter smiles indulgently as she watches him skip across the sands.

At the base of the dome, Returning Daughter accesses one of the outer chambers created by Joseph Go-Between and enters a capsule. The cylinder closes and cleans her with a vile, stinging fluid. Returning Daughter is so offended by the procedure that she momentarily forgets what comes after the sterilising. Caught off-guard, she screams in agony as a machine wraps her in a sheath-shape, forcing filters into the appropriate cavities so she can breath and speak without infecting anyone, then seals the membrane with a blast of heat.

There is a five-minute wait while the machine gauges her reaction to the process. Returning Daughter stands hunched in the capsule regretting that she has come. Enveloped by Oldhome materials, her body convulses and she dry retches. Fortunately, there is no spillage; even though liquids cannot pass through the mouth filter, regulations dictate that vomiters can go no further. Many of the Children can never visit their parents because they are serial pukers.

A green light gives the all-clear. The capsule revolves and opens. Returning Daughter falls forth and stumbles about the inner chamber. She wants to rip off the ghastly sheath-shape and spit out the membranous gag and scream and yell and weep, but instead puts out a hand and steadies herself against a wall; she clings also to the reason for her visit while she regains control of her senses. As her body adjusts to the constant physical discomfort, Returning Daughter's mind likewise settles.

She continues, navigating a corridor to the second point of entry.

Returning Daughter searches her memory for the password. A phrase gushes out, initially an awkward noise that the gateway will not accept and which she must discipline into distinct bursts, contorting her face for the shaping of each word and carefully regulating the flow of air and sound through the mouth membrane. Finally she gets the words right and a blue light blips acceptance. The security system scans to double check that she is indeed contained within a sheath-shape. Weapons on either side of the threshold clang and grind as they put on a showy production of targeting her, ensuring that she alone enters the dome. A red light flashes and the metal door rises.

Returning Daughter hesitates, taking a moment to prepare for the shocks ahead before she pushes through the barrier of gritty air that seals in the colonists, an additional quarantine precaution which seems to grow more abrasive with each visit. Returning Daughter cries out in pain as she enters the world of her childhood.

Everything within the dome is of Oldhome. Even the air and soil is assembled from the recycled remnants of another world. Inside the sheath-shape, Returned Daughter squirms. Once more she overrides her body's reflexive reactions and wills her vision to understand the colony. The smooth, sliding sands that should be travelling across this plain are diverted for now, replaced by a jumble of closed dwellings. The air is numb, the ground beneath her perversely paved over; even deeper down, the floor of the dome seals Dilmun off from the world upon which it rests. No energy flows, no whispers carry.

A throng of tall beings move about. This is some kind of gathering place. A market. Shops and stalls. Recognition floats up from the past. Returned Daughter recalls a doll she yearned to own. Shiny beads and coloured ribbons. Ice cream. Spicy food wraps. Warm, cinnamon-dusted sweetbreads. Games with friends. A black-and-white kitten that Happy Mother purchased for Beloved Daughter's fifth birthday. Returned Daughter basks in the pleasant memories and relives why a fondness for this place has remained with the Children for so long, often luring them in from the desert the way sparkly toys once enticed the birthday kitten. Then she remembers the terrible price paid by the Children who had returned too soon, before Joseph Go-Between had organised a truce and built the decon chambers, and she shrinks back from the honeyed trap. It takes Returned Daughter many minutes to calm down enough to reclaim those three surrendered steps.

People are stopping to stare at her. Returned Daughter is overwhelmed by their many hysterical features. Long ago, she understood the expressions. Now she tentatively conjectures guiding images, pairs their wide eyes and slack mouths with emotional labels. These reflect fear. Or awe. Or disapproval.

The last guess triggers a cue and Returned Daughter remembers the Virtue of Modesty. She turns to a rack of clothing left by the access point and strokes the robes hanging there, filmy garments which do not overly constrict or grate against the sheath-shape she is already wearing. The robes are another of the comprises designed by Joseph Go-Between. Many Oldhomers think the garments scandalously improper. The Children, already suffocated by a sheath-shape, find yet another layer of senseless covering stretches their sensibilities to almost breaking point, but they obey the propriety as a mark of respect for those who first gave them life.

Returned Daughter reaches for a garment that vibrates joyous blood hues before another, long ago learnt lesson in etiquette rises to reprimand her. Red is not an appropriate tone to wear for this visit. Returned Daughter lets her finger run the spectrum of colors and finally dons black for Dead Mother's burial.

Concerned she has made other blunders that might offend—it has been many years since she last moved amongst these people—Returned Daughter steps up to a shop window and regards her reflection. She sees the featureless exterior of the sheath-shape, a dour image that reveals nothing of her true self, and thinks she should find some crayons in the market and put on pretend lipstick, draw rosy circles for cheeks, sketch brows over the eye sockets and colour in the hollows with blue. Returned Daughter giggles, enjoys the idea so much that she also imagines sticking on a red ball for a nose and finding a wig of curly, orange clown hair to pop on top of her head. Laughter flows and lightens the stolid air about her.

She notices a man staring from inside the shop. This experience is a common one and easy to interpret—he wonders whether she is his own Returned Daughter restored to him for a while. Not wishing to torment the man, Returned Daughter turns away. She finds that people are closing in on her now and she shudders, fearful they might touch her. Most Oldhomers are oblivious to the agony they cause the Children with their clumsy petting; much worse is the fact that some do realise, yet still choose to satisfy their own needs at the cost of another's pain.

Returned Daughter ducks through a gap in the big bodies. An abrasive cacophony erupts in her wake. Wails? Abuse? She has not been back long enough yet to distinguish the different sounds. Returned Daughter runs and runs until the noise dissipates.

Anamnesis grows stronger and the neighbourhood gradually segues from the alien into the familiar. Returned Daughter navigates a maze of dwellings along preordained pathways until she sights the construction once designated as her habitat. Two men sit on its outer ledge. Its verandah. One is Mournful Father, grey haired, wrinkled, but still straight of back and strong of hand. On his lap rests an old black-and-white cat, a descendant of the birthday kitten Happy Mother bought at the market long ago. The other man has many names, but to Returned Daughter he is first and foremost Young Love. His presence still makes her spirit glow.

Returned Daughter greets the men with a bow of sorrow rather than Joyous Feet, the whirling dance of reunion that would only upset Mournful Father in his present condition.

"Debbie?" says Mournful Father. His speech grates the air, sets Returned

Daughter twanging with hundreds of aches. His gaze scans her doubtfully. "Are you my Deborah?"

"Yes, Father. Condolences for your grief. I come to pay respects for the life I owe."

"Mother wondered whether you would."

Returned Daughter is puzzled by the remark. "We always do."

"Indeed. You never come to celebrate weddings or birthdays, but you always turn up, on the dot, for funerals. How do you do that? How do you know?"

A curious question. How can one not know, wonders Returned Daughter. She struggles to articulate something that is so obvious but cannot, so a horrible groan wafts out through the mouth membrane instead. Mournful Father frowns and looks over her sheath-shape in a searching way that makes Returned Daughter glad she did not carry out her amusing crayon notion.

Mournful Father growls, "Some Oldhomers claim you can smell it. They don't call you the Children, they call you the Carrion. Is it true? Did you smell Mother's death and come running to sniff her carcass?"

Returned Daughter suspects that Mournful Father is insulting her, although the offense is not obvious. Of course the Children can smell death. They can also see it, taste it and hear it, even when it is locked inside the dome. Returned Daughter steers away from the subject.

"Your grandson sends his respects," she says, which is not true. Missed Son would not understand the concept of a transportable courtesy. Returned Daughter is surprised at how quickly she is reverting to deceitfulness, yet she also acknowledges the expediency of manipulating Mournful Father's inadequate comprehension as best she can to save him from too much anguish.

"Ah, yes, my grandson. How is the little tyke?"

Returned Daughter easily recognises the bitterness in Mournful Father's voice. The longer she is in his world, the more she reconnects. To avoid further animosity, Returned Daughter does not use a single aspect of the ever-changing name for her offspring that Mournful Father could not pronounce anyway, but simply replies, "Beloved Son is well."

"Hello, Deborah," says Young Love.

His face is no longer smooth, his once dark hair is as grey as Mournful Father's, and the small hands which long ago cooled her brow as she lay ill with fever have become huge, rough mitts, but Young Love's voice is still soft and lilting, a caress which pleasantly washes over her. Because she wishes to make Young Love happy, Returned Daughter tries to look and sound the way she once did.

"Hi there, Joey," she chirps, hands on hips and shoulders waggling.

"Not Joey," says Young Love. His expression is one of beseeching. "Don't call me Joey, please."

Returned Daughter acquiesces. She stills her body and breathes Young Love's true name for this moment, a long susurration which caresses the air between them, joins them for a second, then dies in a sigh of yearning. Young Love's face relaxes, opens, blooms with serenity even as sadness creeps forth to reclaim his eyes.

"Thank you," he whispers.

"Ah, it's just like the good old days, Joey and Debbie together again, happy as can be," sings Mournful Father as he strokes the cat. The words gallop along in a friendly enough fashion, but there is a sharp note of discord tucked within the heart of each syllable. Returned Daughter cringes at the onslaught.

"Don't, sir," pleads Young Love. "You're hurting her. She'll run off again if you don't stop."

It is Young Love's great blessing that he can see such things and act as a link between the Children and their parents. It is also his great curse. Returned Daughter pities him. She feels again his sorrow, the torment of being trapped between worlds, for though Young Love senses the pulse of Newhome, too much of Oldhome clutters his cells. Newhome can never subsume Young Love so Young Love can never wander the desert as one of the Children. When it occurs, his death will be an act of finality.

"How is it out there?" Young Love asks.

"It is beautiful," Returned Daughter says, and she is about to sing of the wonders beyond the dome when she catches the emanations of anger from Mournful Father swirling amidst the even darker miasma of grief that clings to him.

Returned Daughter bows her head in surrender. She hears Young Love's sigh of disappointment and murmurs an apology. How strange, she thinks, that Young Love should be denied the desert when he was the first to grasp its true nature. She remembers Joey, the child made on Oldhome from selected seeds and assembled for labour, revivified right off the ship to be Leader Father's servantson. Also Deborah, the blessed offspring of Leader Father and Happy Mother conceived on Newhome, the doting mistressdaughter following the servantson everywhere. As the colony grew, the two children had wandered the dunes and listened to the winds and found secret things in hidden places; they had returned each evening with sand in their clothes and between their bare toes and in their ears and up their noses, and Happy Mother had cheerfully scolded them. There had been no fear then, no dome, just innocence and hope and love and curiosity.

Remembering the love, Returned Daughter smiles.

"You can still feel joy," says Mournful Father softly. He drops his gaze, pats the old cat. "I'm glad."

The remark confuses Returned Daughter. Her life is full of laughter, songs, stories and dancing. She struggles for a suitable response.

"Happy Mother smiled often when I was very young, and she sang happy songs and danced in the garden. But then she stopped singing. And she stopped dancing. I often wonder why."

Mournful Father strokes the cat's chin and the animal rumbles approval. "She stopped singing because you got sick, remember?"

"But then I got better," says Returned Daughter.

Mournful Father snorts. "Sometimes I think you Children only come in from the wastelands to mock us."

"Why would we mock you?" asks Returned Daughter.

"For hoping. For being stupid. For loving too much. How should I know what goes on inside your warped little heads?"

"Sir, please, stop it," begs Young Love. "You're upset. Don't say something you might regret later."

"The way I regret now that Mother and I couldn't leave this world?" says Mournful Father.

Returned Daughter is confused by this untruth. "Others left," she points out.

Mournful Father's eyes dart up, sparking with . . . hatred?

"The ones who left were all childless," he snaps.

Returned Daughter flinches, teeters on the verge of fleeing from the blame that batters her more fiercely than any desert wind, but remains. She notes that she is enduring Mournful Father's emotions more ably the longer she stays in his company. She watches Mournful Father haul his hands roughly across the cat's fur, troubled by the vehemence fuelling the act. The old creature, however, does not seem to mind but arches into Mournful Father's bowed palms.

"Besides," says Mournful Father, "There was nowhere to go from here. We signed up for a one-way trip to the stars, and this forsaken ball of sand was the end of the line. Those who left as good as committed suicide. But they knew that, I think."

Mournful Father puts the old cat aside and gives it a final caress, a gesture that sends a ripple of yearning through Returned Daughter. She finds she is shaping the odd wish that she might become the cat for a while so Mournful Father would treat her with such kindness. Amazed at how quickly she is reverting, a brush of panic unsettles her. What if she forgets who she is? What if she forsakes Beloved Son?

Mournful Father rises, says with great weariness, "Well, let's get this farce over and done with."

As head of their household, Mournful Father strides to the fore, making it clear that he expects Returned Daughter and his servantson Joseph Go-Between to respect propriety. They dutifully fall in behind him. Young Love walks beside Returned Daughter, tall and massive like all the Oldhomers who grew to adulthood. He moves close but knows better than to touch her. Returned Daughter relaxes, knowing she is safe with Young Love. They walk in silence, enjoying the happiness which comes from simply being together again.

The cemetery lies at the edge of the settlement between the buildings and the dome, a wide swathe of graves sweeping off in both directions to encircle Dilmun. It is hedged by a white picket fence, the headstones are neatly arranged in an impossibly green lawn, and the trees are permanently weighted with pink blossoms to complete the illusion of a seasonal rotation on Oldhome called Spring. None of it is real. The cemetery is like a dollhouse, a collection of fake furniture for the Oldhomers to play with while they pretend that all is well. They can do this as long as they keep their eyes lowered and do not look outwards.

For here, beyond the streets and dwellings, it is difficult to deny Dilmun's predicament. A gigantic wave of golden sand arches overhead and presses down against the dome. The breaker is much higher than the fake trees and the church, higher even than the crooked steeple to which the Oldhomers once kept adding extra height in a desperate bid to keep its apex above the rising sand. The cemetery, Returned Daughter knows, is a wellspring of hope for the colonists; offspring interred within the dome have stayed in the ground as they should and thus confirmed the Oldhomers' prejudices about the world beyond. Perversely, the Oldhomers rejoice over each child who remains buried.

Returned Daughter studies the closest graves. There, in alien soil under fake grass, lie Younger Brother and Baby Sister, who never felt the world beyond the dome. Mournful Father counts them as pure and blessed. Returned Daughter knows that too much time has passed for their reforming and that there was too much of Oldhome in them anyway for a viable restructuring, but a childish part of her still hopes that one day, when all the original Oldhomers are gone, Younger Brother and Baby Sister will wake up, jump from the ground and run out into the desert to play with her.

Two gravediggers stand by a hole. One of them hisses at Returned Daughter and raises his shovel. Leader Father sharply reprimands him, then waves off both men and tells them to come back later. The gravediggers trudge towards the church, shovels over their shoulders.

Dead Mother is already in the hole, encased in a metal box. Mournful Father speaks ritual words while Returned Daughter and Joseph Go-Between stand silently by. It is a strange farewell, a bloodless and joyless celebration of an existence. Returned Daughter regrets that she cannot set the air sparkling with her story-memories of Happy Mother.

Mournful Father ends the ceremony with a lifeless dedication: he kneels by the open hole, extends a hand and lets dirt dribble from his fist. The earth spreads over the coffin and becomes a dusty shroud.

"My poor beloved," he says. "She always hoped for a funeral with many children and grandchildren gathered to remember her life."

"I am here," says Returned Daughter.

"Yes," sighs Mournful Father.

Returned Daughter also kneels, scoops up a handful of soil and sprinkles it into the hole.

"Will you ever accept me as your issue?" she says.

"How can I? Just look at you," says Mournful Father.

"Must a child always be similar to its parents?"

"No." Mournful Father looks across the open grave at Returned Daughter with a hint of desperate amusement that surprises her. "But it should at least be of the same species."

"But I am your offspring, you know that," insists Returned Daughter. She can no more avoid the imminent argument than Mournful Father can.

Mournful Father snorts. "When I plant beans, I expect beans, not pumpkins," he says. It is his favourite saying.

"That is a false analogy. We are a variant, not a different genus." Returned Daughter's response is also depressingly familiar.

"Deviation is extinction," says Mournful Father. His pale eyes study Returned Daughter. "And sometimes I think that deep down you also acknowledge that you're an abomination. I think that's why you never bring your own child to visit his Grandpa. You're ashamed of him."

"I have told you many times that he cannot enter the dome because his generation cannot tolerate the chambers made by Joseph Go-Between," says Returned Daughter.

A crooked smile appears on Mournful Father's face. "Convenient that, eh?"

Returned Daughter easily comprehends the insinuation. "Why would I lie? Come outside the dome and meet him if you wish. The desert will not harm you. That is your excuse."

Mournful Father looks past her, stares into the distance. "And just what would I see, I wonder?"

"Your grandson, of course."

"Would I?" Mournful Father shakes his head. "Best to leave an old man a few delusions."

Returned Daughter cannot feel the grains of Oldhome soil still sliding between her fingers because of the sheath-shape. She opens her hand and dumps the last of the dirt onto the casket. "I do not understand this constant invocation of delusions. Living Mother did it all the time too."

"They provide us with comfort."

"Yet you continuously compose delusions which do not console you but instead cause much misery."

Mournful Father's eyes go cold, his face sets in stern lines. "Could we please forego the usual proselytising? Grief makes me vulnerable but it has not made me suddenly more stupid."

Returned Daughter dusts off her empty hands and stands to look down at Angry Father. "But why not devise joyful delusions? Why not suppose that since you have conducted your life correctly, the Children must be a reward rather than a punishment?"

"You think we should consider it a blessing that our children walk an alien wasteland as lepers?" says Furious Father.

"We are not diseased or possessed. We are saved. Newhome was moved when it heard you weep for your inert offspring, so it cleansed our remains of the Oldhome residues which had clogged our growing bodies and gave us back to you in a more compatible form."

"Who is the deluded one now?" taunts Furious Father.

Returned Daughter tries not to feel anger, but her voice sharpens as she reminds Leader Father of his past crimes. "When you cast out the Children and sealed yourselves off inside this dome, it was Newhome that looked after us."

"Here we go again. Great Mother saves the day, Great Mother knows best, the Great Child Murderer and Corpse Stealing Bitch loves us all," says Mournful Father wearily.

He falls silent. Returned Daughter waits for the rest of the speech but Mournful Father stares into the open grave rather than refute the charges of abandonment and neglect as he usually does. Returned Daughter hesitates, bemused by this change in routine, then forges on.

"Through practicing the Virtue of Compassion, by which you also abide, Newhome discovered the joys of progeny. Newhome loves us and so honours those who made us first. If you switch off the dome, we can all live together. We will laugh and sing and the Children can tend the Oldhomers as you grow old and provide comfort as you die."

"Self-serving lies," sighs Weary Father. "If we turn off the dome, we not only die, but we lose our souls as well."

Sadness fills Returned Daughter. She has failed to give Mournful Father any comfort, and she has failed yet again to reunite the Children with their parents. She slumps in defeat and also stares down at Dead Mother's coffin.

"Let's go, Debbie," says Young Love, his voice taut. "Hurry!"

Returned Daughter looks at Young Love, then follows his fearful gaze. She sees that Composed Father is holding a knife, turning it slowly in his hands.

Composed Father stares at the blade as he says, "Your mother was a good woman, Debbie, and she never stopped hoping that her little girl would be returned to her."

Composed Father rises from his knees and holds forth the knife as if offering a precious gift.

"On her deathbed, Mother begged me to free you, Debbie. She wants to stand at your side as you are judged and petition on your behalf. Please, let me do this for you, Debbie. Long ago, I failed as your father and your protector, but now I can make up for my many mistakes. Please, honour your mother's wishes and obey your father's command, my dearest daughter. Come, Debbie, please come to me."

Returned Daughter is much moved. She knows of the terrible torments that Composed Father believes this act will cost him, yet Composed Father is willing to endure eternal damnation so that she might be saved.

By his standards, this sacrifice is the greatest gift he can bequeath. The old bonds between them tighten. Love for Cherished Father wells up within Returned Daughter-Debbie. She wants to make him happy, she wants to abide by the Virtue of Obedience and walk into the blade so that Cherished Father might delight in her salvation. She sees him smile, rejoicing already. Exultant Father nods encouragement, eyes burning brightly with the desire to set things right. Returned Daughter-Debbie takes one step around Dead Mother's grave, then another.

"Look up, Debbie," cries Young Love. "Look up at the sky."

Only because it is Young Love who has uttered these words does Returned Daughter-Debbie respond. Her gaze lifts from Exultant Father, rests upon the adhoc steeple of the church, then is pulled higher. A tiny face pokes over the edge of the sand leaning against the dome. It is Willful Son impishly peering into the world of his forefathers. Cheeky Son waves, delight sparking from him when she waves back. Returned Daughter laughs, her spirit refreshed, her memory revitalized.

"I am sorry, Father, but I cannot," she says, then turns and walks away with Young Love.

"Please, Debbie, stay with Mother, please keep her company," cries Despairing Father.

Returned Daughter looks back just once, and sees that Defeated Father has collapsed by Mother's grave and is sobbing. Leaving Daughter feels great pity but knows she cannot go back and offer him comfort. She has already lingered for too long.

Young Love leads her safely through the market place and back to the chambers he created. He kneels before her, very gently rests his forehead against hers, and they remain thus for a while. Then Leaving Daughter and Young Love move apart and look into each other's eyes. They bid each other farewell with a simple nod.

Leaving Daughter pushes through the barrier of gritty air and enters a capsule. Within a recess in the outer chamber, she shucks the hated sheath-shape, watches it dissolve and wash down a drain. She is saddened by the futility of it all. The dome, the sheath-shapes, the procedures, they are all useless for there is no disease or hostile presence lurking outside. These tokens and rituals serve only to make the Oldhomers feel safe.

As soon as Leaving Daughter steps outside, the external door slides shut behind her. Sand and heat assault her. Delighted Son comes racing around the dome and throws himself into her arms, singing with relief because Mother Love has come back to him. They turn towards home. Naughty Son runs ahead, chuckling to himself, still delighted with his joke and thrilled by the fact that he has seen Mother's Father, even if it was from a distance. He scampers up an embankment, outline shimmering in the heat, and vanishes over the top. His cries of joy waft on the breezes that wend between the dunes.

Leaving Daughter looks back. Sand presses high about the dome. A few more storms and the desert will conquer the peak and cover the colony. Long after the last Oldhomer has died, when the engines of the great starship finally run out of fuel and the dome fails, the desert will collapse upon the empty city. Sand will stream into the streets and houses, salvage plains for the dunes to slide along and reclaim airspace for the wind, but under it all, in her grave, will be Dead Mother, her corpse encapsulated within a world that cannot absorb her alien tissue, forever apart and far, far from Oldhome.

Leaving Daughter pities these lost children of another world. They should store their dead in the old ship, she thinks, and as a final act, launch the barge into the starsea above towards the world that birthed them. They should let the Oldhomers drift back to the place that Mother missed so much, send them back to rest beneath a loving earth that would grow green shrouds over their bodies and tenderly reclaim them, return them to the place where trees bud pinkly in the springtime, where rains fall mercifully and birds whistle merrily and sweet flowers fill the air with gentle perfumes.

Leaving Daughter reaches the crest of the dune. She glances back at Dilmun. The visit has taken a heavy toll on her for she sees and hears all around her the same barren landscape that once taunted Happy Mother and Leader Father. Leaving Daughter breaths deeply, reminds her spirit that it is no longer confined by the sheath-shape or trapped within the dome. The wind caresses her and carries away her anxieties. She feels herself expanding. Her vision shifts. The beauty of Newhome overwhelms her and she tunes into the sounds of the water deep below, the sand in between, the sky above and the stars beyond. Buoyancy returns to her being. Her true name for the moment forms as she walks into the desert, following the sound of Cherished Son's laughter.

I shall return twice more, Mother Daughter thinks with a twinge of dread, for Dead Father's funeral and for the death of Joseph-Young-Love-Go-Between.

Then I will be free of them forever.

MUO-KA'S CHILD

INDRAPAMIT DAS

—◆—

Ziara watched her parent, muo-ka, curl up and die, like an insect might on Earth.

muo-ka was a giant of a thing, no insect. Ziara was the one who'd always felt like an insect around it. Its curled body pushed against the death shroud it had excreted in its dying hours, the membrane stretched taut against rigid limbs. She touched the shroud. It felt smooth but sticky. Her fingertips stuck lightly to it, leaving prints. It felt different from her clothes. muo-ka had excreted the ones she wore a month ago. They smelled softer than the death shroud, flowers from Earth on a distant, cosmic breeze. She raised her fingers to her face, touching them with her tongue. So salty and pungent it burned. She gagged instantly, coughing to stop herself retching.

"muo-ka," she said, throat thick. "You are my life." Ziara thought about this. "You *are* my life, here." She meant these words, but felt a hollow, aching relief that muo-ka's presence was gone.

She closed her eyes to remember the blue rind of Earth, furred with clouds, receding behind the glass as she drifted into amniotic sleep. Orphan. Volunteer. Voyager. A mere twenty years on that planet. When she had opened her eyes after the primordial dream of that year of folding space, the first thing she saw and felt was muo-ka pulling her from the coma, breaking open the steaming pod with predatory lurches. Its threaded knot of limbs rippling like a shredded banner in the sweltering light, stuck on the leviathan swell of its dark shape. She had opened her mouth, spraying vomit into the air, lazy spurts that moved differently than on Earth. muo-ka had pulled her out of the pod and towards it, its limbs sometimes whiplashes, sometimes articulated arms, flickering between stiffness and liquid softness so quickly it hurt her eyes to see that tangled embrace. Stray barbed limbs tugged and snapped at the rubbery coil of her umbilicus, ripping it off so pale shreds clung to the valve above her navel.

muo-ka had grasped at Ziara's strange, small, alien body, making her float in the singing air as she tried and tried to scream.

Ziara watched the shroud settle over muo-ka. Already the corpse had shrunk considerably as air and water left it. Its body whistled softly. A quiet song for coming evening. With a bone knife, she cut small slits into the shroud to let the gas escape more freely, even though the membrane was porous. The little rents fluttered. A breeze ruffled the flat waters of the eya-rith basin into undulations that lapped across muo-ka's islet, washing Ziara's bare feet and wetting the weedy edges of the stone deathbed. The water sloshed in the ruined shell of the pod at the edge of the islet, its sleek surfaces cracked and scabbed with mossy growth. Inside was a small surveying and recording kit. She had discovered the kit, sprung free of its wall compartment, shattered and drowned from the rough landing. Even if it had worked, it seemed a useless thing to her now.

When the pod had once threatened to float away, Ziara had clung to it, trying to pull it back with her tiny human arms, heaving with frantic effort. muo-ka had lunged, sealed the wreck to the islet with secretions. Now it stood in a grassy thatch of fungal filaments, a relic from another planet.

muo-ka had no spoken words. Yet, its islet felt quieter than it had ever been. Ziara had learned its name, and some of its words, by becoming its mouth, speaking aloud the language that hummed in a part of its body that she had to touch. It had been shockingly easy to do this. What secret part of her had muo-ka unlocked, or taught to wake? muo-ka's skin had always felt febrile when she touched it, and when it spoke through her she felt hot as well.

The first thing it had said through her mouth was "muo-ka," and she had known that was its name. "Ziara," she had said, still touching it. "Jih-ara," it had said in her mouth, exuding a humid heat, a taste of blood and berries in her head. Ziara had disengaged her palm with a smack, making it shiver violently. Clammy with panic, she had walked away. It had felt too strange, too much like becoming a part of muo-ka, becoming an organ of its own.

Ziara rarely spoke to muo-ka in the time that followed. When she got an urge to communicate, she'd often stifle it. And she did get the urge, again and again. In those moments she'd hide in the broken pod on the islet's shore. She'd curl into its clammy, broken womb and think of the grassy earth of the hostel playground, of playing catch with her friends until the trees darkened, of being reprimanded by the wardens, and smoking cigarettes by the barred moonlight of the cavernous bathrooms, stifling coughs into silent giggles when patrols came by. Daydreams of their passing footsteps would become apocalyptic with the siren wail of muo-ka's cries. It never could smell or detect her in the strange machinery of the wrecked pod. She assumed the screams were ones of alarm.

"You've fed me," Ziara said to the corpse. "And clothed me. And taught me to leap across the sky." Those stiffened limbs that its shroud now clung to had snatched her from the air if she leaped too high, almost twisting her shoulders out of their sockets once. She'd landed on the mud of the islet safe, alive. In the shadow of muo-ka she'd whispered "Fuck you. Just, fuck you. Fuck you, muo-ka."

She had tasted the sourness of boiled fruit at the back of her throat. muo-ka covered the sky above her, and offered one of its orifices. Gushing with the steam of regurgitate cooked inside it. She'd reached inside and took the scorching gumbo in her hands. The protein from dredged sea and air animals tasted like spongy fish. It was spiced with what might have been fear.

Ziara didn't have an exact idea of how long it had been since muo-ka had pulled her into the air of this world from the pod. She had marked weeks, months and years on a rock slick with colonies of luminescent bacteria. Left a calendar of glowing fingerprints that she had smeared clean and then restarted at the end of every twelve months, marking the passing years with long lines at the top. She had three lines now. They glowed strongest at dusk. If they were right, they told her she was twenty-four years old now. muo-ka had been her parent for three years.

Not that the number mattered. Days and years were shorter here. muo-ka had always lingered by that rocky calendar of fingerprints, hovering over it in quiet observation when it thought she wasn't looking, when she was off swimming in the shallows. Watching from afar in the water, she could always taste an ethanol bitterness at the back of her throat and sinuses. A taste she came to associate with sadness, or whatever muo-ka would call sadness.

muo-ka had never washed the calendar clean. It had never touched it. It had only ever looked at that glimmering imprint of time mapped according to a distant world invisible in the night sky. The dancing fingertips of its incredible child.

The evening began to cast shadows across the shallow seas. Across the horizon, uong-i was setting into mountains taller than Everest and Olympus Mons. uong-i at this time was the blue of a gas flame on a stove, though hot and bright. Sometimes the atmosphere would tint it green at dawn and dusk, and during the day it was the white of daylit snow. But now it was blue.

Ziara touched muo-ka's shroud again. It was drier, slightly more tough as it wrapped around the contours of the moaning, rattling body. She lit the flares by scratching them on the mossed rocks. The two stalks arced hot across the water, sparks dancing across her skin. She plunged them into the soil by the deathbed.

Her eyes ached with the new light. Again, she remembered her first moment with muo-ka, remembered her panic at the thing ensnaring her in blinding daylight. The savagery with which it severed her umbilicus, the painful spasming of its limbs around her. She remembered these things, and knew muo-ka had been in as much panic as she had. She had long since realized this, even if she hadn't let it sink in.

From her first moment here, muo-ka remained a giant, terrifying thing. The days of recovery in the chrysalid blanket it wove around her. She'd been trapped while it smothered her with boiling food from its belly, trying and failing to be gentle. Fevers raging from nanite vaccines recalibrating her system, to digest what her parent was feeding her and breathe the different air, the new soup of microbes. "Stop," she would tell muo-ka. "Please stop. I can't eat your food. I'm dying." But it would only clutch her cocooned body and tilt her so she could vomit, the ends of its limbs sharp against her back. It would continue feeding her, keep letting her shit and piss and vomit in that cocoon, which only digested it all, preventing any infections.

Sure enough, the fevers faded away and one day the cocoon came off in gummy strips. Ziara could move again, could move like she had on Earth. At first it was an aching crawl, leaving troughs in the rich mud of the islet. But she'd balled that mud in her fists and growled, standing on shaking legs. She watched her human shadow unfurl long across the silty islet, right under the eclipsing shape of muo-ka above her, its limbs whipping around her, supporting her until she shrugged them off.

Ziara had laughed and laughed, to be able to stand again, until phlegm had gathered in her throat and she had to spit in joy. So she walked, walked over this human stain she had left on the ground, walked over the wet warmth of muo-ka's land. She walked until she could run. She was so euphoric that she could only dance and leap across the basin, flexing her muscles, testing her augmented metal bones in this low gravity. Sick with adrenalin, she soared through the air, watching the horizon expand and expand, bounding from rock to rock, whipping past exoskeletal flying creatures that flashed in the sun. muo-ka watched, its leviathan darkness suddenly iridescent. Then Ziara stood in one place panting, and she screamed, emptied her lungs of that year of deep sleep through a pierced universe. She screamed goodbye to the planet of her first birth. As this unknown sound swept across the basin, muo-ka's limbs glittered with barbs that it flung into itself.

Ziara nodded at this memory. "muo-ka. Leaping? You taught me to walk," she said with a smile.

She had avoided muo-ka's oppressive presence by hiding in the pod. She would shit and piss, too, under the shade of the tilted wreck, in its rain of re-leaked tidal water. When she didn't want the smallness of the pod, she slipped into the basin's seas, walked across the landbridges and glittering sandbars to swirling landscapes of rock and mud fronded with life-colonies that clung like oversized froth. But always her parent would be looming on the horizon, its hovering shape bobbing over the water, limbs alternating in a flicker over the surface as it dredged for food. Sometimes it would soar over her in the evening, its blinking night eyes flickering lights, stars or aircraft from the striated skies of Earthly dusks. With those guiding lights it would lead her back to the islet. Her throat would throb in anger and frustration, at the miles of watery, rocky, mountainous horizon she couldn't escape, but she'd know that straying far would likely mean she'd be killed by something on land,or sea that was deadlier than her.

It took her a while to have her first period on the planet, because of the nanite vaccine calibrations and the shock of acclimatisation. All things considered, it hadn't been her worst. But she had recognized the leaden pain of cramps immediately, swallowed the salty spit of nausea and gone to the pod again. She'd squatted under it and bled into the unearthly sea.

Looking at that, she'd wondered what she was doing. Whether she was seeding something, whether she was changing the ecosystem. She'd felt like an irresponsible teenager. But looking at those crimson blossoms in the waves, she'd also felt a sudden, overwhelming longing. She'd become breathless at the thought that there was nobody else in the world. Not a single human beyond that horizon of seas and mountains and mudflats. Only the unbelievably remote promise that the mission would continue if the unmanned ship that had ejected her pod managed to return to Earth, with the news that the visitation had been successful. Another human might be sent, years later, maybe two if they could manage, hurtling down somewhere on the world with no means of communicating with her. Or a robot probe sent to scour the planet until it found and recorded her impact, just like the first probes that had seeded messages and artifacts to indicate Ziara's arrival.

But at that moment, she was as alone as any human could be. It was conceivable that she might never see a human again. Her eyelids had swollen with tears, and she'd watched her blood fall into the sea. She hadn't been able to see muo-ka from under the pod then. But she'd heard it secreting something, with loud rattling coughs. She'd sat and waited until her legs ached, until the rising tide lapped at her thighs.

Later she'd found fresh, coarse membranes strewn across the ground next to her rock calendar. They were waterproof.

New clothes.

Ziara had wrapped the membranes around herself like a saree, not knowing how else to wear them. She became light-headed when she caught the scent of flowers in them. It was a shocking sensation, a smell she'd never encountered on this world before.

muo-ka had been absent that whole day. When it returned, lights flickering in sunset, she held out her hand. It lurched gracelessly through the air as if caught in turbulence, before hovering down to her, curtaining her in softened limbs. Her palm fell against the familiar spot behind the limbs. She flinched at the heat.

"Thank you," Ziara said.

It said nothing through her, only unfurling, drowning the back of her throat in bloody sweetness.

muo-ka had been dying for months. It had told Ziara, in its sparse way, a cloying thick taste of both sweet berried blood and bitterness in her head.

"Sick?" she had asked.

"Sh-ikh," it had said in her mouth. "Ii-sey-na," it said, and when the word formed in her throat she knew it meant "death."

"Sorry," she had whispered.

"Euh-i," it had said. No. Not sorry.

Ziara had let it talk for longer than ever before. For hours, her hand flushed red from its heat. It had told her several words, sentences, that made up an idea of what to do with its dead body. Then it went on, forming concepts, ideas, lengthier than ever before. muo-ka told her many things.

Ziara thought about her relief, now, looking at dead muo-ka. It disturbed her, but it was the truth. There was a clarity to her world now. To this world. She would move along the mudflats and sandbridges and mountains. She would make blades of her parent's bones, as it had told her, and explore the world. She would finally go beyond that horizon, which now flared and dimmed with the setting of uong-i.

She was an alien, and the world would kill her, sooner rather than later. Even if by some miracle the second human arrived in the coming months, he'd be too weak to help. If one of the leviathans adopted him—and it would be a man that fell this time—it might even violently keep Ziara away from him as its own child, and she had no chance of fighting that. She knew nothing about the dynamics of this adoption. She was the first, after all. They had come into this without much knowledge, except their curiosity and gentle handling of the initial probes.

Until and unless Earth sent an actual colonization team that could touch down a vessel with equipment and tools on the surface, humans wouldn't be able to survive here without the help of muo-ka's kind. As muo-ka's child, she wondered if she might be able to befriend one of them, or whether she'd be killed in an instant.

Ziara shook her head. It was no point overthinking. She would walk this world, and see what came. She had chosen this, after all. She hadn't chosen her parent, but there it was, in front of her, dead as she was alive. And she was alive because of it.

The blue dome of the gas giant appeared over the horizon, filling the seas with reflections. In the sparking light of the flares, Ziara waited. The shroud had fossilized into a flexible papyrus, with an organic pattern that looked like writing, symbols. The shrunken behemoth finally vented its innards as the stars and far moons appeared in the night sky, behind streaks of radiant aurora. Ziara clenched her jaw and began to scoop the entrails up to give to the sea, as was dignified. For a moment, she wondered what the deaths of these solitary creatures were normally like. She had seen others on the horizons, but always so far they seemed mirages. They lived their lives alone on this world, severed from each other. It had to be the child that conducted the death rites, once it was ready to move on. Perhaps they induced death in themselves once their child was mature enough.

She stopped, recoiling from the mess.

In the reeking slop of its guts, she saw muo-ka replicated. A small muo-ka. But not muo-ka. A nameless one, budded in its leviathan body. It was dead. The child's limbs were tangled in the oily foam of its parent's death. The body was crushed. Her hands slid over its cold, broken form.

muo-ka had budded a child. A child that would have done muo-ka's death rites once it had matured, ready to go on its own.

"Oh," she said, fingers squelching in the translucent mud seeping out of muo-ka's child. "Oh, no. My muo-ka. My dear muo-ka," she whispered, to both corpses.

muo-ka had budded a child, and finding a mature child already ready to venture out into the world, it had crushed the one growing inside it. Only ziara was muo-ka's child.

"You brought me to life," ziara said, leaning in her parent's guts, holding her dead sibling, wrapped in clothes her parent had made. Her face crumpled as she buried it in the remains of muo-ka's life, her body shaking.

ziara left her sibling in the sea with muo-ka's guts. Using the bone-knife, she cut away the death shroud carefully and wore it around her shoulders. One day, ziara swore to herself, she would translate the symbols it had excreted on it. Her parent's death letter. She sliced off a part of the deflated hide, scrubbed it in the sea, and wore it as a cowl to keep her head warm during nights. The flares had smoked out. She looked at muo-ka curled dead. It had told her the creatures of the air would come and consume it, slowly, as it should be. She felt bad leaving it there on that stony deathbed, but that was what it had told her to do. She wiped her eyes and face. A bone knife and a whole world she didn't belong in, except right here on this islet.

A fiery line streaked across the sky. A human vessel. Or a shooting star. ziara gazed at its afterimage for a moment, and walked off the islet and across the shallows and mudflats of the basin. She had named that basin once, or muo-ka had, with her mouth.

eya-rith. Earth, so she would not be homesick.

THE DISMANTLED INVENTION OF FATE

JEFFREY FORD

The ancient astronaut John Gaghn lived atop a mountain, Gebila, on the southern shore of the Isle of Bistasi. His home was a sprawling, one-story house with whitewashed walls, long empty corridors, and sudden court-yards open to the sky. The windows held no glass and late in the afternoon the ocean breezes rushed up the slopes and flowed through the place like water through a mermaid's villa. Around the island, the sea was the color of grape jam due to a tiny red organism that, in summer, swarmed across its surface. Exotic birds stopped there on migration, and their high trilled calls mixed with the eternal pounding of the surf were a persistent music heard even in sleep.

Few ever visited the old man, for the mountain trails were, in certain spots, treacherously steep and haunted by predators. Through the years, more than one reporter or historian of space travel had attempted to scale the heights, grown dizzy in the hot island sun, and turned back. Others simply disappeared along the route, never to be heard from again. He'd seen them coming through his antique telescope, laboring in the ascent, appearing no bigger than ants, and smiled ruefully, knowing just by viewing them at a distance which ones would fail and which determined few would make the cool shade and sweet aroma of the lemon groves of the upper slopes. There the white blossoms would surround them like clouds and they might briefly believe that they were climbing into the sky.

On this day, though, Gaghn peered through his telescope and knew the dark figure he saw climbing Gebila would most definitely make the peak

by twilight and the rising of the ringed planet in the east. He wanted no
visitors, but he didn't care if they came. He had little to say to anyone, for
he knew that Time, which he'd spent a life abusing on deep space voyages
sunk in cryogenic sleep and hurtling across galaxies at near the speed of
light, would very soon catch up and deliver him to oblivion. If this visitor
wanted to know the history of his voyages, he felt he could sum it all up in
one sentence and then send the stranger packing. "I've traveled so far and
yet never arrived," he would say.

After his usual breakfast of a cup of hot water with the juice of a whole
lemon squeezed into it, a bowl of tendrils from the telmis bush, and the
still-warm heart of a prowling valru, he tottered off, with the help of a
cane, into the lemon grove to sit on his observation deck. He settled his
frail body gently into a bentwood rocker and placed upon the table in
front of him a little blue box, perfectly square on all sides, with one red
dot in the center of the face-up side. His left hand, holding in two fingers
a crystal the shape of a large diamond, shook slightly as he reached
forward and positioned the point of the clear stone directly above the
red dot.

When he drew back his hand, the crystal remained, hovering a hair-
breadth above the box. He cleared his throat and spoke a word—"Zadiiz"—
and the many-faceted stone began to spin like a top. He leaned back in the
rocker, turning his face—a web of wrinkles bearing a grin, a wide nose,
and a pair of small round spectacles with pink glass lenses—to the sun. As
the chair began to move, a peaceful music of flutes and strings seeped out
of the blue box and spiraled around him.

He dozed off and dreamed of the planets he'd visited, their landscapes
so impossibly varied, the long cold centuries of frozen slumber on deep
space journeys filled with entire dream lives burdened by the unquenchable
longing to awake, the wonderful rocket ships he'd piloted, the strange and
beautiful aliens he'd befriended, bartered with, eluded, and killed, the suit
that preserved his life in hostile atmospheres with its bubble helmet and
jetpack for leaping craters. Then he woke for a moment only to doze again,
this time to dream of Zadiiz.

He'd come upon her in his youth, on one of the plateaus amid the sea
of three-hundred-foot-high red grass covering the southern continent on
the planet Yarmit-Sobit. He'd often wondered if it was random chance or
destiny that he'd chosen that place at that time of all the places and times
in the universe to set down his shuttle and explore. The village he came

upon, comprised of huts woven from the red grass, lying next to a green lake, was idyllic in its serenity.

The people of the village, sleek and supple, the color of an Earth sky, were near-human in form, save for a ridged fin that ran the length of the spine, ending in a short tail. They had orange eyes without irises and sharp-edged fingers perfectly suited for cutting grass. In their sensibility, they were more than human, for they were supremely empathetic, even with other species like his, valued friendships, and had no word for "cruelty." He stayed among them, fished with them off the platforms that jutted out over the deep sea of grass for the wide-winged leviathans they called hurrurati, and joined in their ceremonies of smoke and calculation. Zadiiz was one of them.

From the instant he first saw her, flying one of the orange kites crafted from the inflated bladder of a hurrurati on the open plateau, he had a desire to know her better. He challenged her to a foot race, and she beat him. He challenged her to a wrestling match, and she beat him. He challenged her to a game of tic-tac-toe he taught her using a stick and drawing in the dirt. This, he finally won, and it drew a laugh from her—the sound of her joy the most vibrant thing he'd encountered in all his travels. As the days went on, she taught him her language, showed him how to find roots in the rich loam of the plateau and how to wrangle and ride the giant, single-horned porcine creatures called sheefen, and explained how the universe was made by the melting of an ice giant. In return, he told her about the millions of worlds beyond the red star that was her sun.

Eventually the mother of the village came to him and asked if he would take the challenge of commitment in order to be bonded to Zadiiz for life. He agreed and was lowered by a long rope off the side of the plateau into the depths of the sea of red grass. In among the enormous blades, he discovered schools of birds that swam like fish through the hidden world and froglike creatures that braved the heights, leaping from one thick strand of red to another. Even deeper down, as he finally touched the ground where almost no sunlight fell, he encountered large white insects with antennae and six arms each that went about on two legs. He'd hidden his ray gun in his boot, and thus had the means to survive for the duration of his stay below the surface.

Upon witnessing the power of his weapon against a carnivorous leething, the white insects befriended him, communicating through unspoken thoughts they fired into his head from their antennae. They showed him the sights of their secret world, cautioned him to always be wary of snakes (which they called weeha) and took him to stay overnight in the skeletal remains of a giant hurrurati where they fed him a meal of red grass sugar and revealed their incomprehensible philosophy of the sufficient. When he left, they gave him an object they'd found in the belly of the dead hurrurati for which they had no name, although he knew it to be some kind of metal gear. Two days later, the rope was again lowered and he was retrieved back to the plateau. Zadiiz could hardly believe how well he'd survived and was proud of him. During their bonding ceremony, Gaghn placed the curio of the gear, strung on a lanyard, around her neck.

It wasn't long before the astronaut's restlessness, which had flogged him on across the universe, finally returned to displace the tranquillity of life on the plateau. He needed to leave, and he asked Zadiiz to go with him. She courageously agreed, even though it was the belief of her people that the dark ocean beyond the sky was a sea of death. The entire village gathered around and watched as the shuttle carried them up and away. Legends would be told of the departure for centuries to come.

Gaghn docked the shuttle in the hold of his space vessel, the *Empress*, and when Zadiiz stepped out into the metal, enclosed world of the ship, she trembled. They spent some time merely orbiting her planet, so that she might grow accustomed to the conditions and layout of her new home. Then, one day, when he could withstand the impulse to travel no longer, he led her to the cryo-cradle and helped her to lie down inside. He tried to explain that she would experience long, intricate dreams that would seem utterly real, and that some could be quite horrendous, but to remember they were only dreams. She nodded. They kissed by fluttering their eyelashes together, and he pushed the button that made the top of her berth slide down over her. In the seconds before the gas did its work, he heard her scream and pound upon the lid. Then came only silence, and with a troubled conscience, he set the coordinates for a distant constellation and went, himself, to sleep.

Upon waking, light-years away from Yarmit-Sobit, he opened her cradle and discovered her lifeless. He surmised that a nightmare that attended the frozen sleep had frightened the life out of her. Her eyes were wide, her mouth agape, her fists clenched against some terror that had stalked her imagination. He took her body down to Eljesh, the planet the *Empress* now orbited, to the lace forest at the bottom of an ancient crater where giant, pure white trees, their branches like the entwining arms of so many cosmic snowflakes, reached up into an ashen sky. He'd intended the beauty of this place to be a surprise for her. Unable to contemplate burying her beneath the soil, he laid her on a flat rock next to a milk-white pool, closed her eyes, brushed the hair away from her face, and took with him, as a keepsake, the gear he'd given her.

When he fled Eljesh, it wasn't simply the wanderlust drawing him onward; now he was also pursued with equal ferocity by her memory. He always wondered why he couldn't have simply stayed on the plateau, and that question became his new traveling companion through intergalactic wars, explorations to the fiery hearts of planets, pirate operations, missions of good will, and all the way to the invisible wall at the end of the universe, after which there was no more, and back again.

He knew many, and many millions more knew of him, but he'd never told a soul of any species what he'd done until one night, high in the frozen mountains, near the pole of the Idiot Planet (so named for its harsh conditions and a judgment upon any who would dare to travel there). Somehow he'd wound up in a cave, weathering a blizzard, with a wise old Ketuban, universally considered to be the holiest and most mystical cosmic citizens in existence. This fat old fellow, eyeless but powerfully psychic, looked like a pile of mud with a gaping mouth, four tentacles, and eight tiny legs. He spoke in whispered bursts of air, but spoke the truth.

"Gaghn," said the Ketuban, "you have sorrow."

John understood the language and moved in close to the lumpish fellow so he could hear over the howling of the wind. Once he understood the statement, the sheer simplicity of it, the heartfelt tone of it, despite the rude sound that delivered it, he told the story of Zadiiz.

When he was finished, the Ketuban said, "You believe you killed her?"

Gaghn said nothing but nodded.

"Some would call it a sin."

"I call it a sin," said the astronaut.

The storm outside grew more fierce, and the roar of the gale hypnotized Gaghn, making him drowsy. As he drifted toward sleep, his memory awash with images of Zadiiz, teaching him to fish with spear and rope and tackle, sitting beside him on the plateau beneath the stars, moving around the dwelling they'd shared on a bright warm morning in spring, singing the high-pitched bird songs of her people. Just before he fell into sleep, he heard his cave mate's voice mix with the constant rush of the wind. "Rest easy. I will arrange things."

When Gaghn awoke, the storm had abated and the Ketuban had vanished, leaving behind, on the floor of the cave, a crude winged figurine formed from the creature's mud. He also realized the Ketuban had taken the gear he'd worn around his neck since leaving Zadiiz on Eljesh. As the astronaut made his way cautiously over ice fields fissured with yawning crevices back to his shuttle, he remembered the mystic alien's promise. In the years that followed, though, he found no rest from his compulsion to journey ever farther, nor from the memories that tormented him, and he realized that this must be the fate that was arranged—no peace for him as punishment for his sin.

More memories of his travels ensued as the ancient astronaut woke and slept, the music from the blue box washing over him, the scent of the lemon blossoms and the heat of the sun, his weak heart and failing will to live, mixing together into their own narcotic that kept him drowsy. One last image came: his visit to the laboratory of the great inventor, Onsing, inside the hollow planet, Simmesia. The aged scientist, whose mind was once ablaze with what many considered the galaxy's greatest imagination, was laid low by the infirmity of age, on the verge of death. The sight of this had frightened John, and he'd thought if he went far enough, fast enough, he'd escape the fate the dying inventor assured him in labored whispers came to all.

Then Gaghn woke to the late afternoon wind of the island, saw the ringed planet had risen in the east, and in the failing light, noticed a tall dark figure standing before him.

"I've traveled far and yet never arrived," he said.

The visitor, nearly eight feet tall, as broad as three men, and covered in a long black cloak, the hem of which brushed against the stone of the deck, stepped forward, and the old man saw its face. Not human, but some kind of vague imitation of a human face, like a mask of varnished shell with two dark holes for eyes, a subtle ridge for a nose, and another smaller hole that was the mouth. Atop the smooth head was a pair of horns whose sharp points curved toward each other.

"You may leave now," said the old man.

The tall fellow, his complexion indigo, took two graceful steps forward, stopping next to Gaghn's rocker. The astronaut focused on the empty holes that served as eyes and tried to see if some sign of a personality lurked anywhere inside them. The stranger leaned over and, quicker than a heartbeat, a long tapered nozzle, sharp as the tips of the horns, sprang out of the mouth hole, passed through Gaghn's forehead with the sound of an egg cracking, and stabbed deep into the center of his brain. The astronaut gave a sudden sigh. Then the nozzle retracted as quickly as it had sprung forth. The old man fell forward, dead, across the table, his right arm hitting the blue box sideways, sending the crystal plinking onto the stone floor of the deck.

The indigo figure stepped away from the body and sloughed its long cloak. Once free of the garment, the two wings that had been folded against its back lifted and opened wide. They were sleek, half the creature's height, pointed at the lower tips and ribbed with delicate bone work beneath the slick flesh. Its entire manlike form suggested equal parts reptile and mineral. From down the mountain came the death cry of some creature, from off in the grove came the sorrowful call of the pale night bird, and beneath them both could be heard, in the distance, the persistent pounding of the sea. The visitor crouched, and with great power, leaped into the air. The wings spread out, caught the island wind, and carried him, with powerful thrusts, into the night sky. He flew, silhouetted before the bright presence of the ringed planet from pole to pole, higher and higher, as the figure of John Gaghn receded to a pinpoint, became part of the island, then the ocean, then the night. Hours later, the winged visitor pierced the outer membrane of the planet's atmosphere and was born into space.

The Aieu, people of the jump-bone animal, blended flawlessly with the white trees in the lace forest. A dozen of them—hairless, perfectly pale, crouching still as stone gargoyles among the branches—silently watched the movements of the dark giant. Its wings, its horns, told them it would be a formidable opponent, and they wondered how their enemies had created it. After it had passed beneath them, the elder of their party motioned for the swiftest of them to go quickly and warn the queen of an assassin's approach. The small fellow nodded, and then, on clawed feet, took off, running through the branches, leaping soundlessly from tree to tree, in the direction of the hive. Those who remained behind spread out and followed the intruder, their leader all the while plotting a strategy of offense for the time his force would be at full strength.

Zadiiz, the powder-blue queen, sat in her throne at the center of the hive, the children of the Aieu gathered around her feet. Nearly too feeble with age to walk, let alone run and climb, she could no longer lead the war parties or the hunt as she once had. She was not required to do anything

at all as her subjects owed their very existence to her, but she wanted
to remain useful for as long as she could, both to pass the time and to
set an example. She instructed the young ones on everything from the
proper way to employ the deadly jump-bone against a foe to the nature
of existence itself, as she saw it. On this day, it was the latter. In her weak
voice, quivering with age, she explained:

"Look around you, my dears. All of you, everything you see, the white
forest, the gray sky, your distant past, and whatever future we have left,
everything is a dream I am dreaming. As I speak to you, I am really asleep
in a great vessel, in the clutch of a cradle that freezes the body but not the
dream, flying through the darkness above, amid the stars, to a far place
where I will eventually awake to be with my life companion, John Gaghn."

The children looked into her orange eyes and nodded, although they
could hardly understand. One of the brighter ones spoke up: "And what
will become of us when you awaken?"

Zadiiz could only speak the truth. "I'm not sure," she said, "but I'll do
everything I can to keep you safe inside my memory. You'll know if I've
done this when, if I appear to die, you are still alive." Upon the mention
of her own death, the children gasped, but she went on to allay their fears.
"I won't have really died, I'll merely have emerged into another dream, or
I'll truly have awakened, the vessel having reached its destination." She
could see she had confused them and frightened them a little. "Go and
think on this for now, and we'll discuss it more tomorrow." The small,
dazed faces, which, at one time, back on the plateau of the red grass lands
of her own planet, she might have considered ugly, now were precious to
her. The children came forward and lightly touched her arms, her legs, her
face, before leaving the hive. She watched them scamper out and take to
the branches that surrounded her palace in the treetops, and then sat back
and tried to understand, for herself, what she had said.

John had warned her that the dreams would come and they would be
deep and sometimes terrible, and there were parts of this one she believed
herself presently imprisoned in that were, but there was also beauty and
the reciprocal love between the Aieu and herself. How many more dream
lives would she need to experience, she wondered, before waking? This
one began with her opening her eyes, staring up into the pale faces of a
hunting party of the people of the jump-bone animal. Later, when she'd
come to learn their language, they told her that even though many of them
thought her dead when they'd found her lying on the flat stone next to the

pool, their herb witch listened closely, placing her ear to the blue queen's ear and could hear, though very weak, the faint murmur of thoughts still alive in her head. Then, slowly, by employing a treatment of their most powerful natural drugs and constantly moving her limbs, they'd brought her around to consciousness.

Zadiiz was roused from her reverie by the approach of one of her subjects. He was agitated and began spouting in the Aieu gibberish before he'd even reached her side. "An intruder, an assassin," he was shouting, waving his needle-sharp jump-bone in the air. She shook her head and put both hands up, palms facing outward to indicate he should slow down. He took a deep breath and bowed, placing his weapon on the floor at her feet. "What is this intruder?" she asked, feeling so weary she could hardly concentrate on his description.

He put the two longest fingers of each of his three-fingered hands, pointing atop his wrinkled forehead. She understood and nodded. He then made as blank an expression as he could with his face, closing his eyes, turning his mouth into a perfect "O." She nodded. When he saw she was following him, he held his right hand up as high as he could and then leaped up to show the stranger's height. Last, he said, "Thula," which meant "deadly." In response, she made a fist, and he responded by lifting his weapon and exiting out upon the treetops to summon the forces of the Aieu.

As old and tired as she was, there still burned within her a spark of envy for those who now swarmed away from the hive to meet the threat of this new enemy. She lit her pipe, ran her hand across the old crone stubble on her chin, and, with a vague smile, found in her memory an image of herself when she could still run and climb and fight. It hadn't taken her long, once the Aieu had brought her around, before she was back on her feet and practicing competing with the best hunters and wrestlers her rescuers had among them. She'd taken to the treetops as though she'd been born in the lace forest, and a few days after they'd demonstrated for her the jump-bone-throwing technique, she was more accurate and deadly with it than those who were still young before the jump-bone animal had been hunted to extinction.

But it was in the war against the Fire Hand that she'd proven herself a general of keen strategic insight and unfailing courage. Utilizing the advantage of the treetops, and employing stealth and speed to defeat an enemy of greater number, she'd helped the Aieu turn back the bloodthirsty hordes that had spilled down over the high lip of the crater and flooded the forest. It was this victory that had elevated her to the status of royalty among them. She drew on her pipe, savoring the rush of imagery from the past. As the smoke twined up toward the center of the hive, a distant battle cry sounded from the forest, and in the confusion of her advanced age, she believed it to be her own.

The victory shouts of the Aieu warriors woke her as they led their prisoner into the hive. The giant indigo creature, wings bound with woven white vine around its chest, hands tied together at the wrists in front, a choker around its muscular neck, strode compliantly forward, surrounded by its captors, who brandished jump-bones above their heads.

"Bring him into the light," commanded Zadiiz, and they prodded the thing forward to stand in the glow of the two torches that flanked her throne. When she beheld the huge indigo form, she marveled at the effectiveness of her battle training on the Aieu, for it didn't seem possible that even all who lived in the treetop complex surrounding the hive could together subdue such a monster. "Good work," she said to her people. Then her gaze came to rest on the emotionless, shell mask of a face with its simple holes for eyes and mouth, and the sight of it startled her. It shared, in its blank expression, the look of another face she could not help but remember.

It was in the dream that had preceded her waking into the lace forest and the people of the jump-bone animal, the first of her sleeping lives that John Gaghn had promised after he'd closed her in the cradle. In this one, she'd lived alone in a cave on a barren piece of rock, floating through deep space. She spent her time watching the stars, noting, here and there, at great distances, the slow explosions of galaxies, like the blossoming of flowers, and listening to endlessly varied music made by light piercing the darkness. A very long time passed, and she remembered the weight of her loneliness. Then one day, a figure appeared in the distance, heading for her, and slowly it revealed itself to be a large silver globe. Smoke issued from its back and it buzzed horribly, interfering with the natural song of the universe.

The vessel rolled down onto the deep sand beside the entrance to her cave. Moments later, a door opened in the side of it and out stepped a man made of metal. The starlight reflected on his shiny surface and he gave off a faint glow. At first she was frightened to behold something so peculiar, but the metal man, whose immobile face was cast in an expression of infinite patience, spoke to her in a friendly voice. He told her his name was 49 and asked if he could stay with her until he managed to fix his craft. Zadiiz was delighted to have the company, and assured him he could.

She offered him some of the spotted mushrooms that grew on the inner walls of the cave, her only sustenance. They tasted to her like the flesh of the hurrurati. 49 refused, explaining that he was a machine and did not eat. Zadiiz didn't understand the idea of a robot, and so he explained that he had been made by a great scientist named Onsing, and that all of his parts were metal. He told her, "I have intelligence, I even have emotion, but I was made to fulfill the need of my inventor, whereas beings like you were made to fulfill your own desires."

"What is your master's need?" asked Zadiiz.

"Onsing has passed on into death," said 49, "but some time ago, while he still lived, he discovered through intensive calculation, using a mathematical system of his own devising and entering those results into a computer that not only rendered answers as to what was possible but also what could, given an infinite amount of time, be probable, that his sworn enemies, the Ketubans, would some day create a mischievous creature that could very likely manipulate the fate of the universe."

Zadiiz simply stared at 49 for a very long time. "Explain 'infinite' and 'probable,' " she finally said.

The robot explained.

"Explain 'fate,' " she said.

"Fate," said 49, and a whirring sound could be heard issuing from his head as he stared at the ground. Sparks shot from his ears. "Well, it is the series of events beginning at the beginning of everything that will eventually dictate what must be. And all you would need to do to change the universe would be to undo one thing that must be and everything would change."

"Why must it be?" she asked.

"Because it must," said the robot. "So, to prevent this, Onsing created a machine of one thousand parts that could, once its start button was pressed, send out, in all directions, a wave across the universe that would eventually find this creature and melt it. When he had finished the machine, he hoped to always keep it running so that it could forever prevent the Ketubans from undermining fate."

"And did he?" asked Zadiiz.

"Poor Onsing never had a chance to start his machine, because it was destroyed by the evil Ketubans, loathsome creatures, like steaming piles of organic waste with tentacles and too many legs. They used their psychic power to automatically disassemble the machine, and all of its individual parts flew away in as many different directions as there were pieces. Onsing, too determined to give up, but knowing he would not live long enough to rebuild the machine or find all of the parts scattered across the universe, created one thousand robots like me to go out into space and fetch them back. Nine hundred and ninety-nine of the robots have found their parts, and they have assembled all of the machine but for one tiny gear that is still missing. That is my part to find, and they wait for my success. Once I find it, I will return with it. It will be fitted into the machine. The robot that has been designed to press the start button on the machine will fulfill its task and the fate of the universe will be protected."

"How long have you searched?" asked Zadiiz.

"Too long," said 49.

Eventually, Zadiiz grew weary, as she always did when eating the mushrooms, and fell asleep. When she awoke, she found that 49 was gone from the cave. She ran outside only to discover that his sphere of a vessel was also gone. Some time later, she realized that the metal gear that had hung around her neck was missing, and the thought of having to live the rest of that lonely dream life without even the amulet's small connection to John Gaghn sent her into shock. Her mind closed in on itself, shut down, went blank. When she awoke, she was surrounded by the pale faces of the people of the jump-bone animal.

She surfaced from her memory, again surrounded by the Aieus' pale faces; this time in the hot and crowded hive. They'd been waiting in expectant silence for her to pronounce the fate of the assassin they'd brought before her. Zadiiz realized she'd had a lapse of awareness, and now tried to focus on the situation before her. She looked the horned figure up and down, avoiding another glimpse at the face. She wondered who could have sent this thing. Because of its unknown nature, its obvious power and size, she could not allow it to live. She was about to order that the creature be drowned in the white pool when she noticed the fingers on its left hand open slightly. Something fell from between them but did not continue on to the floor. It was caught and suspended by a lanyard looped through one of its small openings.

Upon seeing the gear, she gasped and struggled to her feet. The fact that she'd just been thinking of it made her dizzy with its implications. "Where did you get that?" she asked. The implacable face remained silent, but her obvious reaction to the sight of the curio sent a murmur through those assembled. "Who sent you?" she asked. Its eye holes seemed to be staring directly at her. She started down the two steps from her throne, and her people came up on either side to help her approach the creature. As she drew near, she felt a flutter of nervousness in her chest. "Did John send you from his own dream?" she said.

When she was less than a step away from the prisoner, she reached out for the amulet, and that is when the indigo creature inhaled so mightily the ropes binding its wings snapped. In one fluid motion, it ripped its wrists free of their bonds, the vines snapping away as if they were strands of hair, and took Zadiiz by the shoulders. She was too slow to scream, for he had already leaned forward and the pointed nozzle had shot forth from its mouth. There was the sound of an egg cracking. The Aieu did not recover from their shock until the nozzle had retracted, and by then the creature had torn the lead from its neck and leaped into the air. At the same moment, Zadiiz fell backward into her subjects' waiting arms. Jump-bones were thrown, but the assassin flew swiftly up and out of the opening at the top of the hive.

The indigo creature flew on and on for light-years through space, past planets and suns, quasars and nebulae, black holes and wormholes, resting momentarily now and then upon an asteroid or swimming down through the atmosphere of a planet to live upon its surface for a year or two, and no matter the incredible sights it witnessed in the centuries it traveled its expression never once changed. Finally, in a cave whose walls were covered with spotted mushrooms, on an asteroid orbiting a blue-white star, it found what it had been searching for—a large metallic globe and, sitting next to it upon a rock, a robot, long seized with inaction due to the frustration of its inability to accomplish the task its master had set for it.

Dangling the gear upon its lanyard in front of the eye sensors of the robot, the indigo creature brought the man of metal to awareness. Robot 49 reached up for the gear, and the creature placed it easily into his ball-jointed fingers. The two expressionless faces stared at each other for a moment and then each turned away, knowing what needed to be done. The robot moved to his globe of a space vessel, and the indigo creature sprinted from the cave and spread its wings. Even before the sputtering metal ball had exited the cave and set a course for the hollow world, the indigo creature had disappeared into the vast darkness of space.

On an undiscovered world where a vast ocean of three-hundred-foot-tall red grass lapped the base of a small mountain, the creature landed and set to work. Time, which had passed in long lazy skeins to this point, now was of the essence, and there could be no rest. At the peak of the mountain, the winged being cleared away a tangled forest of vines, telmis, and wild lemon tress, uprooting trunks with its bare hands and knocking down larger ones with its horns. Once the land was cleared, it set about mining blocks of white marble from a site lower down the slope, precisely cutting the hard stone with the nail of its left index finger. These blocks were flown to the peak and arranged to build a sprawling, one-story dwelling, with long empty corridors and sudden courtyards open to the sky.

When all was completed upon the mountain peak, the creature entered the white dwelling, passed down the long empty corridors to the bedroom, and sat down upon the edge of a soft mattress of prowling valru hide stuffed with lemon blossoms. It could see through the window opening the ringed planet begin its ascent as the day waned. Twilight breezes scudding off the sea of red grass rushed up the slopes and swamped the house. The indigo creature folded its wings back and stretched its arms once before lying back upon the wide, comfortable bed it had made.

As the horned head rested upon a pillow, many light-years away, at the center of the hollow planet, robot 49 fitted the small gear into place within Onsing's remarkable machine. Cheers went up from the 999 metallic brethren gathered behind him. And the 1,001st robot, designed solely to press the start button on the machine, finally fulfilled its task. A lurching, creaking, clanging of parts moving emanated from the strange device. Then invisible waves that gave off the sound of a bird's call issued forth, instantly disabling all of the robots, traveling right through the hollow planet and outward, in all directions across the universe.

The indigo creature heard what it at first believed to be the call of the pale night bird, but soon realized it was mistaken. It then made the only sound it would ever make in its long life, a brief sigh of recognition, before it began to melt. Thick droplets of indigo ran from its face and arms and chest, evaporating into night before staining the mattress. Its horns dripped away like melting candle wax, and its wings shrank until they had both run off into puddles of nothing. As the huge dark figure disintegrated, from within its bulk emerged a pair of forms, arms clasped around each other. With the evaporation of the last drip of indigo, John and Zadiiz, again young as the moment they first met, rolled away from each other, dreaming.

In the morning they were awakened by the light of the sun streaming in the window without glass and the sounds of the migrating birds. They discovered each other and themselves, but had no memory, save their own names, of their pasts or how they came to be on the mountain peak. All they remembered was their bond, and although this was an invisible thing, they both felt it strongly.

They lived together for many years in tranquillity on the undiscovered planet, and in their fifth year had a child. The little girl had her mother's orange eyes and her father's desire to know what lay out beyond the sky. She was a swift runner and climbed about in the lemon trees like a monkey. The child had a powerful imagination and concocted stories for her parents about men made of metal and dark-winged creatures, of incredible machines and vessels that flew to the stars. At her birth, not knowing exactly why, John Gaghn and Zadiiz settled upon the name of Onsing for her and wondered how that name might direct her fate.

JAGANNATH

KARIN TIDBECK

Another child was born in the great Mother, excreted from the tube protruding from the Nursery ceiling. It landed with a wet thud on the organic bedding underneath. Papa shuffled over to the birthing tube and picked the baby up in his wizened hands. He stuck two fingers in the baby's mouth to clear the cavity of oil and mucus, and then slapped its bottom. The baby gave a faint cry.

"Ah," said Papa. "She lives." He counted fingers and toes with a satisfied nod. "Your name will be Rak," he told the baby.

Papa tucked her into one of the little niches in the wall where babies of varying sizes were nestled. Cables and flesh moved slightly, accommodating the baby's shape. A teat extended itself from the niche, grazing her cheek; Rak automatically turned and sucked at it. Papa patted the soft little head, sniffing at the hairless scalp. The metallic scent of Mother's innards still clung to it. A tiny flailing hand closed around one of his fingers.

"Good grip. You'll be a good worker," mumbled Papa.

Rak's early memories were of rocking movement, of Papa's voice whispering to her as she sucked her sustenance, the background gurgle of Mother's abdominal walls. Later, she was let down from the niche to the older children, a handful of plump bodies walking bow-legged on the undulating floor, bathed in the soft light from luminescent growths in the wall and ceiling. They slept in a pile, jostling bodies slick in the damp heat and the comforting rich smell of raw oil and blood.

Papa gathered them around his feet to tell them stories.

"What is Mother?" Papa would say. "She took us up when our world failed. She is our protection and our home. We are her helpers and beloved children." Papa held up a finger, peering at them with eyes almost lost in the wrinkles of his face. "We make sure Her machinery runs smoothly. Without us, She cannot live. We only live if Mother lives."

Rak learned that she was a female, a worker, destined to be big and strong. She would help drive the peristaltic engine in Mother's belly, or work the locomotion of Her legs. Only one of the children, Ziz, was male. He was smaller than the others, with spindly limbs and bulging eyes in a domed head. Ziz would eventually go to the Ovary and fertilize Mother's eggs. Then he would take his place in Mother's head as pilot.

"Why can't we go to Mother's head?" said Rak.

"It's not for you," said Papa. "Only males can do that. That's the order of things: females work the engines and pistons so that Mother can move forward. For that, you are big and strong. Males fertilize Mother's eggs and guide her. They need to be small and smart. Look at Ziz." Papa indicated the boy's thin arms. "He will never have the strength you have. He would never survive in the Belly. And you, Rak, will be too big to go to Mother's head."

Every now and then, Papa would open the Nursery door and talk to someone outside. Then he would collect the biggest of the children, give it a tight hug and then usher it out the door. The children never came back. They had begun work. Soon after, a new baby would be excreted from the tube.

When Rak was big enough, Papa opened the Nursery's sphincter door. On the other side stood a hulking female. She dwarfed Papa, muscles rolling under a layer of firm blubber.

"This is Hap, your caretaker," said Papa.

Hap held out an enormous hand.

"You'll come with me now," she said.

Rak followed her new caretaker through a series of corridors connected by openings that dilated at a touch. Dull metal cabling veined the smooth pink flesh underfoot and around them. The tunnel was lit here and there by luminous growths, similar to the Nursery, but the light more reddish. The air became progressively warmer and thicker, gaining an undertone of something unfamiliar that stuck to the roof of Rak's mouth. Gurgling and humming noises reverberated through the walls, becoming stronger as they walked.

"I'm hungry," said Rak.

Hap scraped at the wall, stringy goop sloughing off into her hand.

"Here," she said. "This is what you'll eat now. It's Mother's food for us. You can eat it whenever you like."

It tasted thick and sweet sliding down her throat. After a few swallows Rak was pleasantly full. She was licking her lips as they entered the Belly.

It was much bigger than the Nursery, criss-crossed by bulging pipes of flesh looping through and around the chamber. Six workers were evenly spaced out in the chamber. They were kneading the flesh or straining at great valves set into the tubes. The light was a stronger yellow here.

"This is the Belly," said Hap. "We move the food Mother eats through her entrails."

"Where does it go?" asked Rak.

Hap pointed to the far end of the chamber, where the bulges were smaller.

"Mother absorbs it. Turns it into food for us."

Rak nodded. "And that?" She pointed at the small apertures dotting the walls.

Hap walked over to the closest one and poked it. It dilated, and Rak was looking into a tube running left to right along the inside of the wall. A low grunting sound came from somewhere inside. A sinewy worker crawled past, filling up the space from wall to wall. She didn't pause to look at the open aperture.

"That's a Leg worker," said Hap. She let the aperture close and stretched.

"Do they ever come out?" said Rak.

"Only when they're going to die. So we can put them in the engine. Now. No more talking. You start over there." Hap steered Rak toward the end of the chamber. "Easy work."

Rak grew, putting on muscle and fat. She was one of twelve workers in the Belly. They worked and slept in shifts. One worked until one was tired, then ate, and then curled up in the sleeping niche next to whoever was there. Rak learned work songs to sing in time with the kneading Mother's intestines, the turning of the valves. The eldest worker, an enormous female called Poi, usually led the chorus. They sung stories of how Mother saved their people. They sang of the parts of Her glorious body, the movement of Her myriad legs.

"What is outside Mother?" Rak asked once, curled up next to Hap, wrapped in the scent of sweat and oil.

"The horrible place that Mother saved us from," mumbled Hap. "Go to sleep."

"Have you seen it?"

Hap scoffed. "No, and I don't want to. Neither do you. Now quiet."

Rak closed her eyes, thinking of what kind of world might be outside Mother's body, but could only imagine darkness. The thought made a chill run down her back. She crept closer to Hap, nestling against her back.

The workload was never constant. It had to do with where Mother went and what she ate. Times of plenty meant hard work, the peristaltic engine swelling with food. But during those times, the females also ate well; the mucus coating Mother's walls grew thick and fragrant, and Rak would put on a good layer of fat. Then Mother would move on and the food become less plentiful, Her innards thinning out and the mucus drying and caking. The workers would slow down, sleep more, and wait for a change. Regardless of how much there was to eat, Rak still grew, until she looked up and realized she was no longer so small compared to the others.

Poi died in her sleep. Rak woke up next to her cooling body, confused that Poi wasn't breathing. Hap had to explain that she was dead. Rak had never seen a dead person before. Poi just lay there, her body marked from the lean time, folds of skin hanging from her frame.

The workers carried Poi to a sphincter near the top of the chamber, and dropped her into Mother's intestine. They took turns kneading the body through Mother's flesh, the bulge becoming smaller and smaller until Poi was consumed altogether.

"Go to the Nursery, Rak," said Hap. "Get a new worker."

Rak made her way up the tubes. It was her first time outside the Belly since leaving the Nursery. The corridors looked just like they had when Hap had led her through them long ago.

The Nursery looked much smaller. Rak towered in the opening, looking down at the tiny niches in the walls and the birthing tube bending down from the ceiling. Papa sat on his cot, crumpled and wrinkly. He stood up when Rak came in, barely reaching her shoulder.

"Rak, is it?" he said. He reached up and patted her arm. "You're big and strong. Good, good."

"I've come for a new worker, Papa," said Rak.

"Of course you have." Papa looked sideways, wringing his hands.

"Where are the babies?" she said.

"There are none," Papa replied. He shook his head. "There haven't been any . . . viable children, for a long time."

"I don't understand," said Rak.

"I'm sorry, Rak." Papa shrank back against the wall. "I have no worker to give you."

"What's happening, Papa? Why are there no babies?"

"I don't know. Maybe it is because of the lean times. But there have been lean times before, and there were babies then. And no visits from the Head, either. The Head would know. But no-one comes. I have been all alone." Papa reached out for Rak, stroking her arm. "All alone."

Rak looked down at his hand. It was dry and light. "Did you go to the Head and ask?"

Papa blinked. "I couldn't do that. My place is in the Nursery. Only the pilots go to the Head."

The birthing tube gurgled. Something landed on the bedding with a splat. Rak craned her neck to look.

"But look, there's a baby," she said.

The lumpy shape was raw and red. Stubby limbs stuck out here and there. The head was too big. There were no eyes or nose, just a misshapen mouth. As Rak and Papa stared in silence, it opened its mouth and wailed.

"I don't know what to do," whispered Papa. "All the time, they come out like this."

He gently gathered up the malformed thing, covering its mouth with a hand until it stopped breathing. Tears rolled down his lined cheeks.

"My poor babies," said Papa.

As Rak left, Papa rocked the lump in his arms, weeping.

Rak didn't return to the Belly. She went forward. The corridor quickly narrowed, forcing Rak to a slow crawl on all fours. The rumble and sway of Mother's movement, so different from the gentle roll of the Belly, pressed her against the walls. Eventually, the tunnel widened into a round chamber. At the opposite end sat a puckered opening. On her right, a large round metallic plate was set into the flesh of the wall, the bulges ringing it glowing brightly red. Rak crossed the chamber to the opening on the other side. She touched it, and it moved with a groaning noise.

It was a tiny space: a hammock wrapped in cabling and tubes in front of two circular panes. Rak sat down in the hammock. The seat flexed around her, moulding itself to her shape. The panes were streaked with mucus and oil, but she could faintly see light and movement on the other side. It made her eyes hurt. A tube snaked down from above, nudging her cheek. Rak automatically turned her head and opened her mouth. The tube thrust into her right nostril. Pain shot up between Rak's eyes. Her vision went dark. When it cleared, she let out a scream.

Above, a blinding point of light shone in an expanse of vibrant blue. Below, a blur of browns and yellows rolled past with alarming speed.

Who are you? a voice said. It was soft and heavy. *I was so lonely.*

"Hurts," Rak managed.

The colours and light muted, and the vision narrowed at the edges so that it seemed Rak was running through a tunnel. She unclenched her hands, breathing heavily.

Better?

Rak grunted.

You are seeing through my eyes. This is the outside world. But you are safe inside me, my child.

"Mother," said Rak.

Yes. I am your mother. Which of my children are you?

The voice was soothing, making it easier to breathe. "I'm Rak. From the Belly."

Rak, my child. I am so glad to meet you.

The scene outside rolled by: yellows and reds, and the blue mass above. Mother named the things for her. *Sky. Ground. Sun.* She named the sharp things scything out at the bottom of her vision: *mandibles,* and the frenetically moving shapes glimpsed at the edges: *legs.* The cold fear of the enormous outside gradually faded in the presence of that warm voice. An urge to urinate made Rak aware of her own body again, and her purpose there.

"Mother. Something is wrong," she said. "The babies are born wrong. We need your help."

Nutrient and DNA deficiency, Mother hummed. *I need food.*

"But you can move everywhere, Mother. Why are you not finding food?"

Guidance systems malfunction. Food sources in the current area are depleted.

"Can I help, Mother?"

The way ahead bent slightly to the right. Mother was running in a circle.

There is an obstruction in my mainframe. Please remove the obstruction.

Behind Rak, something clanged. The tube slithered out of her nostril and she could see the room around her again. She turned her head. Behind the hammock a hatch had opened in the ceiling, the lid hanging down, rungs lining the inside. The hammock let Rak go with a sucking noise and she climbed up the rungs.

Inside, gently lit in red, was Mother's brain: a small space surrounded by cables winding into flesh. A slow pulse beat through the walls. Half-sitting against the wall was the emaciated body of a male. Its head and right shoulder were resting on a tangle of delicate tubes, bloated and stiff where they ran in under the dead male's body, thin and atrophied on the other. Rak pulled at an arm. Mother had started to absorb the corpse; it was partly fused to the wall. She tugged harder, and the upper body finally tore away and fell sideways. There was a rushing sound as pressure in the tubes evened out. The body was no longer in the way of any wires or tubes, that Rak could see. She left it on the floor and climbed back down the hatch. Back in the hammock, the tube snuck into her nostril, and Mother's voice was in her head again.

Thank you, said Mother. *Obstruction has been removed. Guidance system recalibrating.*

"It was Ziz, I think," said Rak. "He was dead."

Yes. He was performing maintenance when he expired.

"Aren't there any more pilots?"

You can be my pilot.

"But I'm female," Rak said.

That is all right. Your brain gives me sufficient processing power for calculating a new itinerary.

"What?"

You don't have to do anything. Just sit here with me.

Rak watched as Mother changed course, climbing up the wall of the canyon and up onto a soft yellow expanse: *grassland,* whispered. The sky sat heavy and blue over the grass. Mother slowed down, her mouthpieces scooping up plants from the ground.

Angular silhouettes stood against the horizon.

"What is that?" said Rak.

Cities, Mother replied. *Your ancestors used to live there. But then the cities died, and they came to me. We entered an agreement. You would keep me company, and in exchange I would protect you until the world was a better place.*

"Where are we going?"

Looking for a mate. I need fresh genetic material. My system is not completely self-sufficient.

"Oh." Rak's mouth fell open. "Are there . . . more of you?"

Of sorts. There are none like me, but I have cousins that roam the steppes. A sigh. *None of them are good company. Not like my children.*

Mother trundled over the grassland, eating and eating. Rak panicked the first time the sun disappeared, until Mother wrapped the hammock tight around her and told her to look up. Rak quieted at the sight of the glowing band laid across the sky. *Other suns,* Mother said, but Rak could not grasp it. She settled for thinking of it like lights in the ceiling of a great room.

They passed more of the cities: jagged spires and broken domes, bright surfaces criss-crossed with cracks and curling green. Occasionally flocks of other living creatures ran across the grass. Mother would name them all. Each time a new animal appeared, Rak asked if that was her mate. The answer was always no.

"Are you feeling better?" Rak said eventually.

No. A sighing sound. *I am sorry. My system is degraded past the point of repair.*

"What does that mean?"

Goodbye, my daughter. Please use the exit with green lights.

Something shot up Rak's nostril through the tube. A sting of pain blossomed inside her forehead, and she tore the tube out. A thin stream of blood trailed from her nose. She wiped at it with her arm. A shudder shook the hammock. The luminescence in the walls faded. It was suddenly very quiet.

"Mother?" Rak said into the gloom. Outside, something was different. She peered out through one of the eyes. The world wasn't moving.

"Mother!" Rak put the tube in her nose again, but it fell out and lay limp in her lap. She slid out of the hammock, standing up on stiff legs. The hatch to Mother's brain was still open. Rak pulled herself up into the little space. It was pitch dark and still. No pulse moved through the walls.

Rak left Mother's head and started down the long corridors, down toward the Nursery and the Belly. She scooped some mucus from the wall to eat, but it tasted rank. It was getting darker. Only the growths around the round plate between the Head and the rest of the body were still glowing brightly. They had changed to green.

In the Nursery, Papa was lying on his cot, chest rising and falling faintly.

"There you are," he said when Rak approached. "You were gone for so long."

"What happened?" said Rak.

Papa shook his head. "Nothing happened. Nothing at all."

"Mother isn't moving," said Rak. "I found Her head, and She talked to me, and I helped Her find her way to food, but she says she can't be repaired, and now she's not moving. I don't know what to do."

Papa closed his eyes. "Our Mother is dead," he whispered. "And we will go with Her."

He turned away, spreading his arms against the wall, hugging the tangle of cabling and flesh. Rak left him there.

In the Belly, the air was thick and rancid. The peristaltic engine was still. Rak's feet slapping against the floor made a very loud noise. Around the chamber, workers were lying along the walls, half-melted into Mother's flesh. The Leg accesses along the walls were all open; here and there an arm or a head poked out. Hap lay close to the entrance, resting on her side. Her body was gaunt, the ribs fully visible through the skin. She had begun sinking into the floor; Rak could still see part of her face. Her eyes were half-closed, as if she were just very tired.

Rak backed out into the corridor, turning back toward the Head. The sphincters were all relaxing, sending the foul air from the Belly toward her, forcing her to crawl forward. The last of the luminescence faded. She crawled in darkness until she saw a green shimmer up ahead. The round plate was still there. It swung aside at her touch.

The air coming in was cold and sharp, painful on the skin, but fresh. Rak breathed in deep. The hot air from Mother's insides streamed out above her in a cloud. The sun hung low on the horizon, its light far more blinding than Mother's eyes had seen it. One hand in front of her eyes, Rak swung her legs out over the rim of the opening and cried out in surprise when her feet landed on grass. The myriad blades prickled the soles of her feet. She sat there, gripping at the grass with her toes, eyes squeezed shut. When the light was less painful, she opened her eyes a little and stood up.

The aperture opened out between two of Mother's jointed legs. They rested on the grass, each leg thicker around than Rak could reach with her arms. Beyond them, she could glimpse more legs to either side. She looked up. Behind her, the wall of Mother's body rose up, more than twice Rak's own height. Beyond the top there was sky, a blue nothing, not flat like seen through Mother's eyes but deep and endless. In front of her, the grassland, stretching on and on. Rak held on to the massive leg next to her. Her stomach clenched, and she bent over and spat bile. There was a hot lump in her chest that wouldn't go away. She spat again and kneeled on the grass.

"Mother," she whispered in the thin air. She leaned against the leg. It was cold and smooth. "Mother, please." She crawled in under Mother's legs, curling up against Her body, breathing in Her familiar musk. A sweet hint of rot lurked below. The knot in Rak's chest forced itself up through her throat in a howl.

Rak eventually fell asleep. She dreamed of legs sprouting from her sides, her body elongating and dividing into sections, taking a sinuous shape. She ran over the grass, legs in perfect unison, muscles and vertebrae stretching and becoming powerful. The sky was no longer terrible. Warm light caressed the length of her scales.

A pattering noise in the distance woke her up. Rak stretched and rubbed her eyes. Her cheeks were crusted with salt. She scratched at her side. An itching line of nubs ran along her ribs. Beside her, Mother's body no longer smelled of musk; the smell of rot was stronger. She crawled out onto the grass and rose to her feet. The sky had darkened, and a pale orb hung in the void, painting the landscape in stark grey and white. Mother lay quiet, stretched out into the distance. Rak saw now that Mother's carapace was grey and pitted, some of the many legs cracked or missing.

In the bleak light, a long shape on many legs approached. When it came close, Rak saw it was much smaller than Mother—perhaps three or four times Rak's length. She stood very still. The other paused a few feet away. It reared up, fore body and legs waving back and forth. Its mandibles clattered. Something about its movement caused a warm stirring in Rak's belly. After a while, it turned around, depositing a gelatinous sac on the ground. It slowly backed away.

Rak approached the sac. It was the size of her head. Inside, a host of little shapes wriggled around. Her belly rumbled. The other departed, mandibles clattering, as Rak ripped the sac open with her teeth. The wriggling little things were tangy on her tongue. She swallowed them whole.

She ate until she was sated, then crouched down on the ground, scratching at her sides. Her arms and legs tingled. She had a growing urge to run and stretch her muscles; to run and never stop.

TEST OF FIRE

PERVIN SAKET

—◆—

Fellow Styonkars,

As SigEv just transmitted to you, the experiment has failed and I have returned. Yes, three hundred and four kosos before I was due. But remaining on Earth would only have wasted precious time. The Planet of Colour did not meet the criteria and I was compelled to ask Dharti to carry me back. We must begin the search for another, more worthy race. I intimate you now, before the official sabha meeting due in the eighth hissa, because it is best we resume the archive searches, choose from the volunteers and draw plan layouts. The time of the bequest approaches and another deserving race must be identified before the 444th Chakker of Larissa around Styon. And this time we must choose more carefully, lest our trial fails, like it did with Earthlok. For the first time since the Rounds of the Bequest, a race has been denied what it should have easily earned. Certainly you will want to know why—particularly the Mantris, whose fate it is now to scout for the next beneficiaries. The matter however, will be much discussed at the sabha, and it is futile to delve into details in so short a correspondence. It'll suffice for now to know that our side of the test went off without a hitch, but they faltered repeatedly. Their last act clearly proved them unfit for such a historic revelation. Mercifully though, they will never know what they have lost.

The answer to the eventual "why?" of existence, the question that plagues every race's soul. It requires either minds that are open enough to grasp its vastness or small enough to live only for the truth of the moment. Earthlok can boast of neither; the Planet of Colour is far too frivolous to deserve or appreciate such a gift. More so because the bequest can never be reversed. On the Planet of Colour, birds talk, chariots fly, humans perform miracles, but their minds are caught in tight webs of mediocrity. The race of Manus is petty.

Subhi and Jaul, my patient trainers, you would have been proud had you seen your pupil merge so seamlessly into the role of a royal Earth princess, complete with all the conventions and ceremonies. Goka, the wisest of Mantris, on your advice we tested not any random Manus but he who was considered The Best among Men—*Purushuttam*. When a race is ready for the reason behind its existence, the particular suffices for the examination. Yet, worried about mistakenly rejecting Earthlok due to the faults of an ill-chosen candidate, we picked the one who they deemed the highest among mortals. One who embodied every value that they cherished; one who acted on their highest principles; one who will, in fact, be hailed the Ideal Man for centuries to come.

Morphed into an Earthwoman, I prayed to their Gods, wore their garbs and accepted their relationships, as planned. Their customs, like those of many Presight races we have already witnessed, are obsolete and reek of fear. I saw Earthwomen, clever but conniving, brave but narrow, their children shackled by tunnelled visions. These however, were not our criteria for the decision, and they were accordingly ignored, allowing for the role of conditioning, the convenience of repetition over rebellion. And in any case, it was *Purushuttam* who counted.

You are already aware, due to Dharti's SigEv transmissions of Significant Events, that I chose him at a special Earthlok ceremony, to be what they call varyingly, *var,* husband or *pati*.

Later, details shall be divulged at the sabha, but subsequently, situations compelled me to live like a nomadic Earthling, wandering alone, isolated save two Earthmen, one of whom was my Earth-*var,* the *Purushuttam*. Strangely, those were blissful moments, spent in picking wild fruit, bathing in sweet streams, feasting on the colours of the famed planet, away from their ritualistic lives. A far cry, of course, from the comforts of the palace, but what do fourteen Earth years of physical difficulties count in a sea of eventual youthful immortality?

Youth. Lust. The flying chariot—you were worried about me, I remember, and it took six SigEv transmissions to assure all Styonkars of my safety. But I did not blame him. For lust is fuelled within the loins and as loathsome as it is, it will never be a perversion of the heart. Isolation again. This time within flowered gardens and perfumes, punctuated by the wise counsel of beautiful women. The role, the test, the mute pretence—I thought it would all end when finally the battle was over and the ten heads smashed, smeared with blood and dust.

Only, it was far from over. A washer-man was all it took and I was sent through the blazing fire. You can imagine not the intensity of those flames, the cold, mocking crackle of the orange, the first sting of human tears. *Purushuttam,* the highest among men fell prey to a mere rumour, and collapsed from his pedestal. The suspicion, the fear, the doubts that lurked in his mind could be forgiven, overlooked. They could be pacified and explained. What doomed Manus was the need to seek approval from even the lowest rung. The desire to be respected by those whom he could never have respected back. The act of giving up every scruple he had, every principle he upheld, only to be adored by one more person. The Ideal Man didn't value his own opinions, only those that others had of him.

I felt then not the heat but the tightening corridors of their minds, lairs too binding for the wisdom of their origins. The weight of all our eternal years crashed down on me, the smallness of humankind pressed against itself.

I activated the Homecoming Hoop and Dharti brought me back. Earth failed. The Planet of Colour shall never know why it exists, why it was really made. Goka, let the next deserving race be found.

Sita.

MY MOTHER, DANCING

NANCY KRESS

—◆—

Fermi's Paradox, California, 1950: Since planet formation appears to be common, and since the processes that lead to the development of life are a continuation of those that develop planets, and since the development of life leads to intelligence and intelligence to technology—then why hasn't a single alien civilization contacted Earth?

Where is everybody?

They had agreed, laughing, on a form of the millennium contact, what Micah called "human standard," although Kabil had insisted on keeping hirs konfol and Deb had not dissolved hirs crest, which waved three inches above hirs and hummed. But, then, Deb! Ling had designed floating baktor for the entire ship, red and yellow mostly, that combined and recombined in kaleidoscopic loveliness that only Ling could have programmed. The viewport was set to magnify, the air mixture just slightly intoxicating, the tinglies carefully balanced by Cal, that master. Ling had wanted "natural" sleep cycles, but Cal's arguments had been more persuasive, and the tinglies massaged the limbic so pleasantly. Even the child had some. It was a party.

The ship slipped into orbit around the planet, a massive subJovian far from its sun, streaked with muted color. "Lovely," breathed Deb, who lived for beauty.

Cal, the biologist, was more practical: "I ran the equations; by now there should be around two hundred thousand of them in the rift, if the replication rate stayed constant."

"Why wouldn't it?" said Ling, the challenger, and the others laughed. The tinglies really were a good idea.

The child, Harrah, pressed hirs face to the window. "When can we land?"

The adults smiled at each other. They were so proud of Harrah, and so careful. Hirs was the first gene-donate of all of them except Micah, and probably the only one for the rest of them except Cal, who was a certified intellect donor. Kabil knelt beside Harrah, bringing hirs face close to the child's height.

"Little love, we can't land. Not here. We must see the creations in holo."

"Oh," Harrah said, with the universal acceptance of childhood. It had not changed in five thousand years, Ling was fond of remarking, that child idea that whatever it lived was the norm. But, then . . . *Ling.*

"Access the data," Cal said, and Harrah obeyed, reciting it aloud as hirs parents had all taught hirs. Ling smiled to see that Harrah still closed hirs eyes to access, but opened them to recite.

"The creations were dropped on this planet 273 E-years ago. They were the one-hundred-fortieth drop in the Great Holy Mission that gives us our life. The creations were left in a closed-system rift . . . what does that mean?"

"The air in the creations' valley doesn't get out to the rest of the planet, because the valley is so deep and the gravity so great. They have their own air."

"Oh. The creations are cyborged replicators, programmed for self-awareness. They are also programmed to expect human contact at the millennium. They . . . "

"Enough," said Kabil, still kneeling beside Harrah. Hirs stroked hirs hair, black today. "The important thing, Harrah, is that you remember that these creations are beings, different from us but with the same life force, the only life force. They must be respected, just as people are, even if they look odd to you."

"Or if they don't know as much as you," said Cal. "They won't, you know."

"I know," Harrah said. They had made hirs an accommodator, with strong genes for bonding. They already had Ling for challenge. Harrah added, "Praise Fermi and Kwang and Arlbeni for the emptiness of the universe."

Ling frowned. Hirs had opposed teaching Harrah the simpler, older folklore of the Great Mission. Ling would have preferred the child receive only truth, not religion. But Deb had insisted. *Feed the imagination first,* Hirs had said, *and later Harrah can separate science from prophecy.* But the tinglies felt sweet, and the air mixture was set for a party, and hirs own baktors floated in such graceful pattern that Ling, even Ling, could not quarrel.

"I wonder," Deb said dreamily, "what they have learned in 273 years."

"When will they holo?" Harrah said. "Are we there yet?"

Our mother is coming.

Two hours more and they will come, from beyond the top of the world. When they come, there will be much dancing. Much rejoicing. All of us will dance and rejoice, even those who have detached and let the air carry them away. Those ones will receive our transmissions and dance with us.

Or maybe our mother will also transmit to where those of us now sit. Maybe they will transmit to all, even those colonies out of our transmission range. Why not? Our mother, who made us, can do whatever is necessary.

First, the dancing. Then, the most necessary thing of all. Our mother will solve the program flaw. Completely, so that none of us will die. Our mother doesn't die. We are not supposed to die, either. Our mother will transmit the program to correct this.

Then the dancing there will be!

Kwang's Resolution, Bohr Station, 2552: Since the development of the Quantum Transport, humanity has visited nearly a thousand planets in our galaxy and surveyed many more. Not one of them has developed any life of any kind, no matter how simple. Not one.

No aliens have contacted Earth because there is nobody else out there.

Harrah laughed in delight. Hirs long black hair swung through a drift of yellow baktors. "The creations look like oysters!"

The holocube showed uneven rocky ground through thick, murky air. A short distance away rose the abrupt steep walls of the rift, thousands of feet high. Attached to the ground by thin, flexible, mineral-conducting tubes were hundreds of uniform, metal-alloy double shells. The shells held self-replicating nanomachinery, including the rudimentary AI, and living eukaryotes sealed into selectively permeable membranes. The machinery ran on the feeble sunlight and on energy produced by anaerobic bacteria, carefully engineered for the thick atmospheric stew of methane, hydrogen, helium, ammonia, and carbon dioxide.

The child knew none of this. Hirs saw the "oysters" jumping up in time on their filaments, jumping and falling, flapping their shells open and closed, twisting and flapping and bobbing. Dancing.

Kabil laughed, too. "Nowhere in the original programming! They learned it!"

"But what could the stimulus have been?" Ling said. "How lovely to find out!"

"Sssshhh, we're going to transmit," Micah said. Hirs eyes glowed. Micah was the oldest of them all; hirs had been on the original drop. "Seeding 140, are you there?"

"We are here! We are Seeding 140! Welcome, our mother!"

Harrah jabbed hirs finger at the holocube. "We're not your mother!"

Instantly, Deb closed the transmission. Micah said harshly, "Harrah! Your manners!"

The child looked scared. Deb said, "Harrah, we talked about this. The creations are not like us, but their ideas are as true as ours, on their own world. Don't laugh at them."

From Kabil, "Don't you remember, Harrah? Access the learning session!"

"I . . . remember," Harrah faltered.

"Then show some respect!" Micah said. "This is the Great Mission!"

Harrah's eyes teared. Kabil, the tender-hearted, put hirs hand on Harrah's shoulder. "Small heart, the Great Mission gives meaning to our lives."

"I . . . know. . . . "

Micah said, "You don't want to be like those people who just use up all their centuries in mere pleasure, with no structure to their wanderings around the galaxy, no purpose beyond seeing what the nanos can produce that they haven't produced before, no difference between today and tomorrow, no—"

"That's sufficient," Ling says. "Harrah understands, and regrets. Don't give an Arlbeni Day speech, Micah."

Micah said stiffly, "It matters, Ling."

"Of course it matters. But so do the creations, and they're waiting. Deb, open the transmission again . . . . Seeding 140, thank you for your welcome! We return!"

Arlbeni's Vision, Planet Cadrys, 2678: We have been fools.

Humanity is in despair. Nano has given us everything, and nothing. Endless pleasures empty of effort, endless tomorrows empty of purpose, endless experiences empty of meaning. From evolution to sentience, sentience to nano, nano to the decay of sentience.

But the fault is ours. We have overlooked the greatest gift ever given humanity: the illogical emptiness of the universe. It is against evolution, it is against known physical processes. Therefore, how can it exist? And why?

It can exist only by the intent of something greater than the physical processes of the universe. A conscious Intent.

The reason can only be to give humanity, the universe's sole inheritor, knowledge of this Intent. The emptiness of the universe—anomalous, unexplainable, impossible—has been left for us to discover, as the only convincing proof of God.

Our mother has come! We dance on the seabed. We transmit the news to the ones who have detached and floated away. We rejoice together, and consult the original program.

"You are above the planetary atmosphere," we say, new words until just this moment, but now understood. All will be understood now, all corrected. "You are in a ship, as we are in our shells."

"Yes," says our mother. "You know we cannot land."

"Yes," we say, and there is momentary dysfunction. How can they help us if they cannot land? But only momentary. This is our mother. And they landed us here once, didn't they? They can do whatever is necessary.

Our mother says, "How many are you now, Seeding 140?"

"We are 79,432," we say. Sadness comes. We endure it, as we must.

Our mother's voice changes in wavelength, in frequency. "Seventy-nine thousand? Are you . . . we had calculated more. Is this replication data correct?"

A packet of data arrives. We scan it quickly; it matches our programming.

"The data is correct, but . . . " We stop. It feels like another dying ceremony, suddenly, and it is not yet time for a dying ceremony. We will wait another few minutes. We will tell our mother in another few minutes. Instead, we ask, "What is your state of replication, our mother?"

Another change in wavelength and frequency. We scan and match data, and it is in our databanks: laughter, a form of rejoicing. Our mother rejoices.

"You aren't equipped for visuals, or I would show you our replicant," our mother says. "But the rate is much, much lower than yours. We have one new replicant with us on the ship."

"Welcome new replicant!" we say, and there is more rejoicing. There, and here.

• • •

"I've restricted transmission . . . there's the t-field's visual," Micah said.

A hazy cloud appeared to one side of the holocube, large enough to hold two people comfortably, three close together. Only words spoken inside the field would now transmit. Baktors scuttled clear of the ionized haze. Deb stepped inside the field, with Harrah; Cal moved out of it. Hirs frowned at Micah.

"They can't be only seventy-nine thousand-plus if the rate of replication held steady. Check the resource data, Micah."

"Scanning . . . no change in available raw materials . . . no change in sunlight per square unit."

"Scan their counting program."

"I already did. Fully functional."

"Then run an historical scan of replicants created."

"That will take time . . . there, it's started. What about attrition?"

Cal said, "Of course. I should have thought of that. Do a seismic survey and match it with the original data. A huge quake could easily have destroyed two-thirds of them, poor seedings . . . "

Ling said, "You could ask them."

Kabil said, "If it's not a cultural taboo. Remember, they have had time to evolve a culture, we left them that ability."

"Only in response to environmental stimuli. Would a quake or a mudslide create enough stimulus pressure to evolve death taboos?"

They looked at each other. Something new in the universe, something humanity had not created . . . this was why they were here! Their eyes shone, their breaths came faster. Yet they were uncomfortable, too, at the mention of death. How long since any of them . . . oh, yes. Ling's clone in that computer malfunction, but so many decades ago. . . . Discomfort, excitement, compassion for Seeding 140, yes compassion most of all, how terrible if the poor creations had actually lost so many in a quake. . . . All of them felt it, and meant it, the emotion was genuine. And in their minds the finger of God touched them for a moment, with the holiness of the tiny human struggle against the emptiness of the universe.

"Praise Fermi and Kwang and Arlbeni . . . " one of them murmured, and no one was sure who, in the general embarrassment that took them a moment later. They were not children.

Micah said, "Match the seismic survey with the original data, and moved off to savor alone the residue of natural transcendence, rarest and strangest of the few things nano could not provide.

Inside the hazy field Harrah said, "Seeding! I am dancing just like you!" and moved hirs small body back and forth,up and down on the ship's deck.

Arlbeni's Vision, Planet Cadrys, 2678: In the proof of God lies its corollary. The Great Intent has left the universe empty, but for us. It is our mission to fill it.

Look around you, look at what we've become. At the pointless destruction, the aimless boredom, the spiritual despair. The human race cannot exist without purpose, without vision, without faith. Filling the emptiness of the universe will rescue us from our own.

Our mother says, "Do you play games?"

We examine the data carefully. There is no match.

Our mother speaks again. "That was our new replicant speaking, Seeding 140. Hirs is only half-created as yet, and hirs program language is not fully functional. Hirs means, of the new programs you have created for yourselves since the original seeding, which ones in response to the environment are expressions of rejoicing? Like dancing?"

"Yes!" we say. "We dance in rejoicing. And we also throw pebbles in rejoicing and catch pebbles in rejoicing. But not for many years since."

"Do it now!" our mother says.

This is our mother. We are not rejoicing. But this is our mother. We pick up some pebbles.

"No," our mother says quickly, "you don't need to throw pebbles. That was the new replicant again. Hirs does not yet understand that seedings do what, and only what, they wish. Your . . . your mother does *not* command you. Anything you do, anything you have learned, is as necessary as what we do."

"I'm sorry again," our mother says, and there is physical movement registered in the field of transmission.

We do not understand. But our mother has spoken of new programs, of programs created since the seeding, in response to the environment. This we understand, and now it is time to tell our mother of our need. Our mother has asked. Sorrow floods us, rejoicing disappears, but now is the time to tell what is necessary.

Our mother will make all functional once more.

• • •

"Don't scold hirs like that, hirs is just a child," Kabil said. "Harrah, stop crying, we know you didn't mean to impute to them any inferiority."

Micah, hirs back turned to the tiny parental drama, said to Cal, "Seismic survey complete. No quakes, only the most minor geologic disturbances . . . really, the local history shows remarkable stability."

"Then what accounts for the difference between their count of themselves and the replication rate?"

"It can't be a real difference."

"But . . . oh! Listen. Did they just say—"

Hirs turned slowly toward the holocube.

Harrah said at the same moment, through hirs tears, "They stopped dancing."

Cal said, "Repeat that," remembered hirself, and moved into the transmission field, replacing Harrah. "Repeat that, please, Seeding 140. Repeat your last transmission."

The motionless metal oysters said, "We have created a new program in response to the Others in this environment. The Others who destroy us."

Cal said, very pleasantly, "Others? What Others?"

"The new ones. The mindless ones. The destroyers."

"There are no others in your environment," Micah said. "What are you trying to say?"

Ling, across the deck in a cloud of pink bakterons, said, "Oh, oh . . . no . . . they must have divided into factions. Invented warfare amongst themselves! Oh . . . "

Harrah stopped sobbing and stood, wide-eyed, on hirs sturdy short legs.

Cal said, still very pleasant, "Seeding 140, show us these Others. Transmit visuals."

"But if we get close enough to the Others to do that, we will be destroyed!"

Ling said sadly, "It *is* warfare."

Deb compressed hirs beautiful lips. Kabil turned away, to gaze out at the stars. Micah said, "Seeding . . . do you have any historical transmissions of the Others, in your databanks? Send those."

"Scanning . . . sending."

Ling said softly, "We always knew warfare was a possibility for any creations. After all, they have our unrefined DNA, and for millennia . . . " Hirs fell silent.

"The data is only partial," Seeding 140 said. "We were nearly destroyed when it was sent to us. But there is one data packet until the last few minutes of life."

The cheerful, dancing oysters had vanished from the holocube. In their place were the fronds of a tall, thin plant, waving slightly in the thick air. It was stark, unadorned, elemental. A multicellular organism rooted in the rocky ground, doing nothing.

No one on the ship spoke.

The holocube changed perspective, to a wide scan. Now there were whole stands of fronds, acres of them, filling huge sections of the rift. Plant after plant, drab olive green, blowing in the unseen wind.

After the long silence, Seeding 140 said, "Our mother? The Others were not there for ninety-two years. Then they came. They replicate much faster than we do, and we die. Our mother, can you do what is necessary?"

Still no one spoke, until Harrah, frightened, said, "What is it?"

Micah answered, hirs voice clipped and precise. "According to the data packet, it is an aerobic organism, using a process analogous to photosynthesis to create energy, giving off oxygen as a byproduct. The data includes a specimen analysis, broken off very abruptly as if the AI failed. The specimen is non-carbon-based, non-DNA. The energy sources sealed in Seeding 140 are anaerobic."

Ling said sharply, "Present oxygen content of the rift atmosphere?"

Cal said, "Seven point six two percent." Hirs paused. "The oxygen created by these . . . these 'Others' is poisoning the seeding."

"But," Deb said, bewildered, "why did the original drop include such a thing?"

"It didn't," Micah said. "There is no match for this structure in the gene banks. It is not from Earth."

"Our mother?" Seeding 140 said, over the motionless fronds in the holocube. "Are you still there?"

Disciple Arlbeni, Grid 743.9, 2999: As we approach this millennium marker, rejoice that humanity has passed both beyond superstition and spiritual denial. We have a faith built on physical truth, on living genetics, on human need. We have, at long last, given our souls not to a formless Deity, but to the science of life itself. We are safe, and we are blessed.

Micah said suddenly, "It's a trick."

The other adults stared at hirs. Harrah had been hastily reconfigured for sleep. Someone—Ling, most likely—had dissolved the floating baktons and blanked the wall displays, and only the empty transmission field added color to the room. That, and the cold stars beyond.

"Yes," Micah continued, a trick. "Not malicious, of course. But we programmed them to learn, and they did. They had some seismic event, or some interwarfare, and it made them wary of anything unusual. They learned that the unusual can be deadly. And the most unusual thing they know of is us, set to return at 3000. So they created a transmission program designed to repel us. Xenophobia, in a stimulus-response learning environment. You said it yourself, Ling, the learning components are built on human genes. And we have xenophobia as an evolved survival response!"

Cal jack-knifed across the room. Tension turned hirs ungraceful. "No. That sounds appealing, but nothing we gave Seeding 140 would let them evolve defenses that sophisticated. And there was no seismic event for the internal stimulus."

Micah said eagerly, "We're the stimulus! Our anticipated return! Don't you see . . . we're the Others!"

Kabil said, "But they call us 'mother'. . . . They were thrilled to see us. They're not xenophobic to us."

Deb spoke so softly the others could barely hear, "Then it's a computer malfunction. Cosmic bombardment of their sensory equipment. Or at least, of the unit that was 'dying.' Malfunctioning before the end. All that sensory data about oxygen poisoning is compromised."

"Of course!" Ling said. But hirs was always honest. "At least . . . no, compromised data isn't that coherent, the pieces don't fit together so well biochemically . . . "

"And non-terrestrially," Cal said, and at the jagged edge in his voice, Micah exploded.

"California, these are not native life! There is no native life in the galaxy except on Earth!"

"I know that, Micah," Cal said, with dignity. But I also know this data does not match anything in the d-bees."

"Then the d-bees are incomplete!"

"Possibly."

Ling put hirs hands together. They were long, slender hands with very long nails, created just yesterday. *I want to grab the new millennium with both hands,* Ling had laughed before the party, *and hold it firm.* "Spores. Panspermia."

"I won't listen to this!" Micah said.

"An old theory," Ling went on, gasping a little. "Seeding 140 said the Others weren't there for their first hundred years. But if the spores blew in from space on the solar wind and the environment was right for them to germinate—"

Deb said quickly, "Spores aren't really life. Wherever they came from, they're not alive."

"Yes, they are," said Kabil. "Don't quibble. They're alive."

Micah said loudly, "I've given my entire life to the Great Mission. I was on the original drop for this very planet."

"They're alive," Ling said, "and they're not ours."

"My entire life!" Micah said. Hirs looked at each of them in turn, hirs face stony, and something terrible glinted behind the beautiful deep-green eyes.

Our mother does not answer. Has our mother gone away?

Our mother would not go away without helping us. It must be that they are still dancing.

We can wait.

"The main thing is Harrah, after all," Kabil said. Hirs sat slumped on the floor. They had been talking so long.

"A child needs secure knowledge. Purpose. Faith," Cal said.

Ling said wearily, "A child needs truth."

"Harrah," Deb crooned softly. "Harrah, made of all of us, future of our genes, small heart Harrah . . . "

"Stop it, Debaron," Cal said. "Please."

Micah said, "Those things down there are not real. They are not. Test it, Cal. I've said so already. Test it. Send down a probe, try to bring back samples. There's nothing there."

"You don't know that, Micah."

"I know!" Micah said, and was subtly revitalized. Hirs sprang up. "Test it!"

Ling said, "A probe isn't necessary. We have the transmitted data and—"

"Not reliable!" Micah said.

"—and the rising oxygen content. Data from our own sensors."

"Outgassing!"

"Micah, that's ridiculous. And a probe—"

"A probe might come back contaminated," Cal said.

"Don't risk contamination," Kabil said suddenly. "Not with Harrah here."

"Harrah, made of us all . . . " Deb had turned hirs back on the rest now, and lay almost curled into a ball, lost in hirs powerful imagination. Deb!

Kabil said, almost pleadingly, to Ling, "Harrah's safety should come first."

"Harrah's safety lies in facing the truth," Ling said. But hirs was not strong enough to sustain it alone. They were all so close, so knotted together, a family. Knotted by Harrah and by the Great Mission, to which Ling, no less than all the others, had given hirs life.

"Harrah, small heart," sang Deb.

Kabil said, "It isn't as if we have proof about these 'Others.' Not real proof. We don't actually *know*."

"*I* know," Micah said.

Cal looked bleakly at Kabil. "No. And it is wrong to sacrifice a child to a supposition, to a packet of compromised data, to a . . . a superstition of creations so much less than we are. You know that's true, even though we none of us ever admit it. But I'm a biologist. The creations are limited DNA, with no ability to self-modify. Also strictly regulated nano, and AI only within careful parameters. Yes, of course they're life forms deserving respect on their own terms, of course of course I would never deny that—"

"None of us would," Kabil said.

"—but they're not *us*. Not ever us."

A long silence, broken only by Deb's singing.

"Leave orbit, Micah," Cal finally said, "before Harrah wakes up."

Disciple Arlbeni, Grid 743.9, 2999: We are not gods, never gods, no matter what the powers evolution and technology have given us, and we do not delude ourselves that we are gods, as other cultures have done at other millennia. We are human. Our salvation is that we know it, and do not pretend otherwise.

Our mother? Are you there? We need you to save us from the Others, to do what is necessary. Are you there?

Are you still dancing?

NATIVE ALIENS

GREG VAN EEKHOUT

——◆——

1945

As Papa stands between the two rows of men holding rifles, he stands as a Dutchman. His shirt is starched white, tucked neatly into khaki trousers with creases sharp enough to cut skin. It is not especially hot today, but sweat pools under his arms and trickles down his back. The Indonesians with the guns are sweating too.

Papa's skin is as dark as the Indonesians', naturally dark and baked tobacco brown from years spent hammering together chicken coops and pigeon hutches in the backyard. He is a good carpenter, and people come to him for help and advice. But carpentry is not his job. He works as a bookkeeper for Rotterdamse Lloyd, the Dutch shipping company. He is a Dutchman with a Dutch job.

The men with rifles stand in two ragged rows, facing one another, before the entrance of the school where we learned our lessons, which now serves as a prison for enemies of the Indonesian revolution.

It is the imprecision of the Indonesians that angers Papa, their sloppy spacing, their relaxed and slovenly postures. They hold their guns as though they were shovels or rakes or brooms, and the Indonesians have no interest in hard work.

He recognizes almost all of them. This one sells satay in front of the train station. Papa's money has helped him buy the shoes on his feet. Another, Rexi, has actually been in our home. When he was a young boy, not so long ago, he slipped on the rocks by the river and hit his head, and when we told Papa of this, Papa carried him in his arms and laid him down in the sitting room until the boy's grandfather came for him. He has sipped water from our well, and now he waits for Papa with a gun slung lazily over his shoulder.

A hand shoves Papa in the back, and Papa, slightly built, pitches forward and goes down to one knee in the dirt. He uses this opportunity to mouth a very quick prayer before being yanked roughly back to his feet.

The man who pulls Papa up is one of those he does not know. He is one of those who pounded on our door in the night and demanded we all assemble in the front room of our sprawling house built on the hill. "Are these the only men?" he asks, indicating Papa and me.

Mama explains that, yes, we are the only men. Ferdinand remains in Tokyo, where he has mined coal for the Japanese since his unit's capture. He mines coal no longer, though, because he was freed when the Japanese surrendered. When he is well enough to travel, he will return home. And there is Anthonie, the next eldest, but he is not here either. He is dead of tuberculosis, contracted in a jail cell of the Japanese occupation army.

And there is Papa. And there is me.

I am eleven years old. Later, there will be a camp for me and Mama and my sisters. But for now, they take only Papa.

The man steadies Papa, who is shaking now, who is so afraid he cannot stop shaking, who hates himself for shaking, who should not have to fear his own neighbours. "I am a bookkeeper," he says. "What have I to do with this?"

"You are a Dutchman," says the man. "Isn't that what you always insist? At your office at Rotterdamse Lloyd? At the train station where you buy your Dutch newspaper? At the cantina where you drink your coffee? At the swimming pool where only the Dutch can swim. At home, where your servants cook your food and clean your house and raise your children? 'I am a Dutchman. My family is a Dutch family.' Isn't that what you always say?"

Three generations ago, a Dutchman came from the Netherlands and married an Indonesian girl. There have been Indonesians and Dutch-Indonesians in our family for three generations, but no one from Holland.

"Yes, I am a Dutchman."

"Yes. You are," the man says to Papa. "And now, you must run."

Papa is not the first to receive this command today. He knows what's expected of him.

The men with rifles change their stances. They spread their legs to shoulder width. They bend at the knees. They raise their guns over their shoulders, inverted with the rifle butts held before them, and they wait.

The dirt at the feet of these men, his neighbours, is dark with blood and vomit and urine and shit. This is the entrance to a new prison.

Papa hopes that if he runs fast enough, maybe only a few of the rifle butts will strike him. Maybe not too hard.

He makes the sign of the cross and takes a step forward.

2367

At school, they tell us about Preparation. It's almost all we talk about. For the last three months, we haven't read stories. We haven't done logic problems. We haven't learned songs or sculpted in clay or played games or done swim-dances. All we talk about is Preparation.

In three months time a ship will arrive, and all 879 of us Brevan-Terrans will board, and we will spend the next four years travelling to Earth.

We need Preparation for the journey, and we need Preparation for the arrival.

At the beginning of the year, our teacher was Mr Daal, a Brevan-Terran like my classmates and me. But after the Re-Negotiation Si Tula, a Brevan man, with eyes so blue they seem to glow even when he shuts his lids, replaced him. He speaks in a deep-horn voice and is very nice.

In a circle, we sit on the floor in trays of warm brine, watching the pictures Si Tula projects before us. There is a planet of blue and white and brown, and I already know this is Earth, because I've been seeing it for months and months now. It's been on the news. Mama has been showing us books about it. Opa has been reading pamphlets about Earth.

Si Tula begins every lesson by showing us Earth. "This is your home," he always says. And then he raises his arms, his long fingers slowly fluttering as though they were underwater, and we know what to say: *This is Earth. This is where we come from. This is where we going. It will be good to be home.*

After that, the Preparation lesson is always a little different. We have seen the cities of Earth, which are big, sprawling fields of light. We have seen the animals of Earth, which are kept inside the cities in houses of their own for all to see. We have seen the great oceans, so much broader and deeper and more powerful than our little lakes on Breva.

"Your home is a mighty world," Si Tula says. And he flutters his fingers, and we respond: *Breva is too small for Earth.*

This is something the Brevan said a lot during the Re-Negotiation. It's the reason why all us Brevan-Terrans must go.

I have a question, so I raise my hand, and Si Tula bows respectfully towards me, his rib-arms lowered. It is odd, seeing my teacher bow to me. It is not something our old teacher would ever do. But Brevans are taught from childhood to bow to Brevan-Terrans.

"You may speak, Dool," he says.

I click my valves. "We have seen Terran habitations and Terran animals and Terran planetary features."

Nervous—and not knowing why—I shift in my tray, water sloshing over the sides. Si Tula nods encouragement, so I continue. "But . . . when will we see Terran *people*?"

Si Tula makes an appreciative click. "Thank you, Dool. I am pleased you asked. For what now follows is the most important part of Preparation. All else is merely knowing. But this, what we are about to learn, will require doing. It will require doing from you. It will require doing from the Health and Wellbeing Authority. It will require doing from all."

The Health and Wellbeing Authority is a new organization formed after the Re-Negotiation. Only Brevans sit on the Health and Wellbeing Authority.

Si Tula moves his hands, and a new projection appears in the middle of the circle. It is a pair of creatures. They are four-limbed—two thick limbs upon which they stand, and two thinner, upper limbs which end in things that look very much like hands. One of the creatures has a large pair of teats in front. The other has much smaller teats, and a penis. Their faces are flat and unexpressive. I have seen enough pictures of Terran animals to know that these creatures would live on land.

The projection progresses, and the creatures now wear clothing of sorts, and they move about in various settings. Here, they fold their legs beneath them and sit on the ground, planting a tree. And then they are in a structure, putting food into their tiny mouths. Here they are holding a baby creature, and despite their alien faces, it is clear they are happy. These are intelligent creatures, perhaps. More like me than like animals.

"This is you," Si Tula says. "This is you. These are Terrans, and this is what you are. This is how you were when you came to Breva. This is how you will be again."

Si Tula pauses. When he does this, we know we are to remain quiet and think about what he has said. This is us, he has told us. This is me. This is how I was.

After a suitable interval, I raise my hand.

Si Tula bows.

"I don't understand," I say. "How can these creatures be us? They have no rib-arms, no dorsals, no valves. They are land creatures. How can this be me? I don't understand."

He smiles, his eyes very blue. "Your confusion is not surprising to me. It is a new concept. It is a new concept for all of you. But you will get used to it. Given enough time, one can get used to anything."

1949

They had told us we'd be coming to a place of colours. There would be fields of tulips, white and pink and yellow and red, a celebration of colours against the blue sky. There would be wonders—windmills and canals and lanes alive with bicycles. This would be a home. We were not Indonesian, we were Dutch, they told us, and this would be our home.

What we find here is stone. The buildings are blocks of neatly stacked stone, and the streets are stone and brick, fitted together, tight and clever. They had told us it would be cold, and it is. They had told us we would get used to it, and they were lying, because how can I get used to this? Even in my jacket, which weighs as much as I do, and the wool hat that scratches my scalp, and the gloves that prevent me from feeling anything I touch, I am cold. "You'll get used to it," they tell us.

We are home. The third floor of a narrow stone building is our home. There is a small sitting area, and we can all sit together if we keep our legs tucked close. There is a room for Mama and Gerda and Anki. Because I am the only boy—the only male in my family who survived the Japanese occupation and the Indonesian revolution—I have a room to myself, shared with the two steamer trunks we brought from Jakarta.

When Mr. Kaarl, the landlord, was showing us the apartment, he realized it was quite different from what we were used to. "The water closet is down the hall," he said, jingling a ring of keys. "That'll be different for you, but you'll get used to it. They make a lot of noise, but it's more privacy than you had in your other life."

Gerda peers down the hall skeptically. "More privacy? But we have to share it with everyone else on the floor."

Mr Kaarl laughs. He has a very friendly laugh. "But it's covered and indoors, at least. No prying eyes."

Gerda frowns, not understanding.

I, however, understand very well.

Mama casts me a sharp warning look, but I don't mind such looks. At fifteen, I am the man of the house.

"Mr Kaarl believes," I explain to Gerda, "that back home we used the river as our lavatory."

When I see terror, rather than anger, in Mama's eyes, I feel a small pang of regret. There have been many moments in the last few years in which the wrong word has had grave consequences. She still thinks Papa is dead because of all his bragging about being a Dutchman. But many of our neighbours are dead, and they weren't all the braggarts Papa was. There was a war, and once the Japanese were defeated there was a revolution, and the Dutch were cast out. Many people died, of course. Blood of all kinds soaked into the ground.

But my comment was spoken in Indonesian, so Mr Kaarl only smiles a happy, puzzled smile. "Chattering monkey," he says, winking. "I'm renting to a lot of chattering monkeys lately. I should have invested in trees instead of buildings." And he laughs, his cheeks very pink.

2367

When Preparation finally happens, it happens in a dry, silver room. It is unlike any room I've ever been in. There are no mollusks clinging to the walls. There is no soft carpet of moss beneath my feet. There is no gentle trickle of water.

I am alone. I am here with only a Brevan doctor, his green-and-black mottled chest blinking with medical devices.

"This is the kind of room Terrans build," he says.

I tell him no, that is wrong, that my ancestors were Terran, and they built no dead rooms like this.

And I am told, Yes, oh, yes, they did. But Breva remained Brevan, and over time, Terran rooms became Brevan. The Terran rooms were changed, sometimes deliberately, to adapt to the Brevan environment. And sometimes Breva simply took what Earth brought into its embrace, and then transformed it. But too often, Brevan rooms were made into Terran rooms, and many Brevan rooms died forever. "Earth is mighty, indeed," says the doctor. "But there is more than simple might, is there not? Is there not also patience? Is there not also resolve? What lasts longer—a heart that beats hard, or a heart that beats gentle?"

This particular room has been drained of water. In this room, the mollusks have been scraped away. In this room, herbicide has killed the moss. This room is once more a Terran room, and it must be this way, says the doctor, for the Preparation.

In the centre of the room is an oval table, shaped like an altar in a bulb-temple. "Recline upon it," says the doctor.

I look at the table. I look above it. Hanging above the table is a cluster of silver arms, dangling down like jellyfish tentacles. Blades glint in the silver room.

The doctor's eyes are blue as Si Tula's, but not at all kind.

And I run. I run towards the door, towards the cool wet air of outside, away from this dry and silver room, away, away, towards home.

I don't get far. The doctor lashes out with his rib-arms, and though I struggle and beat at his arms and try to pry loose from his suction with my soft fingers, he is too strong, and he pulls me in and lifts me and sets me on the table. And once on the table, I cannot move.

"How do you feel?" the doctor says.

"I feel nothing."

He moves his hands, and the silver arms overhead descend.

"Good," says the doctor. "We can begin now."

He begins by severing my rib-arms.

When I scream out—not in pain, but in something else, something worse—he adjusts the table and I am silent.

"Yes," he says. "That is good. Your life has been good and comfortable, and it will be so in continuance. You have no cause to cry."

1969

It occurred to me some time ago that my backyard is a re-creation. The chicken coop, with the half dozen Leghorns and Rhode Island Reds, is a plywood attempt at something Papa might have built. Only, he was a carpenter, and I just began playing with wood and nails seven years ago, when we came to California. My work is a mess of crooked surfaces and ill-fitted joints, but it keeps the chickens inside, and that's what's important. I fear once the pigeon hutch is done, only the fattest and stupidest cats will fail to find a way in.

But this is my backyard. In Holland, we shared a courtyard. Here, we have something: A rambling, cluttered, wild backyard that I can think of as home.

To have a home of your own—something that can't be taken away—this is no small thing. We rent now, but someday, perhaps, it will be ours.

Of course, anything can be taken away. Even here, in this country, anything can be taken away from any person.

It's important to keep that in mind.

I turn satay kambing on my barbeque grill while across the fence, the neighbour flips hamburgers on his. Between the pickets, I see the neighbour's boy watching me. He wrinkles his nose as if he smells something foul, and I say, loud enough for him to hear, "Mmmm. Good dog. Good, delicious dog." Even louder: "Say, I wonder where Ranger is?"

Ranger is the boy's sweet-faced mutt.

The boy runs to complain to his father, and the neighbour scowls at me.

I smile and wave.

2371

To be Terran is to walk without water. Earth is a wet world, but our home is a dry building. There is water in the walls—sometimes I can hear it course through pipes—but it comes out only in faucets, and it can be collected only in small vessels. There is a tub in the bathroom, roughly the size of a coffin, but it is dead water and I will not stay in it.

My family is fortunate. We have been located near the sea, only twenty minutes by rail, and I have a job on the shore. I sell tourist items to those who visit the water. They like to buy clothing and sensations that remind them of their travels. I sell these items well, and someday, perhaps, I will have a business of my own. I often wonder if people who come to the sea might like to have sensations that don't remind them of where they've been, but instead show them where they cannot go.

In the shop's changing room is a mirror, and I always volunteer to clean it. It is not pleasant to examine myself, but doing so is like the kind of meditation we did back home in the bulb-temples.

My body is made for work. My two arms are stronger than my rib-arms ever were, which were made for sculling. My lungs don't take in as much air as they used to, but I get enough oxygen by inhaling often. Sometimes I stand and look at myself as I am now, and then I try to imagine myself as I was. Neither body seems quite right. My new body is alien to me, and my old body is alien to this world. When I clean the mirror, I see a puzzle that cannot be solved, or an out-of-place object that has no place.

In times that are not busy, I can look outside the shop, out over the ocean. The surf can be violent here, and the waves boom against the sand, fingers of white foam reaching out and grasping, as if the ocean were trying to pull itself up on the land. Twice a day, the ocean gets as far as it can go, but then it recedes. Despite its strength, the ocean must always return to itself.

1969

Last night, we went to the Moon. Three men were packed like the last pairs of socks into an overstuffed suitcase and then they went to the Moon. I didn't stay up to watch, but Anthony did. From down the hall, I could dimly hear the voices from the television, and the sound of Anthony clapping and bouncing in the squeaky-springed chair.

He's a dreamer, my son. He believes in better places.

He comes out of the house and I hand him an unseasoned lamb skewer. Satay kambing should be made with goat, but nobody eats goat here.

"How are your spacemen?"

"Astronauts," he corrects. "I don't know. Mama made me turn off the TV. She thinks I need more sunlight."

"The spacemen can get by without you watching them."

"The most important moment in the history of humanity, and Mama's worried about my Vitamin D."

I bite my lip to keep from laughing. He's a funny kid, my son. And smart. Much smarter than I was at twelve. Or smart in other ways, I suppose. By the age of twelve, I'd lost two brothers. I'd seen Japanese Zeroes fly over my house. I'd seen my father taken away by our neighbours to die. Not much time for jokes when I was his age.

"So, first we walk on the Moon," I say. "And then what? We come back home? We use what we learned to build better adding machines? New and improved vacuum cleaners?"

He gives me a look that, had I ever given to my Papa, would have earned me a slap across the face. And I let it pass. I have learned to let so much pass. It is a better way of getting through life, I think.

"It's not about . . . *things*," Anthony says. "It's about going places. There's so much out there, Dad." About a year ago, he stopped calling me Papa and started calling me Dad. I understand why—it's what American boys call their fathers—but I have yet to get used to it. I will, in time, but not yet. "We can't stay here forever. First, the Moon. Then, by the time I graduate college, Mars. Then the asteroid belt, maybe. And the moons of Jupiter. By the time I have kids, the stars. There'll be other planets. Other worlds. Maybe with intelligent life. We have to go there."

"We can barely live on the Moon," I argue. "Billions of dollars and space suits and thousands of people to make it happen. And the Moon is just next door, isn't it? It's just a few thousand miles away."

He gives me that look, and I chide myself for baiting him. The Moon is 240,000 miles away. I've been following everything too.

Anthony clamps down his molars on a chunk of lamb and tears it from the skewer. "Things'll be different by the time we get to the stars," he says. "We'll be different. I read a story about it. If we find life out there, we'll change ourselves to be more like what we find. We'll make our bodies and brains different. We won't even have to come back home. We'll be so well adapted that we can survive wherever we land as efficiently as the native aliens."

Native aliens.

I let the paradox pass.

Removing the satay from the grill, I lay the skewers down in neat rows on a plate. "But, what if the life we find out there doesn't want us? What if they see us as a threat? People come to a new land, and they want to change it. They want to make it like the place they came from, and they want to be top dog. Visitors who refuse to go home aren't really visitors."

"We'll be welcome," he says, with so much confidence that I feel my heart fissure, "because we'll come with peaceful intentions."

This is a moment, now. This is a moment in which I could press the issue. I could bring to bear my thirty-five years of life experience, of scratches and bruises and scars and calluses. I could strip away every one of my son's naive sentiments and make him see the world as it is. I have seen blood in the dirt. I bet I could make my son see it too.

I hand him the plate of satay. "Bring this to the kitchen. And then watch your spacemen walk on their rock."

"Astronauts," he says, taking the plate. "And it's not just some rock. It's a world."

I pierce more lamb chunks onto skewers. "Okay. Have it your way. A world. Tell me if the astronauts find something good on their new world."

He gives me his look and takes the satay kambing into the house.

I stay in my backyard and look to the sky.

There's nothing to see there, but I look on my son's behalf, praying that he'll never have to see what I see.

COVENANT

LAVIE TIDHAR

—◆—

"And there we saw the Nephilim, the sons of Giant, which come of the Nephilim: and we were in our own sight as grasshoppers, and so we were in their sight."

—In the Desert, 13:33

Ya'el had been gone for the length of nearly fifteen cigarettes and Miriam was getting worried. No—it was fifteen cigarettes now, exactly. Her breathing had been getting short for the past few hours, and she felt the familiar feeling of helplessness that always combined with that strange feeling of calm when blood flowed slower. With shaking hands—she had really left it too long again—she adjusted the yarmulke on her bald head, feeling the little beast resist as it moved. The tingling sensation in her scalp was not a good thing; it meant the yarmulke was getting hungry, was beginning to sink feelers deeper into her head.

As always when she had been gone too long without smoking, hallucinations have started to occlude her vision; impossibly-tall creatures with a countenance of pure light seemed to walk around her, through her, passing with an inhuman grace through shining streets that had never existed, through broad avenues and past gigantic buildings that never were.

She abandoned the struggle with the yarmulke and with careful, slow movements unwrapped the small wooden box and took out a cigarette. With a feeling of distaste she had never been able to be rid of she put the grey, organic tube in her mouth and lit it, throwing the match on the sand as soon as the flame touched the fungal material.

Where *was* Ya'el?

The smoke poured into her body; in an instant, the alien feeling at the top of her head disappeared and her breath returned. She sucked on the cigarette, the way she had been taught since childhood at the *cheder*, trying to get as much of the smoke in as possible with each breath. The visions slowly receded.

It was her fifteenth since Ya'el had gone. Almost a week of planetary rotation, and really she should have been smoking more. She had to stop fighting it.

She finished the cigarette down to the stub. Only after making sure there was nothing left in it, nothing at all, did she throw it on the sand, where it joined the burnt match in a single testament to human life. The desert air calmed her, and she scanned the horizon with hooded eyes, unable to stop the feeling of exhilaration that was momentarily overcoming her, as it did after each hit of the fungus.

As long as she kept smoking, she would live.

She looked back, where the city of New Jerusalem squatted uncomfortably in the oasis, and then forward again, at the never-ending expanse of the desert. Migdal lay over seven cigarettes in that direction, if you walked. But Ya'el had a vehicle, and knew the terrain, and had done that journey before. She should have been back by now.

Miriam wished they didn't have that fight before Ya'el left. It made her absence all the more painful, and in her dreams, Miriam was forced to re-enact that fight again and again, with the smoke-induced vividness she had found offensive since childhood.

It was only a silly argument; they have been through it enough times before, but this time Ya'el was particularly upset, and when she called Miriam an atheist bitch and slammed the door as she rushed outside Miriam was left unable to speak, unsure how this particular argument could have gone so wrong.

They were sitting together at Miriam's apartment in the Old Quarter, built as tradition demanded it of stone; built when the Tikvah first arrived at the planet and when the machines still worked. When cutting stones from the remote quarries of newly-named Har Even—Mountain of Stone—was still possible. That, at least—as Ya'el was fond of arguing—was the prevailing theory. No one really knew when the city was built; no one really knew why the machines have died.

They had just finished making love; Ya'el was smoking a cigarette (her own body time had always been much faster than Miriam's) and they watched the people below as they made their way in the streets. The sun was setting behind the Temple, and the movement of people had a purpose in it, a singular direction. They looked the same, from above, men and women and children all wearing the grey, shapeless yarmulkes.

"I don't see how you can say that," Ya'el said. Smoke covered her face like a grey mask. "I just don't understand how you can come up with those things sometimes."

Miriam shrugged, tracing a finger on Ya'el's smooth inner leg. "*I don't understand why you're so positive they had any form of religion. I mean, I don't,* and I have to conclude that, therefore, religion is *not* a natural state of being. I don't see it being any different for an alien species." She withdrew her hand as Ya'el's muscles tightened. "In fact, since the only species we *have* studied are humans, it's quite likely we're alone in having developed religion."

Ya'el almost threw her cigarette down. Miriam saw, not for the first time, the anger in her eyes, and felt bitterness rise in her. Lovemaking was definitely over.

"You utter, utter . . . " Ya'el struggled for words. "Atheist *bitch*." The yarmulke on her head pulsated, as if feeding on the turmoil in Ya'el. Miriam didn't need to look at a mirror to know her own beast was doing the same. She knew where this was heading even before Ya'el silently got up, put out her unfinished cigarette, and began to dress. The words left her mouth all the same, knowing she would regret saying them later, yet saying them anyway. "You have no proof. None. And you want to know what I think? I think the Nephilim were fucking *sensible*. They didn't have any superstitions. *Like you*."

Then, as Miriam knew would happen, Ya'el called her that thing again, and put away the half-smoked cigarette in her own, metallic case, and left, slamming the door to the flat behind her.

"You want proof?" Ya'el had shouted at her when she reached the street. "Come with me to Migdal and you'll have proof. Or better still, wait right here in your cushy little apartment, writing your angsty little poems, until I come back."

People's heads were turning. Miriam realised suddenly that she was leaning over the balcony completely naked, and that this confrontation would most likely be in the gossip columns the next day. NAKED POET FIGHTS LEADING ARCHEAOLOGIST. She opened her mouth to shout to Ya'el, to call her back, but there was a new look on Ya'el's face, a victorious look fused with the angry one, and Miriam, not knowing anymore what to say, didn't say anything.

Come with me to Migdal and you'll have proof, Ya'el had said. But Miriam didn't, and now Ya'el was missing, and no one seemed to care.

She had tried. When Ya'el hadn't come back Miriam went to the Archaeology Department, but in that imposing building where the ruins of the Nephilim lay on display like an incomprehensible alphabet no one was willing to help.

"You're the . . . " Professor Yagil said curiously, then checked himself. "The poet, right? I read some of your stuff." His tone was cautious, neither complimentary nor negative. Despite the recent return of democratic life many people—especially those employed by the civil, rather than Rabbinic, authorities—still stepped cautiously. And Miriam's work made many people uncomfortable. "Look," he said when she directly asked him about Ya'el. "Don't worry about her. She knows the desert like the back of her hand, and she's been to Migdal dozens of time. Tell you the truth, I have no idea why she went there this time. We've been through the place with a comb. If there was anything there we would have found it by now."

"Maybe it's not something obvious," Miriam had argued, desperate to break the man's unconcerned mask. "Maybe it's something she just realised, something you've overlooked."

"Don't worry." Yagil smiled at her, his grey teeth, like Ya'el, showing he was a heavy smoker, something that characterised the archaeologists and the rare traders, the people who spent most of their time in the outside, away from the cities. "She'll be back before you know it." His expression made it clear he thought Ya'el was just wasting time, probably thinking she had wanted to get away from Miriam for a while. She had no doubt that Yagil read the articles that inevitably appeared after their fight.

The police were not much help either. "If she doesn't show up in a month let us know, and we'll send someone over there," the inspector had said, "but I don't see what could have gone wrong. It's not as if the Nephilim got her, eh?" and he laughed as he walked off.

If it was up to her, Miriam *would* have blamed the Nephilim. Their artefacts were scattered haphazardly across the planet like broken toys left by unruly children. *Large* unruly children. While no skeleton was ever found of that vanished race, their buildings towered over humans. Their few dwellings have become places of industry, the commerce centres of the planet's small population. Not for the artefacts, though a trade in those curiosities did go on, only half-heartedly regulated by the civil police—though not by the Rabbinic authorities, who took such matters with extreme seriousness—but for the fungus. That grey, moist substance grew wherever the Nephilim once lived. It grew like moss, like weeds, on the side of buildings and inside them and in the avenues of abandoned towns.

And the fungus provided the planet's new occupants with life.

Miriam felt the rush of euphoria ease; the cigarette's initial, overwhelming effect had passed. She looked again towards New Jerusalem, and again at the desert's horizon. Seven cigarettes to go.

She hoisted her small pack on her back and began to walk towards Migdal.

The road to Migdal was cut through the desert in the early years of settlement. That, at least, was what the legends had said. The crew that first arrived on the planet were many generations removed from the ones who first left the Israeli colony on Mars on their uncertain way to the stars. Current debate ranged over whether the crew still had technological capabilities on crash landing. Those in favour cited the roads, ruler-straight and cut through the desert the way a scalpel cuts through skin. Those against only had to point at contemporary life.

Miriam thought of the debates with a feeling of bitterness. Ya'el was so involved in them, her cheeks flushing when she got excited, her voice growing louder, more confident.

"Does it matter?" Miriam had pleaded with her one night. "What difference does it make if they had technology or not?"

Ya'el was looking at her, impatience simmering behind her eyes. "The question," she said, "is not whether they still retained control of the technology they brought with them. The question is what happened."

"What happened . . . " Miriam prompted her.

"To bring us to our current level of technology," Ya'el completed the sentence for her. "You may have noticed, it's not exactly of a star-faring level."

"Don't you dare use sarcasm on me," Miriam said, and made Ya'el smile.

No records were left, and that had frustrated Ya'el, Miriam knew, more than she was willing to admit. There was no record left of the first years of settlement, nothing to indicate what had happened, not even who the people who first reached the planet were. The words "Israel" and "Mars" have gained an almost mythical resonance amongst the settlers; of their physical presence remained only intangible names.

Miriam's pace was measured. She walked the way she wrote the rebellious poems that had made her name, with care and not a little wariness. The sun was level on the horizon, a red globe blinking like a sore eye. She opened her senses to the silence around her, mentally cataloguing every detail.

The silence, first and always. The utter, invasive quiet of the desert, where nothing lived, where nothing moved. So different to the city, where the press of people always provided noise, conversation, a reassuring background hum to her life. Ya'el loved the desert and the quiet, but Miriam found it almost offensive, as if the world was mocking her with its total lack of life. *At least New Jerusalem has birds*, she thought, *cats, even, amazingly, those strange animals called horses that somehow came with the Tikvah and which only the very rich ever kept.*

But nothing lived on the planet that wasn't brought. It was as if, Miriam had written in one of her early poems, they were trespassers on holy ground, squatters in a morgue. The visions she always saw when not smoking enough seemed to reinforce that in her, as if what she was seeing was not exactly a hallucination but an alien memory, of the planet as it was before the Nephilim have disappeared.

But few enough people saw them. Most simply became weak and sluggish, dull-witted until they smoked again and were revived.

She abandoned this train of thought with difficulty and returned to cataloguing. She may have a poem of this trip yet, she thought with sudden, icy guilt. *Don't think about it*, she warned herself, *don't think about Ya'el until you get to Migdal. Don't fall apart now.*

She took a deep breath. A clean, warm air, like liquid oxygen. Almost clinical in its purity. She hated that, the lack of life in that scent. Nothing alive, no plants, no animals—only the smell of stone and sand and silence.

"It's not natural," Ya'el had insisted in one of their many, tempestuous arguments.

They were sitting on the balcony of the Temple, the stone cool against their backs, whispering. Below, the Rabbis performed the evening prayers of Ma'ariv, their yarmulkes seeming to absorb the fading light into their grey bodies. A woman sitting above them shushed loudly.

Ya'el ignored her. "There should be life on this planet, love," she said, "plants, animals, forests. Something to produce enough oxygen for us to be able to breathe. The whole eco-system of this place is missing, and yet we are able to live her quite comfortably."

"I don't know about *comfortably*," Miriam said as the woman behind shushed again, "though it's a living, I'll grant you that. Still," she added, "for all you know there are whole continents filled with forests and trees and flowers and, and—" her imagination abandoned her for a moment— "and *shrubs* and stuff."

They both smiled, and for a moment, Miriam felt they were united again, spiritually entwined in shared laughter. Below, the Rabbis finished the song and were parading the effigy of a life-sized Nephilim around the altar. Its body was covered in the grey lichen of the smoke.

The Rabbis then dispersed to the four corners of the enclosure below, and cast more of the grey fungus onto burning braziers; the pungent aroma of the burning weed circled lazily upwards, engulfing the crowd of worshippers.

Ya'el took a deep, shuddering breath as the smoke reached them. All around them, the crowd sighed, inhaling smoke. The woman who shushed them before lay back with eyes closed, a lazy smile playing on her podgy face.

Miriam remembered that smile. Complacent, she deemed it then, and so it still seemed to her, especially here, in the aloneness of the desert. She and Ya'el have never been complacent; that, probably, was part of the problem.

She walked throughout the day, stopping only occasionally, in those rare moments her body rebelled and she had to eat or to relive herself, which she did with a sort of angry impatience.

She stopped when the sun was low on the horizon, and settled down to camp besides the road in a makeshift crater of sand. She had heard stories that the word desert, originally, had signified strange shifts in temperature; they were places burning hot during the day, freezing cold at night. She wondered briefly what it was like, to experience such climatic shifts and whether there was a poem in that, then abandoned the thought.

She felt lethargic, weakened by the walk, then realised she had not smoked since the morning, outside of New Jerusalem. She knew she should light up, knew she should reach for the box, but the lethargy took her, and she lay back and stared at the world as it shifted around her.

Once more, she saw the beings of light walking about her, sometimes going through her as if she was not there. There were buildings, now, great yet delicate things that resembled nothing she knew; and everywhere the light, pouring out of everything around her.

With shaking hands, Miriam reached for the box and opened it. She ran her tongue along her dry lips and with an effort put a cigarette in her mouth. She tried to ignore the vision around her, just as she tried to ignore the pain in her head as the yarmulke hungrily moved.

She fumbled for the matches, lit one on the second try, and quickly inhaled. She hated the ritual; and yet, her body could not deny its need. She felt her head clear, the power coming back into her limbs.

The hallucinations receded.

Miriam prepared herself a light meal, washing the bread and cheese down with a few mouthfuls of water. She thought again of Ya'el and of their plans together, the dream of moving one day to one of the small farms around Har-Even, grow sheep and make cheese and make love every night. She wondered if they were ever to do that again, dream together, make love, then berated herself for her pessimism.

She fell asleep still thinking of Ya'el.

Morning, she felt, had sprung on her unfairly.

She woke up and for a moment was unable to move. Slowly, with cautious, careful movements, she began stretching her arms, then her legs, until she was able to stand up. Her whole body ached; she fell as if an army of tiny people had at work on her during the night, hitting her again and again with small, metal hammers.

She swallowed a mouthful of water again, then lit up a cigarette and waited as the pain ebbed from her body.

The second day's walk was harder. She stopped frequently, smoking a new cigarette during each break. In the evening she sank, exhausted, against the sand, smoked a last cigarette and was immediately asleep.

On the eve of the third day Miriam reached Migdal. The huge, sand-coloured buildings towered over the horizon like gigantic statues. She walked in their shadow for a long while before reaching the outskirts of the city.

Miriam's heart pounded as she neared the first buildings. Even from afar, the buildings looked somehow broken, lifeless. Up close, she could see the chinks in the walls, the broken masonry that had fallen off and was no lying haphazardly on the ground. She passed between two buildings, her mouth dry at the thought of Ya'el lying somewhere, dead or dying.

She followed the wide avenue inward, into Migdal. The town remained unused; devoid, somehow, of the fungus, and of the shapeless animals they called yarmulkes that lived on the fungus until they were harvested and used. It was but another mystery.

She began calling out, shouting Ya'el's name, her voice arid and small in the emptiness of the place. But there was no answer, and the sun had completely disappeared over the horizon she was plunged into an inky, total darkness. Overhead, the stars glistened with a cold light that illuminated nothing.

Miriam found the thought of going into one of the buildings unnerving; as dark as it was outside, it was not as dark as inside one of the windowless buildings, and she found the idea of being enclosed in one of them too much like being inside a cave.

No, she decided. She would remain in open space.

She camped by the wall of one of the buildings, finding the way by touch, feeling the panic she had tried to stomach all evening rise. Where *was* Ya'el?

She pictured her lover lying nearby, unable to speak or move, and nearly got up again to look for her. But it was no use. She would have to remain here until daylight returned, and hope.

And pray, she decided, knowing as she did that it was her last measure, a desperate childhood instinct she has been able to suppress until now. Praying, she once wrote, was hope's unsightly cousin. One she now desperately held on to.

She lit two small candles from her pack; their small illumination seemed to reflect her mood, desperate and fragile in the great abandoned space. She knelt on the ground, her knees sinking into soft sand, and carefully made a small crater in front of her, which she filled up with the grey fungus of a cigarette.

She lit a match, edged it close to the weed until it began to catch fire, then kneeled close, inhaling the smoke. She closed her eyes.

Why she prayed with her eyes closed she didn't know. The words, when at last they came, were a jumble of broken sentences, of flickering images, dull and ragged: nothing like the poetry for which she was known. She prayed—to whom, that, also, she didn't quite know—asking only for Ya'el to be alive, to be well, to be back with her.

But prayer brought her no relief, and as the last vestiges of smoke faded away she remained empty, crouching in the darkness, eyes still closed against the world.

She fell asleep at last, curled against the ancient wall the Nephilim built. She didn't dream.

Morning rose about her like a temple. She woke at first light, and sat with her back to the wall as the sun came up, lighting the buildings around her in a measured pace, from the foundations up to the skies. They towered over her, those monuments for a vanished race, and her heart caught with the twined beauty and futility of it, and the sudden conviction, like a rush of blood to the head, that they were responsible for the vanishing of her beloved.

She stood up abruptly, pain flaring in her legs, numb from her uncomfortable slumber. Not waiting for the blood to circulate, not waiting to light a cigarette from her diminishing box, not waiting for anything but driven by an urgency she now sensed in everything about her, Miriam began to walk away.

She shouted Ya'el's name, over and over as she walked, her eyes moving across the alien landscape as if starved of anything but that she was looking for. The silence oppressed her. The shadows gradually shortened until it was midday, and the sun high in the sky. Still there was no sign of Ya'el.

She became dizzy with hunger and the pangs of not smoking. On her head, the yarmulke moved restlessly, sending shocks of pain through her scalp.

Still she wouldn't stop.

She began to see the visions again: the movement of light coalesced into living beings; they occluded her vision, their movement like the drifting of leaves, their buildings strangely real, unchanged.

The buildings were the same, she realised. Unlike in the desert, where the phantoms of habitation rose around her. Here, the buildings were the same, sand-coloured and broken. *Why did she not hallucinate buildings?* She wondered, then a bark of laughter escaped her, sudden and unwelcome. *What did it matter?*

She had to find Ya'el.

She searched all throughout the day, getting lost in the identical-seeming avenues of Migdal, seeking her beloved. At last, when the shadows again lengthened and the brilliance of the day subsided, Miriam reached—by accident or design, she couldn't later say—the seeming heart of Migdal. The tall tower that gave the place its name rose above her, disappearing into the rising darkness above.

"Ya'el!"

She was huddled against two stone boulders, looking like a rag doll thrown aside in a fit of pique. Blood was coming out of her head, her nose, her mouth, and for a moment Miriam was unable to identify the source of the wrongness about Ya'el's shape, a wrongness she felt immediately was there.

She knelt besides her lover, running shaking hands over her inert body. "Ya'el?"

Then realization hit her, and unseated deep buried fear. Ya'el's yarmulke was gone, and in its place was an eroded, bleeding crater.

"Can you hear me? Are you ok?" She was shouting, her voice echoing weakly against the tower.

Ya'el's head turned, and her open eyes—and only now did Miriam realise that Ya'el's eyes have been open throughout—stared at Miriam. There was something terrifying about her features, a look of terrible victory etched in her face, yet also, Miriam thought, one of a desperate longing.

"What happened to you?" Miriam said, tears burning her face with salt. The air was still, the sun growing lower on the horizon. "Oh, shit." She frantically searched for her box of cigarettes, trying to extract one, light it and shove it into Ya'el's mouth all at once.

"Don't." Ya'el's voice was a distant murmur.

"You don't know what you're saying," Miriam said, trying to hold the cigarette in Ya'el's unresponsive mouth and strike a match at the same time. She changed tack, put the cigarette in her mouth and lit it, then pressed it into Ya'el's mouth and held her nose closed, forcing her to smoke.

"I know exactly what I'm saying." Some of the smoke must have gone through, Miriam thought as Ya'el's voice rang with sudden anger in the still air. Her eyes have lost their intensity, and Miriam felt that for the first time they were really looking at her and were seeing her there.

"What happened?"

"Can't you see them?" Ya'el's face set in a grimace of a smile. "But of course you can." Dhe coughed, and blood splattered Miriam's front. "you always could."

"See what?" Miriam asked. Their was a sudden sensation of falling inside her head, as of an inevitable but unwanted outcome finally materialising.

"*Them*." Ya'el pointed in the air, before energy abandoned her and her hand dropped back to her side.

Miriam reluctantly looked around her. The space around the tower was thronging with beings of light; they shimmered and flickered in and out of her field of vision, gliding past them and through them, moving between the gigantic buildings like ghosts.

"You're hallucinating."

Ya'el laughed, and before Miriam could stop her she buried the cigarette in the sand, extinguishing it.

"Not anymore."

A silence fell between them. Miriam felt sudden anger flare. To have come all this way, and to be helpless: that she couldn't stomach. She held Ya'el's hand in hers and tried not to think of the meaning behind Ya'el's words.

"What happened to you?" She didn't know how she meant it, but the words came out choked and coated in bitterness, like wrongly-inhaled smoke.

"I wanted to know the truth," Ya'el said. The effect of the smoke Miriam had forced on her seemed to have dissipated. She looked bright and feverish, her pupils moons swimming in a milky sky.

"What truth?" Miriam demanded. She felt a sudden, irrational urge take her, to slap Ya'el and bring her to her senses. Ya'el's words hovered at the back of her head; she refused to understand them.

"For a poet," Ya'el said, "you have a remarkable ability to ignore what your eyes tell you." Her eyes tracked the moving beings of light and her face relaxed into a childish mask of pure fascination. "*Their* truth," she said at last.

Miriam didn't answer.

Darkness fell. The ghostly figures of the Nephilim shimmered in the blackness, illuminating Ya'el's fragile, dying body. At last Miriam spoke, and when she did, bitterness again threatened to overwhelm her, making her voice quaver, disobedient to her wants. "Why Migdal?" she demanded at last. "Why come *here* to kill yourself?" she remembered Professor Yagil's vague smile, his assurance there was nothing left in Migdal of any worth.

Ya'el coughed. On Miriam's head, the yarmulke squirmed, hurting her.

"Because this is where we landed."

It came out as a whisper.

"Miri . . . " Ya'el held her arms out, shaking as she did so. There were no words left. Miriam stooped down to her and held Ya'el in her arms, holding on to her tight, trying to cover her, to protect her from the world.

Her face searched Ya'el's, inhaling her aroma, the mixture of sweat, smoke and blood. Ya'el's lips, in a last physical act, found Miriam's and they kissed, lips dry and wordless.

Miriam felt Ya'el let go as their lips touched. She kissed her nevertheless, praying uselessly, and when she lay the body of her lover back on the sand there was nothing of Ya'el but that. A body.

Miriam found she couldn't cry.

She sat, cross-legged, in the sand, holding the hand of her lover entwined in hers. As she watched she knew her own body could not be deprived much longer, that she herself would soon die if she did not feed the yarmulke, if she did not let smoke enter her body. And still she resisted.

Her mind, unable to stop working, was composing a poem, and as she sat in the darkness of Migdal she knew that, had she but written it down, it would have been her greatest work. It was a narrative poem she was writing in her head, the story of a ship arriving at a far and strange planet after crossing space itself; the story of those first people, landing here in this alien city, consumed by excitement, curiosity, and a confidence in themselves that was overwhelming.

There are some things we are not meant to see, she thought. It was a line of Talmudic scripture, written a generation after landing. It was drummed into her in the *Cheder* every day for years. She tried to construct that first meeting, between people and those who were more than people.

It must have seemed a lush planet, to the people of the Tikvah. They brought hope with them, and hope was what they saw. And that hope, she thought as her hands, independently, it seemed, of her conscious mind, began searching for the cigarette box, that hope was not a futile one.

She put a cigarette in her mouth and, with shaking hands, struck a match.

They were allowed to live, after all. They settled and raised children and worked and prayed. They wondered at the curious artefacts that littered the small space of their habitation, asked themselves why the machines stopped working, why no records remained, and they formed scholastic societies and played with archaeology and raised furious debates.

She lit the cigarette and inhaled, and inhaled again, until her eyes filled with tears.

The burning figures of the Nephilim receded, as if they never were.

Her head cleared. The world around her was once again the world she knew, silent and peaceful and empty. She knew grief would come, later, and that she might be ready for it then, and she wondered again at the contracts one makes, the bonds between lovers and the pacts between a woman and a God she no longer believed in. And she wondered, also, at the covenant that must have been struck all those years ago, on landing, and at the way that which is commonplace may live with that which is truly alien.

She sat holding Ya'el's hand in hers and waited for the sun to rise and end the long night.

A VECTOR ALPHABET OF INTERSTELLAR TRAVEL

YOON HA LEE

The Conflagration

Among the universe's civilizations, some conceive of the journey between stars as the sailing of bright ships, and others as tunneling through the crevices of night. Some look upon their far-voyaging as a migratory imperative, and name their vessels after birds or butterflies.

The people of a certain red star no longer speak its name in any of their hundreds of languages, although they paint alien skies with its whorled light and scorch its spectral lines into the sides of their vessels.

Their most common cult, although by no means a universal one, is that of many-cornered Mrithaya, Mother of the Conflagration. Mrithaya is commonly conceived of as the god of catastrophe and disease, impartial in the injuries she deals out. Any gifts she bestows are incidental, and usually come with sharp edges. The stardrive was invented by one of her worshipers.

Her priests believe that she is completely indifferent to worship, existing in the serenity of her own disinterest. A philosopher once said that you leave offerings of bitter ash and aleatory wine at her dank altars not because she will heed them, but because it is important to acknowledge the truth of the universe's workings. Naturally, this does not stop some of her petitioners from trying, and it is through their largesse that the priests are able to thrive as they do.

Mrithaya is depicted as an eyeless woman of her people, small of stature, but with a shadow scarring the world. (Her people's iconography has never been subtle.) She leans upon a crooked staff with words of poison scratched into it. In poetry, she is signified by smoke-wind and nausea, the sudden fall sideways into loss.

Mrithaya's people, perhaps not surprisingly, think of their travels as the outbreak of a terrible disease, a conflagration that they have limited power to contain; that the civilizations they visit will learn how to build Mrithaya's stardrive, and be infected by its workings. A not insignificant faction holds that they should hide on their candled worlds so as to prevent Mrithaya's terrible eyeless gaze from afflicting other civilizations, that all interstellar travel should be interdicted. And yet the pilgrims—Mrithaya's get, they are called—always find a way.

Certain poets write in terror of the day that all extant civilizations will be touched by this terrible technological conflagration, and become subject to Mrithaya's whims.

Alphabets

In linear algebra, the basis of a vector space is an alphabet in which all vectors can be expressed uniquely. The thing to remember is that there are many such alphabets.

In the peregrinations of civilizations grand and subtle, each mode of transport is an alphabet expressing their understandings of the universe's one-way knell. One assumes that the underlying universe is the same in each case.

Codices

The Iothal are a people who treasure chronicles of all kinds. From early on in their history, they bound forest chronicles by pressing leaves together and listening to their secrets of turning worm and wheeling sun; they read hymns to the transient things of the world in chronicles of footprints upon rocky soil, of foam upon restive sea. They wrote their alphabets forward and backward and upside down into reflected cloudlight, and divined the poetry of time receding in the earth's cracked strata.

As a corollary, the Iothal compile vast libraries. On the worlds they inhabit, even the motes of air are subject to having indices written on them in stuttering quantum ink. Some of their visionaries speak of a surfeit of knowledge, when it will be impossible to move or breathe without imbibing some unexpected fact, from the number of neutrons in a certain meadow to the habits of aestivating snails. Surely the end product will be a society of enlightened beings, each crowned with some unique mixture of facts and heady fictions.

The underside of this obsession is the society's driving terror. One day all their cities will be unordered dust, one day all their books will be scattered like leaves, one day no one will know the things they knew. One day the rotting remains of their libraries will disintegrate so completely that they will be indistinguishable from the world's wrack of stray eddies and meaningless scribbles, the untide of heat death.

The Iothal do not call their starships ships, but rather codices. They have devoted untold ages to this ongoing archival work. Although they had developed earlier stardrives—indeed, with their predilection for knowledge, it was impossible not to—their scientists refused to rest until they devised one that drank in information and, as its ordinary mode of operation, tattooed it upon the universe's subtle skin.

Each time the Iothal build a codex, they furnish it with a carefully selected compilation of their chronicles, written in a format that the stardrive will find nourishing. Then its crew takes it out into the universe to carry out the act of inscription. Iothal codices have very little care for destination, as it is merely the fact of travel that matters, although they make a point of avoiding potentially hostile aliens.

When each codex has accomplished its task, it loses all vitality and drifts inertly wherever it ends up. The Iothal are very long-lived, but even they do not always survive to this fate.

Distant civilizations are well accustomed to the phenomenon of drifting Iothal vessels, but so far none of them have deciphered the trail of knowledge that the Iothal have been at such pains to lay down.

The Dancers

To most of their near neighbors, they are known as the dancers. It is not the case that their societies are more interested in dance than the norm. True, they have their dances of metal harvest, and dances of dream descending, and dances of efflorescent death. They have their high rituals and their low chants, their festivals where water-of-suffusement flows freely for all who would drink, where bells with spangled clappers toll the hours by antique calendars. But then, these customs differ from their neighbors' in detail rather than in essential nature.

Rather, their historians like to tell the story of how, not so long ago, they went to war with aliens from a distant cluster. No one can agree on the nature of the offense that precipitated the whole affair, and it seems likely that it was a mundane squabble over excavation rights at a particular rumor pit.

The aliens were young when it came to interstellar war, and they struggled greatly with the conventions expected of them. In order to understand their enemy better, they charged their masters of etiquette with the task of interpreting the dancers' behavior. For it was the case that the dancers began each of their battles in the starry deeps with the same maneuvers, and often retreated from battle—those times they had cause to retreat—with other maneuvers, carried out with great precision. The etiquette masters became fascinated by the pirouettes and helices and rolls, and speculated that the dancers' society was constricted by strict rules of engagement. Their fabulists wrote witty and extravagant tales about the dancers' dinner parties, the dancers' sacrificial exchanges, the dancers' effervescent arrangements of glass splinters and their varied meanings.

It was not until late in the war that the aliens realized that the stylized maneuvers of the dancers' ships had nothing to do with courtesy. Rather, they were an effect of the stardrive's ordinary functioning, without which the ships could not move. The aliens could have exploited this knowledge and pushed for a total victory, but by then their culture was so enchanted by their self-dreamed vision of the dancers that the two came instead to a fruitful truce.

These days, the dancers themselves often speak admiringly of the tales that the aliens wrote about them. Among the younger generation in particular, there are those who emulate the elegant and mannered society depicted in the aliens' fables. As time goes on, it is likely that this fantasy will displace the dancers' native culture.

The Profit Motive

Although the Kiatti have their share of sculptors, engineers, and mercenaries, they are perhaps best known as traders. Kiatti vessels are welcome in many places, for they bring delightfully disruptive theories of government, fossilized musical instruments, and fine surgical tools; they bring cold-eyed guns that whisper of sleep impending and sugared atrocities. If you can describe it, so they say, there is a Kiatti who is willing to sell it to you.

In the ordinary course of things, the Kiatti accept barter for payment. They claim that it is a language that even the universe understands. Their sages spend a great deal of time to attempting to justify the profit motive in view of conservation laws. Most of them converge comfortably on the position that profit is the civilized response to entropy. The traders themselves vary, as you might expect, in the rapacity of their bargains. But then, as they often say, value is contextual.

The Kiatti do have a currency of sorts. It is their stardrives, and all aliens' stardrives are rated in comparison with their own. The Kiatti produce a number of them, which encompass a logarithmic scale of utility.

When the Kiatti determine that it is necessary to pay or be paid in this currency, they will spend months—sometimes years—refitting their vessels as necessary. Thus every trader is also an engineer. The drives' designers made some attempt to make the drives modular, but this was a haphazard enterprise at best.

One Kiatti visionary wrote of commerce between universes, which would require the greatest stardrive of all. The Kiatti do not see any reason they can't bargain with the universe itself, and are slowly accumulating their wealth toward the time when they can trade their smaller coins for one that will take them to this new goal. They rarely speak of this with outsiders, but most of them are confident that no one else will be able to outbid them.

The Inescapable Experiment

One small civilization claims to have invented a stardrive that kills everyone who uses it. One moment the ship is *here*, with everyone alive and well, or as well as they ever were; the next moment, it is *there*, and carries only corpses. The records, transmitted over great expanses against the microwave hiss, are persuasive. Observers in differently equipped ships have sometimes accompanied these suicide vessels, and they corroborate the reports.

Most of their neighbors are mystified by their fixation with this morbid discovery. It would be one thing, they say, if these people were set upon finding a way to fix this terrible flaw, but that does not appear to be the case. A small but reliable number of them volunteers to test each new iteration of the deathdrive, and they are rarely under any illusions about their fate. For that matter, some of the neighbors, out of pity or curiosity, have offered this people some of their own old but reliable technology, asking only a token sum to allow them to preserve their pride, but they always decline politely. After all, they possess safe stardrive technology of their own; the barrier is not knowledge.

Occasionally, volunteers from other peoples come to test it themselves, on the premise that there has to exist some species that won't be affected by the stardrive's peculiar radiance. (The drive's murderousness does not appear to have any lasting effect on the ship's structure.) So far, the claim has stood. One imagines it will stand as long as there are people to test it.

One Final Constant

Then there are the civilizations that invent keener and more nimble stardrives solely to further their wars, but that's an old story and you already know how it ends.

ABOUT THE CONTRIBUTORS

An (pronounce it "On") **Owomoyela** is a neutrois author with a background in web development, linguistics, and weaving chain maille out of stainless steel fencing wire, whose fiction has appeared in a number of venues including *Clarkesworld, Asimov's, Lightspeed*, and a pair of year's bests. An's interests range from pulsars and Cepheid variables to gender studies and nonstandard pronouns, with a plethora of stops in-between. Se graduated from the Clarion West Writers Workshop in 2008 and attended the Launchpad Astronomy Workshop in 2011.

Ken Liu (kenliu.name) is an author and translator of speculative fiction, as well as a lawyer and programmer. His fiction has appeared in *F&SF, Asimov's, Analog, Clarkesworld, Lightspeed*, and *Strange Horizons*, among other places. He has won a Nebula, a Hugo, a World Fantasy Award, and a Science Fiction & Fantasy Translation Award, and been nominated for the Sturgeon and the Locus Awards. He lives with his family near Boston, Massachusetts.

Catherynne M. Valente is the *New York Times* bestselling author of over a dozen works of fiction and poetry, including *Palimpsest*, the Orphan's Tales series, *Deathless*, and the crowdfunded phenomenon *The Girl Who Circumnavigated Fairyland in a Ship of Own Making*. She is the winner of the Andre Norton, Tiptree, Mythopoeic, Rhysling, Lambda, Locus and Hugo awards. She has been a finalist for the Nebula and World Fantasy Awards. She lives on an island off the coast of Maine with her partner, two dogs, and an enormous cat.

Zen Cho was born and raised in Malaysia, and now lives in London. Her short fiction has appeared in various publications in the US, Australia and Malaysia, most recently in *Andromeda Spaceways Inflight Magazine*, and anthology of urban fantasy and fashion *Bloody Fabulous*, edited by Ekaterina Sedia. Find out more about her work at zencho.org.

Vandana Singh is an Indian science fiction writer living in the U.S., where she also teaches physics full-time at a state university. She has published short stories in various anthologies and magazines, including *Strange Horizons* and *TRSF*, many of which have been reprinted in year's best volumes. Her novella *Distances* (Aqueduct Press) won the 2008 Carl Brandon Parallax award. Most recently she has been a columnist for *Strange Horizons*, where her reflections on science and the environment can be found.

Paul McAuley is the multiple award-winning author of more than twenty books, including science-fiction novels, thrillers, and short-story collections. Having worked for twenty years as a research biologist and university lecturer in Britain and America, he's now a full-time writer, and lives in North London. His latest novel is *In the Mouth of the Whale*.

Ursula K. Le Guin has received five Hugo Awards, six Nebula Awards, nineteen Locus Awards (more than any other author), the Gandalf Grand Master Award, the Science Fiction and Fantasy Writers of America Grand Master Award, and the World Fantasy Lifetime Achievement Award. Her novel *The Farthest Shore* won the National Book Award for Children's Books. Le Guin was named a Library of Congress Living Legend in the "Writers and Artists" category for her significant contributions to America's cultural heritage and the PEN/Malamud Award for "excellence in a body of short fiction." She is also the recipient of the Association for Library Service for Children's May Hill Arbuthnot Honor Lecture Award and the Margaret Edwards Award. She was honored by The Washington Center for the Book for her distinguished body of work with the Maxine Cushing Gray Fellowship for Writers in 2006.

Molly Gloss is the author of four novels, including *Wild Life* (Tiptree Award) and *The Dazzle of Day* (PEN West Fiction Prize). Several of her short stories have been anthologized in *The Year's Best Science Fiction*. For more about her work, see her website, mollygloss.com

Desirina Boskovich has published fiction in *Realms of Fantasy, Fantasy, Clarkesworld,* and *Nightmare,* with stories forthcoming in *Lightspeed* and *Kaleidotrope.* She is an '07 graduate of the Clarion Science Fiction and Fantasy Writers Workshop. Find her online at desirinaboskovich.com.

Genevieve Valentine's first novel, *Mechanique: A Tale of the Circus Tresaulti,* won the 2012 Crawford Award and was nominated for the Nebula. Her second novel, *Glad Rags,* a 1927 retelling of the Twelve Dancing Princesses, is forthcoming from Atria in 2014. Her short fiction has appeared in *Clarkesworld, Strange Horizons, Journal of Mythic Arts, Lightspeed,* and others, and the anthologies *Federations, The Living Dead 2, After, Teeth,* and more. Her nonfiction and reviews have appeared at *NPR.org, Strange Horizons, io9.com, Lightspeed, Weird Tales, Tor.com,* and *Fantasy,* and she is a co-author of pop-culture book *Geek Wisdom* (Quirk Books). Her appetite for bad movies is insatiable, a tragedy she tracks on her blog.

Caitlín R. Kiernan is the author of several novels, including the award-winning *Threshold, Daughter of Hounds, The Red Tree, The Drowning Girl,* and, most recently (as Kathleen Tierney), *Blood Oranges.* Her short fiction has been collected in *Tales of Pain and Wonder; From Weird and Distant Shores; To Charles Fort, with Love; Alabaster; A Is for Alien;* and *The Ammonite Violin & Others.* Her erotica has been collected in two volumes, *Frog Toes and Tentacles* and *Tales from the Woeful Platypus.* Subterranean Press published a retrospective of her early writing, *Two Worlds and In Between: The Best of Caitlín R. Kiernan (Volume One)* last year. She lives in Providence, Rhode Island with her partner, Kathryn.

Jamie Barras is a London-based academic who investigates fake drugs masquerading as the genuine article; and masquerades are a frequent subject of his fiction, which has appeared in magazines in the UK and US.

Robert Reed has published eleven novels. His twelfth, *The Memory of Sky: A Novel of the Great Ship,* will be published in spring 2014. Since winning the first annual L. Ron Hubbard Writers of the Future contest in 1986 and being a finalist for the John W. Campbell Award for best new writer in 1987, he has had over two hundred shorter works published in a variety of magazines and anthologies. Collections include *The Dragons* of *Springplace, Chrysalis, The Cuckoo's Boys*, and the upcoming *The Greatship*. Reed's stories have appeared in at least one of the annual year's best anthologies in every year since 1992, and he has received nominations for the Nebula and the Hugo Awards, as well as numerous other literary awards. He won a Hugo Award for his novella "A Billion Eves."

Elizabeth Bear was born on the same day as Frodo and Bilbo Baggins, but in a different year. She is the multiple-Hugo-Award-winning author of over a dozen novels and nearly a hundred short stories. Her hobbies include rock climbing, running, cooking, archery, and other practical skills for the coming zombie apocalypse. She divides her time between Massachusetts, where her dog lives, and Wisconsin, the home of her partner, fantasist Scott Lynch.

Sofia Samatar is the author of the novel *A Stranger in Olondria* (Small Beer Press, 2013). Her poetry, short fiction and reviews have appeared in a number of places, including *Strange Horizons, Clarkesworld, Stone Telling* and *Goblin Fruit*. She is the nonfiction and poetry editor for *Interfictions: A Journal of Interstitial Arts*.

Karin Lowachee was born in South America, grew up in Canada, and worked in the Arctic. Her first novel *Warchild* won the 2001 Warner Aspect First Novel Contest. Both *Warchild* (2002) and her third novel *Cagebird* (2005) were finalists for the Philip K. Dick Award. *Cagebird* won the Prix Aurora Award for Best Long-Form Work in English and the Spectrum Award also in 2006. Her books have been translated into French, Hebrew, and Japanese, and her short stories have appeared in anthologies edited by Julie Czerneda, Nalo Hopkinson, and John Joseph Adams. Her current fantasy novel, *The Gaslight Dogs*, was published through Orbit Books.

Jeremiah Tolbert is a writer, photographer, and web developer living in rural Kansas. His stories have appeared in magazines such as *Interzone* and *Lightspeed*, and anthologies such as *The Way of the Wizard* and *Federations*. He's also responsible for the websites of some of your favorite science fiction and mystery authors.

Alastair Reynolds was born in Barry in 1966. He spent his early years in Cornwall, then returned to Wales for his primary and secondary school education. He completed a degree in astronomy at Newcastle, then a PhD in the same subject at St Andrews in Scotland. He left the UK in 1991 and spent the next sixteen years working in the Netherlands, mostly for the European Space Agency, although he also did a stint as a postdoctoral worker in Utrecht. He had been writing and selling science fiction since 1989, and published his first novel, *Revelation Space*, in 2000. He has recently completed his tenth novel and has continued to publish short fiction. His novel *Chasm City* won the British Science Fiction Award, and he has been shortlisted for the Arthur C Clarke award three times. In 2004 he left scientific research to write full time. He married in 2005 and returned to Wales in 2008, where he lives in Rhondda Cynon Taff.

Brooke Bolander is a chaos-sowing trickster being of indeterminate alignment. Originally from the deepest, darkest regions of the southern US, she attended the University of Leicester from 2004 to 2007 studying History and Archaeology and is a graduate of the 2011 Clarion Writers' Workshop at UCSD. Her work has previously appeared in *Lightspeed*, *Strange Horizons*, and *Reflection's Edge*.

Nisi Shawl's collection *Filter House* won the 2009 James Tiptree, Jr. Award. Her work has been published at *Strange Horizons*, in *Asimov's*, and in anthologies including *Dark Matter, River,* and *Dark Faith*. She was WisCon 35's Guest of Honor. She edited *Bloodchildren: Stories by the Octavia E. Butler Scholars*, and co-edited *Strange Matings: Octavia E. Butler, Science Fiction, Feminism, and African American Voices*. With classmate Cynthia Ward she co-authored *Writing the Other: A Practical Approach*. Shawl is a cofounder of the Carl Brandon Society and serves on the Board of Directors of the Clarion West Writers Workshop. Her website is nisishawl.com.

Samantha Henderson lives in Covina, California by way of England, South Africa, Illinois and Oregon. Her short fiction and poetry have been published in *Realms of Fantasy, Strange Horizons, Goblin Fruit* and *Weird Tales*, and reprinted in *The Year's Best Fantasy and Science Fiction, Steampunk II: Steampunk Reloaded, Steampunk Revolutions* and *The Mammoth Book of Steampunk*. She is the co-winner of the 2010 Rhysling Award for speculative poetry, and is the author of the Forgotten Realms novel *Dawnbringer*.

Sonya Taaffe's short stories and poems have appeared in such venues as *Beyond Binary: Genderqueer and Sexually Fluid Speculative Fiction*, *The Moment of Change: An Anthology of Feminist Speculative Poetry*, *Here, We Cross: A Collection of Queer and Genderfluid Poetry from Stone Telling*, *People of the Book: A Decade of Jewish Science Fiction & Fantasy*, *Last Drink Bird Head*, *The Year's Best Fantasy and Horror*, *The Alchemy of Stars: Rhysling Award Winners Showcase*, and *The Best of Not One of Us*. Her work can be found in the collections *Postcards from the Province of Hyphens* and *Singing Innocence and Experience* (Prime Books) and *A Mayse-Bikhl* (Papaveria Press). She is currently senior poetry editor at *Strange Horizons*; she holds master's degrees in Classics from Brandeis and Yale and once named a Kuiper belt object.

Eleanor Arnason published her first story in 1973. Since then she has published six novels, two chapbooks and more than thirty short stories. Her fourth novel, *A Woman of the Iron People*, won the James Tiptree Jr. Award and the Mythopoeic Society Award. Her fifth novel, *Ring of Swords*, won a Minnesota Book Award. Her short story "Dapple" won the Spectrum Award. Other short stories have been finalists for the Hugo, Nebula, Sturgeon, Sidewise and World Fantasy Awards. Her blog address is eleanorarnason.blogspot.com

Born and raised in Australia, **Gitte Christensen** also lived in Demark for twelve years before returning to study journalism at the Royal Melbourne Institute of Technology. Her speculative fiction has appeared in *Aurealis*, *Andromeda Spaceways Inflight Magazine* and other publications, including the anthologies *The Tangled Bank: Love, Wonder, and Evolution*, *The Year's Best Australian Fantasy and Horror 2010*, *Dark Tales of Lost Civilizations*, *Return of the Dead Men (and Women) Walking* and *Mark of the Beast: New Legends of the Werewolf*. To escape keyboards, she regularly grabs a horse and a tent and goes trail riding through distant mountains.

Indrapramit Das is a writer and artist from Kolkata, India. His short fiction has appeared in *Clarkesworld*, *Asimov's*, *Apex*, *Redstone*, and the anthology *Breaking the Bow: Speculative Fiction Inspired by the Ramayana* (Zubaan Books), among others. He is a grateful graduate of the 2012 Clarion West Writers Workshop and a recipient of the Octavia E. Butler Memorial Scholarship Award. He completed his MFA at the University of

British Columbia, and is currently in Vancouver working as a freelance writer, artist, editor, extra, game tester, tutor, would-be novelist, and aspirant to adulthood. Follow him on Twitter (@IndrapramitDas).

Jeffrey Ford is the author of the novels *The Physiognomy, Memoranda, The Beyond, The Portrait of Mrs. Charbuque, The Girl in the Glass, The Cosmology of the Wider World*, and *The Shadow Year*. His story collections are *The Fantasy Writer's Assistant, The Empire of Ice Cream, The Drowned Life*, and *Crackpot Palace*. His short fiction has appeared in numerous journals, magazines and anthologies, from *MAD Magazine* to *The Oxford Book of American Short Stories* (2nd edition).

Karin Tidbeck lives in Malmö, Sweden, and writes in Swedish and English. Her stories have appeared in *Weird Tales, Shimmer, Unstuck Annual* and the anthologies *Odd?* and *Steampunk Revolution*. Her short story collection *Jagannath* was published in English in November 2012. She recently received the Crawford award for 2013.

Pervin Saket writes poetry and prose. Her fiction has been published in *Breaking the Bow, Kalkion, Page Forty Seven, Katha, Ripples* and others. She has written a collection of poems, *A Tinge of Turmeric*, and her poems have featured in *Kritya* and *The Binnacle*. She lives in Pune, India.

Nancy Kress is the author of thirty-two books, including twenty-five novels, four collections of short stories, and three books on writing. Her work has won four Nebulas, two Hugos, a Sturgeon, and the John W. Campbell Memorial Award. Most recent works are *After the Fall, Before the Fall, During the Fall* (Tachyon, 2012), a novel of apocalypse, and *Flash Point* (Viking, 2012), a YA novel. In addition to writing, Kress often teaches at various venues around the country and abroad; in 2008 she was the Picador visiting lecturer at the University of Leipzig. Kress lives in Seattle with her husband, writer Jack Skillingstead, and Cosette, the world's most spoiled toy poodle.

Greg van Eekhout is the author of the contemporary fantasy novel *Norse Code*, and the middle-grade novels *Kid vs. Squid* and *The Boy at the End of the World*. His short stories have appeared in *Asimov's, Strange Horizons, F&SF*, and several year's best anthologies. His work has received nominations for the Nebula Award and the Andre Norton Award. For "Native Aliens," he drew on his family's history in Indonesia and the Netherlands. Greg currently lives in San Diego, California. Visit his website at writingandsnacks.com.

Lavie Tidhar is the World Fantasy Award winning author of *Osama*, of The Bookman Histories trilogy and many other works. He won the British Fantasy Award for Best Novella, for *Gorel & The Pot-Bellied God*, and a BSFA Award for non-fiction. He grew up on a kibbutz in Israel and in South Africa but currently resides in London.

Yoon Ha Lee lives in Louisiana with her family and has not yet been eaten by gators. Her works have appeared in *Clarkesworld, Lightspeed, F&SF*, and other venues.

PUBLICATION HISTORY

ABOUT THE EDITOR

Alex Dally MacFarlane lives in London, where she is pursuing a MA in Ancient History. When not researching ancient gender and narratives, she writes stories, found in *Clarkesworld Magazine, Strange Horizons, Beneath Ceaseless Skies, Shimmer* and the anthologies *The Mammoth Book of Steampunk* and *The Other Half of the Sky*. Poetry can be found in *Stone Telling, Goblin Fruit, The Moment of Change* and *Here, We Cross*. She is the editor of *Aliens: Recent Encounters*, out in June 2013 from Prime Books, and *The Mammoth Book of SF Stories by Women*, due out in late 2014.